PRINT EDITION

Crimson Winter Vol. 2: Lands of Jade

© 2022 by Mirror World Publishing
Edited by: Robert Dowsett

Cover by: Justine Dowsett

Published by Mirror World Publishing in April 2022

Mirror World Publishing
Windsor, Ontario
www.mirrorworldpublishing.com
info@mirrorworldpublishing.com

ISBN: 978-1-987976-87-8

For Adam, Sabrina, Robert and Christine.
For all the memories.

LANDS OF JADE
CRIMSON WINTER
VOL.2

JUSTINE ALLEY DOWSETT

"When something you care about is threatened, your first instinct is to guard it with everything you have. Sometimes that instinct is what leaves you most vulnerable to losing the very thing you want to keep safe. The answer to this lesson is harder than the lesson itself – give that which you seek to protect the means to defend itself and then let it have the opportunity to try. I don't think I'll ever stop struggling with that philosophy, but how I learned it in the first place is a story worth telling...

Ch. 1 – Picking up the Pieces

There were many wounded among the survivors in the green fields of Taiyou outside the Temple of Jade. I walked among the lucky, and the not so lucky, to see if I was needed by anyone, but by now the wounded had been treated to the best of my abilities and those of the magical healers from the former school of the Oujou sorceresses.

Perhaps it had been working together against a common foe, or their shared losses, but the soldiers of the Lion Brigade and the Roughlanders were intermingled now like they hadn't been on the journey here. And, although their wounds may have been treated, bandaged, and in some cases their flesh magically knitted back together, they were still feeling the effects of the brutal assault they had faced at the hands of an unidentified assailant.

As I made my way toward the imposing mountain temple, I was greeted by friendly nods of acknowledgment from almost everyone I passed. I was known now, to these people at least, whereas less than a week ago I had been a stranger in this land, hiding who I was.

There was no more hiding now – Yukari Namikoya, Chosen of Sapphiros, was a name most people would soon know, and my frizzy bob of pale blue hair and intense blue eyes had never made it possible for me to fade into the background.

Hotaru, Kaji, Yue, and I – the four Chosen of Sapphiros – were still feeling the effects of the assault as well, though in our case those effects were more emotional than physical. The strain was getting to all of us, watching the pain and suffering of the people we had brought here with us, but had been unable to defend.

"We can't just stay here," I announced, tired beyond belief as I slowly climbed the temple's steps to where Kaji sat conversing with the young, white-haired leader of the Lion Brigade, Sir Leon Rama. "That woman could come back at any time. We still don't know what she was after or where she went."

"That's true, but on the move or sitting here, we'd still have a large number of wounded people to protect," Kaji pointed out. "If she wants to come after us, she's going to."

"We need more supplies, the more seriously injured need shelter, and we're like sitting ducks out here."

The metaphor slid right out in my frustration before I remembered where we were and that Rama had likely never seen a duck in his life. The four of us had arrived here from Earth – Tokyo, Japan to be precise – and after only two months on this world, I was starting to forget we were foreigners here. Of course there were times where I was forcefully reminded of the truth and a wave of not exactly homesickness, but more like nostalgia, would pass over me, leaving me feeling disoriented and out of place.

I grimaced at my error, but Rama let it slide with no more than a raised eyebrow. It was common knowledge Chosen were from other worlds, and by now I assumed the people we had been travelling with were more or less used to our strangeness.

"We can't go anywhere for the present," Rama interjected, his tone polite, "but you are correct in saying we need more supplies and reinforcements would be welcome. Would it be possible for you to send a message to my father? He could have men here in a few days, I'm sure."

I nodded, considering this. As a Chosen of the gem god Sapphiros, I, like my friends, had developed certain abilities that allowed us to do things most people couldn't. Our powers were each unique, and mine tended to center around forming various types of arrows with the force of my mind. One arrow type would be particularly useful in this situation, as Rama well knew, having been on the receiving end of one of my messages in the past.

"I believe I could send him a message, but I would have to send it through your captain – the one that travelled with Yue to get supplies – as I have never met your father. I assume he would deliver it to Lord Rama?" Rama nodded. "Okay, I'll do that. Where's Narlhep?" I looked around, confused by his absence from the temple stairs where he'd been seen most often since we had emerged from the temple. "I'd like to ask him if he has anything he'd like to add."

I was referring to the prince of the land we currently found ourselves in – a country called Taiyou. We had recently managed to ally ourselves with Prince Narlhep by helping to capture his traitorous regent, Lord Viron, and defeat the regent's pet sorceress, the Oujou. Now Narlhep needed only to convince the council of Viron's treachery and, I assumed, undergo some form of coronation ceremony, before he would be King in advance of his sixteenth birthday, which was a few months away.

"Prince Narlhep is within the temple," Rama stated with particular emphasis and I looked past him to the temple doors beyond – they were sealed shut.

"No!" I gasped, noticing Narlhep's sword lying at Kaji's side as a sudden realization dawned on me. "He didn't…"

"I'm afraid so." Rama grimaced.

"But he knows how to open the doors now, right?" I looked past Rama and Kaji to our prisoner, still tightly held, bound in a rope net and creatively gagged with bandages from the medical supplies. "He made Viron tell him, didn't he?"

"I don't think it's going to work that way," Kaji informed me. "Narlhep went in there with the intention of facing Jedeite and proving his right to the throne of Taiyou."

"He did what? But we proved Viron is a traitor. Surely the council wouldn't require…"

"The council is not the only approval Narlhep believes he needs right now, and I, for one, agree with him," Rama stated. "The confirmed existence of the gem gods is going to take some getting used to. Most Taiyouns, if they believe in Jedeite at all, believe he abandoned us long ago. Now that the Oujou have been defeated and Jedeite's power returned to him, Prince Narlhep is likely doing the right thing by solidifying his claim through Jedeite first. It's the first step to the acceptance that this land is not only ours, but His as well."

I contemplated the ornate and magically sealed Jade doors, with their Jade pillar statues of the form of the Oujou decorating either side of the entrance. There was no objection I could make to Rama's arguments as this land was not my own, but I sincerely wanted to protest against the prince having gone in there to face the gem god who was said to represent 'civilized savagery'.

I was not a religious person, despite being the Chosen of Sapphiros, and until perhaps as late as the other day I would have said I believed as many of the Taiyouns do – that the gem gods were a myth, or were, at the very least, absent from the day to day affairs of this world. Now, I wasn't so sure. Certainly their power was evident; I was proof of that with my newfound abilities, as was the magic infesting this world. Also, Yue claimed she had spoken with Jedeite himself in her mind, which left me with no choice but to accept my friend's claims or believe she was losing her hold on sanity.

I had seen any number of things I would have believed impossible before coming here, but I had never heard Sapphiros' voice or seen the evidence of his presence, other than the power that now coursed through me and my friends, and the blue diamond-shaped marks upon our chests that marked us as his Chosen.

Now Narlhep, someone I had known only a short time, but whom I had come to consider a friend, had willingly sealed himself inside the Jade mountain to face his god. Despite my desire to continue denying the presence and influence of the gem gods, I found myself worrying for his safety, hoping the doors would open any moment now and he would emerge. Unfortunately, that didn't seem like it was going to be the case.

"How long has he been in there?" I asked.

"He went in at change," Rama replied and I quirked a brow in confusion.

"He means the bounce," Kaji clarified. "In Taiyou, that's when they change shifts – like night and day."

I looked up to find the sun directly overhead; on this world the sun never set – which took some getting used to – but the endless days were broken up by the moment the sun touched the horizon and started its return journey through the sky. The Roughlanders – who lived out in the harsh deserts of this planet – called it the bounce, but I suppose, like many other things, it was different here in the fertile and protected lands of Taiyou.

I nodded, absorbing this new information. "So we're stuck here for the time being, then?"

Kaji and Rama nodded. "But that will at least give our reinforcements time to get here," Rama added. "There's little use trying to move all of the injured without help."

I nodded and took the time to carefully compose the message to Lord Rama in my mind, requesting aid in the form of soldiers, supplies, and pallets to carry the more seriously wounded, before forming an arrow made of glowing energy between my hands and letting the message fly.

"Sabien, where is everyone?" I asked.

Sir Sabien, the Knight Commander of Sapphiros, was a tall and imposing man in his white armour with two swords strapped to his back – the black-bladed one had, until recently, belonged to the traitor, Viron.

"Adel is guarding Aysel personally. There has been no change."

Lady Adel was the one Knight I did know the location of very well. The formidable Knight had been injured in the fight with the mysterious assailant, but that wasn't what kept her immobile. Her twin sister and squire, Aysel, had been badly wounded, losing her sword arm and some of the right side of her body with it. The Kumori healers – a race of silent, bat-like people – had done their best work amputating her arm and removing what was left of her armour with their magic, but Aysel had remained unconscious ever since the operation. Adel had not left her sister's side, unless commanded by Sabien to take her turn scouting.

"Ris and Masaru are ranging out a little further north and east today," he continued, "and Jeth has gone southwest. I'm staying here in the centre, in case she evades the others and returns here."

"Is there still no sign of her, then? Or the reinforcements I sent for?"

Sabien shook his head, "No, but Ris informed me Masaru believes he has found her trail. They are following it now."

"Should they really be going after her?"

"They are simply following her trail to see which direction it leads," he responded. "They have no intention of engaging her. With any luck, she will already have left Taiyou entirely. If we can confirm that, I will rest a little easier."

I nodded, though I wasn't entirely reassured. Like Sabien worried for Ris, my feelings toward Masaru were quite similar, only in my case Masaru wasn't aware of them yet. Ever since I realized how I felt, I had been trying to find the words to explain it to him, but there had yet to be an appropriate time. After I had emerged from the confrontation with the Oujou to discover the carnage that took place while we had been occupied within the temple, I realized just how important it was to tell him while I still had the chance. Still, it had been difficult to find him alone for even a minute; as one of the less injured Knights, he was always off scouting.

"Do you think I should join them? I should be able to fly just as quickly as Ris does, and I could help them scout."

I had been feeling the need to be on the move now for several days and if anyone was going to have to face this deadly woman, it should be one or more of the Chosen – which is not to say I was looking forward to the experience – but also, I wanted my chance to speak to Masaru. I had been forced to realize just how dangerous this world was and it was a simple fact that our positions didn't help matters. We would have to fight to stay alive and we had plenty of enemies besides. There was no benefit to waiting any longer, as much as I was afraid to tell him the truth in case it wasn't something he wanted to hear.

Sabien levelled his gaze on me. "Yukari, I know you wish to be of use, but I think your place right now is here with the people that need to be defended."

My mouth settled into a grim line at the reminder that Sabien seemed to be able to see right through me. "Fine. I'll be waiting near the temple. If you hear anything at all from Ris, I would appreciate it if you could let me know."

Sabrine nodded and I stalked impatiently back to the temple steps. Rama was there, as were Kaji and Hotaru, and a number of the currently unoccupied Lion Brigade. As I approached, I noticed they were sharing bread for their midday meal and I climbed the steps, accepting my own slightly stale bun to join them. The rations were not improving as the days wore on; we hadn't anticipated an extended stay at the Jade mountain.

"So it's a children's toy that goes down the stairs?" Rama asked. "On its own, you say?"

I listened only half-heartedly as Hotaru tried, once again, to explain another tidbit of Earth culture to someone who had no frame of reference for what she was talking about. Hotaru was my best friend, but I was often exasperated by her lack of good judgment. I prided myself on having a solid grasp on the facts of any given situation, but it was not lost on me that my round-faced, dark-haired friend was my complete opposite. It was a wonder we got along at all.

Beyond Hotaru, Kaji rolled his eyes to indicate what he thought of the current topic of conversation and I smiled at him, despite myself. Like Hotaru, I had known Kaji my entire life. We didn't talk much, but when we did we often saw eye to eye, which was refreshing compared to the arguments I often had with Hotaru.

Yue, the other one of us who had been chosen by Sapphiros, was another matter altogether. I looked up as I saw my friend appear at the base of the staircase and grab a couple of buns from the soldier handing them out, her impossibly long, chestnut brown hair falling down to cover her face in shadow. Yue and I had been close enough on Earth, though even then she had been quiet and generally preferred to be on her own, rather than socialize or study. Since arriving on this world, she had, if anything, become more distant from the rest of us. In the last three days she had been mostly silent, using her power to increase her walking or running speed until she was no longer visible as she passed from place to place, in order to avoid having to actually encounter anyone.

She turned, buns in hand, and made as if to flash-step back in the direction she had come when she stopped suddenly, her back stiffening. I sat up straight in alarm before I realized what had caused Yue to pause. A familiar grating noise filled the air and I looked over my shoulder in disbelief to see the doors of the temple were opening at last.

The group of us on the steps hurried to our feet as two at a time, sorceresses and sorceresses-in-training emerged from the massive temple, fanning out from the doors themselves and down the sides of the staircase. Prince Narlhep emerged slowly into the light of day from the dark confines of the Jade mountain. He walked stiffly, but I was glad to see him exiting the temple under his own power – after three days of his continued absence, I had begun to worry he would not emerge at all. The prince took a few more steps and stopped between Kaji and Rama, but he didn't make any move to take his helmet off, nor did he speak.

"All hail the new King of Taiyou!" Kaji called out, his voice amplified by his power so everyone could hear him. "All hail King Narlhep!"

"King Narlhep!" The cheer was repeated by those of us on the steps, Rama's troops, and the Roughlanders beyond, though the many sorceresses remained silent and stony-faced.

My eyes were trained on Narlhep, who still had not made any move to remove his helmet – something was amiss here. After a long moment, Narlhep retrieved his sword from Rama and started making his way down the stairs. I fell in step beside him as the sorceresses began to disperse and the others talked excitedly amongst themselves.

"Narlhep, are you all right?"

He didn't answer me, confirming my suspicions. I quickened my pace to keep step with him as he broke free of the crowd at the bottom of the stairs and continued on away from where we had set up our encampment. Ahead of us lay the partly-destroyed small village that decorated the one side of the mountain, where we had commandeered most of our remaining supplies.

"Narlhep?" I tried again as he marched deliberately toward a wooden cabin, which was slightly larger than the majority of the huts still standing in the village.

I entered the cabin on the heels of the prince – or the king now, I suppose. The cabin was still not very big, despite being larger than most of the buildings in this village. The main room – perhaps the only room, I couldn't tell – contained only a few rickety chairs facing a wooden desk. Behind the desk was a woman I had met before, but didn't much like. She was small of stature and elderly, with a bun of grayish-white hair held atop her head by a black net of spider-like webbing. As the armoured King of Taiyou entered her presence, the matronly sorceress stood and gave a slight bow of her head in his direction. Narlhep did not wait for the woman to finish acknowledging him before he removed her head with a single, powerful swipe of his sword.

I gasped, my eyes widening in shock. Narlhep, like me, was only fifteen. I had never killed anyone before, though since coming here I had seen my share of death. I had read in the museum of Taiyou that

Prince Narlhep, like the other princes of his line before him, had been responsible for the death of his father, but until now I hadn't fully believed my friend to be capable of murder. Her head rolled to the ground as her body crumpled and a slight green mist, like a gas, wafted from out of her body to dissipate in the air.

"She was the last of the Oujou." Narlhep's voice sounded muffled from beneath his helmet, but I could hear him struggling to keep his voice controlled. "I had no choice."

"Narlhep, please, talk to me," I pleaded with him, wanting my friend back. "Tell me what happened in there."

He gave no response, but stood tightly gripping his bloody sword a moment in his gauntleted hand before walking past me. I couldn't let him just walk away. I tried a different tactic, though it would cost me to do it. "Your Majesty?"

He stopped with his back to me and he didn't turn his head. "Don't call me that," he said. "I'm not the King of Taiyou."

"If you're not the King of Taiyou, then who is?"

Narlhep took a deep breath, audible through his helmet. "The Chosen of Jedeite. I'm to act as Regent until he returns to Taiyou, then my time is finished."

I thought this through as quickly as I was able, though I was certain there was something I was misunderstanding about this. Narlhep was acting very unlike himself; he had always said he wasn't certain if he even wanted to be king, or if he was suited for it.

I shook my head to clear it. "Well, you'd better get used to people addressing you as King anyway. The people think you are the King, thanks to Kaji, and I don't think you should disappoint them just yet. Taiyou needs to be strong, especially now. We have a civil war on our hands and the possible threat of this woman who seems to have walked right through Taiyou's defenses to attack our people here in the centre of the country."

"It's worse," Narlhep said, barely above a whisper. "The defenses are down, or as good as, anyway. I'm not the King and I'm not Viron. I can't feel the Leyins like I should and without Kosetsu—" he choked on the name of Viron's daughter, whom Narlhep had loved and Viron had killed, "I can't fire the weapon. Taiyou has never been this vulnerable – we *need* the Chosen of Jedeite."

"What Taiyou needs is a strong king and for now that person is you." I didn't spare his feelings, his country needed him to snap out of this state of self-pity and step up to the responsibility of his role. "We can't know how long it will take for the Chosen of Jedeite to be found, or for that person to come to Taiyou. In the meantime, for all intents and purposes, you are the King of Taiyou. Your enemies will not hesitate to take advantage of your weaknesses if you let on they exist."

His shoulders slumped, the erect posture he had been holding since he had come out of the temple relaxing at last. I took a step forward with the intent of placing a hand on his shoulder and trying to say something comforting to make up for the harsh words I had used to make him see reason, but he snapped to attention as soon as he heard my foot drag across the ground, and it was like his moment of vulnerability had never shown. It was what I had asked for, but it was difficult to watch regardless.

With Narlhep gone, I couldn't stay in the cabin. The knowledge of what had been done there – even if it was to an agent of the Oujou – weighed too heavily on my conscience. Emerging into the light of day, I looked about the tiny village of huts and wondered where to go next. I sighed in frustration, realizing the only choice I had was to go back to the encampment at the base of the mountain and discover what Narlhep intended to do, or continue to wait for the reinforcements to arrive. It had been some time since I had sent the message to Lord Rama; providing he was willing to acquiesce to my request, more of the Lion Brigade should have been arriving any time now.

I started back in the direction of the temple with a sense of apprehension that couldn't quite be explained by Narlhep's new demeanor or his shocking revelation, when I noticed a lone Roughlander running through the village huts in the same direction I was headed. He was blond and fit and the combination of his filthy white shirt over hide pants held up by too many belts was nearly unmistakable.

Masaru was running hard. I ran to intercept him. "What's going on?"

"It's the Lion Brigade. They've been slaughtered."

His words struck me like a blow to my midsection. "You mean the ones I sent for?"

He nodded solemnly. "Ris is still in the woods, keeping an eye on things and watching for survivors, but I thought I should come back and let everyone know before we investigate further."

"Do you think it was her, then?"

"I think so, aye – who else could it have been? Unless some ran, there doesn't seem to be a man left standing."

I cringed at the thought of what Masaru had likely come across. A few days ago, I had emerged from the temple to a similar scene of carnage and destruction, but at least in my case there had been survivors left to find.

I swallowed visibly. "I'm coming with you. If there are any survivors, I can help Ris."

"Aye, I hoped ye would," he agreed, "but I need to tell Sabien at least beforehand. If she is still there, we'll need more than just the three of us to face her."

"I'll let him know."

I closed my eyes briefly and composed the message I wanted to send, detailing what Masaru had just told me, and then I let it loose in the form of an arrow directed to Sabien. Then Masaru and I took off running back the way he had come. Masaru slowed down considerably once we reached the trees, giving me a chance to catch my breath – I wasn't nearly as athletic as he was. As I recovered, I began to notice the care with which he picked his way through the foliage and the noise he was making, despite his efforts.

"Are we getting close, then?" I whispered.

"It's a ways yet," he answered.

"Then why are we going so slowly?"

Masaru glanced back over his shoulder and I saw his grimace. "It's all this green stuff, I'm just not used to it."

I smiled at him, despite myself. After growing up in a desert, of course Masaru would be completely out of his element in the forests of Taiyou.

"Is it straight ahead?" As Masaru nodded, I pushed past him and began leading the way through where the greenery was less dense.

Eventually Ris found us. The beautiful part bat, part woman Kumori drifted silently down from where she had been perched in a tree. She put her index finger to her lips to direct us to remain silent and then used that same hand to point forward through the trees. Masaru nodded and guided me forward, taking me by the hand. We moved quite slowly, but much more quietly than we had before. As we neared a ridge Masaru gave my hand a tug, and we dropped to a crouch and began to crawl forward.

The edge of the ridge revealed a ghastly scene in a clearing below. The pile of corpses decorated with flies had once been the men Lord Rama had sent to escort us back toward the city. The white armour with the lion head symbol was identifiable even from this distance, even if the number of bodies could not be accurately counted due to their mutilated state. Thankfully we were upwind of the scent of death, but I felt nauseous all the same and I couldn't bring myself to get a closer look, even though my power would have enabled me to do so. There was little reason to look for survivors – no one living would have remained here if they had the strength to move.

I reached for Masaru's shirt and gave it a slight tug. When he looked my way and saw my expression, there was no need for further communication; we started back the way we had come.

Ris frowned as we rejoined her. I didn't know whether it was for the deaths of the soldiers or for how unsettled I looked, but her sentiment was clear enough. I shook my head sadly and Ris nodded her silent agreement – she had seen no one living either.

A sudden gust of wind rustled through the trees around us.

"Yue," Masaru gasped, following the motion with a sharp turn of his head. Evidently Masaru's vision was much quicker than mine if he could see Yue when she was at her top speed. "And she's got Kaji on her back."

Without waiting for a response, Masaru headed back toward the ridge. With a 'wait here' gesture to Ris, I reluctantly followed him. I didn't want to look out over the battlefield again, but I wanted to know what Yue and Kaji were up to.

Yue had stopped in the middle of the bloody aftermath and Kaji was standing beside her by the time I joined Masaru at the top of the ridge. Neither Kaji nor Yue were looking about at the death surrounding them, but both had their faces turned up to the eastern sky instead.

High in the sky, but rapidly descending, were four comets of equal size. The fiery balls flew too low to the ground and too steadily to be in any way natural. What was going on here?

Masaru looked dumbfounded and I returned his expression, but out on the battlefield Kaji scrambled back onto Yue's back and in a flash they disappeared, only to reappear on the ridge with us.

"It's Lady Mikura and her Deathsquad," Kaji informed us worriedly. "There are four comets, so that means she's bringing about two thousand troops. We have to warn Narlhep – maybe we can take shelter in the temple?"

"Who's Lady Mikura?" Masaru asked the question on my mind.

"She's a Deathsquad General. We ran into her before, on our way to Taiyou," Kaji replied. "She may not look it, but she's strong. We were lucky to get away from her before."

Deathsquad, here? We had known our enemy – the Vile Emperor of the Ruby City – would try again to conquer Taiyou, especially now we were here, but we hadn't thought the attack would come so soon. Two thousand Deathsquad soldiers might not be enough to take Taiyou, but it was certainly more than we could handle at present.

"I'll warn Narlhep." I formed the arrow that would send him the message and watched it worriedly as it sped through the trees. "We should head back. If the Deathsquad is headed for the mountain, they'll need us back there."

"I don't think they're headed for the mountain, Yukari," Masaru informed me. "Look."

Masaru was right; the comets weren't going any further – they were landing right here.

Just beyond the field of carnage, the first of the four comets crashed, followed closely by the other three. In the place where the comets landed, there stood legions upon legions of Deathsquad soldiers in their black full-plate armour. And in front of them all stood a little girl in a black dress.

She looked to be about twelve years old with long limbs and a graceful appearance. Her ankle-length black dress was decorated with red and white trailing ribbons and thick black ribbons held her long golden-blonde hair up in two pigtails. Lady Mikura stood nonchalantly between her Deathsquad and the pile of corpses, and faced the soldiers with her hands clasped behind her back.

"I saw something blue between the trees." We could hear her high-pitched voice clearly from here as she addressed her troops. "You and you," she said, indicating two Deathsquad soldiers, "go and find it for me."

The two of them separated themselves from the ranks and the four of us scrambled down the ridge as quietly as possible. I silently cursed myself for forgetting that my arrows were so visible – of course Lady Mikura would have seen my message from the sky.

We were separating to hide in the foliage when I noticed Yue was not with us. I paused to look around for her when I felt hands grab my shoulders and I was hoisted upwards. I suppressed a yelp and Ris settled me on a sturdy tree branch, before placing her finger to her lips. I nodded and noted that from this vantage point I could see the Deathsquad. Other than the two soldiers who were almost to the treeline, the others had not moved. In the centre of the field of carnage, Yue approached the Deathsquad General with her arms held out where Mikura could see them. One of the Deathsquad soldiers stepped forward and took up a defensive position beside his General in the pose I had seen Deathsquad soldiers use before – shield out front and sword held over the opposite shoulder – ready to strike, or shoot a deadly beam of energy from his blade.

Lady Mikura tilted her head to the side as she contemplated Yue and then held up a hand to forestall her fervent defender. "Yue?" she called out, her childish voice crossing the distance easily. "What are you doing here?"

Whatever Yue's reply was, I couldn't hear it, but it was obvious the two were acquainted. I wondered briefly why Kaji or Yue hadn't mentioned encountering a Deathsquad General when they had recounted their adventures to us before.

I felt Ris' furred hand on mine and I turned to look at her. She was already looking down and I followed her gaze to realize the two Deathsquad soldiers Mikura had sent into the trees were directly beneath us now.

The Deathsquad soldiers were just as intimidating up close. Their armour was made of overlapping plates of jet black metal and combined with their black helmets and ruby-coloured visors, there was no real indication a person existed within the suit of armour. I caught a sudden flash of blue and had to stop myself from gasping in recognition of one of Masaru's blue energy knives he could summon with his powers as a Knight of Sapphiros.

Thankfully, the Deathsquad soldiers hadn't seen what I had – their viewpoint was different – but if they pressed on even the tiniest bit further, I knew Masaru would be discovered.

"Hey guys!" Mikura's voice rang out and the Deathsquad soldiers stopped to listen. "You can come back now! Yue says it's okay!"

I let out the breath I was holding in relief as the two Deathsquad soldiers left off their search. Masaru's blue knife winked out of existence and I turned back to see what was happening out in the clearing.

Yue's hair streamed out behind her as she dodged and weaved at regular human speed through the ranks of Deathsquad soldiers, Mikura trailing gleefully behind her. Were they playing tag?

Ris squeezed my hand this time and I tore myself away from watching Yue. She pointed at herself, then down. Below, Masaru was already out of his hiding spot and standing with Kaji. Ris hopped down out of the tree to join them. With one last look over at Yue – who had allowed herself to be wrestled to the ground by Mikura and was now rolling around, laughing – I, too, climbed down from the tree, albeit not as gracefully as the winged Kumori.

Masaru led the four of us further into the forest so we could speak without worry of being overheard. "Kaji," I addressed him as soon as Masaru indicated it was safe to do so, "who is Lady Mikura? Why is she acting like Yue is her long lost friend?"

He grimaced. "It's a long story – one we don't have time for right now. Don't be fooled by Yue's lack of concern, Lady Mikura is a very dangerous individual – with or without her Deathsquad."

I would have questioned him further, but Yue flashed to a stop beside us with the Deathsquad General in question upon her back.

"Hi!" Mikura said brightly.

Kaji took a step back, despite himself.

"Don't do anything rash," Yue cautioned us. "I'm taking her to Narlhep. She's willing to talk to him. I'll be back in five minutes."

And before any of us had the chance to reply, Yue was off again, the trees moving slightly with her passing.

"Kaji, tell me about Lady Mikura," I directed him.

"We met her at the outpost far to the north," he grimaced. "You know the last one we were supposed to stop at before crossing into Taiyou? Well, it wasn't exactly an outpost – it was a weapons factory run by a man who owed his allegiance to the Ruby City and it was operated by Croatin slaves…"

Yue had the man in her grasp, which meant she could take memories straight from his mind with her Sapphiros-given powers. Unfortunately, just as she had a hold of him, the man's robot assistant had her by the back of the neck. It was a standstill, only no one knew Kaji was there, invisible, thanks to his own power.

"Unhand me," the man commanded, "or my Binoid will have your head and I'll feed it to the Croatin brutes!"

Yue's eyes flashed cyan as she took what memories the man's mind had to offer. "He's sent a message to the Ruby City," she gasped. "He knew who we were the moment we walked in here. He hacked into Binaris' system – he's the one who told the Ruby City about our arrival."

"Kill her!" the man commanded his Binoid.

The Binoid raised his bladed right arm – this model was equipped for combat, being stationed in a weapons factory – and swiped it...

"I had a decision to make and I'm ashamed to say I made the wrong one," Kaji recounted with difficulty. "I could have stopped the Binoid, but I killed the man instead..."

The man levitated into the air slowly, held aloft by Kaji's magic. Frost crept along his skin, freezing him more solidly in place as his struggles subsided. Kaji's held his hand open and outstretched before him with his power holding the treacherous slave driver aloft. Rage rolled off Kaji in waves and the force of the emotion made him visible once more so the man he was killing would see his face.

Yue had never really been in any real danger. She caused the bladed arm of the Binoid to disappear with no trouble at all and stood frozen, watching with a horrified expression.

"Kaji, no! It's not worth it."

Kaji didn't listen; he closed his outstretched hand into a fist and the man exploded in a spray of blood and ice.

"Hey, thanks!" a new childishly-feminine voice exclaimed. "I really hated him!"

Kaji and Yue both stared dumbfounded at this new arrival, though Kaji still couldn't shake the horrible rage gripping him.

"Who're you?" Yue asked.

"I'm Lady Mikura – Deathsquad General, and you are?"

"I'm Yue," Yue answered, politely cautious, "and this is Kaji."

Kaji didn't wait for any more signal than that. The slave driver he had just killed had sent for a Deathsquad General to come for them; he wasn't going to just stand there and let a twelve year-old girl capture him and take him back to her master, or kill him if that was her intention. Kaji leapt at Mikura to deliver a powerful blow to any part of her he could reach.

The Deathsquad General made no attempt to move out his way. His fist impacted with her face, or at least the air around it, and he was filled with a sudden, intense pain all over his body. Kaji was flung backwards by the force of Mikura's personal defenses to land stunned on his backside, several feet away.

"If you're not going to play nice," Mikura exclaimed, pouting. "I'll just have to explode this factory with you still in it."

"But the Croatins are still inside," Yue protested. "They're kept locked up. Surely you'd at least let them out?"

"Hmm...I'm just supposed to destroy the factory. No one said anything about any Croatins."

"Will you let us get them out, then?" Yue asked. "You can have the factory, we don't want it."

"Sure, I can do that...if," Mikura added, "he apologizes."

"Long story short, Yue made me apologize," Kaji explained with a rueful expression, "and then Mikura let us free the Croatins and leave. We watched her destroy the factory and part of the mountain it was built into. She had her Deathsquad stationed outside, but she didn't even need them. She simply floated up into the air, formed a ball of red-black energy in one of her hands, and let it loose on the building. The whole place went down in no more than two explosions."

I pursed my lips, considering this while Ris leaned past me to pull Kaji into a hug.

Masaru, however, was looking about. "She's back," he informed us a split-second before a familiar gust of wind passed us in the direction of Mikura's Deathsquad.

The four of us followed much more slowly. If the Deathsquad was going to attack, there was an unspoken agreement we would have to fight, even knowing what we did about Mikura's capabilities and how far outnumbered we were – if only to buy Sabien and Narlhep some time to flee with everyone else.

Yue rejoined us before we had even made it so far as the ridge. "They've made an agreement," she announced. "There's not going to be any fighting today. Come on, let's get back to the temple. We have work to do."

She was off again without further explanation, and after ascertaining the Deathsquad were starting to march, we decided we didn't want to be found in the woods, so we had no choice but to follow Yue's direction and head back. Once we had put a little space between us and the Deathsquad, Ris and I flew for added speed – I wanted to know what was going on.

When we reached the mountain encampment, it was buzzing with activity. Narlhep was addressing a crowd of sorceresses and students from the former school of the Oujou. "You are free now to live within Taiyou and make your own way. You may remain here in this village if you wish, but you are no longer bound to the service of the Oujou and the Temple of Jade is off-limits to you. I ask that any of you who wish to do so, accompany me to the city of Taiyou. I will need your abilities in the times to come, but I won't force any of you – it is your life and your choice."

The sorceresses were of mixed responses to this, but to my surprise a large number of them chose to accompany us back to the city. There wasn't much time for explanations and 'King' Narlhep wasn't very forthcoming, as with the help of the sorceresses, and what pallets we could fabricate from anything we could find in the village, we prepared to leave the Temple in all haste.

"It's Lady Mikura's mountain now," Narlhep stated in a controlled voice. "She doesn't know it's Jedeite's temple – she just thinks it's a pretty mountain and wants to make it her new home. I've denied her the top floor where I've left the Kumori and some able-bodied soldiers with enough supplies to last them. The Kumori she knows about and they are allowed to come and go at will. The others are there to guard the weapon from her – that hall is a defensible position."

"So you're just letting his advance troops stay until the Vile Emperor can send reinforcements?" I asked.

"I had no other choice – but at least I've bought us some time."

CH. 2 – CRUMBLECAKES

It was a long, hard walk back to the city with the wounded in tow and the knowledge we had left a Deathsquad on Taiyoun soil behind us. In the interest of getting Narlhep back to the palace as quickly as possible, so he could inform the council of the change in leadership and begin preparing the country for war, we left the sorceresses and the able-bodied with Adel and Jeth, while the rest of us forged on ahead with the King.

Upon returning to the city of Taiyou, we discovered our troubles were far from over. Our path from the northern edge of the city to the palace was unobstructed, and devastatingly so; the city street and buildings that used to stand in our path were no longer present.

In place of the once beautiful boulevard of shops, benches, treed walkways, and gardens, there was now only a swath of destruction and rubble. It was possible someone or something else was responsible for the destruction of property, but the most logical explanation was that the blue-haired murderess that had attacked us at the Temple of Jade had also left this in her wake as she passed through town. We didn't spare the time to investigate the extent of the damage, however; we headed straight for the palace drawbridge where we encountered yet another problem – Lord Fuzen.

We had encountered Fuzen before. The image of the tall and imposing man with his thigh-length brown jacket, long black hair, sinister eye-patch, and mocking European accent was engraved in my mind ever since he tried to kill me and I had fled to save Masaru's life. He was one of the four Talons of the Vile Emperor and so far the only one of them we had run into on this world, though we had been accosted by all four back on Earth.

Fuzen was also the unwelcome Ambassador to Taiyou from the Ruby City. Thanks to a decree by Narlhep's father, Fuzen was the only Talon, and indeed the only agent of the Vile Emperor – until Mikura, that is – to gain access to Taiyou. Until now, Narlhep hadn't had the authority necessary to expel Fuzen from the city, which had been a major stumbling block in our negotiations with him.

Narlhep took a single step forward so he was standing just ahead of the rest of us. I was wary of Fuzen's dangerous expression; his uncovered eye betrayed his rage at seeing us with Narlhep. "Lord Fuzen, you are hereby expelled from Taiyou," Narlhep decreed, his voice ringing through the helmet he still had not removed. "Your interference will no longer be tolerated by the crown–"

Narlhep was, I was sure, beginning a very impassioned speech, but I could see Fuzen was shaking with rage and about to lash out like a cornered animal. In any case, I had heard as much as I needed to – Fuzen, agent of the Vile Emperor, was no longer protected by the laws of Taiyou. He had tried to kill Masaru and I both, and he had been responsible for the death of a Roughlander in my care. He was a criminal and our enemy; he deserved no mercy and no second chances. I formed an arrow, made it as sharp as the force of my will and loosed it on him. I held nothing back – I shot to kill.

Fuzen saw the arrow coming for him, but he had no chance to move out of its way and his sword wasn't even drawn. My aim was true – there was no doubt of that – and my arrow sunk directly into his chest. He cried out and his back arched involuntarily. Following my lead, Hotaru and Kaji both sprung into action. Hotaru summoned her two blades – one made from water and the other ice – and Kaji raised his right hand and made a fist. A cracking sound filled the air as ice spikes formed like a cage around Fuzen.

"You made one very big mistake this time, Fuzen," Kaji said. "There may be four of us and four Talons, but right now you are all alone."

In a flash, Yue appeared between us and Fuzen, her arms held out to either side. "Kaji, no! Stop it!" She didn't wait any longer to see if her words had sunk in; she flash-stepped again, and in the space of a heartbeat she had leapt onto Fuzen and was trying to break the ice surrounding him.

It took me no time at all to form another arrow, but I hesitated as Yue tried to save the Talon. Did she have some reason for protecting him, or was it just she couldn't bear to watch Kaji kill again after what had happened in the factory?

My view of Fuzen was partially blocked by Yue, who had latched on tightly to his front, her legs propped between two of the pillars of ice, but I could still make out the side of his face. As Yue fought against Kaji's ice, I caught a glint of red around the edge of Fuzen's eye patch and watched as the red glow strengthened with a mounting power. Whatever Fuzen was doing, he didn't intend to wait peacefully until his unlikely rescuer broke him free.

I formed five more arrows and fired at Fuzen, locking onto him as my target, so there was no chance of hurting Yue. The arrows split up in the air and surrounded the Talon before curving inwards to strike him in the back.

Yue must have taken note of the red glow because she ripped off Fuzen's eye patch and threw it aside. There she saw not a damaged eye, but a hollow socket containing only a glowing red ruby, twirling rapidly in place and pulsing with energy. With the ruby revealed, Fuzen grinned wickedly, despite his obvious discomfort.

But Yue was not intimidated. On Earth, before our powers were known to us, Yue had wrestled the armoured Vile Emperor – when compared to him, what was Fuzen to her? Without hesitating, she reached her hand into his exposed eye socket and plucked the glowing ruby out with her fingers. Yue's other hand shot straight up into the air, pointed index finger held aloft, and the power of the glowing ruby seemed to pass right through her body, only to be propelled upward and released in a waving ribbon of red energy. Fuzen stared blankly after the trail of red energy in the sky, until at last the flow stopped and he crumpled, his strength gone.

Yue lowered her arm slowly and stumbled back from the rapidly melting ice. Her shoulders slumped tiredly and she swayed with the effort of trying to remain upright. With a last spurt of energy she lifted up the now dull, lifeless ruby, and threw it down with as much strength as she could muster. It shattered easily, like it was no more than powerless red glass.

The rest of us, Chosen, Knights, and newly-made King included, stood motionless with the gravity of what had just occurred on the drawbridge of the palace of Taiyou. Beyond the mound of melting ice where the body of Fuzen lay, his blood colouring the ice beneath him, there stood several Legionnaires, hesitating as they waited for orders.

Yue, oblivious to her audience, took one step forward and then another, before she was close enough to kneel at Fuzen's side. Slowly, and not without effort, she lifted one of his limp arms to roll him over. Even from here I could tell he was unconscious, maybe even dying, but it was also clear something was happening to him. Fuzen was changing. His features were softening and the lines of age on his face fading, causing a sense of familiarity to build. I knew this person from somewhere – I was sure I had seen him before.

Kaji beside me gasped in sudden recognition and that was enough to tell me who I was looking at – Goji Nakamura, president of Shinjuku high school's student council…but how?

"Arrest Fuzen," Narlhep commanded.

"No, don't!" I called out. "He needs medical attention, let me see to him."

Narlhep nodded and held up his hand to stop the Legionnaires from advancing.

Sabien left the prisoner he had been escorting – Viron – to Rama and walked forward. "I'll carry him."

As I followed after Sabien, my mind was whirling and it was all I could do to put one foot in front of the other. I didn't know Goji well, but he was someone from back home – someone I had gone to high school with. That had only been two months ago, but it felt like forever. I gave a sidelong glance to Kaji who simply looked tortured; I could understand why – Kaji had been student council treasurer and had worked very closely with our affable, yet eccentric student council president.

My hands trembled and I clenched them into fists so no one would see just how shaken I was – I had almost killed Goji. He was not some faceless Deathsquad soldier, or a Talon of the Vile

Emperor, or even someone who was trying to kill me first. I hadn't fired those arrows in self-defense; I had tried to kill with them – never mind that I hadn't known who I was really attacking at the time.

I forced myself to look at Goji in Sabien's arms as we walked through vaguely familiar palace hallways. His face was unmistakable now, though his right eye was missing, his hair long and unkempt, and the clothes all wrong. But was it really Goji? Was it even possible he could be here on this distant world in the guise of one of our enemies?

Or was this the guise? Was it that the Vile Emperor, or the Talons themselves, sought to look like people we knew in order to confuse us, to make us hesitate in killing them?

The questions whirled in my mind, but as I had yet to understand the circumstances of our arrival, I had no hope of understanding this. It was possible Goji had left Earth when we had, or had been taken by the Vile Emperor at some other point. It was also possible Goji really was Fuzen and had been so all along. All I could do was hope I could help save his life to make reparations for the damage I had caused him, so I could ask him and figure out the truth for myself.

Sabien lowered Goji onto a bed in a spare room of the palace, presumably one Narlhep was allowing us to use. I had been too preoccupied with my thoughts to pay attention to what had been decided. Ris accompanied us, as had Kaji and Hotaru, but I didn't know where Yue or the others had gone.

Looking about the room, I snapped into focus. I had a patient and it was time for me to work. "This room is small, I can't have everyone crowding it. Ris, if you'll stay and help, I would appreciate it. Hotaru, Kaji," I said, turning to them, "I'll need bandages and clean water. After that, I have to ask you to stay outside. You'll only be in the way."

As soon as they had left, their presence in the room was replaced by two palace guards and a person who introduced himself to me as a palace medic. "Prince Narlhep requested they be sent in case Fuzen should awake and cause any problems," the medic informed me, referring to the guards.

"Very well," I agreed, seeing the logic in this – Goji could, indeed, still be Fuzen, though his appearance had changed. It was part of the reason I hadn't wanted Kaji or Hotaru in the room. Of the three of us, I was the only one I thought would not be lulled into a false sense of security by Fuzen's new face.

Sabien took up position with the guards as Ris and I got to work. It made it simpler to know where his injuries were when I was the one to have inflicted them. I tried not to think about that as I did my initial inspection. I placed my hand upon Goji's neck to check his pulse and I froze in terror – there was no heartbeat. My own heart skipped a beat in my chest – I had killed him.

I felt a shallow intake of breath beneath my hand and I stared at Goji in confusion, before moving my shaking hand to hover over his mouth and nose. After a moment, I felt the warm air from his breath; against all logic, he was still breathing.

"Ris," I called the attention of the Kumori, "his heart."

Ris placed one of her delicate hands on Goji's chest just over his heart. She paused a moment and then looked back up at me with a shake of her head. Her expressive face showed both her confusion and the pity she felt for the patient before her. She put her hands to her own heart, then mimed taking it and throwing it away, and then shrugged as if to say she knew how impossible it seemed.

I looked from Ris back to Goji in confusion – he had no heart? His heart had been thrown away? I didn't fully understand what she was trying to tell me, but maybe there was a way I could see for myself.

Back on Earth I had worn glasses for reading and focusing on details close up, but since I began developing my powers, I discovered I didn't need them anymore, and my vision had actually improved beyond what a person would call normal. With my power I could now focus on something extremely far away, or zoom in on something before me, almost to the microscopic level. I had also found that when magic was present, especially in the case of an illusion, I could sometimes see through it if I concentrated on it the right way.

I don't know how I managed it exactly, but I twisted my vision and all of a sudden, I was looking into Goji's chest and the hole where his heart should have been. My vision flickered; for a moment, I saw the heart as it should be and I felt a shiver go through me, as if the room had abruptly gone cold. Startled out of my focus, I lifted my head to look around and the room I saw wasn't in the palace of Taiyou...

I heard the familiar beeping of a heart monitor and tasted sterile hospital air. The room was stark white and perfectly clean. Goji lay still on a hospital bed, his arm hooked up to an I.V. and his body hooked up to various machines blipping and whirring softly. The early morning light streamed in through the hospital window, warring with the fluorescent bulbs. I caught a glimpse of movement as someone – a nurse, most likely – crossed my field of vision through the pane of glass on the door.

I blinked and was staring at the marble wall of the makeshift sickroom in the palace of Taiyou, trying desperately to hold on to the vision of a hospital room in Japan.

I forced myself to breathe again; the moment, whatever it had been, had passed. I was not in Japan, but in Taiyou. But maybe for Goji it was different. I looked down at my patient again as Ris helpfully used her magic to lift Goji and the palace medic began to remove his jacket and shirt in order to access his wounds. Goji was here, or at least this body that looked like him was, but he had no heart, which wasn't exactly possible. The hospital room I had seen so briefly had been too real and too detailed for me to have invented it, and when I had seen it I had been using my power to try and see beyond Goji to where his heart was.

Perhaps Goji was also in Japan where he had a heart beating to keep him alive here. It was no more impossible than anything else, but the questions remained of how Goji had gotten this way and why he had been masquerading as Fuzen.

Facts and suppositions still churning through my mind, I helped Ris and the medic clean Goji's wounds and then stood back to let Ris do what she could to mend them with her magic. She could do nothing for his missing eye, but I was somewhat relieved to watch the damage my arrows had caused disappear under Ris' direction.

I'm not exactly sure how much time passed while I sat by Goji's side, listening to the sound of his breathing. Ris came and went, checking on his progress and frowning each time she discovered he had not yet woken. There was nothing physically wrong with him after Ris' ministrations, but no matter what we tried he remained as he was. I tried more than once to see the hospital room again, to prove to myself what I had seen, but all I could manage by twisting my vision was seeing into the unnatural hole in his chest. Once or twice I caught glimpses of the heart that should be there and heard the faintest of beeps I might have been inventing.

After a time, Goji's continued breathing became a very soothing sound. I must have drifted off only to be awoken by a sudden, sharp intake of breath. Goji – long-haired and disheveled looking – was sitting bolt upright in the bed and looking around himself in a panic.

"Calm down, you're all right," I told Goji – or Fuzen, whoever he was.

"Where am I? What's going on here?" The heavy European accent broke my heart – perhaps this was Fuzen after all.

"You're in the palace of Taiyou," I answered as calmly as possible, "You've been gravely injured, but you're going to be okay."

"Yukari?" Goji's one blue eye locked onto me as if trying to identify who I was. "Is that you? I recognize the voice, but…you look so different."

The dreaded accent faded in and out as he spoke, and I could almost recognize Goji's voice underneath. I wasn't yet fully convinced either way as to his identity, but the possibility this really was Goji was strengthening.

"It's me," I choked a little on the words. "You've never seen me with my hair down before, or without my glasses."

"Ah." Goji leaned back and closed his eye. After a moment his eye opened again to look at me. "Where's Taiyou?"

"It's a long story," I answered evasively. "What's the last thing you remember?"

"It all seems really fuzzy and far away, but I guess it was walking down the street with Tim – you know, Harford-san?" I nodded – Tim Harford was an exchange student who had been in my class. "Hotaru called me on my cell phone…something about Shuzhue? I think she was looking for her. I told her I didn't know where she was, but I would head back to school and check…"

My heart pounded in my chest at Goji's words. Accent notwithstanding, this couldn't be Fuzen. Goji had known all of us on Earth – especially Kaji – and Shuzhue was Kaji's girlfriend. The night we left, Shuzhue had been missing, and Kaji and Hotaru had been searching for signs of her. There was no way Fuzen could have known that, but it was certainly possible Hotaru had called Goji to check for Shuzhue's whereabouts and it would be a simple matter to confirm Goji's story with Hotaru.

Before I could question Goji any further, Kaji, Hotaru, and Yue chose that moment to return. The guards, on edge due to the presence of such an infamous prisoner, immediately spun around to the open door to face the three remaining Chosen of Sapphiros.

"Let them in," I said tiredly.

"We have orders," one of them responded.

Yue handed the man a rolled up document. "He's not Fuzen and King Narlhep has given his word he will be guarded, but not treated as a prisoner until proven otherwise."

The guards read the document and, seemingly satisfied, let the three of them into the room. I stood aside as Kaji, Hotaru, and Yue crowded around Goji, who looked pleased to see them, and I backed away from the reunion until I was out of the room. Kaji and the others could decide how to fill their friend in on all that had happened; I needed some time to think this all over and I couldn't do that here.

I left the palace and my feathered wings, made from blue energy like my arrows, sprung from my back and carried me into the air without me making a conscious decision to fly. As I had learned the hard way, sometimes powerful emotion triggered our powers and at other times that same level of emotion could inhibit them.

I flew over the city of Taiyou, subconsciously following the path of destruction that cut through the city in an unerring straight line. I realized my destination as soon as I caught sight of it: the Roughlander Sanctioned Outpost. Located on the southern edge of the city of Taiyou, it would be the perfect place to go to be alone and really, it was the closest thing I had to a home here in Taiyou.

The outpost building, similar in design to all the other Roughlander outposts I had been to, only on a smaller scale, stood in a fenced-in compound near the bridge of Taiyou, which crossed the only sizable body of water on this world. The Sanctioned Outpost had formerly been a prison for diseased Roughlanders who crossed into Taiyou from the desert wastes outside, but since our coming that, among many other things, had changed. Now the outpost stood empty, as the Roughlanders who had been there had accompanied us north to the temple and were now on their way back to the city with Adel and Jeth.

Landing at the outpost, I discovered the compound wasn't as empty as I had believed; the wounded were back. I found Sabien in the outpost yard by the fountain conversing with Jeth.

"Has there been any change, then?" Sabien asked.

"He's awake and he's not Fuzen. He's actually someone we knew from Earth."

He nodded. "Everyone is back and settling in here now that it is safe to do so again. Adel and Masaru have gone out to the bridge to investigate how far the damage goes."

I absorbed the possible ramifications of this. There was a Deathsquad encampment on the far side of the bridge of Taiyou as a result of the ceasefire agreement between the two countries, and determining whether they had suffered losses might indicate whose side the blue-haired woman was on. In either case, both the deadly woman and the Deathsquad were dangerous, and now that Taiyou's defenses were down thanks to Virons' treachery, a close eye would have to be kept on them to ensure they didn't try to enter and discover that the magic barrier that had held them at bay for so long no longer existed.

"I'll go join them," I told Sabien, "just in case."

"Make sure you return to report what you find. The King will have to be informed of the situation on his border."

I took off like I had before; flying seemed as easy and natural as breathing now. I had little trouble locating Masaru and Adel, as they were the only people in the vicinity of the bridge, and that worried me. When I had crossed into Taiyou before I had taken the ferry, but from that vantage point I had seen people on the bridge from all walks of life, making their way to and from the city, with Legionnaires posted at either end as border guards. Now, the lengthy bridge over the lake was silent and empty, save for Masaru and Adel who were almost at the middle of the bridge's length by the time I reached them.

I drifted down to land beside them and together we crossed the rest of the distance to where the Deathsquad encampment had been, but no longer stood – there were no survivors here, either.

The stench was overpowering and I gathered these bodies – so similar to the ones we had found in the forest – had been here for some time now, as there had been no one left alive to report the tragedy that had occurred here. The Deathsquad soldiers were the legions of my enemy and the enemies of Taiyou, but even knowing that, I couldn't help feeling all this death and carnage was a horrible waste.

Masaru had gone down to investigate the docks to see if the ferry still remained and if anyone had taken refuge there, leaving Adel and I standing and looking over a battlefield filled with mangled corpses. Walking off a ways, I turned to stare out over the empty wasteland instead; I had seen enough death today.

"Yukari," Adel spoke my name with a hint of uncertainty as she joined me, looking out over the featureless rock with its light dusting of sand blown in from the desert. "I have to ask you something and I want your honest opinion."

"I'll do my best, Adel," I frowned. I wasn't sure if I was up to helping anyone else with their problems.

"Aysel was never made a Knight of Sapphiros, but I was," she began. "Sometimes I wonder why that is – what Sapphiros saw in me that isn't present in my sister. My question is…do you think I am worthy of this position…of being your Knight?"

"I know your opinions on the matter, so you may not agree with me, but I believe both you and Aysel are more than worthy of being Knights," I told her truthfully. Until being informed otherwise, I had assumed Aysel was a Knight like the others we had found waiting for us at the Temple of Sapphire. "You are the strongest woman I know, and I don't just mean in the physical sense of the word, either. Aysel is strong too, but in a different way. I don't know why she wasn't Knighted like the rest of you. I don't know what qualities made a Knight in those days, but her dedication since I've known her qualifies her in my eyes, if nothing else does."

Adel looked stricken. "I must admit my own dedication is waning. The world as it is now is not the one I am used to and this war isn't my own. With Aysel injured…I was thinking I might try to return to our home and see if it still stands, or maybe find a safe place where she can recover."

Adel's words hurt me in a way I couldn't fully explain. I hadn't known the Knights very long and I hadn't realized I was growing so attached to them, especially Adel, whose proud nature I identified with. Out of all of the Knights, I hadn't expected her to feel this way or want to leave when things got tough, though I understood the sentiment when she said this war wasn't her own. We had been dragged into this due to circumstances beyond our control, but the

Knights were from eight hundred years in this world's past, just as we were from another world altogether.

"I can't make you stay," I told her, "any of you. This isn't our fight, I know that. But do you think anywhere on this world will be any safer? It's dangerous here. The world is in turmoil and if it's known who you are, you'll be hunted. I know you're not the type to hide and I doubt you want to spend the rest of Aysel's life and yours running.

"We need you, Adel. I need you. We're not strong enough on our own. I won't tell you to stay, but I'm asking you to."

Adel considered this and then nodded. "All right. I'll stay for the time being and think it through – and Yukari…thank you."

Adel and I rejoined with Masaru and we began the trek back to the Sanctioned Outpost. I sent off a message arrow to Narlhep to let him know his southern border was unguarded and he should rectify the situation as soon as possible. When we got back to the outpost building, Adel left Masaru and I inside, while she went to find out where Sabien had gone.

The outpost was bustling, but not as much as it used to be. We had lost so many Roughlanders at the temple and the sorceresses had decided to accept King Narlhep's hospitality at the palace. Masaru and I found ourselves with a rare moment alone on the ground floor of the outpost building, though I could see past him to the open archway, which led to the outside courtyard where the occasional Roughlander walked by.

I had promised myself I would take the next available opportunity to talk to him and it looked like this was it. I felt woefully unprepared, but the scare of not knowing if he had survived the battle of the temple had taught me I had to seize the moments I had and not squander them.

"Masaru, can I talk to you for a moment?"

"Aye, of course ye can."

I turned my back to him to hide my embarrassment and started my way up the stairs to the second floor of the outpost for a little bit more privacy. By the sound of his footsteps on the stone stairs behind me, Masaru followed my lead. I stopped suddenly, only halfway up the rounded stairwell, when I heard voices and laughter coming from the common room, and I turned back to Masaru.

"I suppose here'll do as well as anywhere," I said nervously, trying without success to meet his eyes.

"Aye," Masaru replied, confused. "What is it, Yukari?"

I forced myself to breathe in and out at a steady rate. "There's been something I've been meaning to tell you for a little while now. I realized something very important when Fuzen tried to prevent me from saving you back at that warehouse." I didn't want to remind him of that time again – Masaru had lost several of his friends that I hadn't been able to save as I had saved him – but it was important for him to understand how I came to realize how I felt about him. "When I first came here I was afraid of everything, but when Fuzen leapt at us with his sword intent on killing us both – I wasn't afraid...not like I used to be, anyway."

In an attempt to prove my own courage, I forced myself to meet his eyes. They were the same startling blue they had turned after he was Knighted and they were filled with confusion. I took another deep breath. I had started this, now I had better finish it in case this was the only chance I got. "I realized then there was something more important to me than being afraid – you were more important." I could see in his eyes he didn't yet understand. "I saved you from that warehouse because I couldn't bear to lose you..."

I watched as sudden realization crossed his features, but then I couldn't read his expression. I waited for what seemed like an eternity as he processed what I had just told him. I hesitated in finishing what I had come here to say, in case he didn't want to hear it.

"There's a saying among the Roughlanders," Masaru said suddenly. "When something happens the first time, it could be by accident. When it happens a second time, it could be a coincidence. But when something happens a third time...well, then...it can only be fate."

When I had first kissed Masaru it had not been an accident exactly, but certainly not something I had planned. I had done it to shock him out of the effects of a curse placed upon him by Oujou magic, and in the moment our lips met I had felt something a little stronger than I had intended. The second time I had kissed him it was as a gift to acknowledge the completion of the Knighting ceremony as he returned to consciousness, his strength miraculously returned by his Knighting after being so close to death only moments before.

This time, when Masaru kissed me, it was completely different and it meant a whole lot more. He took hold of both of my hands and pulled me closer to him as he stepped up one of the stairs to meet me in the middle. His lips on mine were as warm and soft as I remembered, but filled with a passion I had never experienced before. We stayed like that until we were interrupted by the sound of someone clearing their throat on the stairs below us.

We broke apart hastily and I looked down to find Adel with her hands on her hips. I flushed beet red and I put another step's worth of space between myself and Masaru. Adel's stern expression evaporated abruptly, leaving a sly smile in its place. "I wouldn't let Sabien catch you at that. You know how he feels about it, Masaru."

"Aye," Masaru said, lowering his head with a hint of shame, "he's made himself pretty clear about it."

I looked from Adel to Masaru in confusion – there was obviously something I was missing.

"Sabien's of the opinion I'll only distract ye, or the other way around," Masaru told me.

"You mean, he knew? And he spoke to you about it?"

"Aye, haven't ye noticed he's been keeping us apart whenever he can? I told him it wasn't like that – I didn't know ye felt that way about me, I mean, but…"

"Adel?" Sabien's voice called from downstairs and we instantly ceased the discussion we were having. I was taken aback by Sabien's interference, but I filed it away as something I would think over later and focused on controlling my features.

Masaru and I followed Adel separately down the stairs, leaving some space between us. The three of us filled Sabien in on all we had learned from the Rubian encampment, which wasn't much. When we were just about finished our discussion, Yue appeared, dressed in Roughlander clothes and with a bundle on her back like she was preparing for a journey.

"I just thought I'd stop off and let you know I'm going," Yue said, affixing her canteen to one of her Roughlander belts. "I'm going to find the Chosen of Jedeite and bring him or her back like Jedeite asked me to."

"You're going out into the Sand Lakes…alone?" I asked.

"I know ye're fast Yue, but I don't recommend for anyone to travel alone across the Sand Lakes – there's more waitin' for you out there than just Deathsquads," Masaru seconded.

"Masaru and Yukari are right," Sabien agreed. "The Sand Lakes are very dangerous. I know you feel you need to do as Jedeite has asked you to, but I would feel better if you took at least Masaru with you as a guide. He knows more about the Sand Lakes than any of us do."

"No." The word escaped my lips before I had a chance to stop it and everyone, including Sabien, turned from Yue to look at me. I had almost lost Masaru once; I didn't want to send him on a fool's errand with Yue through the deadly Sand Lakes so I might never know what became of him. "I mean, yes, you shouldn't go alone, but if we are to split up again, don't you think it would be best to do it in groups like we did before? The Sand Lakes are dangerous, we don't know who that woman was or where she went, and there could be more Deathsquads waiting out there for us, or preparing to attack Taiyou now that they have a foothold here. I'd even go so far as to say we're needed here – as a group – to defend Taiyou like we promised. We're stronger together."

"We need to grow stronger apart as well," Yue countered, "and this is an excellent chance to do that."

"I don't feel I should leave Taiyou, but at least take Hotaru or Kaji with you," I pleaded. "Have you even told them you're leaving?"

A sudden shift of Yue's eyes betrayed the truth. "I was going to stop there next," she lied. "But I'm going to be travelling fast – really fast. I don't think anyone else would be able to keep up with me and I should be able to outrun anything that tries to stop me."

"Hotaru or Kaji would be no better than Yue out in the Sand Lake," Masaru said. "I mean no offense to any of ye, of course."

"With your method of travel is it possible for you to take someone else with you, Yue?" Sabien asked.

"Well, it'll slow me down, but I suppose I could carry a lighter person on my back like I did with Sir Rama's captain before. Who do you have in mind?"

"You can take me," Razor offered, coming down the stairs onto the main floor of the outpost building, "though I might have to go on a diet." He patted his perfectly flat stomach with a self-deprecating smile.

Masaru watched Razor like a hawk as he presented himself before Yue. Razor, with his rugged eye patch, aged Roughlander leathers, and missing pinky finger, appeared rough and ready for action. In truth, he was a charmer and a rogue, but an all around useful person to have on your side. Masaru would disagree with my assessment, but there seemed to be some bad blood between them that neither of them would explain. Masaru might not think Razor was a good choice for Yue's companion in the desert, but compared to a lot of other options, I thought Razor would do a fine job.

Yue inspected Razor before nodding. "You'll do, hop on."

"Hold your mount, there – Yue, is it?" Razor cautioned. "You're going to want to let me get a few supplies together first. I doubt whatever you have in that rucksack will be enough to get us by."

"Yue," I tried one last time, "please, don't do this. There's no need for us to separate. I meant what I said about us being stronger together."

"I'll be fine." She dismissed my worries with a wave of her hand. "I'll only be gone for a few days, five at the most. Two days out, one to look around, and two days back. I won't go any further and if I don't find the Chosen of Jedeite in that amount of time, I'll come back."

"That sounds like a solid plan to me," Sabien agreed, "but I would make sure you inform King Narlhep about your intentions first, Yue. You did make an alliance with him on the grounds you would be here to defend Taiyou if it was attacked. I know we are not in battle currently, but there is an occupying force in the temple."

"Fine, I'll tell him," Yue conceded. "Can I go now?"

Sabien nodded and with a look to Razor and a mumbled, "I'll be back for you," Yue flashed away, disappearing through the open doorway.

Razor made to follow after her, though at a normal human pace, and I started after him. "I know you'll look after her and that I don't have to ask, but I was actually wondering if you could do me a favour while you're out there. If you happen to stop by Lord Hex's outpost, could you see if Dahlia made it there? Do you know who she is?"

Razor gave a half-smile. "Everyone knows Corporal Dahlia."

I nodded; in my short association with the Roughlander Corporal, I had seen she left quite an impression on people. "Good. Apparently, she split up from Kaji and Yue after their visit to the

Croatin home base to ride across the Sand Lake and warn us about the Deathsquad encampment on the border of Taiyou. She never caught up with us and she's not in Taiyou, so I thought maybe she followed our trail to Hex's outpost and decided to stop there, instead of trying to sneak past the Deathsquad soldiers to follow us into the city."

"It's possible. Dahlia won't be happy to see me again, but I'll find out if she's there or not for you."

"Thank you...and take care of Yue for me."

"Of course," Razor agreed with a wry smile. "It would be my pleasure."

When I went back inside, Adel and Sabien had left with the suggestion we all return to the palace to meet with King Narlhep and decide our next course of action. Masaru had waited behind to tell me this and offer to accompany me on the walk back. "I thought maybe ye'd walk with me if ye didn't mind. I know flyin' is a bit faster for ye, but I don't figure ye're in too much of a hurry."

I nodded somewhat shyly. I had finally told Masaru the secret I had been guarding and now that my feelings were out in the open, I didn't quite know how to act around him. Masaru put his hand on mine as we exited the outpost compound and began our walk through the city. I was inordinately pleased with this turn of events and I realized suddenly I had done it; I had finally revealed how I felt to Masaru and for a wonder, it seemed he had accepted me and possibly felt similarly towards me. For some of the distance as we walked hand in hand through the bustling streets of Taiyou, I was lost in an unfamiliar state of bliss.

"Masaru, Yukari!"

It was quite a surprise to hear my name called out in the city streets of Taiyou. Looking around for the source of the call, I discovered it was Marc, an ex-Roughlander who had settled in Taiyou after a stint as a city guard. Masaru and I both had spent some time, albeit separately, squatting in Marc's storehouse, but he had been more than understanding, doing what he could to help us while we were faced with difficult times. Marc was smiling and waving us over to where he stood near a partially destroyed building with his young daughter, Sally. We changed course and joined Marc and Sally as he lifted up a plank of wood to hand to someone on a ladder above him.

Sally, whom I had only seen once, and from a distance at that, looked extremely excited to see me. The little red-haired girl was practically dancing from foot to foot and occasionally tugging on her father's sleeve while she regarded me with wide eyes.

"What is it, honey?" Marc asked.

"Is she going to do the thing?" Sally asked, miming with her hands something disappearing in a puff.

Marc smiled a little at my uncomfortable expression; he now knew I was a Chosen and capable of things average people weren't. "I'm afraid she saw you at whatever you were doing and she hasn't stopped asking about it since."

"It was amazing!" Sally exclaimed.

I laughed suddenly, I couldn't help it. Despite all the hardships I had faced and the worries I still carried around with me, the recent conversation with Masaru had made me somewhat giddy. We said goodbye to Sally and Marc, and continued on along the destroyed patch of the city. I was pleased and impressed to note the citizens of Taiyou were already working together to make repairs to the homes and businesses that had been affected. We saw average people, city guards, and Legionnaires building and clearing debris, and even Masaru and I stopped more than once to lend a hand when it was needed.

The city and the country, whether they all knew the news or not, had just taken a few major hits – the destruction in the city; the presence of a Deathsquad on Taiyoun soil; the discovery of a traitorous regent; and the untimely death of his daughter, Kosetsu, the woman formerly destined to be Narlhep's queen. Even through all that, the people struggled on and had the spirit to help each other rebuild and reclaim what was theirs. Taiyou wasn't out of the woods yet by any means, but I was glad to see Narlhep had good people who were worth protecting, and would not just lie down and let their homes be taken from them.

As we continued our walk, I took hold of Masaru's hand once more and he turned his head to smile at me. I didn't have a home here, but I determined I wasn't going to lose what little I had managed to gain. The world might fall apart around us, but I was going to hold on to Masaru and keep him safe no matter what else it might cost me.

CH. 3 – FACING IN ALL DIRECTIONS

"Where're they going?" Masaru asked, referring to the citizens of Taiyou, who all seemed to be flocking to the marketplace, leaving behind the tasks they were working on or closing down their storefronts temporarily to do so.

We pushed through the busy streets after them and made our way to the crowded marketplace. Taiyou's market square was a busy place at almost any time of day; the sun never set and so the market never closed, operating in shifts instead, but now every inch of space was filled with people. Some, like Masaru and I, were wondering what was going on, while others were talking animatedly amongst themselves. At the centre of the market square, before an elaborate fountain, was a table manned by two individuals.

I was surprised enough to see Kaji, but Mifa was by far the bigger shock. Mifa had long, brown hair to the middle of her back and was pretty in a reserved way in her modest Taiyoun-style robes. My shy and quiet friend, with her controversial theories, was the last person I expected to find at the centre of a crowd of people vying for her attention.

"What's going on here?'

"Yukari!" Mifa smiled, noticing me for the first time. "We're having a raffle and collecting names of volunteers."

"Volunteers for what?" Masaru asked.

"Well, for defense of the city mainly," she explained, "but we won't turn away anybody who wants to help. Everyone has something they can do."

I looked to Kaji, who was just finishing up talking to someone while taking notes. "Was this his idea?"

"Oh, no – it was Goji's," Mifa answered, before being interrupted by someone else with a question about the raffle. "Excuse me a minute."

Goji Nakamura, president of Shinjuku High's student council, had always been ambitious and somewhat of an organizational genius. Last year – his first year as president – he had managed to organize a fundraiser that brought in enough money to construct the new swimming arena over the summer. Goji had a way of rallying people behind him and using his social contacts to accomplish whatever he set his mind to. Even though he had woken up earlier today disoriented and out of place it seemed he had somehow miraculously already regained his footing and was plowing forward doing what it was he did best.

As I watched, Goji himself came into view. Thankfully, he had managed to cut his hair back to the way I remembered it, and he had exchanged the jacket Fuzen had been wearing for a set of Taiyoun robes. There was nothing he could do about the eye patch – he needed it now – but at least he didn't look like Fuzen anymore.

"It's a brilliant idea, really," Kaji informed me. "Goji spoke to Narlhep as soon as he was feeling up to it. He told him he wanted to help. Naturally, Narlhep wasn't inclined to trust him. The King told Goji that if he could prove himself useful, then he could stay on in an advisory capacity as Fuzen had before. So Goji's offering a raffle to gain interest and let people know what's going on. If they want to help or have some useful skills to contribute, we take their names down along with what they have to offer and we enter them into the draw. Goji will then be able to offer these names to the King as a sort of civilian army to help in the defense of Taiyou."

"You told him everything?" I asked.

"Yue did," Kaji answered. "She gave him her memories. I gather it was faster that way and he was able to see it for himself."

I shook my head. I was so far from home that Goji was one of the last people I ever expected to see again and I was a little taken aback by how fast he had gotten this all underway.

"Speaking of Yue," I began, "are you coming back to the palace? I believe we're organizing a meeting to discuss what our plans are. I know Yue plans to go find the Chosen of Jedeite. I've already told her I don't want her to go alone, but she's at least conceded to taking Razor with her."

"I'd like to continue giving Goji a hand here, but I'll come back later. If a time gets scheduled for the meeting, you'll let me know, right?"

I nodded my agreement and together, Masaru and I returned to the palace.

When we eventually gathered to speak with Narlhep it was in the throne room, but it was set up as a meeting room, as it presumably had been for the council meeting earlier in the day. There was a long, wide, wooden table that had been brought in and it was well able to accommodate all of us Knights and Chosen, as well as King Narlhep and the few council members who had decided to stay, including Rama who was filling in for his father. The council members in the room were each introduced to us, but the only one whose name stood out to me was the one woman who seemed to be a prominent member of the council, Lady Rhine.

The elegant woman carried herself with a confident bearing. She stood to Narlhep's right, with a long staff with an intricately carved head held in her right hand. Her pink and burgundy dress was medieval in style, and its costume-like strangeness immediately reminded me of the oddness of our circumstances. However used to this world I thought I was getting, it struck me suddenly that we were meeting with a medieval king in full armour – Narlhep had still not removed his helmet – in a far away land, on the brink of war.

Had the circumstances not been so real, they might have been comical, but as it was the reminder only served to make me apprehensive of how this meeting would go. I had to remember I had very little idea of what to expect here, especially now that Narlhep's disposition seemed to have changed so drastically since he had emerged from the Temple of Jade.

"Before anything else," he began, his voice reverberating slightly as he spoke through his helmet, "I should inform you I received a request today from the man formerly known as Lord Fuzen, Talon of the Vile Emperor. Due to a set of extraordinary circumstances, he claims he is no longer the person he once was and is, in reality, a friend of the Chosen of Sapphiros."

I gathered he was not talking directly to us, but making a formal announcement to the room at large. His words were unfeeling, but it seemed Narlhep was fitting into his role as King of Taiyou a lot faster than anyone would have predicted.

"I am allowing him the chance to prove his resourcefulness and dedication before I decide if he will be allowed to remain in Taiyou," Narlhep continued. "Enter, Goji Nakamura."

Kaji had given me the impression Goji had approached Narlhep and asked for an opportunity, but it seemed the reality was the opposite. The double doors opened to reveal Goji and a small team of people, one of whom was carrying a wheelbarrow filled to the brim with krevels, while each of the others held onto orderly stacks of paper. Mifa stood to Goji's left, looking nervous but hopeful.

"Your Majesty, I would like to introduce you to your new advisory council," Goji announced and I did a double take as I was abruptly reminded of another place and another time.

Where Shuzhue had once stood at Goji's side, there was now Mifa, and though Kaji was, I suppose, still a part of Goji's team, now he was a Chosen of Sapphiros and sat with the King. Things had changed so much, but yet I suppose there were a few things that remarkably remained the same. It struck me suddenly that if Goji was here, maybe he wasn't the only one. We knew Shuzhue had gone missing. If Goji was one of the Talons, then who were the other three?

"I know you have a lot to discuss with your council and the Chosen of Sapphiros, so I'll make this as brief as possible. As you can see," Goji was saying, referring to small booklets he had handed out to each person at the table, which were cleverly written in Japanese for us and Taiyoun for everyone else present, "through speaking to the general populace, I have garnered an interest in the war effort and also compiled a comprehensive list of volunteers for a reserve force, as well as possible skills and trades that could be of use to us. In addition to the obvious benefits of such an exercise, this list has allowed me to gain contact information with the intention to organize these people and their businesses for the use of the crown if necessary.

"My team and I have also sold a number of war bonds," Goji continued, indicating the barrel, "thereby gaining additional krevels the crown can use to fund the war effort. All you have to do, your Majesty, is award a tour of the palace to the lucky winner of the raffle."

"You did this all today?" Lady Rhine asked.

"We did," Goji confirmed, sharing credit with his team. "And this was just the marketplace. If given leave to survey the rest of the city or to contact the provinces, I'm certain much more can be accomplished in short order."

The room fell silent as Narlhep considered Goji through his armoured helmet. "Kaji did say you were industrious, but there is still one problem – you haven't yet given me any reason to trust you."

"I know you have no reason to trust me, aside from my word. I understand my presence in Taiyou could be seen as a ploy by your enemies. I apologize for what Fuzen did while he had control over my body, but I assure you I am not him and I have no connections with the Ruby City, nor do I want them." Goji faced Narlhep's impassive helmet with a determined pride. "I am far away from home, but while I am here I would very much appreciate the chance to make a difference. I know I can be of use to you, King Narlhep, if you'll let me."

"I think there is something you all must be made aware of," Narlhep said as he stood, the metal of his armour grating as he pushed back his chair and got to his feet. He drew his sword and took a few steps closer to the throne, until he was standing with one foot on the raised dais. "I am not the true King of Taiyou. By the council's decree and by the will of Jedeite, I will be King in name only until the Chosen of Jedeite returns to claim his lands."

Narlhep gripped his sword with both hands and raised it above his head, only to plunge it downwards with all of his strength into the middle throne – the throne where the rightful King of Taiyou would sit.

"Only the true king can draw this sword and when he does – I will die."

Shocked silence greeted this awful pronouncement.

"So Fuzen – Goji, whoever you are, you can stay and be my advisor, but you'll have to renegotiate your position with the future King of Taiyou when he arrives."

"Yes, Your Majesty," Goji said with a bow.

"Goji," Narlhep spoke once more, and Goji stopped and turned to face him, "your team may go, but you will stay – my advisor should be present during official meetings."

Goji smiled slightly – a small look of triumph – before crossing over to take a seat to Narlhep's right. With proud smiles in Goji's direction, the newly-made advisory council wheeled out the barrel of krevels and left the throne room, so the real meeting could begin.

"The Rubian encampment to the south of the city is no more," Sabien informed everyone. "It appears it suffered a similar fate to the damaged areas of the city. No survivors were found, but that is not to say some did not flee. I have already informed King Narlhep of this, and he sent a platoon of Legionnaires to guard the southern border. Also, I have been informed Yue intends to head southward into the Sand Lakes to search for the Chosen of Jedeite. Yue?"

Yue snapped to attention, as if this was a lecture back in science class and she had been fighting against sleep. She stood abruptly and all eyes were drawn to her, which is when I noticed the difference. Yue's hair was darker – much darker. She had somehow found the time and supplies to dye her hair; it was now black on top and I could see a vibrant red flowing out from underneath. Back in Tokyo, Yue had dyed her hair often. Other than where we found ourselves, Yue dying her hair was not something to remark upon; it was her choice of colours that gave me pause – red and black – the colours associated with the Deathsquads, the Talons, and the Ruby City.

"Jedeite told me to," Yue sated boldly. "I plan to head two days out and spend a day or so searching, before making the journey back. I should be gone for about five days."

Yue stared at Narlhep as if daring him to defy her. Narlhep sat as still as a statue for a moment, before the suit of armour suddenly came to life once more. "Bring him home," he stated. "Tell him his country needs him – do whatever it takes, Yue.

"As for everyone else," he continued, "I can't tell you what to do. We have an alliance, yes, but I am nobody's king. But I ask a favour of you – we need allies. Even if the Chosen of Jedeite does come, there is no way of knowing if that will be enough. The magic that has protected Taiyou for as long as can be remembered is no longer present. If the Vile Emperor gains word of this – and we have to believe he already knows, thanks to Lady Mikura's presence…" Narlhep gathered himself. "Lady Mikura has agreed to warn me if she receives news the Vile Emperor is marching, but the attack may come at any time."

"Then shouldn't we be here to help?" I asked.

"You four have more chance of travelling quickly and safely across the desert than anyone I could send from Taiyou. You can convince others the way you convinced me to form an alliance with you. Please," the word contained the most emotion I had heard from Narlhep since he had emerged, changed, from the temple, "bring whoever will come to Taiyou to help us and as quickly as possible. I will mobilize every Legionnaire and try to hold out until you return."

"You may not like it, Your Majesty, but you did ask for help," Kaji began. "I can bring you an army of Croatins."

Some of the Taiyouns around the table looked decidedly uncomfortable, but Narlhep only nodded. "I assume they will want something in return for their help?"

"They'll want a piece of Taiyou. They want their home back."

"I'll go with him, Your Majesty," Rama volunteered. "I've been given leave by my father to do what's necessary to protect Taiyou. If I can be a diplomat to the Croatins and gain their support, then I will be fulfilling that request."

Narlhep nodded his agreement. "Go, then. You have my voice, offer what amount of land you deem appropriate to the Croatins for their help."

"I can go to Espearia," Hotaru suggested. "When we met Lord Hex at his outpost on our way to Taiyou, he told us there were other potential allies we could call on for help like the Espearians and the Kumori. I don't know where the Kumori live, but the Espearians should be in Espearia, right?"

I looked around the table at Yue, Kaji, and Hotaru. This was all getting very rapidly out of control – before long the four of us would be scattered to the winds.

"How do you intend to get all the way to Espearia, Hotaru?" I asked, pointing out an obvious flaw in my eager friend's plan. "It's on the other side of the map."

Hotaru looked mulish at my interference, but to my surprise Narlhep interjected on her behalf. "If we can find someone from Espearia who is willing to go with her, the Visionaries' magic is capable of sending a few people great distances nearly instantaneously."

"Jeth, you're from Espearia!" Hotaru suggested excitedly.

"Hey, hold on a minute, I never said I wanted to go back there," Jeth protested.

"I'll go," Adel suggested suddenly to everyone's surprise. "I'm not from Espearia, but I lived there for a number of years and know it well. If that's enough for the Visionaries to get us there, I'll accompany Hotaru. She's right in saying they would be powerful allies."

"That's three out of four," Sabien said, turning to me. "Speaking of Hex, Yukari, you left a rather large force of Roughlanders there that could be of use to us."

"I can send word to them that they can now join us in Taiyou," I offered; my message arrows could travel unerringly to their destination and no one could doubt who they were from, if they had seen me fire an arrow before.

"I was hoping perhaps you and Masaru could make the journey back there," Sabien suggested. "I wasn't well enough to look around or speak to Hex while we were there, but I can tell you from past experience I believe he is holding back on us. He has far more at his disposal than just those Roughlanders we saw."

"I don't believe Hex was lying to us, Sabien." I frowned.

"I didn't say he was lying," he amended, "just that there is more to Hex than he lets on. Just talk to him and see what you can find out."

"All right, I'll go," I agreed, "but I would feel better knowing you, at least, will be staying here to help Narlhep organize the defenses."

"Ris and I will stay," Sabien confirmed. "Ris will continue to look after Aysel and I will be here with Narlhep should any of you need to contact me. Yukari, I know you can send arrows – may I suggest everyone else work on a way to communicate, should it become necessary."

With everyone in agreement, we didn't waste any time in wrapping up the meeting and getting preparations underway. In less than an hour, we met once more before the palace drawbridge to say our goodbyes before we embarked on yet another dangerous journey. Despite the fact I would have Masaru all to myself, I wasn't exactly looking forward to the next few days, for fear I would spend them worrying about Hotaru and the others. I resolved I would try and put them out of my mind and focus – it would help no one if I were to fall prey to a sand shark because I was distracted.

"I won't be gone long and I'll make sure to look in on Aysel when I come back to see if there is anything I can help Ris with. She's in good hands, though," I told Adel as she and Hotaru headed inside to meet with the Visionaries for their trip to Espearia. No matter how things went for them, they would likely be gone the longest as they would have to make their way back on their own somehow.

Yue, I noticed, had fashioned a sort of backpack out of wound strips of cloth. The cloth sack struck me as odd, knowing Yue's power allowed her to make whatever she chose vanish and store it – even she didn't know where – until she called it forth again. I had watched her store two full barrels of water and one barrel of food only moments ago, so she was set for her journey already.

I watched as Jeth passed by Adel and then suddenly he was gone and there was only a dog in his place. The large dog was mostly black, with unnatural red tufts here and there and a red tip to his tail. Yue crouched down so he could climb into the sack on her back. I opened my mouth to ask her about Razor, but before I had even started to speak Yue disappeared before my eyes, going her usual speed.

"Are ye ready to go?" Masaru asked.

"Can we stop by the Sanctioned Outpost first? I figure that would be the best place to get supplies and since we've got the shortest distance to go, we don't have to leave right away. It might be better if we rested a bit before we head out."

"Aye, that's what I was thinking," Masaru agreed. "I'd also like to see if I can get my hands on a couple of mounts – that would make our trip a little easier."

I nodded absently, my thoughts churning over Yue's change of mind about Razor, but I resolved the best way to find out would be to ask him, seeing as asking Yue was no longer an option.

Masaru and I returned to the Roughlander Sanctioned Outpost to find it bustling with the good-natured liveliness of the Roughlanders, even if a large number of them were still recovering from their injuries.

"Razor? He left with his band," a Roughlander woman informed me. "Said he was off to see Corporal Dahlia and didn't know when he'd make it back. He's got a new recruit though, in his gang. Have you met Neva? Never took her for the type to join up with a pack like Razor's."

So Razor had gone on ahead, despite Yue not taking him along as her guide. It seemed he had taken my request to locate Dahlia seriously enough to take his men out of Taiyou and across the Sand Lake to Hex's outpost. I wished Yue had told me her plans had changed; I could have saved Razor a trip, or he and his gang could have come with Masaru and I. As much as Masaru and Razor did not get along, there was something to be said about safety in numbers, especially out in the Sand Lakes.

While Masaru asked after supplies and saw about getting us mounts, I took a moment to myself out in the outpost garden. Most of the Roughlanders were in the common room, having gathered for meal-time, so I had the yard to myself.

Fuun,

I addressed a message arrow to the one ally I wasn't really sure of. When we had last met at the Temple of Sapphire, he had held me precariously off the edge of a building and only my fast talking had prevented him from slaughtering us. I wasn't looking forward to having to face him again – Fuun was a dangerous man and the self-proclaimed Chosen of the gem god Machalite, who was said to represent order through chaos.

> *The Vile Emperor may be planning an attack*
> *on Taiyou. We will need all of our allies to repel*
> *his advance.*

I thought a little bit about what else I wanted to say and then realized a curiosity of mine might well be solved by asking Fuun. Like Jeth and the others, he, too, had been around for the last eight hundred years – except he had been awake and active, instead of in a cryogenic stasis.

> *We encountered someone you may know – blue-haired, extremely powerful, and with a taste for chaos and death – is she a friend of yours?*

I signed the mental message with *Chosen of Sapphiros*. I formed it into an arrow with my mind and then loosed it into reality. I watched the blue energy arrow shoot off to the southwest until I could no longer see it over the fenced outpost yard.

Next I began a letter to Sabien, which I knew wasn't going to be any easier to write than the one I had sent to Fuun, but for an entirely different reason.

> *Sabien,*
> *I will be careful with my heart, but know it was given the very minute I saved Masaru's life. I have seen the way you place Ris' well-being before your own. We are all of us only human, but when the time comes for difficult decisions to be made, believe I will not falter and I will believe the same of you.*
> *Be well,*
> *Yukari*

I took a deep breath; with that off my mind, I could proceed with my test. Fitting for this garden, I chose a target I knew was no longer among the living – Tathos, the mindless Roughlander for whom this place had once been cursed.

> *Tathos, may your spirit rest in peace.*

The arrow formed and I shot it directly above me; it went no more than a few feet before exploding like a firework, sparks of blue energy showering down around me like glitter – my question answered.

I stood up and dusted myself off. My Roughlander clothes had seen better days, but soon I would be very grateful for their sturdiness when I was back to travelling across the desert. Remembering the last time we had set out across the Sand Lakes reminded me of Corporal Dahlia and the fact she was still missing.

My message arrows flew straight to their targets. It would be a simple matter to fire one off and see if it went in the direction of Hex's outpost, or elsewhere. He hadn't said anything, but I knew Masaru was worried about Dahlia – the two of them were very close – and it would be a kindness to him if I could confirm where she was.

I formed an arrow with another simple message. *Dahlia...we are coming.*

I sent my suitably cryptic message off into the air and felt my heart catch in my throat when it, too, exploded into a multitude of blue sparks. I stood staring as the energy rained down around me. Not Dahlia...

It had never even occurred to me for a minute the reason Dahlia hadn't turned up was because she was dead; it was too difficult of a thought to form. Corporal Dahlia was tough and resourceful, and the only time I had ever seen her show a moment of weakness was when she had thought Masaru had lost his life.

Masaru...Dahlia was his Corporal, but also his friend. The way they treated each other was like family. Just as she had been a wreck when she thought she had lost him, I knew Masaru would be crushed by the news Dahlia was gone – but now that I knew, I had to tell him, didn't I?

I didn't have any trouble avoiding Masaru on my way up to the sleeping area of the Sanctioned Outpost. I saw him sitting with the other Roughlanders and enjoying their company, which he must have missed since I had Knighted him and whisked him away to this world of responsibility and loss. Not that Masaru's life before had been easy, but it seemed since I had come into his life he'd had to leave everything he cared about behind, including his outpost, his friends, and now Dahlia...

I couldn't stop the tears from falling as I crawled into a cot on the top floor of the outpost building. I still hadn't gotten used to what time of the day was what on this world, but I was thankful for it, as it meant there was no one else in the sleeping area to see me cry.

I may have managed to sleep for a few hours, but when I woke I felt more exhausted than I had before, and what was worse was Masaru was there to greet me with a contented smile on his face. I wiped away the tear-stains on my face, like I was rubbing the sleep out of my eyes, as Masaru handed me a small teacup filled with a clear liquid.

"I ordered it from one of the catalogs. I thought we might as well make use of them before Narlhep discontinues them and I thought ye might like it."

I took the cup from him, feeling shy and unable to really understand why. Masaru and I, along with everyone else, had been travelling together for a while now, sleeping and eating whenever and wherever we were able with no regard for privacy, but somehow it was different now.

"Thank you." I took a cautious sip – I had seen some of the strange things the other Roughlanders, primarily Razor, had ordered from the catalogs and I wasn't sure what to expect. I was immediately surprised at the sweetness and the slight tang. "What is this?" I asked, surprised there was anything like it on a world where sugar was a rarity – but then again we were in Taiyou where rare things were often plentiful.

"I think they called it a fizzy drink. It's made in the Raman province. Do ye like it, then?"

I nodded, feeling tears welling up in my eyes again. "It reminds me of home. We have something like it."

Masaru beamed at me, thankfully not noticing my distress. "We should probably be going. I've got everything ready and I've got another surprise for ye."

Not having anything to get ready myself – I didn't have any belongings except those I carried around with me – I followed Masaru out of the outpost building and into the yard, where I found two mounts waiting for us.

They looked like armoured horses. In reality they were only part horse – or a horse-like animal, anyway – and the rest of them was metal. They were essentially organic machines. I wasn't sure how or why the Roughlanders made them that way, but they didn't tire, rode more like a vehicle than a creature, and ran on steam power, and they were fairly handy things to have for an extended trip across the Sand Lakes.

"Do ye remember how to ride one?" Masaru asked and I nodded.We had spent days on mounts riding away from Deathsquads hunting us and Dahlia had personally taught me everything I needed to know.

"I remember," I said softly, climbing up without assistance.

We left the city with no further ado and crossed the lengthy bridge out of Taiyou without incident. Before long, we were travelling at a good speed across the wasteland, headed for the expansive Sand Lake in the distance.

I shook my head to try and clear it of the memory of Dahlia's message arrow exploding around me, unable to find its target, but no matter how hard I tried to forget, the image kept haunting my thoughts. I had hoped when Sabien had first asked me to go on this mission I was going to be able to spend a few days getting to know Masaru better as we travelled, but even though he tried to initiate conversation once or twice as our mounts walked side by side, I found myself unable to face him. Eventually he stopped trying, leaving me to my own thoughts, and we rode together in silence.

"This is the edge of the Sand Lake," Masaru broke the silence suddenly, drawing his mount to a stop. "We've travelled a long way, but if we're going to rest we should do so here, where we're less likely to be found by a shark or crawler."

I nodded, feeling numb, and stiffly climbed down from my mount. Masaru did the same, but with much more finesse, and together we led our mounts down a path in the ravine to the sand below.

We sat in the sand with our backs to the ravine wall, looking out over the empty expanse of the Sand Lake bathed in the glow of the sun as it rose from its bounce. Having taken his pack from his mount, Masaru reached into it and pulled out a cloth bundle and handed it to me, taking a second one out for himself.

I unknotted the bundle and opened it to reveal a carefully wrapped sandwich. I stared at it a moment in surprise. The fresh white bread with a leaf of what could only be lettuce sticking out of the side of it was far too normal for the setting I found myself in. I was far away from home, sitting in a desert, watching the sun rise in the west over the back of a mechanical horse, but looking at a perfect sandwich that could have been made back in my kitchen in Japan. I looked from the sandwich in my lap to Masaru in surprise and found he was smiling tentatively in my direction.

"I made it for ye," he said. "Just like Hotaru described. They have all sorts of things in the catalogs – I didn't know what all of them were, but I had some help from some of the Roughlanders who'd been in Taiyou longer."

I gripped the cloth in my lap tightly. "Masaru, I have something I need to tell you."

His face fell, and I wondered briefly just how awful my expression must look. I regretted having to be the one to give him more bad news, though it seemed lately that was all I was able to offer him. I remembered vividly the distance in his eyes the last time I had to tell him someone he knew had died and I wasn't looking forward to seeing it again – especially knowing this time would be so much worse because of who it was.

"I tried sending a message arrow to Dahlia before we left, but when I fired it…" I hesitated, but I had to continue, "…it didn't go anywhere. It exploded."

His brow furrowed. "But what could that mean? Have yer arrows ever done that before?"

I nodded, trying to contain the emotions threatening to overwhelm me again. "Just once – Tathos," I said the name out loud as I lifted my arms and formed a message arrow between them. I made sure Masaru was watching and then closed my eyes as I let it go; it didn't help, I could still see the arrow explode in my mind and feel the energy rain down upon us.

"…Dahlia couldn't be dead," Masaru said with obvious disbelief. "It's not possible. There's not much out there that could get the better of her."

"I'd like to believe that," I said truthfully, "but I don't know what else it could mean."

"If it's possible it could mean something else, then it probably does. I won't believe she's dead until I have proof."

"I'm so sorry, Masaru," I said sincerely, "but I had to tell you, it was tearing me apart."

Masaru met my eyes. "I didn't think about how ye must be feeling – Dahlia's important to ye as well, isn't she? She'll come back, she always does."

I nodded. I didn't want to argue with him about it; truth be told, it was a relief to have told him and better by far to believe she was okay somewhere. Masaru stood suddenly with his back to me, shielding his eyes to look out over the desert.

"Get some rest then," he suggested.

"What about you?"

"I'll keep a look out for a little while," he answered a little distantly, before walking a ways out into the sand.

I watched him go then looked down at the sandwich he had left behind. There was one bite taken out of it, but it was otherwise untouched. It broke my heart that he had so painstakingly tried to make this trip a pleasant one and I had ruined it by focusing only on the unfortunate things we could do nothing about. I silently apologized to Masaru once again and tried to take a bite of my own sandwich, but I couldn't bring myself to eat; I was feeling too wretched.

The mound of sand I was leaning up against was comfortable enough, but I found that like eating, sleep wasn't an option for me either, so I watched Masaru as he paced back and forth out in the Sand Lake.

Unexpectedly, his back stiffened. I sat up straight and focused in the direction he was looking, but all I could make out, even at my increased range, was a cloud of sand rapidly closing in on our position. That was enough for me – I had seen fast-moving clouds of sand before and knew they meant something dangerous was quickly approaching. I surged to my feet and my wings appeared to lift me up into the air to get a better look at what was coming for us.

Masaru summoned his blue energy knives and took a defensive stance. He almost wasn't fast enough as the cloud of sand slammed into him and engulfed him completely, blocking him from my sight for an instant before it continued on past him, leaving Masaru standing bewildered in its wake.

I watched the cloud with disbelief – even Yue could not have been fast enough to cross the open desert as quickly as it had – and it was still moving. The cloud enveloped where I had been resting not a moment before and when it moved again our two mounts and our supplies had been reduced to a splotch of pink-tinged remains.

Inexplicably, the cloud started back the way it had come. Masaru, meanwhile, had whirled about and had his knives ready to face it head on. The cloud sped unerringly towards him and before I could even react, he was swallowed up in it once more.

Hovering high above, I tried to pierce through the whirling sand with my magically enhanced vision, but all I got for my trouble was a glint of one of Masaru's blue knives as it slashed at something within the cloud. I concentrated on what Masaru's knife had been striking at and I designated it as my target using my power. Within the cloud, a cyan glow formed.

Then, as suddenly as it had appeared, the cloud began to move again back the way it had come – away from the ridge – only this time, it took Masaru with it.

The cloud, with its fitful cyan glow, raced westward, leaving only disturbed sand behind it and no sign of Masaru. I raced after it with all the power and speed my wings could provide me, but it was very quickly leaving me behind. I formed arrow after arrow and let them loose after my target, hoping at the very least I might be able to slow it down.

The arrows – as sharp as I could make them – struck their target, of that there was no doubt, but the still-unexplained cloud was getting away from me until I had to rely on my power to focus my eyes on things far away to make it out at all. Panicking now, I tried the only other thing I could think of; I fired an arrow trailing a length of rope behind it that would make a net around the target when it struck.

I watched the arrow soar with perfect accuracy, chasing after the cloud of dust, but just before it struck the worst possible thing happened – the dust cloud disappeared in a shower of sand and my cyan glow went with it.

My heart racing, I continued flying at top speed until I was over the place where it had disappeared from view. My rope net lay dejectedly on the sand where it had struck. There was no sign of movement, no hint of cyan light, and worst of all, no indication Masaru had ever been there at all.

I circled the spot, my thoughts racing; it simply didn't make any sense. I wasn't an expert on the creatures that lived in the Sand Lakes, but nothing I knew of could move that quickly and even Masaru had looked completely baffled by the attack. That left people – we did have a number of enemies – but I simply couldn't understand who could have found us. Also, anyone I could think of – with the possible exception of the mysterious blue-haired woman

Masaru and the others had faced back at the Temple of Jade – would have been after me and not Masaru.

I flew around somewhat uselessly in a state of shock; I was alone now like I had not yet been on this world. There had always been someone with me – Masaru, Dahlia, Sabien, or one of the others. Unbidden, my wings carried my back to the spot where our mounts had once stood. When I saw what remained of the place Masaru and I had decided to make camp and the untouched sandwich lying on its cloth, soaked pink with discharged mount water, the reality of the situation came crashing down on me. My worst fear had come true – I had lost him – and this time even my powers hadn't been enough to keep him safe.

My wings faltered – strong emotion never failed to interfere with the use of a Chosen's power. Using the last of my will, I forced myself to form an arrow and directed a message to Masaru with the words I hadn't yet been able to say to him – *I love you.* If it was possible, the arrow would tell me where to find him.

The arrow shot up into the air directly above the remains of the mounts as I began to fall from the sky. It went no further than Dahlia's had before it, too, burst into a multitude of sparks. Tears began falling down my face and the blue energy feathers from my wings fell apart to drift down beside me as I fell from the sky. My knees struck the ground forcefully and I fell to my hands, the useless remnants of my power raining down around me. I couldn't see much past the blur of my tears, but my hands gripped the ground before me for a hold on something real as I cried, my heart bleeding out onto the sand.

Ch. 4 – Darkness Falls...

66 It is unbelievably hot out here," Rama commented drily, wiping sweat from his brow. "I knew it was different outside of Taiyou, but I've never been quite this far away from home before."

"I'll be honest, I was a little surprised you volunteered to come," Kaji told him. "I thought you considered the Croatins monsters, like most people in Taiyou."

"I'll admit I have been prejudiced," Rama stated, "but I've been doing some thinking on the matter and I've come to realize even monsters have women and children to protect."

"That we do..." Pine commented in a whisper from beneath the cowl of his dark robes.

Rama craned his neck to look back at the Second Spawn Croatin who was accompanying them. Even covered from head to toe, it was evident Pine was not human. For one, he was too small; his thin frame reached no more than four feet tall, and the hands that occasionally reached out from beneath his voluminous sleeves were lime green in colour, with delicately pointed fingers.

"So I was thinking it might be time I changed my views," Rama continued, still speaking to Kaji, but with enough volume it was evident Pine was meant to be included, "and what better way to do that than to visit the Croatin home with an open mind."

Pine tilted his head up to look Rama in the eyes and his cowl slid back a little to reveal his smooth, lime green features with their sinuous, purple markings. The Croatin grinned wickedly, his mouth stretching tight at the corners, wider than a human could manage. "We'll see what they think of you, then. Remember that in our home, you are the monster."

"Duly noted," Rama commented stiffly.

The three unlikely travelling companions continued along the ravine edge separating the rocky wasteland from the western Sand Lake until Kaji, noticing movement beyond a rocky outcropping ahead, put out a hand to halt their procession. Using his power, he made a double of himself to head forward and investigate what had caught his eye. The ravine curved rather sharply ahead, creating a rocky promontory from which he could get a better view while still concealing himself from anything waiting out there for them. He realized they were downwind when he caught a sudden gust of rancid air as it wafted up from the desert below.

Far below on the floor of the Sand Lake, sand sharks swarmed intermittently between three dark splotches staining the sand, and he recognized metal parts in two of the piles of mangled flesh as belonging to Roughlander mounts. Due to the attention of the sand sharks, the third splotch was by now unrecognizable, but at one time it may have been human.

Kaji swallowed hard and looked away from the pitiful remains of whoever had fallen as he allowed his clone to splash to a puddle on the rocks. "We're going to want to circle wide around this next patch," he informed Pine and Rama. "There are sand sharks in a frenzy down there and we don't want to give them any reason to think we'd make a good meal."

Rama and Pine nodded their assent and the three of them started forward again, following Kaji's lead away from the edge of the ravine.

"What's that over there?" Pine asked, indicating what looked to be a dark hunk of metal caught between two rocks.

"It's away from those sand sharks you mentioned," Rama indicated. "It can't hurt to look."

"I've seen something like this before," Kaji noted as they reached the metal hunk. "There's the rest of it ahead, there," he pointed. "It's the wing of a Skyraider."

They found the rest of the downed Skyraider easily; the main body of it was still intact, though in no way serviceable, and bits and pieces of the discarded machine littered the rocky ground the closer they got to where it had crashed.

"What's a Skyraider?" Pine asked, examining the wreckage curiously.

"I've never seen one up close like this," Rama answered, "but it's a flying machine. The Deathsquads use them for aerial patrols and each of the Talons has one to themselves."

Kaji wasn't listening to Rama's explanation, nor was he examining the Skyraider. He had seen something else just beyond the ridge where the Skyraider had skidded to a final stop. Lying on the smooth rock floor in a patch of sand was another dead mount – this one intact. As he approached, he could see the mount's neck was clearly broken and jutted out at an impossible angle. On Earth, the dead creature would have been buzzing with flies, but here all was silent. What gave him pause wasn't the carcass, but what lay on the ground next to it. It was a golden rod with a hammer-shaped head he knew full well was both a weapon and a telescope, which belonged to Corporal Dahlia of the Roughlanders – a woman he had not seen since he had last left the Croatin base.

Kaji hadn't known Dahlia long, but he knew her well enough to know she wouldn't have left her hammer-scope behind without good reason. He picked the device up and noticed a web-like crack on the surface of the lens. Turning his head back over his shoulder, he examined the Skyraider once more and mentally recreated the scene.

Fiery, red-headed Dahlia, mounted and with her goggles pulled down over her eyes to protect them from sand-spray, raced along the ravine edge. The Skyraider was catching up to her quickly and there was no way she would be able to outrun it. It simply wasn't possible – she had already watched it run two of her comrades off the ravine edge for trying – but maybe if she was lucky, she could trip it up.

Dahlia checked the way ahead, making sure it was clear for a stretch before twisting her body around and drawing her bolt-

thrower in one fluid motion. She took an instant to thank her foresight for having restocked her ammo at the last outpost, before she took aim and fired off two bolts in rapid succession. The first bolt clipped her assailant off the side of his helmet and the second struck his shoulder, disorienting him momentarily and setting him off balance. The Skyraider veered left with the pilot's loss of concentration and Dahlia swerved her mount suddenly to the right.

The pilot recovered immediately and reacted just as Dahlia had hoped, correcting its course suddenly to chase after her. The right wing of the Skyraider dipped down to complete the turn, but the pilot was too fixed on his quarry to realize he was too close to the surface for such a maneuver. The sound of tearing metal filled the air as the outstretched wing of the Skyraider was caught between two rocks and removed forcefully from the body of the machine.

Dahlia leaned forward and relied on every ounce of speed her mount could give her to put some distance between herself and the failing Skyraider, but she hadn't been anticipating the ingenuity or skill of the pilot.

The pilot abandoned the Skyraider before it struck ground, leaping from the wreckage for the back of Dahlia's mount in a daring maneuver. The pilot landed skillfully behind Dahlia, grabbing hold of the Corporal for purchase. Dahlia wasted no time at all grabbing hold of her hammer-scope – which she always kept before her while riding – and whipping it around to hook on to one of her attacker's arms. With a sharp yank, Dahlia threw the pilot from her mount, but the effort cost her a moment of focus and her mount collided solidly with something before her, tossing her from her seat onto the sand.

If both Dahlia and her assailant survived the fall from the mount, a scuffle would have ensued, but the question remained – where was Dahlia now?

Considering the Corporal's combat prowess, it was unlikely the Skyraider pilot had emerged the victor of this encounter. However, Kaji sincerely doubted a Skyraider patrol would consist of only one unit. There was no corpse to be seen and not enough blood to indicate a death other than the mount's had occurred on this spot, but there was also no further sign of where Dahlia might have gone. He had to consider the only obvious alternative – she had somehow been captured.

Whatever the reality of the situation, he knew one thing for certain. Krox – Dahlia's mate – was going to have his head if he ever learned of this, and the massive First Spawn Croatin was still at the Croatin base where they were currently headed.

An impossibly loud, inhuman scream split the silence, causing Kaji to whip his head southward. There in the Sand Lake, terrifyingly close, was the largest creature he had ever seen. The part of it visible above the sand stood about the size of the Sanctioned Outpost building back in Taiyou. Its body was wide and segmented, with a dun-coloured outer carapace and a lighter tan underbelly, so it would blend into the sand and rocks, though he could see no reason why a monster that big would need to hide. Its head was bulbous, and with its mouth now open to scream, he could make out row upon row of teeth beyond the thing's powerful mandibles.

The sandcrawler arched its head downward and dove for the sand, using its multitude of little legs to propel itself forward sinuously, like a snake, or more accurately, a gigantic millipede. Every Roughlander he'd ever talked to had mentioned how large and deadly sandcrawlers were, but the reality was something else again. It moved faster than Kaji would have believed possible – and it was headed straight for the ravine upon which he stood.

A moment later the sandcrawler dove once more, this time going beneath the sand, solid ground not slowing it in the least, and as the creature's body followed downward after its head, Kaji took a moment to regain control of himself and get free of the terror that had gripped him.

"Run!" He yelled, waving his arms frantically in Rama and Pine's direction as he charged toward them. "Sandcrawler!"

Kaji had almost reached Rama's side when the ground beneath them began to rumble and shake with increasing intensity. Where he had been inspecting Dahlia's fallen mount, the rock split open with a crunching sound. The massive head of the sandcrawler emerged, swallowing the mount and the ground around it whole, before diving into the rock once more.

The shaking caused by the passage of the sandcrawler through the rock at their feet made it difficult to keep their footing, but Kaji, Rama, and Pine persevered, running at top speed. Behind them, the ground gave way suddenly and the mouth of the sandcrawler – more than large enough to swallow all three of them at once – appeared, its mandibles chewing away at the rock before it with terrifying efficiency.

Pine, seeing the three of them were fighting a losing battle, stopped suddenly and whirled about, drawing up the sleeves of his robes to reveal long, green fingers held poised to attack.

"Pine! What are you doing?!" Kaji called out, alarmed.

Pine ignored Kaji and swiped his fingers through the air, as the sandcrawler before him reared up for another dive. Greenish-yellow beams shot from each of the Croatin's outstretched fingers and arced through the air toward the massive beast. The beams made contact and sliced through the sandcrawler's tough hide with ease; the smell of seared flesh and the pitiful cries of a wounded animal filled the air.

A double of Kaji appeared next to Pine, while the other continued distancing himself from the threat with Rama. Copying the Croatin's motions, he tried his best to duplicate Pine's finger-beams with his own power. Kaji was a firm believer there was nothing another could do that his power could not also accomplish; so far, he had not been proven wrong.

Blue beams fired from Kaji's fingers, but the power lasted no longer than a short burst, doing minimal damage to the now enraged sandcrawler. The sandcrawler dove after its attackers and Pine did a noble, but foolish, thing and shoved Kaji with all the might he could muster. The Kaji-clone, made of water, had been in no real danger, but there had been no way for Pine to know he was not dealing with the original. As the sandcrawler crashed into the ground, the Second Spawn Croatin was swallowed up in the creature's gaping maw while Kaji could do nothing but watch in horror.

He was forced to abandon his water clone as the ground beneath its feet continued to give way due to the passing of the colossal beast. The clone splashed onto the crumbling rocks and Kaji's awareness returned to his body next to Rama. He stopped dead, whirling about to watch the sandcrawler's plunge deeper and deeper into the rock.

"Kaji! Don't stop," Rama yelled over the crashing of rocks. "Don't make Pine's sacrifice worth nothing – move!"

The ground rumbled harder, but this time Kaji knew what it meant. Picking up the pace again, he ran desperately to keep up with Rama as the rock behind them once more began to crack and break. Not ten feet behind Kaji, the first of the sandcrawler's mandibles broke ground, followed quickly by the other. The rocks crumbled under the inconceivable power of its jaws and the ground beneath their feet heaved, breaking apart.

Thinking fast, Kaji used his power to harden the air beneath them, so when they fell it was only a short distance before they were lying on a platform in mid-air. Suddenly on ground of his own making, the world stopped shaking. Rama helped pull him to his feet.

"I don't know how you managed to keep us from falling, Kaji, but keep up the good work," Rama commented.

Behind them, the sandcrawler continued to rise up out of the ground, but instead of preparing itself for another dive it seemed to be writhing in agony, its keening cries becoming shriller every moment.

Greenish-yellow beams of light shot outwards, cutting through the thick hide of the sandcrawler's exposed underbelly. The creature arched back in pain and the cuts split open, oozing profusely. As one, Kaji and Rama dove to the side as the massive creature crumpled.

When the dust cleared, the sandcrawler lay deflated; its body half-in and half-out of the rocky ground and oozing a sickly, yellow substance. Rama helped Kaji to his feet once more and together they cautiously approached the fallen beast.

"Pine?" Kaji called, creating a clone of himself to help pry open the belly of the sandcrawler.

Rama drew his sword and made the hole somewhat larger, and together they were able to pull Pine out of the sandcrawler he had killed. The clone did most of the work, as it was poison for either of the humans to touch the Second Spawn's skin. Pine was in bad shape; an enormous and wicked-looking tooth was lodged through the Croatin's middle and his breathing was shallow. Pine's blood was also yellow, making it difficult to tell how much of what coated him was his, and how much belonged to the sandcrawler.

"He's alive," Kaji noted, "but I don't know how long he has, and I don't think removing that tooth is a good idea right now."

"How far are we from the Croatin base?"

"Too far," Kaji replied with a shake of his head, "but there's an outpost nearby. We'll have to make a detour and hope they have someone there who can help him."

On Earth I had always felt alone, even when I was surrounded by other people. When I came to the desert, all of that changed – there were people who relied on me and whom I could rely on.

This planet was harsh, but it was also brighter than anything I had ever known. It was different and challenging, and definitely not safe, but almost better for it. Now the light I had found in it was gone. Only darkness was left. I was alone now, truly alone…and the horror of it was too awful to contemplate…

The ceiling was a twinkling field of stars made up of a multitude of lights glimmering on a black backdrop. At the end of the rather large and mostly empty room, there was a large, white screen framed by rich, red curtains, held back on either side by thick, golden cords. Hotaru assumed people were meant to be impressed, but the maker of this room had no way of knowing she had seen much more impressive uses of technology back home.

"I AM THE HEAD!" A booming voice filled the room and a rather large round head appeared on the screen. "I AM THE TERROR–"

"Adel, why does this Head-person have a statue of Jeth in his house?" Hotaru spoke, ignoring the voice booming over the speakers.

"As I told you before," Adel responded tiredly, "Jeth used to rule here, sort of. He's known as the Demon of Espearia, they both fear and revere him. And, as I also already told you, I have no idea who this 'Head' is supposed to be. There was no such person when I was here last and Espearia was ruled by the priestesses."

"Well we tried them already and they said they would have to speak to the Spirits of Espearia," Hotaru countered, "so there's no harm in figuring out if this person can help us. He's supposed to be in charge of the city too, or something."

"WHAT BRINGS YOU BEFORE THE HEAD?"

"Oh, uh…I'm here to request your help on behalf of Taiyou," Hotaru began. "Would we be able to meet with you in person? I feel kind of silly talking to a giant head on a screen."

"WHAT?"

"Well, you know, your screen and lights and speakers are all very impressive, but I'm from Earth and we see this kind of stuff all the time. So you don't need to worry about impressing me...I'd just like to meet you, that's all."

"WELL, I NEVER..." the voice trailed off suddenly and the lights in the room flared to a more normal level of illumination. Hotaru and Adel could hear clattering from behind the curtain, before it was suddenly tossed aside and a portly Japanese-looking man emerged.

"Hi, I'm Hotaru. Nice to meet you. Do you have a name other than 'The Head'?"

"Zukatoya," the man responded, his accent sounding more southern-American than his Japanese appearance would suggest.

"Are you from Japan by any chance?"

A slow smile spread across Zukatoya's face. "Why no, I'm not," he answered, "but my ancestors were. Lots of us in Espearia are descended from the Japanese who settled here from their home world. I'm surprised you could recognize that about me, most people don't know much about our history, though you look like you might be of Japanese descent yourself."

"Oh, I am," Hotaru said, "from Japan, I mean. I just arrived here recently. We're apparently eight hundred years late, but I'm a Chosen of Sapphiros."

"Well, well! Isn't that somethin'? You seem like a nice young lady, Hotaru. What exactly is it The Head can do for you?"

"Lady Adel and I are here on a diplomatic mission on behalf of the King of Taiyou," Hotaru informed him. "We're looking for help to defend Taiyou's borders."

"We haven't heard from Taiyou in a long time. I'd be real happy to re-establish trade with Taiyou again, but I don't know how much help Espearia can be from all the way over here."

"Well I was hoping that as many of your troops as you can send would be able to accompany me back to Taiyou when I leave," Hotaru answered. "The King would be very grateful and of course he'd be able to house you in Taiyou while you're there and I'm sure you'll be able to talk to him about re-establishing trade routes or whatever."

Zukatoya nodded and stroked his chin. "That doesn't sound like too bad of an idea. I'll tell you what. I'll come with you myself and

I'll bring along my personal guard. I've got near to six hundred soldiers who'd be glad to come out, get some exercise, and see the world a little while they're at it. Whaddya say?"

Six hundred soldiers were certainly better than nothing, but Hotaru found herself hoping the priestesses might be able to promise a little bit more. "That would be wonderful, Zukatoya-san. Thank you."

Adel and Hotaru left The Head to his preparations and retired back to the house Adel had once lived in over eight hundred years ago. Remarkably, the stone building was still more or less intact; even more remarkably, it was empty, with no apparent owner and no furnishings to speak of.

"I wonder if 'The Head' will object to me claiming ownership of this place again," Adel commented as they entered the dwelling through an open archway, the wooden doorway having long since rotted off.

"I don't see why he would, he seems agreeable enough," Hotaru replied.

"I'm going to go take a thorough look around," Adel announced.

Hotaru was left alone in the main room. There was a crack in the floor where the foundation of the house had settled and broken the stone somewhat. Lacking a bowl, or really anything else, she knelt down beside the crack and used her power to create some fresh water within it, before leaning over to take a sip and splash some on her face.

"Hello?" Hotaru spun about to see a newcomer standing somewhat hesitantly in the doorway. "I'm lookin' for someone named Hotaru?" Her voice was softly accented with a southern drawl reminiscent of Zukatoya-san, which seemed to be common in Espearia.

"I'm Hotaru," Hotaru supplied, heading over to the doorway.

"I'm here to let you know the Head Priestess Arashi has spoken with the Spirits and she's agreed to meet with you to discuss what you came here for. I also have to let you know they are going to administer a test to you – the Spirits, that is. If you pass, then Arashi will agree to help you however she can."

"A test?" Hotaru asked. "I'm glad she wants to talk to me, but what kind of test is it?"

"That's a matter between you and the Spirits," the woman replied somewhat cryptically, "but before you go and meet with Arashi..."

70

She pulled a small compact out of her belt pouch and opened it to reveal a round mirror which she held out for Hotaru to look into. "...you've got a bit of a smudge, just there."

Hotaru looked into the mirror the woman held outstretched for her and sure enough there was a dark smudge of dirt above her left brow. She used her still-wet hands to rub at it until it was gone.

"Thanks," Hotaru said. "Well, I suppose I better get going then."

"Good luck to you, Hotaru," the woman responded.

Out on the street, Hotaru abruptly remembered Adel was still upstairs and would be worried about her, should she just leave without a word. Running back inside, she took the stairs two at a time in her excitement – whatever this test was, she was now much closer to her goal of bringing back powerful allies to help Taiyou.

"Adel?" Hotaru called. "Adel!"

All was silent on the second floor. Hotaru stuck her head in each of the rooms with mounting confusion, but she didn't find any sign of Adel. "There's only one door to this place," she commented to herself aloud, "and I didn't see her go by..."

Hotaru wandered over to the window in the hall and looked out. The ground was a ways away, so it was unlikely Adel had jumped, and she figured she would have heard that too, if it were the case. On a whim, she looked upwards; sure enough, it wasn't far to the roof, and the vines that had grown up over the ancient building looked sturdy enough to climb. "There isn't anywhere else she could be," she muttered as she reached out to grab hold of a vine. "Adel? Are you up there?"

The climb proved to be fairly simple, but Adel wasn't on the building's flat rooftop either. Hotaru looked out over the view of the city of Espearia with its short buildings – mainly constructed of stone, metal, and some wood – and its high exterior wall, wondering where else Adel could have gone, when she noticed something odd.

Off in the distance there were four comets hurtling through the sky toward Espearia. The fiery balls were angled downwards, and it seemed as if they were going to crash into the city at any moment. As Hotaru watched in horror, two much smaller specks became visible, heading rapidly towards her. She hid herself quickly and watched as two Skyraiders whizzed by, near enough that she could feel the wind of their passage.

She had only gotten a glance at the pilots of the Skyraiders, but they had been close enough for her to recognize who they were – the Talons.

The first had been Zai-Aku; busty, red-haired and gorgeous in her black, bell-shaped dress that fanned out around her ankles. The second was Arocoth; a youthful-looking person in simple armour with a long katana. They, along with the blond teenager Kai-Een, who wasn't present, and Fuzen, who was now Goji, made up the four Talons of the Vile Emperor.

She waited until the Skyraiders were well clear before running down through the empty house and out onto the street once more. At the next intersection, an imposing suit of spiked, deep purple armour rounded the corner, terrified citizens scattering before him – the Vile Emperor himself stood in the streets of Espearia, lava dripping from his outstretched hands.

Hotaru watched in horror as the Vile Emperor's gauntleted hand reached out and grabbed an Espearian man by the head. The heat of the Vile Emperor's hands melted his victim's head immediately, molten lava dripping down over the man's body as he screamed. Shocked out of her immobility by the atrocity, Hotaru broke to the right and fled before the Vile Emperor could see her. Despite her newfound powers, she doubted she would last any longer than that man had in that monster's hands.

She ran as fast as her legs would carry her in the direction of the priestesses' temple. She was re-routed more than once by troops of Deathsquad soldiers as they rounded corners, herding the frightened people of Espearia before them or slaughtering them where they stood. Her panic and determination to reach the temple rose in equal measure until she came across a larger platoon of Deathsquad soldiers blocking her path and she realized her power might be the only thing to see her through this. Hotaru splashed to a puddle and whooshed through the legs of the Deathsquad soldiers as fast as she was able – which, as water, was at a pretty good speed.

She made it past the Deathsquad soldiers without trouble, but they had been alerted to her presence now, and as one they turned to follow her. Hotaru raced up the temple steps, looking less and less like natural water, and before long she made it to the main doors, racing through the crack between the floor and the ornate door. She had been this way once before when she had first arrived and asked to speak with the Head Priestess, so she knew the way to Arashi's office. There was fighting within the temple, priestesses and guards trying to hold off Deathsquad soldiers, but here the Espearian forces were winning and the battle had not yet reached the area of the building where Hotaru hoped Arashi would still be safe.

As water, she dodged and weaved her way but she found the doors wide open and Arashi sitting calmly, reading over a scroll on the desk before her. The Espearian Head Priestess was a beautiful woman with long, white-gold hair and elegant, ageless features. Her posture was relaxed. Hotaru rushed forward, only to splash against an invisible barrier between herself and the Head Priestess. Confused, she reformed herself.

"Arashi!" Hotaru rammed her fists against the wall she couldn't see.

She looked up from her scroll and a pleased smile crossed her face. "Well, hello there Hotaru, glad you could join us."

"We have to get out of here," Hotaru exclaimed, running back to shut the double doors. "The whole city is under attack!"

"Don't you think I know that, dear?" Arashi asked, her smile developing a hint of condescension. "It's my city after all."

Hotaru faced the priestess once more, flabbergasted, "But the Vile Emperor–"

"He's payin' us a visit," Arashi interrupted her, her southern belle accent sickeningly sweet. "I ought to know, I invited him."

"He's murdering people in the streets!" Hotaru declared hotly, waving her arms to emphasize her point and getting as close to the invisible barrier as she could. "And there's even fighting in the temple. People are dying!"

"I know all that, dear. Most of it in the temple is for show, and out in the streets – well, who cares? Those who are foolish enough to oppose him ought to die for it. Besides, Hotaru, don't you think it's time you joined the winning side?"

Hotaru stared at Arashi in disbelief. "What are you talking about?"

"She's talking about doing what we have to do, Hotaru." Adel's voice came suddenly from above.

Hotaru looked up past the bookcases lining the walls of Arashi's office to the second floor balcony to see Adel standing there. Instead of the Lady Knight's usual attire, she was wearing full Deathsquad armour, the helmet, with its signature ruby visor, held under one arm and her sword in her other hand.

"What are you saying, Adel?" Hotaru questioned.

"The Lady Kusabana has already seen what you and the other Chosen of Sapphiros are too stubborn to admit," Arashi responded in Adel's place. "The Vile Emperor will win, there is no doubt. The only question is whether or not you will join him and stand at his side, or fall before his power."

Hotaru whirled as behind her there was a sudden heavy footfall, followed closely by another. The booming footsteps grew louder as they approached and the air in the room immediately grew much warmer.

"Adel, he's coming, we have to leave!"

"You don't understand, Hotaru, we can't win. Giving in is our only option," Adel insisted. "The only alternative is death."

"I don't believe that!" Hotaru declared, putting her hands up before her and summoning her power to create a shield – like a bubble around herself – as thick as she could make it.

The wooden doors crashed inward under a flow of lava and the Vile Emperor himself was revealed in the doorway, lava flowing freely from his hands. When he spoke, his voice reverberated from deep within his helmet, distorted until it sounded less than human, "In Rubia's name – Die."

Lava filled the room, coating the floor and setting all the books on fire. Hotaru could feel her shield failing as the lava lapped against it, eating away at her strength, but that only made her hold on more tightly and pour as much of her power into it as she could. The lava rose until the red-hot intensity of it was all she could see through the cyan shimmer of her shield.

Adel appeared beside her suddenly, almost making Hotaru lose her concentration, until she remembered how Adel could make clones of herself wherever she wished – like Kaji's, except made from snow, instead of water.

"Give in, Hotaru," Adel pleaded. "It's the only way. If you let me capture you, we can live to fight another day."

The lava was still eating away at the strength of her shield. Hotaru cried out as her shield began to fail and a pinprick of lava dripped through to land on her shoulder, searing right through her flesh.

"I trust you, Adel," Hotaru replied, sagging with the effort of holding the shield together under the Vile Emperor's onslaught. "I trust you."

Adel nodded and raised her sword hilt to strike Hotaru over the head. Hotaru closed her eyes and let the blow come, trusting in her friend to see her through this.

The Espearian woman shut the compact mirror with an audible click. "Guess I was wrong about that smudge."

"What?" Hotaru asked, blinking as her vision came back into focus. Her body hurt all over; she had a pounding headache, an intense pain in her shoulder, and she was beyond exhaustion.

"Not everyone who goes through that comes back conscious, let alone alive," the woman commented inexplicably. "You must have done well."

"Comes back from what?" Hotaru asked.

"Their test with the Spirits of Espearia, of course. Now I know it's disorienting, I've been through it myself. None of it was quite real exactly, though it was at the same time, d'you understand?"

Hotaru slumped to the floor where she was, unable to stand any longer. "Not really, no. Was it some kind of loyalty test or something?"

"Well, sort of. It's a test of character. See if you're someone strong enough to be worth helpin' I guess." She shrugged. "Take some time to rest and absorb it all. The Head Priestess'll be reviewing what you went through and she'll let you know soon enough when she's ready to talk to you. All right?"

Hotaru nodded numbly and the woman left her to her own devices.

I had told Sabien I would be careful where I placed my heart, but it seemed as if that hadn't been my decision to make. Masaru had unwittingly claimed my heart the moment I had saved him from Fuzen and I had let him keep it when I made the choice to Knight him. Now it felt as though Masaru had taken my heart with him when he disappeared. The pain in my chest was so intense; it was as if my heart had been torn out, leaving only a gaping hole where it had once been and a resounding silence where there should be a

comforting rhythm. My tears soaked the desert sand around me and my cries filled the silence until they were all I could hear...

A hand touched my shoulder, snapping me out of my despair just long enough to take in a sharp breath.

"Yukari...?"

I focused past the blur, hoping against hope the familiar voice was the one I wanted to hear. It wasn't.

I shied back from Razor, taken aback by the rage I saw in his eyes, before I realized I wasn't alone with him. There were four others behind him – three men and a woman – all looking concerned. My dazed mind supplied me with the facts I needed – this was Razor's gang and the new girl with the short, brown hair was its newest member, Neva.

I looked back to Razor, realizing something was wrong with this image – Razor shouldn't have been here in the middle of the desert, he should have been at Hex's outpost by now.

"Yukari, what happened here? Where's Masaru?"

I wanted to answer him. I wanted to ask why he was here and not where I expected him to be, but Razor had said the one thing I couldn't bear to hear right now. *Where's Masaru?* I didn't know, and that was the problem and what had happened all in one. The tears started again, but curiously this time they weren't as fierce, now that I was no longer alone. Razor took me by the wrist and pulled me into his embrace. I didn't have the will or the strength to resist and I let him fold me into his arms.

"Shh...it's all right, you're safe now." He held me close as I cried and he tried his best to fill the hole Masaru had left, even if only for the moment.

"Jeth, do you think I did the right thing?" Yue regarded Jeth over her sandwich, which had been taken from one of the barrels of supplies she had retrieved from the place where she stored such things with her power. They sat across from one another, with two barrels standing upright in the sand nearby. One contained food, the other water, and they were both lidded to keep the sand from getting into them.

"Well, that depends on what thing you're talking about and what you think was right or wrong about it," Jeth answered in his usual, roundabout fashion.

"I mean separating us, sending everyone off in different directions," she explained. "It was my idea, you know. I didn't think it was going to work until Hotaru jumped on board with her Espearia plan and Narlhep supported her."

"Well, what was so wrong about it?"

"Let me tell you a story, Jeth," Yue began.

"Ooh, I love stories."

"Once upon a time there were four friends who were stranded on a desert planet far from home."

"This one sounds kind of familiar."

"Just let me finish…" Yue rolled her eyes. "The four of them had access to great power, but deep down in their hearts they were still just lost and confused teenagers. They travelled the desert and learned how to use their powers and work together until one day, one of them suggested they split apart. She knew there would be great dangers to face and the four of them were stronger together. She also knew if they didn't learn to be strong on their own, they may not become strong enough to survive.

"So they split up and each went their separate ways and the one who suggested it worried she had done the wrong thing by making them face what was against them on their own, but at the same time she hoped it would be enough to make them grow stronger apart…"

"That wasn't much of a story," Jeth commented, "but I think I get what you're saying. You're worried your friends won't understand why you did what you did, but you only did it because you want to make sure they're strong enough to face what's coming for them, right?"

"I guess what I'm saying is I'm worried about them, Jeth, but I know we have to learn to rely on ourselves – we won't always be together."

Jeth nodded, deep in thought. "You did the right thing, kiddo."

"Thanks Jeth," Yue responded quietly and slowly got to her feet. "Enjoy your lunch, there's something I need to do."

Leaving Jeth by the barrels, Yue headed off a little way out into the sand. They had been running for quite some time now and had encountered the occasional sand shark, but here there was nothing to bother them or mar the empty perfection of the golden sand stretching as far as the eye could see.

The sun was nearing its bounce, the golden orb dimming somewhat as it neared the horizon. Yue knew from experience that out here, with nothing to hide behind, the sun would no more than touch the horizon before beginning its return journey through the sky, continuing to bake this world until one day, even the lake of Taiyou would no doubt be swallowed up by the endless sand.

Though Yue's mother was a Shinto priestess and Yue had been practically raised in a shrine in Shinjuku, it wasn't often she heeded the knowledge her mother had tried to impart. Sometimes, though, there were occasions where doing so helped her to centre herself and focus.

Facing the setting sun, so Jeth would get no more than a silhouette at best – if he was even looking at all – she took her time and undid her Roughlander belts. The Shinto robes she had worn while staying in Taiyou would have been better for this purpose, but it was too difficult to move fluidly in her Roughlander clothes and she needed to feel more connected with the world right now. She let her sturdy Roughlander clothing fall to the ground and stepped forward, dismissing the pile from her mind. Closing her eyes and centering herself, she began to dance.

The point where she began became the middle; as she danced, Yue spiralled outwards, wider and wider, until she had formed a circle. The dance was a combination of what her mother had taught her and of her own making; it was something she had done for herself whenever she needed to reconnect with the world around her for as long as she could remember. This time, as the dance spiralled outward, she felt the sand beneath her feet and the wind on her naked skin dance with her. Her movements became if anything more focused, more intense, and as Jeth would have described from his vantage point over by the barrels – more beautiful.

The dance came to a close at last. Yue was back in the centre where she had begun, her leg stretched out behind her and her hand brushing the sand lightly, as she stood once more and opened her eyes to take in the last light of the setting sun before it dipped beyond the horizon, blanketing the world in sudden and complete darkness.

"Oh no," Yue's breath escaped her in a whoosh. "What have I done?"

CH. 5 – ...SO I CAN...

The darkness was as absolute as the silence in the surrounding desert.

"Hey, who turned out the lights?" Yue heard Jeth ask from a little ways behind her, breaking the stillness.

Using his voice as a guide, she cautiously inched her way back over to where she thought the barrels might be. Her foot encountered a familiar pile of cloth and she paused for a moment to dress herself in the privacy of total darkness.

"You okay, kiddo?" he asked, coming up beside her now.

"Yeah, I think I've got everything," she replied, feeling disoriented. "I can't see a thing, though."

"That's because the sun set."

Yue snorted, trying to stifle her impulse to laugh because, truth be told, the situation wasn't exactly funny – the sun, which had shone constantly for nearly eight hundred years had just set, against all expectations.

"Can you see, Jeth?" she asked him, curious because Jeth was not human – he was apparently part demon and sometimes a dog – so it might be different for him.

"Yeah, probably better than you can, anyway."

"Good. Lead me over to the barrels. We should probably get going, we're too exposed here."

Jeth placed a hand on Yue's shoulder and spun her about, before giving her a little nudge in the right direction. "Thanks Jeth–" she began and then paused; she had heard something echo across the open desert. The sound, like a distant inhuman scream, had seemed somehow hauntingly familiar to her, but she couldn't immediately place why or how.

"Why'd you stop?" he asked. "The barrels are right there."

Yue took the last few steps to the barrels and placed a hand on the lid of each, her head cocked to the side as she listened intently, in case the sound should repeat itself. She was not disappointed – she heard it again, only much closer this time.

"What is that?" she asked herself aloud, feeling somewhat frustrated. "I know that sound."

Whatever it was, the unnatural screaming sounded in no way human or friendly – and it was coming closer. As she struggled to figure out where she had heard it before, the sound was repeated from several other directions at once.

"We're being surrounded," she said as she placed the barrels back into storage.

"It sure seems that way."

"Get on, Jeth, we're leaving."

"Woof!" Jeth barked, having made the transition to dog again in no time at all, before wriggling into her backpack.

In a flash Yue was off, doing what no enemy force or stalking animal would predict: running incredibly fast and straight for the threat.

The cries got louder and echoed with a decidedly feral quality from all directions as they closed in, not on their prior position as she assumed they would, but on a point straight ahead. Yue thanked her luck she had noted the desert free of obstructions before darkness fell, so she could run without fear of smacking into anything.

"There's a wall up ahead," Jeth commented from his vantage point over Yue's shoulder.

Yue strained her vision trying to pierce the darkness. Her eyes caught onto the only thing they could. Ahead and to the right, there was an inexplicable pillar of green light; in the resulting glow, she could make out a section of cliff edge.

"All right!" she exclaimed, happy to have a destination she could aim for.

She adjusted her course slightly, and quickly lost herself in the physical challenge of propelling herself from ledge to ledge in the barely lit darkness, so she didn't notice the change until she landed solidly on the top of the cliff. The strange screaming noises – though still faintly audible in the distance – had stopped entirely in the area before her, although this was where they had been the loudest only moments before.

"Jeth, I think we've found what we've been looking for."

The green light emanated from a person on his knees in a pool of sand. He was a Roughlander by his dress, with more than one canteen strapped to his copious belts. His face was partially covered by a thick, once-white scarf, embroidered with a pattern of green and brown leaves. Even through this covering, the mark of Jedeite – a stylized green diamond, with a rounded ball on the bottom – shone through.

At the sound of Jeth barking his agreement, the man or boy – whatever his age – snapped to attention. The green fire emanating from his eyes burned even brighter as the Chosen of Jedeite – for there was no doubting who this was – took notice of them. Or did he? Yue wasn't convinced he could see anything at all through the fiery light in his eyes. With the pupils glowing so fiercely, he appeared sightless; it seemed as if he was reacting more to the sound of their presence than their appearance.

"Hello," Yue called out gently. "I'm Yue and this is Jeth. We've been sent by Jedeite to help you."

The Chosen of Jedeite jerked forward suddenly. His eyes shut, briefly dimming the source of the light. He doubled over, clutching at his left side and crying out.

"Are you all right?" Yue asked, flashing forward. "It's all right. I'm here now, you're not alone."

She tugged his arm away to his side to check for wounds. Sure enough, there was a bloody patch on his clothes, the dark wetness barely visible on the dark brown cloth. Probing swiftly, she discovered a puncture wound just under the ribs, going all the way through his body. She didn't know how long he had been this way, but as far as she could figure, this sort of injury would have taken most men down, if it wasn't enough to kill them outright.

"You should lie down or something," she suggested. "Let me look at it."

His intense green eyes locked onto her face, the fiery brightness of them boring into her vision and making her see spots. She noted the sickly pallor of his skin and the awkward way he moved, moments before she recalled where she had heard those sounds before – from the relentless undead guardians of Lilyth's valley.

Then the unnatural scream of the undead ripped out of the Chosen of Jedeite's throat as he lunged for Yue.

Reacting on instinct, Yue grappled with him until she had him pinned, careful to keep his teeth away from any vital part of her. The guardians were infectious, but as far as she could remember, a person had to be mortally wounded before their undead curse took hold.

She only knew of one person who had been saved from becoming a guardian – Masaru – but that had been with the help of Little Lilyth, the one who lived in the valley and controlled the guardians, her protectors. It had only been possible because he was on the verge of turning, but perhaps the same was true in this circumstance. All Yue knew was she had to try; Jedeite wouldn't be too pleased to discover his Chosen had been turned into a zombie before he even made it to Taiyou.

She focused inward, willing her power to help her. The way she figured, it was similar to the way she had made herself able to touch the poisonous Second Spawn Croatins; she simply burned the poisonous radiation out of her system. If his eyes were any indication, this Chosen had some affinity with fire, so there was no reason he shouldn't be able to do the same thing with this curse, especially if it really was a sort of infection.

"You're going to have to fight this," Yue spoke directly into his ear, as she held his arms pinned tightly to his sides.

The only response she got was a struggle and the unexpected sound of flesh tearing; Yue's eyes widened as she watched a new appendage sprout from his shoulder blade. It was made entirely of bone, and segmented so it rose like a pincer and then hovered menacingly like a scorpion's tail, the pointed tip facing downwards.

Yue's hands and arms were already committed to holding his other limbs in place, so there was nothing she could do to avoid the dangerous new talon.

"Woof!" Jeth caught the talon in his teeth before it could pierce Yue's flesh,

Yue let out her breath in a whoosh of relief – and then she heard the flesh begin to tear on the other shoulder. "No!" she stated with determination. "You can fight this, I know you can. You're a Chosen – use your power and burn it out!"

She could see her own power as a thin lick of blue fire, surrounding her skin and burning off anything foreign that came too near. She concentrated on the fire, trying to share it with this stranger. Try as she might, her fire would not spread beyond her own person, but soon enough a mirroring green fire sprung up around the Chosen of Jedeite.

Yue loosened her hold on him, feeling the heat of his flames. The fire surrounded every inch of him, but the bone in Jeth's mouth remained uncovered. Then, just as suddenly as it had appeared, the strange new appendage broke off and turned to nothing but sand in Jeth's mouth.

"Ew," Jeth commented.

The light in the newfound Chosen's eyes winked out and his glowing symbol went dim, returning the world to absolute darkness as he crumpled limply in Yue's arms.

I heard footsteps on the sand in the sudden, and otherwise silent, darkness. I needed to see, so I formed an arrow made of cyan light and fired it in the direction of the sound. I followed it closely with another arrow and another, lighting a path between myself and whoever was approaching. Even in this inexplicable and unnatural darkness, I determined I would not be caught off guard again. As I went to fire the fifth such arrow, my heart caught in my throat.

He staggered forward, leaning to one side, his steps unsteady. The cyan light reflected off of his white shirt, revealing it to be torn down one side with one sleeve was missing entirely. There was dried blood on him here and there, but he was walking under his own power – he was alive and back, that was all I needed to see.

"Masaru!" I was on my feet and running towards him before Razor and the others had even reacted to the sudden fall of night.

He looked up at me before he crumpled to the ground. Within moments I was by his side and checking him over with shaking hands. I felt for his pulse first – it was dangerously weak and sluggish. I checked for broken bones, cuts, and bruises, but by the light of my cyan arrows I only found what looked to be incisions made with frightening precision. They were all over his body, but centred mainly over veins, with most of them on his right arm below the elbow. I couldn't make any sense of them, but I did notice immediately that although the cuts were not exactly shallow, none of them were bleeding like they should be. I used my power to see past Masaru's skin to what lay beneath. I forced myself to do so with as much clinical detachment as I could muster – he had been bled almost dry.

Masaru needed blood and he needed it now.

Instinct took over and I began doing what was necessary. I drew a needle from the medic's supply kit I carried. I knew I had what I needed to try to save Masaru's life – again – and I was going to do everything in my power to ensure it worked. My surroundings, the darkness, and everyone else around me be damned.

"Yukari," Razor said, approaching with everyone else in tow, "we should move him. We're out in the open and your arrows are like beacons."

"We're doing this here – now," I told Razor bluntly. "Keep a look out if you want."

I made a few more arrows of light around us. Then, after cleaning the tip of my needle with a sanitary wipe from my pack, I pierced the tip of Masaru's finger and brought the finger with the drop of blood as close to my eye as I dared and used my power to focus on it. My vision sank deeper and deeper into the drop of blood, until I couldn't possibly see it any closer. I memorized the shapes I saw and the patterns they made and then blinked to clear my vision and return back to normal sight.

The girl with Razor's pack – I had been told her name was Neva, though I had never been properly introduced – was before me, applying a damp cloth to Masaru's other arm, trying to clean his cuts.

She looked up and faced me, feeling my eyes on her. "I'm only trying to help," she said.

"Give me your hand," I commanded.

Confused, she held her hand out to me. Wiping the needle off on the sanitary wipe I was using, I gripped her hand in mine and pricked her finger in a quick motion.

"Hey!" Neva protested and tried to pull her hand away, but I held tight and brought her finger closer to my eye the way I had done with Masaru's.

Using my power, I inspected the patterns of the cells in her blood. If I was being honest with myself, I didn't even know if Roughlanders were truly human, or in any way the same as those of us from Earth. I wasn't exactly looking to identify blood types or anything quite so advanced, but if I could ascertain that one of the people here had blood similar to Masaru's, then maybe, just maybe, I could perform a transfusion and give him the blood he so desperately needed. Neva's blood was different from Masaru's though – markedly so. I let go of her hand and blinked to bring my eyes back to focus before looking around for my next victim.

Razor was standing over me with a worried expression, the rest of his gang having fanned out, presumably at his request, to stay alert for any signs of danger.

"Give me your hand, Razor," I ordered..

"If it'll help him, I'll do it," Razor said and I realized abruptly it wasn't me Razor had been worried for – it was Masaru.

I nodded and Razor placed his hand in mine. I repeated the procedure and let out a relieved sigh – it was a match. This, of course, left only the hard part…

When darkness fell, there was chaos in the streets of Espearia. After centuries of constant sun, the only darkness the citizens had really ever seen was in their own windowless closets or basements. Now their whole world had gone black and no one knew when – or if – the light would return.

Confused and befuddled after her harrowing ordeal, Hotaru had gone out into the city looking for Adel. Her body aching about as much as her head, she had been slowly making her way back to the Kusabana house when the world was plunged into darkness.

"This isn't still part of the test, is it?" she asked no one in particular.

Hotaru wasn't far from The Head's mansion – thanks to his use of his technology, she could see a light in his doorway – and from there it was only across a courtyard to get back to Adel's house. Being from Earth, Hotaru was no stranger to darkness, but Tokyo had been fairly well lit, as cities go, and never truly this dark.

She started forward and stopped in her tracks when a familiar noise filled her with a sudden, overwhelming terror – the chilling cry of the guardians of Lilyth's valley.

Instinct honed by her training with the Knights was the only thing to save her as she dove out of the way of the undead's attack. As it crossed between her line of sight and The Head's lit doorway, she was surprised to see this creature – whatever it truly was – looked different from any guardian she had ever seen. The silhouette had looked like a man in shape, but with strange protrusions from its back, giving the impression of wing bones without wings attached. Shaking her head to clear it of the image of the creature in the dark, she ran, her senses alert to danger.

She skidded to a stop in the pool of light before The Head's mansion. She scanned the courtyard for her attacker, but all was silent, and there was nothing to be seen in the darkness. She allowed herself enough time to catch her breath, before taking off toward the house as fast as she could.

"Adel!" Hotaru almost ran into the formidable Knight as Adel was coming off the porch of the house, a concerned look on her face.

"There you are. Where have you been?"

"I was looking for you," Hotaru explained, trying to catch her breath. "But Adel, there are guardians in the city – except they look different, they have these bone things." She held up her hands to imitate the extra appendages she had seen. "At least I think they're guardians, they make the same sounds as them. Why would there be guardians in Espearia?"

"They're called Lillem, not guardians, and by the sound of things, the city is infested with them, which is why I was trying to find you. You said you've come across the Lillem before?"

"Lilyth called them her guardians," Hotaru answered. "They were in her valley. Masaru almost became one, but Lilyth saved him."

Adel let out a relieved breath. "I keep forgetting you said you befriended this Little Lilyth person. Whatever you faced before, these Lillem were made by Lady Lilyth and I don't know why they are here now, nor why the sun has mysteriously set all of a sudden.

"What I do know," she continued in a lecturing tone, "is the Lillem were Lady Lilyth's personal servants and very loyal, but not very intelligent. I'm going out into the city to see if I can be of some help in fighting them off and I would suggest you do the same."

"But how do I fight them? What works against them? I know they fear fire, but I don't have any of that."

"If you see one, Hotaru, walk tall," Adel instructed. "Command them like you were born to. If you're lucky maybe they'll confuse you with someone they're supposed to obey."

Out in the city, the guards were cleverly stringing up lights to keep the monsters at bay; unfortunately they had to concentrate on the outer wall, as hordes of Lillem creatures were shambling from out in the sand to converge on the gates of the city. Within those very same walls, citizens who were unlucky enough to be caught outside when the darkness fell were being cut down by the creatures that had inexplicably appeared within the city itself. The worst part of it all was any time a civilian fell, whether the blow was lethal or not, moments later that same person would rise again – only this time as one of the mindless invaders.

Hotaru, exhausted, had no power left in her to use, so she didn't even have her swords drawn as she faced down the Lillem in her path. A woman she had just saved by interrupting the creature dove into the nearest open doorway to take shelter from the deadly night.

"Go!" she commanded the Lillem with all the authority she could muster. "Leave the city and go back where you came from."

The Lillem, its contorted facial expression only vaguely human, regarded her with curiosity, rather than the mindless hunger it had shown before. For what it was worth, Hotaru considered that a success. She smiled at her triumph, but one moment out of the character she had established was enough to tip the monster off.

The Lillem roared at her. Hotaru, knowing the infectious nature of the creatures and not having any weapons to fend it off with, turned to flee its deadly reach. Out of nowhere a massive hammer swung through the air, wielded by a short, older man in armour. The hammer smashed through the body of the Lillem, which immediately turned into no more than a pile of lifeless sand.

"Knights of the Blue Moon – at your service, young lady," the man said, stroking his lengthy, grey beard with a gauntleted hand.

Hotaru peered through the darkness as she became aware the man was not alone – there were four others with him. All were of varied descriptions and no two were alike, but they all carried ornate weapons and wore pieces of armour decorated in a blue and silver motif, etched with a moon and stars design.

"Nice to meet you," Hotaru replied politely, "I'm–"

The introductions were cut short as Lillem poured into the street from several directions at once. It saddened Hotaru immensely to see a number of these Lillem were transformed Espearian citizens – she could tell by their clothes and the amount of flesh that still remained on their now undead bones. They fought bravely, but within moments the Knights of the Blue Moon were completely overrun. Hotaru, on the edge of the fray and with no weapons to defend herself, found she had no choice but to flee or fall to the Lillem herself.

She hesitated, watching as the Knights of the Blue Moon were stabbed and beaten down by Lillem. She didn't want to just leave them behind, but she knew within moments they would turn into Lillem themselves, and then they, too, would be doing their best to kill her. As a Lillem talon came for her, she did what she had to and dove to the side, making a break for it and leaving the Blue Moon Knights to their fate – there was nothing she could do for them now.

As far as I could tell, the process was working, but then the screaming started. The sound was straight out of my nightmares. I stood quickly, alert to danger, as the wordless, haunting screams were repeated from several other directions, closing in on us in the centre.

Razor, Neva, and the others heard it too, so I hadn't just imagined the sound filling the darkness around us. Taking a deep breath, I summoned five arrows made of bright cyan light and shot them out around. The arrows stuck into the sand in a wide circle around us, instantly illuminating a larger portion of the Sand Lake and revealing what I had feared to be true. I knew these creatures, or something like them, anyway. These were different; they had extra, deadly-looking bone protrusions sprouting from their backs, which they used to propel themselves even faster along the sand. It didn't make any sense for little Lilyth's guardians to be here now, but I wasn't going to question my misfortune – I was coming to expect it.

Just like in my nightmares, the multitude of guardians shambled and clawed their way forward, crying out for my blood with their unnatural voices. I knew full well how deadly just one of the creatures could be; I could never forget the fear in Dahlia's expression when she had loosed every bit of ammo she had on one and still hadn't even managed to slow it down. There was no doubt in my mind this many would be more than enough to tear us to shreds.

My lit arrows were nothing compared to the intense light of the sun, which would have driven the guardians away, but they gave the creatures pause. I pulled the needle from Razor's vein and my wings appeared at my back, giving me the strength I needed to lift Masaru, and I took both of us up into the air as Razor's gang moved to put their backs together, weapons facing outwards at the horde surrounding them.

Neva shot me a murderous glare as I lifted off with Masaru. "Are you kidding me?! She's just going to leave us here to die?"

"Let it go, Neva," Razor instructed. "Yukari's got something more important to do right now."

Their words hurt, but I hardly took them in. Razor was right in saying Masaru was more important, but Neva was wrong – I didn't have it in me to leave anyone behind to be killed by the guardians or by any other means. Hardly knowing where I found the strength, I used my power to turn all five of Razor's gang, including Neva, into mist, and took off what I hoped to be southwest. I knew the mist, guided by my power, would follow behind me as long as I concentrated on it.

I held the unconscious Masaru tightly in my arms and let my wings carry me over the horde of guardians that had somehow appeared in the sand to devour us. We headed away from the blood-soaked sand, where I had lost Masaru so abruptly, and regained him somewhat worse for wear in the same fashion. The world was dark now and nothing made sense, but I had Masaru in my arms and I had so far managed to fight to keep him – and I wasn't through fighting yet.

I raced through the endless blackness, Razor and his pack trailing as mist behind me, until I had long since left the howling guardians behind. I don't know how long I flew for, but I began to feel the strain of the constant use of my power, until my wings began to slow and the mist seemed to drift further and further, until I was only distantly aware it still followed.

In the distance, my eyes caught onto a glow on the horizon – was the sun returning? Whatever it was, I angled for it and willed my power to last. That glow of light meant safety from the guardians and if we were to survive this incomprehensible night, I needed to reach it.

Kaji and Rama – and Kaji's double, carrying Pine – had been fortunate enough to encounter a pair of mounted Roughlanders on their way to the nearest outpost just as the darkness was falling. The Roughlanders, shocked by the falling night and the army of undead creatures it unleashed upon them, were more than happy to escort the travellers in return for their help in ensuring they all survived.

The outpost was not much further ahead; the well-lit building a shining beacon in the darkness. Kaji, running with Rama, turned and created a veritable army of clones of himself between their group and the undead creatures, and with an impressive display of power he caused them all to explode in sprays of ice shards, cutting through the enemy ranks and buying them the necessary time to flee.

The grotesquely-altered guardians, with their ungainly bone appendages, stopped abruptly in a line, as if prevented by an invisible barrier, although nothing had changed as far as Kaji or Rama could see or feel.

"Oh good, the field is still operational," one of their Roughlander escorts commented with relief.

"Och, that's welcome news," the other responded in a thick Roughlander accent.

"Field?" Rama asked.

"Keeps the sandcrawlers and other nasty beasties away," the first responded.

"Aye and it seems it works on those things too," the other added. "We're lucky it does."

Kaji was only half-listening to the conversation as they rode and walked along, their pace much slower now that the threat was held at bay. The past hour had been one of the longest of his life and he was feeling the effects. Still, he found himself staring at the creatures as they threw themselves at the unseen barrier, trying to get at their prey. He studied them, trying to understand where they had come from and why they were here all of a sudden.

As he watched, a glow began on the horizon beyond the enemy horde. Within moments, the rising sun swept its orange glow across the flat desert landscape until it illuminated the raging creatures. One by one, the undead fell and cascaded into piles of unmoving sand, returning to the element that had birthed them and there they lay, dormant once more. Kaji stared at the rising sun in disbelief – it appeared this world had more hidden horrors than anyone knew, and another had just been revealed.

The massive outpost and its outlying city were bustling with activity by the time they reached it. The surprised citizens, having remained safe throughout the unanticipated dark period, were eager to gossip about the possible cause of the blackout – now that it was safely past.

Kaji and the others were led to the infirmary, deep within the main outpost building, where they were greeted by an oversized Sixth Spawn Croatin with a bionic hand. The infirmary was a sterile-looking series of small rooms, with metal walls and a metal door that slid open and shut with the use of technology. Kaji was immediately impressed with the array of computers and advanced-looking medical tools; he was somewhat relieved they had decided to detour here, instead of trying to make it to the Croatin base with their wounded companion.

Pine was still unconscious, the Second Spawn Croatin's usually vibrant green skin looking dull and colourless, and the yellowish blood continuing to seep around the giant sandcrawler tooth, jutting out from his midsection.

"What do we have here?" The Sixth Spawn's voice sounded less guttural and more refined than most Croatins Kaji had met.

"Sixth Spawn?" Kaji asked, speaking in the basic Croatin he had picked up during his stay at the Croatin base and his association with Krox.

"Yes, how did you know?" the Croatin responded in the common human dialect. "I'm afraid I've been a long time away from home and my grasp on the Croatin language has faded somewhat."

"Sorry, I didn't mean to presume." At Kaji's direction, his double placed Pine carefully on the worktable for patients. "Our friend was wounded by a sandcrawler. I was hoping you might be able to help him, but I should warn you – he's a Second Spawn."

The Croatin doctor hissed and raised his hands in what Kaji could only presume to be a sign to ward off evil. "That's unfortunate," he said after a moment, regaining his composure. "I'm not an expert on Second Spawn biology – I mainly deal with humans here." He considered the problem, inspecting Pine without touching him. "I'll do what I can for him," he said at last, lifting his own metal hand and looking at it. "I suppose I'd be the best one to examine him, even if I only have the one hand that can touch him."

"Thank you," Kaji responded. "It's all we can ask for."

"Leave him with me and come back in a few hours. I'll see what I can do in the meantime, and I can at least give you a status report then," the Croatin doctor suggested. "And if I may ask, how is it your twin is able to touch him?"

Kaji smiled ruefully, regarding his clone out of the corner of his eye. "He's a special case."

Rama and Kaji left the infirmary, taking the clone with them, but they were careful not to touch it, in case it had become irradiated by carrying Pine. Heading outside, they found a quiet corner where Kaji could dispose of his clone, allowing it to splash to a puddle and soak into the sand.

"Do you have a name other than 'Sir Rama'?" Kaji asked suddenly as the two of them made their way through the footpaths between the buildings that made up the outpost's town. "If we're going to be friends, I feel a little strange always calling you by your family name."

Rama smiled. "I can't believe I've been so rude as to not mention it earlier. It's Leon. And as for your offer of friendship, I accept. It's an honour."

"Well, Leon, I think you should know that Yukari told me a little about this place. Apparently, this was one of the outposts she and Hotaru stopped at on their way to Taiyou. The way she tells it, this place is practically owned by the Rubians." Kaji spoke quietly now, for Rama's hearing alone, as they walked along the crowded walkways. "She received no welcome here once they learned who she was, so I think it best if we do nothing to cause us to stand out and leave as soon as Pine is well enough to travel."

As if to lend credibility to Kaji's words, there was the sudden whine of engines as several Skyraiders flew by overhead. Kaji watched them as they docked high above on a platform built into the side of the main outpost building.

"Speaking of which," he noted with distaste, eyeing the Skyraider pilots as they disembarked from their aircraft. He led Rama to a nearby bench where they took a seat. "I'm going to go investigate what they're here for. I'll be back."

Rama regarded Kaji oddly for a moment as, contrary to his words, he didn't move an inch. "Are we having that kind of conversation?" Rama questioned, watching Kaji for a response, but getting none. "Yes, I see, we are having that kind of conversation. Very well...did I ever tell you about the time..."

Meanwhile, Kaji had used his power to turn himself invisible and was walking away from the spot where he had left a clone of himself with Rama. He headed into the main outpost building, following after a rather large man and a boy, and scooted into the entrance behind them before the automatic door could close on him.

"What could they want this time?" the fat man grumbled in distaste as he ambled down the hall. "I already paid them their krevels, they've got no reason to be giving me trouble now."

The man before him was large enough that he took up a sizeable portion of the hallway, so Kaji was forced to follow along behind him at his slow pace, or else risk bumping into him.

"The rumour is the Deathsquads are looking for some people," the boy answered excitedly. "Remember when we had those people here who called themselves the Chosen of Sapphiros? I bet you it's them!"

"Don't be silly boy," the fat man said. "Those girls are long gone and even if they were rather pretty, I don't think the Ruby City would worry overlong about their ragtag army of malnourished Roughlanders. No, if the Skyraider patrol is here for anyone, it'd likely be some Roughlander rebels that took refuge here when the darkness fell, nothing more exciting."

Kaji's brain worked furiously. It seemed as if somehow this Skyraider patrol already knew they were here, or at least suspected it. Or, if his suspicions were false, then the arrival of the Skyraider patrol at this time was at the very least an awful coincidence. As the man and boy continued in the direction Kaji wished to go, he continued to follow them, hoping for other tidbits of information.

"It could be the weird Croatin Roy and Garrett brought in with them just after the sun came back," the boy theorized. "I hear he's real small and almost got eaten by a sandcrawler out there!"

"No need to worry about sandcrawlers around here," the fat man said, reaching a closed door. "Open for Big Daddy, code zero-one," he instructed the door, which whooshed open at his command before he returned to the topic of discussion. "But I do wish they'd stop bringing in Croatin strays. I say let 'em fend for themselves out there. They're animals anyway, they belong out in the wild! Alright, go get one of them and bring them here," the fat man instructed the boy. "I hope they didn't send that Kichigai woman. She's a handful, that one."

The boy nodded and ran off and Kaji, still invisible, scooted into the room 'Big Daddy' had revealed. The room took up most of the top floor of the outpost building and was lavishly decorated in rich brocade, with a feast of various foods displayed on a table in the centre and the walls lined wastefully with krevels – presumably to display the fat outpost leader's wealth.

Big Daddy headed over to a corner of the room and drew back a red velvet curtain to reveal a high-tech-looking computer monitor and a series of keypads and buttons. "Big Daddy, code zero-one, checking in," Big Daddy announced jovially to the computer system, which lit up in response.

"Greetings Big Daddy," a feminine-sounding robotic voice responded. "What is your pleasure?"

The fat man smiled, "Status report, Betty."

"Certainly master," Betty began. "Shields are at eighty percent efficiency. Sensors are–"

"Eighty percent?" Big Daddy interrupted,"Why aren't they at a hundred?"

"The system experienced a cut off for one hour's time," Betty informed Big Daddy. "Shields are now at eighty-two percent efficiency and increasing. Main power source is back online."

Solar-powered? Kaji wondered.

"See it stays that way," Big Daddy commented, not understanding. "Continue."

"Sensors are fully operational. Land mines are fully operational–"

There was a sudden knock on the metal door. "That will be all, Betty," Big Daddy instructed the computer, before hefting himself to his feet as the monitor's lights grew dim. Big Daddy closed the curtain around his computer station before wobbling to the centre of the room. "Open."

The door whooshed open to reveal a woman in red and black armour. She had a large, two-bladed axe strapped to her back, and she regarded Big Daddy with an unforgiving expression on her angled features. Her hair was a fiery orange, reminiscent of Corporal Dahlia's, but much longer and held back in a high ponytail.

"Lady Kichigai," Big Daddy greeted the woman, "how good it is to see you again, General."

"I have to say I don't feel the same pleasure at seeing you again," Kichigai commented sourly, regarding Big Daddy with obvious distaste. "I hear you're harbouring fugitives again? I hope you've detained them this time for pickup. I don't want to have made another wasted trip."

"Of course, my dear, of course," Big Daddy replied congenially. "I've got one detained right now down in the infirmary. A Croatin type – it seems he was travelling with the ones you were looking for! Isn't that the biggest coincidence?"

Kichigai drew a small, curved dagger from a sheath at her waist. "I'm getting really sick of you and your games," she said, advancing dangerously upon the fat man with her dagger held out in a menacing fashion. "I think it's about time I get rid of you once and for all and put this outpost under the control of a competent leader."

"Now, let's not be hasty," Big Daddy spoke quickly, sweat forming on his brow as he took a few steps backwards.

"Oh believe me, it wouldn't be in haste," Kichigai threatened, "I've been thinking about ridding the world of you for quite some time, but there have always been too many witnesses – not that I think anyone would miss you."

Big Daddy looked around himself, suddenly realizing he was indeed alone with this woman – invisible Kaji notwithstanding – and he began to sweat more profusely. Kaji, watching this scene play out, was still lost in trying to figure out who was the greater evil here and whether or not he had a right to interfere with what was about to happen. On the one hand, Big Daddy was a scoundrel and a waste of skin, but on the other hand, this woman was presumably a Deathsquad General, and therefore his enemy. Could he stand there and watch her kill someone, even someone like Big Daddy?

As the dagger came down to the fat man's neck and he squealed as its razor-sharp point pricked him, Kaji made another clone of himself appear in the room before Lady Kichigai's eyes.

"Stop," the clone simply said.

Kichigai froze, startled by the sudden appearance of another person in the room; thankfully, there was no recognition in her eyes – the description of the Chosen of Sapphiros had not yet been made common knowledge, apparently.

"Who're you?" Kichigai demanded, not yet releasing the fat man from her clutches.

"A witness," Kaji spoke through his clone, "and if you kill this man, I'll let everyone know who's responsible for it."

"And what's to stop me from killing you as well?" Kichigai demanded, calling his bluff.

Kaji made sure he had the General's full attention before he dismissed his clone, letting it splash to the floor as nothing but the water it was created from. "Because killing me won't matter," he answered, using his power to project his voice from where the clone had been standing. "I'll still be a witness and you'll still be a murderer."

Kichigai stepped back from Big Daddy and relaxed her posture, sheathing her dagger. "All right, you win. What now?"

"Big Daddy, I suggest you run," Kaji hinted to the fat man, whose eyes were quickly darting around the room, like an animal driven wild by fear. "Leave the outpost and get as far away as you can, it's the only chance you'll get."

He nodded, his motions frantic, as he lunged past Kichigai and pleaded with the door to open for him. Within seconds, the fat man was gone – hopefully forever – and the door closed behind him, leaving the invisible Kaji alone with Lady Kichigai, the Deathsquad General who had been sent to retrieve the elusive Chosen of Sapphiros.

"This is Big Daddy, code zero-one, checking in," Kaji announced suddenly in his best impersonation of Big Daddy's jovial tone.

"Greetings, Big Daddy," Betty's voice responded from her corner of the room behind the red velvet curtain. "What is your pleasure?"

Kichigai was looking around the room in obvious confusion.

"Full lockdown of this room, please, Betty," Kaji continued with his Big Daddy impersonation. "Don't let anyone in or out, not even me."

"Yes master," Betty responded. "Lockdown initiated."

Not only did an additional metal panel slide down in place over the door, but also – to Kaji's intense amusement – metal panels slid down in place over the balcony and the other window-sized openings to the outside world. Kichigai would have some trouble getting out of here now.

Her expression was mutinous. "I hardly think you're going to find this so amusing when I get a hold of you."

"You can have the outpost for now," Kaji ignored the General's threat, "since you won't be going anywhere for a little while. But don't get too comfortable, because I'll be back for it."

With that promise, Kaji switched his awareness back to the clone he had left with Rama. He smiled to himself as he became aware of his new surroundings, and then he remembered the rest of the Skyraider patrol and the news he had for Rama.

"Leon, we have to go."

"Hey, maybe he wasn't napping after all," an unfamiliar voice commented.

"No, he just does that sometimes," Rama countered. "Just pops in and out of sleep whether his eyes are open or not – it's a condition."

Kaji took in the change in the scene before him. He and Rama were still seated upon the same bench, but now a small group of Roughlanders had gathered around them to socialize.

"Yeah, sorry," Kaji said, playing along. "Happens to me all the time. But it's best we get going, because of my little nap we're running late."

Kaji and Rama took their leave of the Roughlanders and made their way somewhat hastily back to the main outpost building. As they headed through the halls toward the infirmary, Kaji sketched in the rough details of his adventure to Rama and let him know they needed to do whatever they could to leave this place as quickly as possible.

"I'm afraid there wasn't much I could do for your friend," the Croatin doctor informed them regretfully. "I've made him as comfortable as possible and bandaged the wound around the tooth. He shouldn't lose too much more blood, but I don't have the expertise necessary to remove it without killing him, and I don't see how there'd be much left of him after I took it out. If I may make a suggestion to you, your friend's a Second Spawn and as far as I know the Second Spawns hardly, if ever, leave their spawning grounds. I'm assuming since he's your friend that you know where that is?"

Kaji nodded at the doctor's open-ended question. "We're actually on our way there. We only detoured here because of Pine's injury."

"Well then, I suggest you take him there as quickly as possible. It's possible the Third Spawn may be able to save him." The Croatin held up his bionic hand. "They saved my hand for me a long time ago and I swear to you it was beyond repair by natural means, much like your friend here."

Kaji grimaced at the painful news. Pine had sacrificed a great deal to save them from the sandcrawler; he was determined the Croatin wouldn't lose his life as well.

"How can we get there quickly? We need to leave now," Kaji told the doctor. "It's a matter of some urgency, if I may confide in you."

"That patrol, you mean?" The doctor caught on immediately. "I don't much like them myself. We fix up a lot of stragglers that come in from the Sand Lakes like yourselves, only to see them picked up by a raiding patrol."

"I'd be out of here quicker than anything if I knew how to fly one of those things," Kaji complained. "They'd certainly be the fastest way out of here."

"And the most daring, too," the Croatin countered, looking Kaji and Rama up and down, "but if there's anyone who'd be capable of making off with a Skyraider right under its pilot's nose – it'd be you. I heard from Garrett and Roy what you did to save them from those creatures that came out in the darkness and I think I know who you are. I can supply you a pilot," he continued. "I know someone who can fly a Skyraider who has been looking for a way out of town lately. I'll have them meet you up at the docking station in fifteen minutes. Just do me a favour and stay safe, all right?"

Fifteen minutes later, seven Kajis and one Sir Leon Rama stepped out onto the windy docking platform with a heavily-bandaged Pine in the arms of one of the clones. They managed to catch the Skyraider pilots who were stationed there by surprise, with the exception of one pilot who stood calmly by his Skyraider, his helmet pulled down and his gloves on, almost like he was waiting for something of this nature to occur. The Kaji with Pine in his arms and the real Kaji strode forward with Rama to this pilot, while the other clones marched purposefully toward where the other Skyraiders were docked.

Before the confused pilots could figure out exactly what was happening, Kaji and Rama had loaded themselves – and the clone carrying Pine – onto the Skyraider manned by the mysterious pilot their Croatin ally from the infirmary had recommended. The other clones, whether they encountered resistance or not, tried to climb onto each of the other Skyraiders at Kaji's direction. The unidentified pilot then brought their Skyraider's engine to life and backed out of the dock, expertly maneuvering away from the building with an abrupt increase in speed.

Kaji did his best to hold on while his focus was almost entirely dedicated to controlling his multiple clones. He was unbelievably tired; it had been an almost surreally long day, but hopefully he had only one last task to accomplish before he could rest easy in the knowledge the other pilots could not chase after his Skyraider.

Summoning one final expenditure of his power, Kaji willed the five of his clones he had left on the Skyraider dock to burst, whether they had gotten close enough to their targets or not. The clones exploded on his command, shattering outwards with concussive force. The multitudes of ice shards caused even larger explosions as one by one, the Skyraiders' engines burst from the impact, shattering their metal frames and taking a section of the landing dock down in flames with them.

CH. 6 – ...SEE THE LIGHT OF DAY AGAIN

As Yue learned when he awoke, the Chosen of Jedeite's name was Ao Kouen.

Instead of telling Ao Kouen the story of Taiyou's plight and why he needed to return there with her, Yue simply used her power to give him every memory she had – from the time she had arrived on this world until the present – to get him up to speed.

"So, you're one of the Chosen of Sapphiros...and I'm the Chosen of Jedeite," Ao Kouen stated more than asked, "and Jeth's a dog?"

"Yeah, you've got it," Jeth replied.

Yue nodded, leaning over the two barrels she had taken out for them to have some breakfast to get a better look at Ao Kouen; his brown hair was wind-tossed and his vibrant green eyes crinkled tiredly around the corners. Although she couldn't see the lower half of his face behind his cloth scarf embroidered with green and brown leaves, he looked to be in good shape otherwise, even if his Roughlander clothes had seen better days. "And I've been commandeered by Jedeite to bring you back to Taiyou with me. Your land needs you."

Ao Kouen nodded slowly, absorbing this. "I can see that. Taiyou needs help badly, but I've never even been there before – how can it be my land?"

"Well, it's Jedeite's land…and you're the Chosen of Jedeite, so now it's yours, too," Yue answered.

"Why would Jedeite choose me?" Ao Kouen seemed genuinely curious. "I'm not even Taiyoun…"

"You'll have to take that one up with Jedeite," Yue responded with a slight grimace, "but it seems the gem gods like to choose people who aren't even from this world."

"That's going to take some getting used to – all of it, I mean," Ao Kouen said. "Your memories in my head, this power you say I have…and I can feel it, now that I know what it is, thanks to your memories of using yours. I don't know if I could refuse anyway, but you saved me during the…night," he stumbled over the new word taken from Yue's vocabulary, "and so you've given me a second chance at life. I'll do what you want of me, though I don't know if I'll be able to be anyone's king."

"Well, don't do it just for my benefit," Yue cautioned. "It has to be your decision."

"It is my decision," Ao Kouen told her. "Until now, I didn't know I had anything left to live for. But if Jedeite chose me, then maybe there is something left for me to do. The least I can do is try to help Taiyou in any way I can."

"In that case," she said, "it's time to show you how to use your powers!" Yue drew a line in the sand before them with her toe and then flashed forward a few paces, until she was a suitable distance from the barrels, to draw another identical line. Flashing back to the barrels, she returned them back into storage."We're having a race."

Ao Kouen's green eyes widened perceptively. "I couldn't possibly beat you."

Yue smiled. "I know. That's why you'll be racing against Jeth."

"Aww man, running?" Jeth whined, slowly climbing to his feet.

"All right," Ao Kouen eyed Jeth up and down, taking in his long limbs and his deeply muscled demon-arm, "that, I could maybe do."

"You remember how I do it, right?" Yue asked. "How I go really quickly, I mean."

"Yeah, I think so," Ao Kouen answered. "I know what it feels like, anyway."

"Good." Yue smiled again, as Jeth and Ao Kouen took up positions behind the line she had drawn. "On your marks, get set," she said as she flashed to the second line in less than an instant, "go!"

Jeth took off running, slow and exaggerated, but Ao Kouen did not move; his eyes were closed and his expression focused. Suddenly, to Yue's immense surprise, the spot where Ao Kouen was standing exploded in a mushroom cloud of green fire and smoke. She felt the heat moments before it struck and dove out of the way, as a second mushroom cloud erupted in the place she had been standing. She rolled to safety, thanking her powers for granting her enough speed to get out of the way in time. She watched in a shocked kind of horror as the green fire dissipated and the smoke cleared to reveal Ao Kouen standing exactly as he had been a moment before – with his eyes screwed shut and an expression of intense concentration.

After a moment, Jeth reached the finish line. "Hey there, Ao Kouen…you can relax now man, you did it."

Ao Kouen slowly opened his eyes and looked around, confused. "I did?"

"Yeah man, you beat me, hands down," Jeth noted.

Ao Kouen took in Yue's horrified expression and the way she was sprawled on the sand as if she had been tossed there. "What happened? What did I do?"

Yue tried to control her expression and she dragged herself to her feet with some effort. Without saying a word, she crossed the distance between herself and Ao Kouen and placed a hand to the side of his face to gave him the brief memory of what she had just witnessed – followed by an image from a television broadcast of a nuclear bomb going off and wreaking its destruction upon an unsuspecting Japanese city.

"On my world, that's a very deadly weapon that destroyed parts of my country and killed many people," Yue whispered.

Ao Kouen swallowed visibly. "I'm so sorry, Yue. I didn't mean…I didn't know it would work that way."

Yue nodded, understanding – there was no possible way Ao Kouen could have known. "Come on, let's try something else."

After a few more attempts, the best Ao Kouen could manage was a short spurt of speed, leaving a trail of green fire burning in the sand behind him. Truthfully, he seemed to be a fast learner and had a lot of power at his disposal. It was more than Yue remembered having when she began training with the Knights at the Temple of Sapphire, but it was obvious Ao Kouen had a lot of learning left to do – especially in regards to controlling that power. With this in mind, Yue decided it was not yet time to bring Ao Kouen back to Taiyou. However, this left the question of where to take him to continue his training.

Calling it a day, she told Ao Kouen to climb on her back and she hoisted Jeth the dog under her arm, then she started off for the nearest place indicated by the map she had copied from Kaji – a city called Sresh. If the three of them were going to go on a longer journey, they would need a little more in the way of supplies.

Sresh was nothing like Yue expected to find. She had been told by Corporal Dahlia that it was a Roughlander city, but still, she had expected it to be more like an outpost with a village around it, or a series of outposts arranged together. In reality, it was a prosperous-looking town set into the base of a cliff, with a small outpost building near the front gates, similar in size to the one in Taiyou. Even more surprising were the Deathsquad soldiers who greeted her and Ao Kouen pleasantly at the gates, as they walked unopposed into the city with Jeth, the dog, at their heels.

In the center of the city, Yue found yet another aspect of Sresh that caught her off-guard – there was a large fountain spouting water into a circular pool. Wagging his tail excitedly, Jeth scurried forward to the fountain, and leaned in to lap up some of the water. Yue watched him for a moment, but when no one seemed to mind, she tugged Ao Kouen in the direction of the fountain. When no one was looking, she caused her barrel of water to appear in the fountain itself and filled it quickly.

"What're Deathsquad soldiers doing here?" Yue asked Ao Kouen quietly.

"They're not known as Deathsquad here. They're called Preservation Squad in Sresh," Ao Kouen answered. "They belong to Lady Anaeth, who rules here."

"Really? I'd like to know if they had any trouble with the guardians here during the night," Yue mentioned. "If she's the one who keeps this place safe, then I'm sure she'd like to know what I can tell her about them in case they come here. Let's pay this Lady Anaeth a visit and see what kind of person she is and if she's willing to trade a few supplies for some information."

When I awoke, it was to the bright light of day and the healthy rhythm of Masaru's heart fluttering against my fingertips. My head rested on his chest, which rose and fell steadily, and I could feel his arm around me as the two of us lay propped up against a rough stone wall. I couldn't remember having placed my fingers to his neck to monitor his pulse or placing myself under his arm. I wondered briefly how we had gotten this way, before I somewhat uncharacteristically gave into the peaceful bliss of it and ceased questioning how it had come about.

I looked out over the expanse of Sand Lake before me, enjoying the unprecedented moment of calm. Though Masaru and I were off a ways with our backs to the curved outpost building, the Sand Lake before us was bustling with Roughlanders; they were crossing to and fro, carrying weapons of all types, though most were the long-ranged high-powered carbine rifles they were so fond of. In the distance, there was a low stone wall and I could see Roughlanders stationed at it, weapons held before them, and still others patrolling along its length. Looking to the far left, I noticed the wall was still under construction, which implied it was a recent addition to the landscape.

I caught sight of Razor talking with Neva out of earshot to my right while the other three of his gang roughhoused a little ways behind them, and I realized we must have all made it to Hex's outpost safely. I let out a sigh of relief – I had kept us alive through the night and it seemed the sun had risen once more.

I felt Masaru begin to stir before he actually woke, so I tried to sit up quickly to give him some room. He didn't let me get away, though, and pulled me tighter into his arms instead. "Yukari, thank the gods ye're all right."

"Me?" I mumbled into his chest, confused. "I wasn't the one who –" I pulled back a little to look him in the eyes, but I didn't break out of his hold – I was happy to be there. "What happened to you? What attacked you in the Sand Lake?"

"I don't know," he grimaced. "I honestly can't remember."

"What do you mean you can't remember?" I asked before I fully took in his pained expression. I pulled away, worried I was hurting him. "Are you okay?"

He didn't let me get too far, but settled me more comfortably back under his arm. "It's just I can't remember much of anything and it's only darkness when I try," he answered with frustration.

"Well, what's the last thing you do remember?"

"I was looking out over the Sand Lake and there was something moving really fast out there."

"Couldn't you make out what it was?" I interrupted. "I know you can see Yue when she's running nearly that fast."

"Aye, usually I can," he answered, "but it was kicking up too much sand – and it was moving quite a bit faster than Yue."

"Go on," I instructed him.

"Well, I drew my knives to protect myself, or you, if it tried to go after ye. It slammed into me and I struck something. I felt it, then it moved past me like it was after something else. You were already safely in the sky, so it destroyed the mounts and then came back for me.

"I remember being carried away and yer blue light, then everything went dark..."

"Well, it was dark for a time," I told him, figuring it was best I let him know what happened. "The sun set – that is, went below the horizon," I explained, realizing immediately it would be a foreign concept to him. "I'm not sure for how long."

His brow furrowed. "Well that might explain some of it, then. I saw yer blue light again in the dark and I followed it. I felt very weak, but I made myself keep going to get to ye. I knew ye'd be worried."

I opened my mouth to tell him just how worried I'd been when I was interrupted by an unexpected, but familiar, beeping noise. "Beep, boop boop?"

"Oh, hello there, Coffee-bot," Masaru greeted the little robot as it sidled up next to us.

We had found the little coffee-serving robot and its android companion, Binaris, at Masaru's outpost when we had first arrived; they had been in a much sadder state then, although Coffee-bot was looking particularly shiny and well-maintained now. The two ancient machines were some of the last working remnants of Japanese technology that had been left behind for us to make use of.

I noticed Coffee-bot's full mug of coffee through his clear glass middle moments before he pulled it out to offer it to Masaru and I remembered just how strong the ancient coffee beans were. Smiling politely at the little robot, Masaru reached for the proffered cup, but I got there before he did.

"I don't think drinking that is a good idea right now," I said, holding the mug out away from him. "You've lost a fair bit of blood and the caffeine would go straight through your bloodstream."

"You should listen to her, Masaru," Razor said with only a hint of sarcasm, having come over upon noticing we were awake. "Yukari knows what she's about. I'll take that if he's not allowed to have it." He plucked the coffee mug out of my fingers. "By the way, X-En mentioned Hex wanted to speak with you as soon as you were awake. Should I tell him you're busy?" he asked with a smirk in Masaru's direction.

I rolled my eyes at Razor. "No, I need to speak with him and now is as good a time as any."

"I'll let X-En know," Razor said, taking a sip of the coffee and spluttering it out. "Ugh, what is this crap?"

Shaking his head at the cup of coffee, Razor walked off in the direction of the main door to the outpost, and Coffee-bot followed him. I got myself to my feet with some effort and spent a moment dusting the sand off my stiff Roughlander clothes, trying to ignore the many and varied stains on them.

"This time I'd like to go in with ye, if ye don't mind," Masaru spoke softly from his spot on the wall. "Though, I might need a hand getting up."

"Of course I don't mind," I answered, remembering the last time we had been here and I had heartlessly left Masaru behind as a hostage for our good behavior. Feeling a little strained myself, I helped Masaru to his feet, but when he went to take his first step I realized he was going to need a little more help than that. Wordlessly, I fit myself back under Masaru's arm and let him lean on me as together we began the walk toward where Hex would be waiting for us.

"I'm proud of you, Hotaru," Arashi said in her southern belle accent. "I knew you had it in you, bein' as you're one of the Chosen of Sapphiros and all, but still, I'm very proud of how you handled your test. It's not every non-Espearian who can make it through that as well as you did...and don't you worry, there are no hard feelings whatsoever about the way you saw me in your vision. You didn't know me, after all, and it was simply your mind inventin' your own demons."

They were well outside the city of Espearia now, though Hotaru could still make out the city wall in the distance behind them. After announcing Hotaru had passed her test with the Spirits of Espearia, Arashi had led her here, saying in honour of their alliance she had something she wanted to show her. Arashi reached a gnarled and dead tree jutting out of a rocky outcropping when she stopped, her blue cape fluttering in the breeze and her white-gold hair fanning out around her head like a halo.

"I hope you don't mind, but I need to stretch," Arashi said suddenly, and with a shift of her shoulders her blue cloak fell to the ground, revealing large, feathered white wings draping down her back. Throwing her arms out to either side, Arashi stretched her magnificent wings out to the sun and wind, waving them slowly through the air like one might wave their arms in water. "That's much better," she stated. "All right now, open up. Let's show our new friend the surprise we've got for her."

To Hotaru's immense surprise, the ground before Arashi's feet opened wide at the priestess' command to reveal a set of stone steps leading downward in a spiral. Looking from the angelic Espearian priestess to the dark tunnel at her feet, Jeth's last words to her before they parted in Taiyou came back to her suddenly. *Whatever you do Hotaru, don't go underground in Espearia.* Arashi was looking at Hotaru expectantly, one arm gesturing forward to indicate Hotaru should go ahead of her.

"What's down there?" Hotaru hesitated, wondering finally about Jeth's cryptic piece of advice.

"Why, it wouldn't be much of a surprise if I told it to you, now would it?" Arashi answered with a smile. "I assure you it's well lit down there and you'll be perfectly safe with me. We're allies now, remember?"

Hotaru looked from Arashi to the entranceway once again, struggling internally. She knew full well how important this alliance with Espearia was to King Narlhep, and she didn't want to let anyone down or risk offending Arashi in any way. She had passed her test with the Spirits of Espearia and in doing so she had gained more confidence in herself and her powers. With a determined nod, she stepped past Arashi and began the descent underground.

The stairs were steep and there were quite a few of them, but at intervals there were sconces on the smooth stone walls lit up with a fiery glow as she neared them. When at last they reached the bottom, Arashi stepped forward and the room lit up completely.

The space was long and rectangular, with the stone walls smooth in some places and rough in others. There were a small handful of Espearian priestesses walking about the room, some entering or exiting through doorways they made appear in the stone walls with a wave of their hand, and others simply milling about. In the centre of the room there was a low stone table, decorated with various metal implements. Beyond the table on the far wall was what really caught Hotaru's attention. Suspended by their arms twisted above their heads were two people she recognized instantly and the recognition caused her heart to leap into her throat.

On the left was Arocoth, whom Hotaru had only ever seen a picture of before now with the exception of her test with the Spirits. Now, seeing them for the first time in person and without their armour, she realized Arocoth might actually be a girl. Her chin-length black hair was plain and straight, and at this moment it was flopped down to hide her eyes. With her more masculine-looking armour gone, slight curves were evident on her frame as she hung by her wrists.

On the right was the one Talon who was decidedly female. Tall and busty, with a long mane of vibrant red hair, Zai-Aku was beautiful even now in her tattered black dress and covered as she was in gruesome cuts and purpling bruises. Neither of the Talons were in good shape. Zai-Aku glared defiantly through a puffy and swollen eye, but it was quite possible Arocoth had been driven unconscious by her numerous injuries.

"I wanted to show you these as a sign of good faith for our new alliance," Arashi spoke after Hotaru had had a chance to take in the Espearians' handiwork. "They have been sentenced to four hundred years of torment for their crimes against Espearia and her allies. And I'll have you know we are quite practiced in ensuring they will live just long enough to complete their sentences."

Arashi's words struck home as Hotaru stared at the captive Talons, unable to look away. In her mind's eye, Arocoth's form was replaced by Goji, strung up and tortured because he was a former Talon. Hotaru watched in horror as one of the Espearian priestesses picked up a curved blade from the table and strode with purpose toward her victims. Not thinking of the possible ramifications to the Espearian alliance, Hotaru summoned her power to throw up a shield around the Talons to protect them from harm –but nothing happened.

Zai-Aku cried out as the curved blade sunk into the flesh of her hip and Hotaru tried repeatedly to shield her from the priestess, but to no avail. She could still feel her power, but for the life of her she could not make it work.

"But they could be people we know from Earth!" She exclaimed. "Fuzen is gone, but he's Goji now. We saved him and we can do the same for these two, they don't have to suffer this way."

"Don't have to suffer?" Arashi looked offended. "Why of course they do. They must pay for the crimes they have perpetrated against Espearia for hundreds of years."

Still staring at the Talons as if she could somehow see beyond their faces to the people they really were, Hotaru struggled to come up with some way Arashi would be able to see the injustice in this circumstance. "I know the Talons have been on this world for eight hundred years and have done awful things, but before that I think they were people we knew back on Earth. Those people are still inside the Talons somewhere. They're being held prisoners while their bodies are being tortured and those people are innocent!"

"Now don't get all worked up, dear. I understand you think the Talons might once have been friends of yours, but that doesn't excuse them from the crimes they have committed. But in case you are right and they can be...reverted back to their original forms?" Arashi checked to see if she had it right and Hotaru nodded, listening closely. "Well in that case, I suppose I can make you a deal."

"What kind of deal?"

"A fair one," Arashi stated, "and the only one I can offer – the Espearian people do want justice, after all, and I am not going to just take that away from them, even in light of our newly made alliance. I'll give you one day to attempt to revert them to their original forms and prove to me you have done so. During this time, their punishment will be put on hold and they will be allowed some temporary respite. If you succeed, they're yours, no questions asked, but you must remove them from Espearia with you when you go. If you fail, they are mine for the rest of eternity to do with them as I see fit."

"And if I refuse your deal?" Hotaru asked, not liking her options.

"Well then, they continue on as they are with nearly four hundred years remaining of their sentence and it would be as if you never learned of their presence here," Arashi responded, her musical southern accent sounding slightly out of place as she spoke so easily of centuries of torture. "What do you say, Hotaru?"

"I'll do it," she answered, seeing no other option. "I'll save them."

"What do you want out of this, Hex?" I demanded.

Masaru and I were seated before a round, metal table on the top floor of Hex's outpost building. Hex, the somewhat bird-like alien creature stood before us.

"Before you answer," I interjected, "I want you to know I'm not doing any of this for me. This war isn't my fight – I'm not even from this world – but I will be putting my life on the line for my allies, the people I care about, and all the people who are suffering on this world. So if my friends and I die because we weren't strong enough, or didn't have enough support to win, then all of you who stood by and watched it happen will be the ones to have to live with the consequences when this world is finally and completely overrun.

"If all you want is to see night again, you should find a way to get to my world – it's still untouched, for now – but if you want this world to be saved, then you're going to have to fight for it. We can either all stand together in Taiyou when the Vile Emperor comes or we can let him pick us off one by one at his leisure."

Hex looked, if anything, slightly amused when I finally finished. "Well spoken, Yukari," he rumbled in his deep voice. "Perhaps I should have made myself clearer. You needn't worry about my loyalty. If the Vile Emperor comes to Taiyou, I will be there with forces uncounted. Until then, I will send with you my prototype Gin-Kouteki unit. He will scout and report back to me the state of affairs in Taiyou, and I will determine whether they are worth helping in their own right. Understand it is not you I doubt, but Taiyou and this king I have never met."

"That would be very much appreciated, Hex. I assume that will allow us to communicate with you as well?"

"Indeed," he responded. "If the Vile Emperor comes, you need only inform me through Gin-Kouteki and I will send you the reinforcements you need."

"Then that's all I can ask for," I stated. "Thank you."

"You are very welcome Yukari," Hex said, taking hold of my hand and enveloping it in his giant one. "I know you will make me very proud…"

The underground facility beneath the outpost near Sresh was exceptionally vast, yet still it seemed cramped with the presence of the two sandcrawlers curled up together, far below on the sandy floor.

Yue, Ao Kouen, and Jeth – still a dog – found themselves high above the enormous beasts on one of the many catwalks suspended from the ceiling. They were out of Sresh proper now and some distance out in the Sand Lake at an outpost Lady Anaeth had advised them was informally known as the 'Sandcrawler Farm'. On the surface, the fenced-in compound with its main outpost tower looked much like any other, but underground was a different matter altogether. It was here that Flaqqers – the miracle cure made from sandcrawler larvae – were collected from two mated sandcrawlers.

"I can trade you this barrel of water for a barrel of Flaqqers," Yue offered politely to the Roughlander caretaker before her, "though Lady Anaeth did say we could pick up whatever supplies we needed free of charge."

She handed the man the requisition letter granted to her by Lady Anaeth for her warning about the guardian-style creatures of the night. Lady Anaeth had already known what they were, though she called them Lillem instead of guardians, but she thanked Yue for her information, regardless.

As the Roughlander looked over the letter in some detail, grumbling to himself about giving away Flaqqers for free, Yue leaned over the barrel she had taken out of her storage space to talk quietly with the other two. "So where d'you think we should head to next?"

"Yue?" She heard her name spoken faintly from somewhere nearby.

"What was that?" Ao Kouen asked, looking from Yue to Jeth in confusion.

Yue pulled the lid off the water barrel with a mounting confusion, certain the voice had come from within.

"Yue, are you there? Answer me!" Hotaru's voice rang out clearly from the water in the barrel.

"Hotaru, is that you?" Yue asked, speaking into the barrel. "If it is, make it quick, this isn't exactly the best time."

"Yes, it's me," Hotaru's voice answered. "Thank goodness this worked. Yue, I need your help."

"Where are you, Hotaru?"

"I'm in Espearia, at Adel's house," she replied. "I'm talking through the water here. I need you to come to Espearia right away if you can, or at least tell me how you turned Fuzen into Goji."

"Why?"

"Because Zai-Aku and Arocoth are being held prisoner here and I don't know if they are actually people we know – like Goji was. Arashi says I have only one day to save them or they'll be tortured forever, so I have to try–"

"Okay, hold on–" Yue interrupted Hotaru's panicked flow. "I'm coming. I'll be there as soon as I can."

"You will?" Hotaru asked hopefully. "You have a way to get here in time?"

"I'll find a way," Yue informed her. "Just stay calm, Hotaru. I'll be there before you know it." She slammed the lid down on the water barrel to indicate their conversation was over before she placed the barrels back into storage.

"Time to go," Yue announced to the others.

"Don't ye want yer Flaqqers?" the Roughlander asked, having returned with a barrel of his own.

"Yeah, thanks," Yue responded and vanished the smaller barrel of Flaqqers out of the man's hands just as easily as she had the barrel of water. "Oh good, I didn't know live things could go into my Noh-space – that's a relief," she commented nonchalantly, ignoring the Roughlander's shocked expression. "Well, we'll be going now – see you!"

"Now what reason do we got of trustin' you?" the smarmy looking man with pointed features and sandy blond hair repeated with more than a hint of disdain. I had trouble placing his accent. It was lilting, but unlike any other Roughlander I had yet come across. "I mean you're pretty and all, but what's pretty blue eyes count for out in the Sand Lakes, eh?"

"It's your choice, I suppose," I answered with an effort at nonchalance. "We leave for Taiyou just after the next bounce, in case the darkness falls again. I'd appreciate it if you'd join the rest of us, but it's up to you if you just want to give up now and let the Vile Emperor rule everything."

"You plan to take 'is men right out from under 'im?" the man's much larger and more muscular companion asked in the same accent, only thicker. "I like 'er, boss. This girl's got character. My name's Yuge," he introduced himself, pointing a metal, gauntleted hand at his deeply tanned bare chest. "This 'ere's 'Itachi – 'e's the outpost leader 'round 'ere."

I smiled at Yuge as I took a seat next to Razor, leaving a metal folding chair open for Masaru to my left. Hitachi glared at me from over the lid of his canteen as I settled myself among the other Roughlanders who had gathered. I was pleased to note I recognized a good portion of them as the people I had brought with me across the Sand Lakes and stationed here, while our small group had continued on to Taiyou.

"Well, we'll see what you've got to offer now, won't we?" Hitachi grumbled.

"Sure, Hitachi," I responded glibly, feeling happy for the moment there was no impending disaster to avert and I could relax for once, "right after you show me what makes you so great to have around."

Yuge snorted with sudden laughter and the rest of the table followed soon after – even Neva, I noticed, took part.

"Oh, she got you there, 'Itachi," Yuge commented, once he had recovered enough to speak.

"Shut up, Yuge," Hitachi retorted.

When Kaji awoke, he felt out of place in a dark, humid, cavernous room he didn't recognize. He was lying on a bed of moss over a cool damp stone slab. The walls were covered in the same unfamiliar, mossy substance and the whole place smelled faintly of water and vegetation. He sat up and blinked a few times to let his eyesight adjust to the dim ambient light, only to realize he was nose-to-nose with a very angry Croatin.

Krox, Head-taker of the First Spawn, was an imposing brute at about seven and a half feet tall, with brownish-green skin and heavy-set, muscular limbs. As Head-taker, Krox was revered among his kind for being the best fighter and a celebrated executioner. Over the years it seemed Krox had taken some injuries, but they had never been enough to slow the him down; he had simply added some mechanical parts and continued on, much as he had before.

"Where is Dahlia?" Krox demanded, his hot breath wafting across Kaji's face.

"I...uh..." Kaji stuttered, finding himself unable to answer when faced with the feared Head-taker. If he lied, he knew the Croatin would know it instantly, but the truth would only serve to get him killed.

"What have you done with her?" Krox asked, his guttural voice deepening dangerously. "Answer me, human!"

Krox's muscled hand closed around Kaji's throat to lift him effortlessly into the air. Kaji spluttered, unable to draw breath or answer the Croatin, even if he wanted to. The worst part of it was Kaji knew he deserved this sort of treatment and worse. Krox's mate, Dahlia, was dead, and it was all because Kaji had sent her off across the Sand Lakes, knowing the forces of the Ruby City would stop at nothing to get their hands on anything or anyone that would lead them to the Chosen of Sapphiros.

He had promised the Croatins his arm should he fail them, it looked like he was going to give them his head...

Kaji gasped awake suddenly. "I killed her! It was my fault."

"Shh...it's all right Kaji, you didn't kill anyone; it was just a dream."

Kaji took in the room around him through lidded eyes and a throbbing head. The room was the same as the one from his dream, except this time it was Rama before him and not Krox.

"I wish it was, Leon," Kaji stated truthfully, "but Krox is going to have my head…"

"Have your head for what, Kaji?" Krox's deep, guttural voice spoke from the open-arched doorway of the cavern. "Should I not be glad to see you?"

Kaji winced somewhat guiltily, eyeing Krox up and down and trying unsuccessfully to judge his mood. He stood, taking a deep breath, and decided he had best admit to the situation and give Krox the honest truth. "It's Dahlia, Krox – she's missing and it's my fault."

Krox crossed the room in two strides with his usual lumbering gait, caused by his one bionic leg; he placed one hand on Kaji's shoulder and the other one on the side of Kaji's head. "Your fault?" Krox inquired, his voice low. "Tell me, is there a reason I should let you keep your head?"

Kaji closed his eyes so as not to betray his fear to the Croatin. "It's yours," he answered just as quietly, "only, I don't believe Dahlia's dead. There were signs of a scuffle, but no body, other than the mounts. I think it's possible she was captured. Dahlia would be too valuable to simply kill."

Krox grunted angrily, but pushed Kaji away so he staggered back into the stone slab where he had woken up. "So it's to be torture, then?" He stated with disgust. "Where did you find the trail?"

Kaji explained the scene he had discovered to Krox in some detail and the lay of the land where he had found it, letting him know it may look different after the sandcrawler chewed through the cliff edge to get to them. As he spoke, he noticed the hammer-scope had been placed near his bed; he reached for it to offer it up to Krox.

"I found this. That's how I knew it was her mount we found," Kaji informed him. "We'll get her back, Krox."

Krox's eyes narrowed, as his massive hand covered the rod of the hammer-scope and he took the device to hold it to his chest. "I'll get her back," he declared with purpose and without waiting for a response, strode forcefully from the room.

"Now that is someone I wouldn't want to cross," Rama commented, "and you're a brave man for standing up to him."

"That wasn't bravery," Kaji responded, rubbing his temples tiredly.

"Well, as you've probably figured out by now, we reached the Croatin base," Rama said, changing the subject. "The Third Spawn carted Pine away somewhere and they won't let anyone see him, and the First of the First Spawn says he looks forward to seeing you again."

Kaji raised a brow in Rama's direction.

"Well, those weren't his exact words," Rama amended with a hint of a smile, "but the sentiment was clear enough that he wanted to speak to you as soon as you were able and he didn't want to deal with 'the likes of me'. I tried not to take offence, considering the circumstances."

Rama's lightheartedness succeeded in bringing a smile to Kaji's lips. "All right, Leon, let's do what we came here to do and then we can hunt down Pine."

"Agreed."

Kaji and Rama met with the First of the First Spawn and his near-constant companion, the First of the Second Spawn, in the main auditorium. The First of the First Spawn was a massive brute, even larger than Krox and more battle-scarred, but much older. His right arm was missing entirely at the shoulder and his left was always taken up by his human skull-topped staff of office, which in his case doubled as a convenient walking stick to help him keep his balance.

"For what reason did you come flying back here on one of the Vile One's contraptions?" the First of the First Spawn demanded gruffly.

"I stole it," Kaji answered simply. "You of all people should know the value of using your enemies' resources against them."

The First of the First Spawn grunted, having no response to this, and the First of the Second, behind him and a little to the left, grinned wickedly, his mouth stretching at the corners. The First of the Second Spawn was a wholly different creature from the First of the First, though just as intimidating and deadly, if not more so. The tiny Croatin, shorter even than Pine, stood slightly less than four feet in height. His purple skin was a rich colour, highlighted by his vibrant yellow spots, which marked him for the poisonous frog-person he was.

"I was told you wanted to speak with me," Kaji hinted, trying to direct the conversation to its purpose, so he could find Pine sooner. Truthfully, he was worried.

"Yes," the First of the First Spawn responded. "This other human tells us you are here to make demands of the Croatins," he said, indicating Rama, whose face flushed.

"I did not say demands, Great First One," Rama protested "I'm here to make arrangements for you in Taiyou."

"Arrangements?" the First of the First Spawn demanded angrily. "There will be no arrangements – we will take back our homeland whether the humans want us to or not."

"Great First One," Kaji spoke with authority, "Rama has come here as a representative of the King of Taiyou to welcome you back to Taiyou as citizens. When I came here before, I promised you the Croatins would return to Taiyou and that day has come."

The First of the First Spawn looked taken aback and his eyes widened as he stared from Kaji to Rama in shock. Behind him, the First of the Second Spawn continued to smile, but now his smile had changed to an appraising one as he regarded Kaji.

"It is time for the world to see a Croatin army march," Kaji informed them. "If the borders of Taiyou can be defended, you have been offered a home there."

"And that's where I come in," Rama began. "I have been given leave to designate the land the Croatins will be given in return for their aid…"

Rama pulled out the map of Taiyou given to him by Narlhep and proceeded to discuss in detail the size and location of the new Croatin province of Taiyou. When all parties were satisfied, Kaji and Rama took their leave of the Croatin Firsts, so the news could be spread among the spawns and plans could be made for departure.

"The spawns will march to Taiyou, but the Sixth will remain behind to guard our home," the First of the First Spawn declared.

"I must also request you release the prisoner you have taken," Rama ventured.

"The Skyraider pilot? Very well," the First of the First acceded, with a nod to two Third Spawn Croatins standing near the door to the central chamber, "bring her here."

Her? Kaji and Rama looked at each other with matching expressions of confusion. Sure enough, when their pilot rejoined them, she lacked the helmet she had been wearing during the entire trip and was revealed to be a woman. She smiled tentatively in their direction once she was released from her Croatin guards.

"Thanks," she said, her voice accented in the Roughlander style. "I knew ye'd manage to get me free eventually. I'm Pyote and it's nice to officially make yer acquaintance."

Staying together, the humans were led by the Third Spawn, who as a whole were more like cyborgs with their varied robotic parts. The Third Spawn were unique among the Croatins for being the most experimental with technology and using it to enhance their already impressive physiques.

The room Pine was in beeped and whirred softly, every wall of the cavern lined with computers and different mechanical devices. Pine lay on a table on the far side of the room, a heavy cloth draped over his form, covering him up to the neck.

"He is not quite finished," a heavily mechanized Third Spawn spoke from his place before a monitor on the wall, his voice sounding more like a Binoid than a Croatin, "but he will wake soon. There will be an adjustment period."

The Third Spawn stood, ignoring the three humans in the room and passing by them to reach Pine's side, and then drew back the cloth. With deliberate, almost mechanical, motions, the Third Spawn reached over and picked up a square metal sheet and fastened it to Pine's chest – Pine's metal chest.

Kaji stared at the Second Spawn Croatin in shock – the only recognizable parts of Pine were his right arm and shoulder, the upper part of his chest, and his head. The rest of Pine's body had been replaced with a robotic one, making him a few feet taller and quite a bit larger than he had been previously.

"Oh dear," Rama commented from slightly behind Kaji. "Adjustment period, indeed."

"But he'll live, right?" Kaji asked the Third Spawn Croatin for confirmation.

"He is alive," the Third Spawn responded. "However, he may no longer be termed a member of the Second Spawn. He may, if the First of the Third Spawn allows it, be termed a member of the Third Spawn."

Kaji approached Pine's bedside respectfully and bowed his head. "Thank you, Pine," he began, even if the former Second Spawn couldn't hear him. "Thank you for your sacrifice. You deserve so much more than the hand you've been dealt." He took hold of Pine's metal hand, knowing it wasn't safe to touch the other one. "If the Second Spawns don't want you like this and the Third Spawns won't have you, know you have a place with me."

Kaji raised his face upwards, looking past the ceiling of the cavern and to the heavens beyond. "Sapphiros, hear me," he demanded forcefully. "If anyone deserves to be granted your power, it is Pine, who paid so dearly to save my life. Please, grant him my power so he may be a Knight and a have a place with us."

Kaji willed his power into Pine, knowing there was a proper way to do this, but not knowing what that way was. A cyan light slowly filled the room before centring in on Pine's chest and sinking into the former Second Spawn Croatin. Pine gasped with renewed life and immediately sat up, to everyone's surprise, looking alert and filled with vigour.

"Kaji, Rama?" Pine whispered, his raspy voice sounding alarmed. "Why do I feel so cold?"

A relieved smile lit on Kaji's face. "I dub thee, Sir Pine."

"What?!"

CH. 7 – INNER STRENGTH

"So what did ye do for fun, back on your world?" Masaru asked, seeming genuinely curious as we passed by the unfinished edge of the stone wall and entered into the open Sand Lake.

We had gone out to search the perimeter of Hex's outpost for any clues as to the sudden appearance and disappearance of the deadly guardian-like creatures that had attacked during the darkness. Also, it gave us the chance to stretch our legs and spend some time together, out from under the knowing eyes of the other Roughlanders.

I flushed a little at the question, feeling suddenly self-conscious. "Fun? My life on Earth was very different from here, but fun wasn't really a big part of it," I answered cautiously. It felt strange to be talking about the world I had come from, but knew I would likely never see again. "I loved to swim," I ventured, a note of longing in my voice for the large, clear pool at Shinjuku High and the diving platform.

Masaru shuddered a little, though he tried to hide his reaction, and I smiled. "Well, I suppose there's always the lake at Taiyou," he suggested helpfully.

"It's not the same really," I answered with a sigh, putting thoughts of the pool out of my mind and returning to the question at hand. "Generally, I spent most of my time studying and learning new things – mostly science."

"Aye, that makes sense, ye're real smart."

"What about you?"

"Ye know, boy stuff mainly." He shrugged. "We used to bait sand sharks or hunt down old caves made by sandcrawlers."

I smiled, imagining a younger Masaru exploring the Sand Lake. "That sounds kind of dangerous."

"Aye, it was, but sand sharks are real cute when they're little. They're not vicious like the adult ones while they're still nesting. Hey, wait a minute, maybe I can show ye."

I quirked a brow at Masaru, but he held out a finger to forestall me before he shut his eyes to better concentrate. It wasn't long before the sand at our feet began to rumble and I made to step back, but Masaru took hold of my wrist to stop me. A dusky-blue fin broke the surface of the sand, followed by a rounded head with saucer-like eyes of a deep liquid blue.

The baby sand shark of Masaru's creation struggled its way free of the weighty sand, until most of its body was on the surface and supported by its back flippers. It reminded me vaguely of a seal, if I were to compare it to an Earth animal. It was large for a baby – somewhere between the size of a large dog and a small pony – and like a young pup, its head and flippers seemed too large for its body, causing it to move in an awkward, yet endearing way. Masaru was right – it was nearly the cutest thing I had ever seen.

"Is it tame?" I asked, curious.

"It is, but it isn't." Masaru shrugged. "It's a part of me and I made it, but it has a mind of its own too…it won't hurt ye, if that's what ye're asking."

I cautiously held out a hand to the creature, as one might when meeting a new dog. To my surprise, the baby sand shark lowered its round nose to affectionately bump against my hand.

"Tira used to love them," Masaru noted with a fond smile as he watched me with the sand shark. "There was a nest not too far from the outpost where we grew up and I used to take her there to visit the baby ones."

"Tira? That's your sister, right?"

"Aye," Masaru answered. I was very much aware I had never even heard him mention her name before; it was possible I only knew of her existence from a passing comment Dahlia had made at some point during our travels together.

"What was she like? If you don't mind telling me," I asked tentatively, knowing loss was a tricky subject with Masaru.

"I don't mind," he answered. "I probably should have told ye about her before now. Tira and I lost our parents when we were very young. There's an outpost where a lot of the children are sent to keep them safe while they grow up – it's why you never really see a Roughlander under the age of twelve or so. I'm not exactly sure, but there may be more than one outpost like that – Dahlia could tell ye better.

"We weren't Roughlanders then," Masaru continued. "Our parents ran a trade caravan, but when they were killed by the Deathsquads, we were sent to that outpost for our own safety. She may not have been born one, but Tira was a Roughlander through and through. She was a few years younger than I, but she was always willing to go on an adventure. She was practically fearless, but smart about it, ye know?"

"What happened to her?"

His mouth thinned into a line of distaste. "Tira and Razor used to be a match – they were in love," Masaru explained at my look of confusion. I motioned for him to go on, my hand still on the neck of the sand shark who had snuggled down for a nap with its head in my lap.

"Razor wasn't always the scoundrel he is now," Masaru began, settling down beside me. "At least we didn't think he was. He's actually Dahlia's younger brother."

"What?!"

"Aye," Masaru confirmed. "All four of us, and Krox o' course, once he met Dahlia, were at the same outpost – the one you saw at the center of the Great Sand Lake. We'd often go out on missions together as a part of Dahlia's crew. Sometimes all four or five of us would go, sometimes less. Sometimes we'd take others with us, but we were like a family back then.

"One time there was a trade caravan coming in that needed us to meet it as an escort across the Sand Lake. I was really sick with something and Dahlia was recovering from a serious injury she had taken the last time we had gone out, so it was up to Razor and Tira to go out and meet them on their own. I would've liked Krox to go with them, but it was a routine mission and Krox refused to leave Dahlia's side.

"So Razor and Tira went out, and only Razor came back," Masaru finished, looking grim – the way he usually did when Razor's name was mentioned.

"But what happened out there? Was it more Deathsquads?"

"Only Razor knows and he won't tell anyone," Masaru said darkly. "All I know is he was supposed to bring her back safely and instead he only protected himself."

I spent a moment absorbing this, thinking there had to be another side to the story. If Razor had loved Tira the way Masaru indicated he had, then there was no way he could have betrayed her – or left her undefended, if it could have been helped.

"It was never the same after that – it couldn't be," Masaru continued, lost in remembering a painful time. "Tira was gone and Razor wasn't the same person anymore. He and Dahlia got into a big fight – I think it was about what happened, though I don't think Dahlia ever got it out of him. Not long after, Razor left the outpost. By the time I had recovered enough to confront him he was long gone, and he never came back."

"So when you saw Razor in the Sand Lake on the way to this outpost and attacked him…that was the first time you had seen him since then?"

"Aye." Masaru's eyes met mine and I could see the shame he still felt about starting that fight with Razor when we had been marching across the Sand Lake. He looked away again after a brief moment, staring out into the sun rising from its noon bounce, deep in thought. "I want ye to know I care about ye a great deal, Yukari, and I think you and I have already become close friends. I…" He hesitated. "I want to be more than just your friend."

This line of conversation caught me slightly off guard. "I thought we already were," I said, thinking of the feeling of Masaru's lips on mine before we had left Taiyou and the depth of my pain when he had suddenly disappeared on the Sand Lake. Then, in case he didn't feel as strongly as I did, I once again amended my statement, "Trying, I mean."

"Aye, we are. I mean, I am," Masaru stumbled over his words a little. "Sabien told me he sees a darkness in me, Yukari, and I'm afraid he might be right."

"I know, he told me as well," I informed him. "And it may be true, but I'll tell you the same thing I told him – I have seen that darkness, but I have also seen you overcome it."

Masaru looked grim. "I don't want to ever hurt ye, Yukari. I don't want to lose control like I did when I saw Razor that day."

"You're stronger than any darkness within you. There's no reason you need to consider it a weakness. That darkness can be an inner strength for you, just as much as the light inside you already is."

The corner of his mouth lifted in a slight smile. "I suppose ye might be right. In any case, there's no use running away from something already inside me."

"Masaru," I suggested softly, "have you ever thought perhaps the reason Razor ran away, and the reason he can't talk about what happened to Tira, is because it hurts him almost as much as it hurts you to think about it?"

Masaru looked as if he wanted to protest this and stand by his opinion that Razor had somehow become a selfish bastard overnight, but after a moment his expression softened suddenly, the tension draining out of his features. "Oh, gods, Yukari...ye're likely right," he said. "Poor Razor, he lost the woman he loved and his entire family at the same time. I've been such a jerk to him, no wonder he hates me."

"I don't think he hates you, Masaru, not at all. He's saved your life more than once."

"I have to go speak to him," he said suddenly, getting to his feet and causing the sand shark in my lap to crumble unexpectedly into a pile of sand. "I have to apologize. D'ye mind?"

"Go on." I gave him an encouraging smile as I stood and brushed the sand from my lap. "I can finish up here."

Masaru took off at a run back toward the outpost. After watching him leave, I shook my head and let my wings appear at my back, taking off into the air to complete my patrol from above.

The mushroom cloud that erupted in front of the old Kusabana residence was visible for quite a distance in Espearia. Leaving Ao Kouen to explain the situation to Adel, Yue took off with Hotaru to see what could be done to rescue the Talons of the Vile Emperor. Deep underground, somewhere below the priestess' temple in Espearia, Yue strode forward and tried to see beyond the faces of the Talons and the marks of their torture to the human beings beneath. The disguises, if that was what they were, did their jobs well. Zai-Aku, the red-headed one, could perhaps be Shuzhue, transformed after eight hundred years of unwilling service to the Vile Emperor; but the other, Arocoth, was unidentifiable.

Regardless, Yue knew what needed to be done – except she had no idea of how she was to accomplish it. Freeing Goji from his guise as Fuzen had been unintentional. She remembered clearly how she had done it, but in the case of Fuzen, there had been a visible ruby, which, when drained of its power, released Goji from whatever had bound him captive as the dreaded Talon. Looking over the two Talons chained to the rock face, she could make out no rubies, not even in the open wounds the Espearian priestesses had inflicted upon them. Without the rubies, she had no idea where to even begin.

Surprising herself, she decided the only course of action was to take a page from her mother's book. She was in a temple and she had already discovered – through a conversation with Jeth and some experimentation – that her powers as a Chosen did not work underground in Espearia. The only powers that would work here were Espearian ones. She doubted she had any of those, but Jeth had told her anyone could speak to the Spirits of Espearia if they chose; it was simply up to the Spirits whether or not they would listen.

Her Shinto priestess mother would have had her implore the spirits of this place for their aid and guidance. She removed her Roughlander belts and her canteen, putting them aside. Then she faced the Talons, who were unconscious, taking this valuable respite from their punishment to rest while they could. Putting the belongings on the ground before her, she began to dance.

The dance she performed was not nearly as complex or elaborate as the one that may have caused the sun to set – she didn't want a similar disaster to occur here; she only wanted the Spirits to hear her. As it came to a close, she knelt before the pile on the ground and addressed the Spirits of Espearia. *Spirits, hear me. I seek to free the souls of the two individuals before me. They have been held prisoner in these forms for over eight hundred years – please do not make them have to suffer for an eternity beyond that.*

I have not involved myself in over a millennia. Tell me – why should I interfere now?

The voice that spoke – Yue assumed it was only in her head, as there were no audible reactions from the priestesses or Hotaru behind her – was decidedly male. She could not be certain of who she was speaking with, but she had asked for the Spirits of Espearia, so she had to assume this was them.

The masks these people are forced to wear – the Talons – deserve punishment, yes, but the people beneath are no more than victims in this circumstance. They have been brought here, their bodies forced to commit crimes against their wills and their knowledge. I ask not that you interfere, Yue added, *but that you* intervene *on behalf of innocent souls.*

Done.

Yue looked up at the surprised gasps of her Espearian audience and Hotaru, to see the two Talons before her encased in a shimmering white light. As she watched, the faces and bodies of the Talons shimmered and changed, revealing two much younger-looking people beneath. Yue's breath caught in her throat as the white light faded and the two former Talons were at last identifiable as two more students from Shinjuku high school – Hotaru's best friend, Mizu, and the new transfer student, Reiki.

It had been one thing to see the damage done to Zai-Aku and Arocoth, Talons of the Vile Emperor, and to suspect those were not their true identities, but it was something else again to see those same wounds on two innocent students stolen from Earth.

Hotaru ran by before Yue had even managed to climb to her feet. She threw herself around Mizu's – formerly Zai-Aku's – feet, as they were the only part of her friend she could reach.

Yue stood. "Satisfied, Arashi?"

"Well, I never," the Espearian Head Priestess stated. "It seems I owe you an apology, Hotaru. I never truly believed the Talons could be simply usin' other people's bodies as you said. Take them down at once," she instructed the other priestesses in the room. "As I told you, I always keep my end of a bargain. Hotaru, your friends are free."

"Are the Spirits of Espearia always represented by a male voice?" Yue asked Arashi curiously.

"Why no, dear, the Spirits of Espearia are a beautiful chorus of female voices. They are the spirits of all the Espearian women who have ever and will ever live."

Yue puzzled over this as she donned her Roughlander belts once more and the Espearian priestesses carried Mizu and Reiki toward the stairs that would lead them back above ground, with Hotaru following after. Soon after, Arashi went with them, leaving Yue alone. Yue turned to leave the awful place behind her, when a grating sound caused her to pause. Turning her head over her shoulder, she saw a door-sized opening in the rock between where the Talons had hung that hadn't been there before. A faint glowing white light pulsed from somewhere beyond the darkened opening.

You want me to go there? she asked internally, but got no response other than the insistent, pulsing white light. *I suppose you did what I wanted, so I owe you one,* Yue decided and stepped forward into the dark hallway.

The rocks behind her slid shut, returning the wall to the way it was before. Swallowing apprehensively, she had no choice but to continue onward. The white light got brighter as she advanced along the slightly curved passage, until the light at the end of the tunnel was revealed for what it truly was. In a featureless cavern at the end of the hidden passage, there was a girl seemingly drowning in her long white hair, which was lengthy enough to bathe the space around her and cover most of her form. As Yue entered the chamber, the white light emanating from the girl's very skin was nearly overwhelming. As the girl's head snapped upwards at the sound of Yue's entrance, her blazing white pupils nearly blinded Yue with their intensity.

The Chosen of Damos, Yue realized, recognizing the similarities between the state this girl was in and the way she had found Ao Kouen. *Is that who you are, then – Damos?*

Chikara...

Yue realized instantly she hadn't been the only one to hear Damos' voice this time. Chikara, the Chosen of Damos, heard it as well, and the gentleness in the gem god's tone when he said her name seemed to quiet her. Chikara's brightness faded to a more manageable level and her eyes dimmed until her light grey irises could be seen.

"Chikara?" Yue ventured and the girl regarded her with intense curiosity. It was then Yue realized Chikara was being held hand and foot to the ground by stone that had wrapped itself around her limbs. "Who did this to you?"

"Mother…" Chikara struggled to make her voice work properly, tugging at her bonds, but getting nowhere with her efforts.

Damos? Yue tried to ask the god for his assistance with the stone, but got no response from him. *I guess I'll just have to do it the old fashioned way.*

She looked about the small room for anything she could use against Chikara's restraints, when a piece of the wall broke off and offered itself to her. *Thank you,* she told the stone, hefting the heavy piece of rock in her grasp, *this ought to do the trick.*

Careful not to strike Chikara's hands, Yue worked at the stone bonds with her rock hammer, chipping away at them one by one, until at last Chikara was freed. The girl's eyes began to glow white once more, as she stood to her full height and directed her gaze upwards toward the stone ceiling and beyond. Physically, she appeared to be no more than twelve years-old, but the unbelievable length of her white hair implied otherwise.

"Sun," she said simply, and her feet began to lift off the floor, her body drifting upwards.

"Uh, Chikara?" Yue tried to get the Chosen's attention.

The stone ceiling split open suddenly, revealing a tunnel heading upwards; as the opening widened, Yue could make out the night sky far above. Chikara looked down at the sound of her name and noticing Yue fully for the first time, she drifted back down to the ground to take Yue into her arms. Directing her gaze skywards again, Chikara shot suddenly upwards, until the two of them were floating above the rooftops of central Espearia, glowing brightly in the night sky.

Chikara looked around herself at the darkness of the night, seeming somewhat panicked, "Sun?" Without waiting for a response, she began to glow brighter and brighter, until she was her own miniature white sun and Yue could see nothing but whiteness all around her.

"Now what have I done?" Yue questioned, lost in Chikara's white light and wondering if perhaps the Chosen of Damos had been kept captive for a reason.

"It wasn't a Deathsquad. It was the Talons, Masaru, and you were right in saying it was my fault she was killed – but it's not what you think."

Razor's words tumbled through my mind as I watched the sun dip below the horizon. Even being from Earth, where the sun setting was a natural occurrence, I still couldn't help but feel a deep sense of unease as shadow blanketed the open sand, reaching for the low stone wall where the majority of the Roughlanders were stationed, their carbine rifles held at the ready.

"There was no trade caravan waiting to meet us out in the Sand Lake. It was a set up. They were looking for us, or maybe it was Dahlia they wanted – I'm not sure."

As the darkness swept across the sand and the last light of the sun faded, the inhuman screams began again. From the endless desert the creatures rose, their bodies and deadly talons forming from the sand itself. I loosed five arrows made of light to land in an arc beyond the wall to give some illumination and hopefully give them pause – that is, if these creatures feared the light the same way the guardians of Lilyth's valley had.

"Did Dahlia ever tell you we're not exactly Roughlanders ourselves? We're from a Rubian province, originally. Our father was what they call their 'Eyes and Ears' – which is not as simple as just being a spy. You don't have any choice – you essentially belong to the Ruby City – and they take your reports, willingly or unwillingly.

"My father didn't want to be a Rubian spy. By the end, he didn't even want to be Rubian, so he left and took his family into hiding with him. As far as I know, they never found him – if they even came looking."

I continued loosing arrows until I had a row of illumination between the gathering horde and the line of Roughlanders. When the first of the pseudo-guardians reached the edge of the cyan light it shied back, but the light either wasn't enough to fully deter it, or these guardians were, indeed, different.

"Fire!" someone, maybe Hitachi, instructed, and the line of carbine rifles went off in unison, shattering a number of the advancing enemy.

Still the creatures came, driving forward and bringing death with them.

"My father taught Dahlia everything he knew before he died. She was the eldest and his favourite, but apparently the reluctant position my father held for the Ruby City is a hereditary one, whether he wanted to pass that along or not. That day, the Talons had decided it was time to harvest their investment and so they came for us – though I'm fairly certain they knew where to find us all along."

Bright lights flickered to life around the outpost building, illuminating the desert just beyond the manned wall and driving the creatures back enough to allow the Roughlanders to aim at them.

Hex leapt from the entrance of the outpost building behind me to join the fray, now that it was full dark and he wasn't held at bay by the light of the sun. The massive, vulture-like alien landed with an audible thud in the crowd of undead, and with arcing sweeps of his muscled arms he cut a swath of destruction through the ravenous creatures, shrugging off their many savage attempts to take his life.

"It was an ambush. Zai-Aku had crushed Tira before I even knew who I was dealing with, let alone what they really wanted. I ran at the red-headed witch, crazed, hardly realizing it was too late for Tira and I was only throwing my own life away. Zai-Aku didn't try to kill me – she didn't need to. She flicked a finger and sent me flying, saying I was too valuable a resource to waste. Fuzen picked me up – he's the one who took my eye – and said he would take part of what I owed the Ruby City, and leave the other as a reminder that when he wanted me, he would be back."

The relentless undead were beyond counting and they swarmed around the light of the outpost like moths to an open flame. My arrows did little against them; no matter what type I tried to use, they kept pushing forward. As I watched them come and engage the Roughlanders, who stayed just out of their reach in the relative safety of the light, I began to notice a deep rumble in the ground beneath my feet – just before Masaru identified the source of the disturbance.

"Sandcrawler – it's comin' in fast!"

"I was surprised they left me alive, but I suppose I could serve no purpose dead. No doubt the person they were really after was Dahlia. She had access to more knowledge and Roughlander secrets than I could give them, no matter what they did to me."

"So that's where you think she is, then?" I asked. "The Ruby City?"

"Aye," Masaru's voice responded in my memory, *"it's common enough knowledge that the Ruby City is surrounded by some sort of magical barrier. No one can pass through it who isn't authorized to. Being that it's magic and all, it's possible it could have interfered with yer arrows."*

I took to the air to get a better idea of what was coming for us. Seeing motion out in the Sand Lake beyond the swarm of undead, I fired five glowing cyan arrows out in the straight line to cut a path through the darkness.

"We're lucky – it's only a juvenile one!" Masaru called up to me from below. "Seems like it's being driven mad by all the activity out there – they don't normally come this near to the outposts!"

The sandcrawler – impossibly large for 'only a juvenile one', as Masaru had called it – was headed straight for the outpost. "It's coming straight for us, Masaru; how can I stop it?"

"We'll have to drive it off!" he called back. "I don't know if this one's big enough to take the outpost down on its own, but it'll do quite a bit of damage if we can't convince it to turn around."

"They'll torture her until she tells them everything she knows about you, about your Knights, and all the secrets of the Roughlanders she's got crammed in her head." Razor's voice was filled with regret. *"She didn't want to listen to me, but I warned her this day would come."*

"But Dahlia knows the location of every secret outpost," Masaru said, stricken, *"including where the children are kept. There's not enough time to warn them."*

"Yes, there is," I told them, stumbling on a sudden flash of insight. *"We have access to Binaris and with her systems fully operational now she's connected to twenty-six outposts. We can send a message to warn them all, and they can spread the word to get everyone moved safely, or at least be prepared for an attack, knowing they've been compromised."*

"Ye're brilliant, Yukari."

The sandcrawler was upon us before I knew it, swallowing more than one Roughlander whole as it surged upwards from the ground and wailing loud enough to drown out the cacophony of the screaming guardians. I let loose with my arrows and peppered its tan-coloured hide, before it dove into the ground once more, my efforts having no visible effect.

As it came up for a second time, much closer to the outpost, I tried something a little different. I aimed for its lighter-coloured underbelly, where I hoped its outer shell was thinner. This time, I charged my arrows with as much power as I could give them so they would explode on contact. One by one, my arrows stuck into the creature and exploded, causing the sandcrawler to waver as it rose into the air. The fifth and last arrow fell unintentionally into its gaping maw and the resulting explosion on the inside of the creature sent it reeling. I called forth another slew of arrows to fire at the sandcrawler again – this time knowing exactly where to aim – when all of a sudden the creature was silenced.

The blade of an axe – almost as large as the sandcrawler's head – had sliced clean through the massive beast, removing the head from the rest of its body and sending it crashing to the ground below. My mouth dropped open in shock, as I took in what wielded the weapon ten men would have had trouble lifting. Standing impossibly tall and wielding a long-poled axe with one hand was a mechanized man – or I suppose on this world he would probably be called a Binoid – though his sheer size put him in a totally different category from Binaris or X-En. The robot was obviously equipped for combat, with its large-bladed axe and rounded cannons mounted on its shoulders. As I flapped my wings subconsciously to stay aloft, the sun rose once again and I found I still couldn't tear my eyes away from the giant who had suddenly arrived before me.

"I am known as Gin-Kouteki," the Binoid spoke from speakers I couldn't see, its mouth not moving to keep up the illusion of humanity the way the smaller Binoids were built to. "You are Yukari Namikoya, Chosen of Sapphiros. I am to accompany you and do as you command. Please speak, so I may recognize your voice commands."

"Nice to meet you…Gin-Kouteki," I stuttered out.

"Is there anyone else whose voice commands you would have me obey, Yukari?"

I looked around, a little at a loss, when my eyes lighted on Masaru far below, helping to pull a man out of the severed head of the sandcrawler. It seemed the two Roughlanders who had been swallowed had survived after all, the horrifying beast not having had the chance to digest them yet.

"Uh, yes," I told Gin-Kouteki, pointing out who I meant below, "Masaru...he's my Knight."

Kaji let out a relieved breath as the sun came up once more, allowing the unfortunately solar-powered Skyraider beneath him to surge back to life and right its course before it nearly collided with the rocky ground below.

"That was longer than last time," Pyote informed them, urging the Skyraider higher into the air where it belonged.

"Was it?" Rama asked.

"Aye," Pyote answered him. "It seemed like it was dark for nearly twice as long."

"That was different," Pine commented in his raspy voice from the rear of the Skyraider, having been unconscious the first time the sun had set.

"Aye," Pyote agreed with him. "Just to let ye know – we're comin' up on the outpost ahead. Did ye want me to try and skirt around it?"

"No," Kaji answered her. "Bring us around to the front and land on the ground. There's someone I want to see."

Pyote did as Kaji requested and landed the Skyraider in the open yard before the main outpost building – or as near as she could get to it while being flanked by the remaining two Skyraiders, piloted by actual Deathsquad soldiers. As their Skyraider came to a final, stuttering stop, Deathsquad soldiers filed in to fill the square yard, boxing them in so they couldn't flee even if they wanted to. Kaji stepped off of the Skyraider; before him, the ranks of Deathsquad soldiers parted to reveal their General, Lady Kichigai, as she strode into the square, her double-bladed axe strapped to her back and her curved knife at her hip as before.

"You dare to show your face here again, do you, Chosen?" Kichigai asked.

"I came back for my outpost," Kaji stated boldly.

"Your outpost?" Kichigai laughed. "I beg to differ."

"I told you I would be back for it and here I am," he reminded her. "Since it seems we are in disagreement, something will have to be done about this."

"I know who and what you are," Kichigai stated. "It is all too obvious how a duel between us would end the moment you used your powers."

"No powers then," Kaji offered. "A test of skill and the winner gets to keep control of the outpost."

"To first blood?" Kichigai suggested.

"To mercy," Kaji amended.

"Weapons?"

"I don't intend to use any."

"Very well." Kichigai unhooked the double-bladed axe from her back with one hand and tossed it by the shaft to a Deathsquad soldier, then she removed the dagger sheathe from her side and handed that over as well.

Kaji and Kichigai regarded one another for a long moment, neither willing to make the first move. Eventually, she shrugged and took up a stance from the fighting style known as Croatin boxing. Lowering his right leg out in front of him and bending his left knee to support his weight, Kaji matched her stance with a slight smile, having spent some time learning the unorthodox style from Dahlia, who was an expert.

"Impressive," Kichigai noted with a raised eyebrow, "but can you follow through?"

With that, she leapt, propelling herself into the air with a powerful kick of her legs. Croatin boxing was a more difficult style for humans, not having the same physical make-up as a Croatin, but Kichigai made it look effortless as she landed before Kaji and brought her fist around her head to drive down on his shoulder. Kaji, having seen Dahlia perform this maneuver with equal grace and deadly efficiency, knew what to expect; at the last moment, he brought his hands up to keep the blow from connecting. He knew better than to catch it with his hands, so he shifted his weight to move in closer and clamp his hands around her forearm and push upwards.

Kichigai grinned, showing teeth, her face close to his, as Kaji felt the fingers of her free hand drive painfully into his right side. With a grunt, he loosened his hold on Kichigai to bat her hand aside and brought his leg up for a close-range kick to her midsection. The blow connected, driving Kichigai back, but she rolled with the impact and managed to land on her feet, ready for the next attack.

"I have every right to this outpost, you know," Kichigai commented, almost conversationally. "Whatever you may think, it is my right to rule here as a provincial lord."

"This is a Roughlander outpost, not a Rubian province," Kaji countered, charging to close the distance between them.

Kichigai blocked each of Kaji's punches, keeping his fists away from her face and thrust her attack low, feinting a kick so Kaji wouldn't expect it when she abruptly changed tactics to stomp on his foot. Getting frustrated by her refusal to stick to one style of combat, Kaji reached for her to grab her in a hold, but Kichigai once again surprised him by letting him get his arms about her upper half. In two quick flicks of her foot, she had driven Kaji's legs apart, setting him off balance and turning the tables, so he was forced to rely on her to stand.

"I'm a Roughlander," Kichigai said forcefully, twisting around to throw Kaji from her back. He let go before she could get a good hold on him, realizing finally just how dangerous this woman was, with or without her weapons. She spun about to face him once more, a scowl on her face. "I was born here. This outpost is my home."

The first Deathsquad General Kaji had met had been Lady Mikura, who seemed to rely heavily on her magic powers, which Kaji had believed to be granted by her station, much like the abilities of the Knights of Sapphiros. As he tried his best to fend off Kichigai's next attack, he also realized she was more than capable of thwarting most of what he tried to throw at her.

"My people will never stand for someone like you coming in here like you own the place," she stated, after having driven a particularly brutal strike to Kaji's midsection.

"After 'Big Daddy', I figured just about anybody would be better," Kaji quipped, smiling through his discomfort and trying not to let her see how much she had hurt him.

Kichigai smiled despite herself, before she went in for another blow to the side of Kaji's head. Then he did the most unexpected thing he could think of and dropped low, swinging his leg around and catching her off balance, knocking the Deathsquad General into the sand. She landed on her back and tried to roll to her feet, but Kaji pressed his advantage to not let her regain the upper hand. He dove for her, intent on hitting any part of her he could reach as long as it would keep her on the ground. She let him get in close, before she tossed a handful of sand into his eyes, blinding him temporarily.

Technically cheating, Kaji mentally switched over to his magic sight to see which direction she would come at him from and was completely bowled over when Kichigai drove her fist into his left side. He hadn't seen her coming, not even a flicker of her magic – was it possible she didn't have any?

He took a fair beating as he fought to clear the sand from his eyes, blinking furiously and ineffectually blocking the multiple attacks the Deathsqaud General threw at him. She was lightning fast, and when she knew she had the advantage she pressed it, seeming to come at him from all directions at once. Eventually, he managed one good hit on her and despite his efforts to control himself, the power behind his attack sent her flying. He hadn't intended to, but his power as a Chosen had manifested on his behalf, making his attack more powerful than someone strictly human would have been capable of.

Kichigai landed and skidded to a halt a fair distance from where Kaji stood, but he did not press his success, instead allowing her to climb to her feet. They were both panting now, but anyone could see Kaji was much worse off than the armoured General.

"So how did you turn from a Roughlander to the General of a Deathsquad army and a Rubian provincial lord, then?" Kaji took the opportunity to ask the question on his mind.

"I was sick of watching Roughlanders be slaughtered by a force greater than them," Kichigai replied, taking a moment to catch her breath, as she watched Kaji closely from across the yard. "I'm a firm believer in the philosophy 'if you can't beat them, join them'."

"So why wouldn't you join me, then?" Kaji asked, grinning through the pain in his face caused by the bashing he had received at her hand.

Kichigai grinned back, appreciating Kaji's attempt at humour. "I might as well say the same to you, considering, though I know you could destroy me if you didn't have a sense of honour."

"Truthfully, all I want is someone competent enough to protect this outpost to be in charge of it," Kaji explained.

"I would guard this outpost with my life, even from you," Kichigai responded.

"I call mercy then," Kaji said, putting his hands out to either side to show he had no will to fight any further. "I leave the outpost in your capable hands."

Kichigai laughed suddenly, relaxing her own stance in the process, the tension draining out of her. "And here I thought you were about to get serious. I don't hold it against you that you used your powers, Chosen. I'm sure that's something that would be very difficult to keep from leaking out."

"My name is Kaji," he informed her.

"Well, Kaji," Kichigai said, "I'd like to continue our discussion about the future of the outpost, if you'll join me in my quarters for a drink?"

"I'd be glad to."

We set out soon after the sun came up, knowing we had a lengthy journey ahead of us across the open Sand Lake and following the new pattern that was establishing itself, we would have one period of darkness to deal with between Hex's Outpost and Taiyou. Before dark, the Roughlanders set themselves up in a circle in a defensible position with torches planted all around, ready to light as soon as they became necessary to fend off the undead. As the sun began to set and we completed our preparations, we received an unexpected visitor – Fuun.

One moment I was alone; in the next, the self-proclaimed Chosen of Machalite was standing before me, his long black jacket rippling in the wind as he regarded me with his usual stony expression.

"I received your message," Fuun informed me, his voice devoid of inflection.

"And?" I inquired, aiming for nonchalance and falling just shy of it.

"Would you have my help this night?"

I looked around at the defenses and the several thousand Roughlanders who were prepared to fight with everything they had to survive the coming darkness, no matter what crawled out of it at them. I thought we had a fairly good chance at holding out against the creatures with everyone so dedicated, and the preparations we had made to ensure there would be enough light to protect us, but even still there would be losses, and I was still uncertain of how best to use Gin-Kouteki to minimize them.

"If you would like to help, I would appreciate it," I told Fuun. "If not here tonight, we will most certainly need your help in Taiyou, which is why I sent for you."

"You will not ask for my help? Do you prefer I stand by this evening?"

"That's not what I said," I protested and then gritted my teeth, "Please Fuun, help us survive the night."

"I will keep the monsters at bay," Fuun vowed. "Do not light your torches or fire your weapons."

I informed everyone else of Fuun's request and his intentions – to the Roughlanders' great amusement. Each of them had heard of the legendary Fuun, self-proclaimed Chosen of Machalite, and knew of his skill in combat; while none of them wanted to cross him, they were perfectly willing to see if he could fight their battles for them. Some of them even went so far as to make a game of it and bet on if they would have to raise their weapons at all during the darkness.

"Just make sure they keep at the ready in case Fuun is not true to his word, or in case they overwhelm him. He is just one man, after all, no matter how great he thinks he is," I told Razor.

The sun disappeared below the horizon and drenched the world in blackness again. Lifting Masaru at his request, I flew the two of us up to perch upon Gin-Kouteki's shoulder to see if we could make anything out.

The screams were distant, but they were coming closer – as if they could sense the direction of their prey. In silence, we waited for them to come for us. Fuun, below with the Roughlanders, did not wait – he disappeared to meet death head on.

"Singular unit moving rapidly northward to engage enemy forces. Would you have me assist?" Gin-Kouteki asked.

"Hold your fire, Gin-Kouteki," I responded.

"You can see Fuun?" Masaru asked the Binoid.

"Affirmative," Gin-Kouteki responded. "Activating vid-screen."

With a slight whirring noise, a panel on Gin-Kouteki's chest flipped around and extended outwards. The panel's screen displayed a green-tinged image. On the screen was Fuun, his sword drawn, as he stood before a cluster of the undead creatures. Fuun remained still and steady as he watched the creatures; they ignored him, as if he didn't exist, while they surged around him. When Fuun was completely engulfed by them, he suddenly began to move and the guardians fell to pieces at the barest touch of his sword.

Fuun decimated another cluster and another, when abruptly he stopped, head tilting to the side. No more than a split second later, Fuun dodged to the side, throwing his body left and tossing up a spray of sand with the motion as a thick, corporeal shadow sliced through the air where he had been standing.

"What was that?" I asked.

"Searching," Gin-Kouteki, being a Binoid, took my rhetorical question seriously. "Target acquired."

The screen faded to black and then came back up in a different location, a rocky wasteland instead of the open Sand Lake. The image showed a woman wearing a floor-length cloak with the hood down, her long hair waving a little in the wind as she swung her arms around. As we watched, the shadow darker than the night around it came back to her as if summoned; she whipped it around her head, before stretching her arms out again to send it forth.

"That's her," Masaru confirmed my suspicions of who this was.

"She's attacking Fuun," I stated. "For the time being, we can hope he holds her attention and she doesn't notice us. Gin-Kouteki how far away is this?"

"Target is at a distance of twenty-eight kilometers. Should I engage?"

"How far can this thing shoot?" Masaru asked incredulously.

"Maximum range, eighty kilometers," Gin-Kouteki responded.

"Don't fire, Gin-Kouteki," I instructed him. "How much warning can you give us if she fires that weapon of hers at us?"

"Three-point-two seconds."

That was less than I wanted to hear, but to be expected. "You have my permission to engage if she fires on us, Gin-Kouteki."

"Noted. Holding fire."

On the screen before us, Fuun suddenly appeared, his sword in place inches from the woman's throat. She did not move; her expression was unreadable at this distance, but Fuun did not withdraw his sword. A brief but tense moment passed before two things happened simultaneously: Fuun drove his sword forward, intent on taking her head, and she disappeared in a cascade of sand, leaving Fuun slashing his sword uselessly through air.

"Target lost," Gin-Kouteki stated unnecessarily – the mysterious woman had once again departed as quickly and inexplicably as she had arrived.

CH. 8 – I DIDN'T KNOW IT WAS GOING TO BE SO HARD

Fuun returned to his task and it seemed the Roughlanders would not need to fight to survive the night after all. Our attention was taken from watching him on the screen, however, as something appeared in the air before it, shimmering into existence.

"Friend-Kajis?" a childish, female voice spoke from the incorporeal image of little Lilyth.

Masaru, startled by the sudden appearance of the red-headed little girl in our midst, almost fell from his perch in surprise, but I took the extraordinary event in stride – the impossible was becoming ordinary for me the longer I stayed on this world.

"What is it, Lilyth?" I asked, wondering what had possessed the powerful little girl to try and contact us so far away from her protected valley.

"Yue's here and she wants me to tell you I don't know anything at all about these guardians running around outside my valley."

Lilyth paused. "Wait – Yue says these guardians are something called 'Lillem' and aren't really guardians at all."

"Yue's with you?" I asked. "She's supposed to be on her way to Taiyou by now, how'd she get all the way down there?"

Lilyth looked distracted, presumably talking or listening to Yue, whom we couldn't see. "She says she found the Chosen of Jedeite and she'll be back to Taiyou soon. But please don't think I had anything to do with these Lillem, okay? I've never seen a guardian with spiky-things on it before."

"That's all right, Lilyth," I told her, "no one's blaming you and we're grateful to you for trying to tell us what you know."

"Oh, one more thing," Lilyth added, "Yue says Adel told her the Lillem used to serve my mother. She made them, that's why they're so much like my guardians!"

"That would make sense – if Lady Lilyth made the guardians, then it's likely she made these too," Masaru commented.

"Oh, and I don't know anything about the darkness either," Lilyth informed us. "I've always had night time here. Speaking of which, it's past my bedtime, so I should probably go. Yue's told me I can come visit you in Taiyou if I want, but I don't know...you should still come here to my valley and see me sometime."

"Uh, we will one day, I'm sure," I agreed reluctantly. I knew little Lilyth was lonely, but I was reluctant to return to that valley – I had no good memories of my time there.

"Gotta go, bye!" The image of little Lilyth waved as it shimmered back out of existence.

"That was something else," Masaru remarked.

"Mmm..." I responded wordlessly, lost in thought. I checked the screen; Fuun was still fighting, dashing through the 'Lillem' with sustained finesse – he didn't seem to be tiring. "Gin-Kouteki, how long do we have left of the darkness?"

"Calculating. At the current rate of progression–"

"Rate of progression?!" I interrupted the Binoid. "You mean the darkness has been increasing in duration?"

"Affirmative, Yukari," Gin-Kouteki responded. "The first dark period was approximately one hour and one minute in length. The second dark period increased to two hours and two minutes in length. At the current rate of progression, it is estimated this dark period will last for three hours and three minutes, leaving approximately four minutes and thirty-two seconds until sunrise." A helpful countdown began on the corner of the screen for us.

Masaru did some quick math on his fingers. "Yukari, that would mean we'd have full darkness all the time in only forty bounces from now."

"Yes, it does," I nodded solemnly, coming to terms with the ramifications of this discovery, "if we live that long."

"Ye mean the Lillem?" Masaru asked.

I shook my head. "No, it's worse than even that, though it is true they might manage to kill us all before then. I never really thought much about it before, but if this side of the world has constant sun, then it must mean the other side is perpetually covered in darkness."

"I'm not exactly following ye," he admitted. "Ye mean the sun doesn't go everywhere?"

As if on cue, the first glimmer of dawn began on the horizon. I checked with the screen and sure enough, Gin-Kouteki's calculations were correct – this night had been one hour and one minute longer than the one before it.

"Come on," I said to Masaru, "let's get down from here and I'll see if I can't find a way to explain it to you."

We left Gin-Kouteki's shoulder as the sun came up and I flew us back down to the sand below. Finding a suitable example, I set about trying to explain the basics of planetary rotation to Masaru and Razor, who had come over to see what was afoot.

"This apple represents the planet," I began, but stopped when I saw their identical, blank looks of incomprehension and realized I would have to start even simpler. "The world is round, like this apple and it floats around in space," I stated. "Just take my word on it, okay?" Razor and Masaru both nodded after a moment and Razor settled down to sit with us, seemingly intrigued by my impromptu science lesson.

When I had their full attention, I continued. "This melon on the ground in front of me represents the sun."

"Is the sun that much bigger than the apple?" Masaru asked. "I mean the world…"

"Yes. The sun is really, really far away, which makes it look small to us here," I explained. "So the planet rotates around the sun," I waved my apple in a wide circle around the melon, "and each full rotation indicates a year has gone by. Are you following me so far?"

Masaru and Razor both nodded, the latter a little more dubiously than the former, but thinking that was the best I would get, I continued. "As the planet makes its way around the sun it also spins," I spun my apple slowly to indicate this. "Each spin of the planet is a day, or I suppose here it would be two bounces."

I indicated my apple once again, cupping half of it with my palm. "Now, this side of the apple is the side of the planet we are currently on and the side my hand is covering is the opposite side. If the side we are currently on is facing the sun," I said, pointing the apple toward the melon, "then the other side has to be facing away from it, which means no light."

"Because it's round," Razor said, pointing out the obvious.

I nodded.

"How is it we're on the dark side now?" Masaru asked.

I stared at the apple in my hands and the melon before me, running through a few different possibilities. I lifted the apple slightly to spin it, trying to put my thoughts together, before I lowered my hands with the apple held between them in defeat. "That's the part I haven't figured out yet."

"You'll get it," Razor said, patting my shoulder and getting to his feet.

I sat there for a little while, holding my apple and contemplating it as around me the Roughlanders buzzed about, taking down their preparations from the night before and getting ready to depart. My thoughts were interrupted, however, when Fuun returned to the Roughlander camp and a cheer went up in his honour. Fuun froze in the center of a crowd of Roughlanders. With a slight smile at Fuun's discomfort, I stood up, pocketed the apple for later consideration, and crossed to where Fuun stood in the centre.

"Thank you for your help, Fuun," I told him. "You did well out there." I was surprised to note, looking at him this closely, his dark eyes had a hint of blue to them.

"I will accompany you to Taiyou," Fuun stated tonelessly.

"As you wish," I told him, wondering how the legendary Chosen of Machalite would be received in Taiyou – as a potential saviour, or an enemy?

"Who is she, Fuun?" I asked abruptly.

"Her name is Ku-Roi," he answered. "I cannot tell you more."

It wasn't much, but now at least I had a name; with that, Fuun left me to have a look at what the Roughlanders were doing. I noted with pride that after his showing last night, the Roughlanders greeted Fuun pleasantly and welcomed him, as if he had earned his right to be among them, instead of giving him the wide berth and wary looks one might expect. Without further delay we set off, hoping to reach Taiyou well before the next darkness could fall. It did not escape my notice that as each 'night' grew longer, the daylight hours grew shorter. But still, if we pressed – and we would – we should reach Taiyou sometime after the noon bounce.

The daylight brought us no further complications and we reached the border of Taiyou without incident. The far side of the bridge was unguarded, but the inner gate was barred and heavily manned by Taiyoun Legionnaires. I had sent a message arrow to Sabien, so I was recognized and let in immediately, while the Roughlanders were given instructions about where they were to be housed. In my letter I had warned Sabien about Fuun's presence in Taiyou, but there was no way to keep track of Fuun's whereabouts, and it was foolish to try and tell him where he could and could not go. So, when we entered Taiyou, I was not exactly surprised to discover he had already made himself scarce.

Masaru and I headed to the Sanctioned Outpost fountain to meet with Sabien and we were accompanied by Razor and the few other Roughlanders who had decided to stay there. When I found Sabien, I realized not all was as I expected it to be in Taiyou. As he waited by the fountain, the Knight Commander was flanked by two armoured Deathsquad soldiers. I approached him slowly, my hackles rising.

"What's going on here?" I asked cautiously, fully aware of the tension of the Roughlanders in the yard and the ones I had brought with me.

"A lot has changed," Sabien informed me, his simple words speaking volumes. "Don't be alarmed. The Deathsquad are not here for any Roughlanders." Sabien put a little extra emphasis on the word and seemed to indicate Masaru with his eyes. "Their orders are to accompany all Knights of Sapphiros. I don't believe that includes the Chosen, either."

I nodded slowly to indicate I understood what Sabien was trying to tell me; the Deathsquads didn't yet know Masaru was a Knight – and it would be best if I kept it that way.

"You should head back to the palace at once," he continued. "You are the first to arrive and I'm glad to see you back safely, but there are matters which require your attention – Goji, for one – and you should see the King to be apprised of the current situation."

"What's the matter with Goji?"

"Goji has been instrumental in the defense of Taiyou," Sabien informed me, "but during the last darkness he fell ill. I'm afraid his condition is worsening rapidly and he could use your particular expertise. Ris' magic doesn't seem to have any effect on him and I'm sure he could use a friend at present."

"Thank you, Sabien, I'll see to him. Are you sure there isn't anything you require?"

"No, I'll be fine," Sabien responded with a sudden smile. "I think I'll take a leisurely walk back to the palace."

I took that as the cue it was meant to be and picked up Masaru, taking off without warning; the Deathsquad soldiers couldn't stop or follow me, even if they wanted to. Masaru took his sudden elevation in stride, perhaps getting used to my method of travel, and Gin-Kouteki, true to his programming, followed us at a distance to the palace.

I stationed Gin-Kouteki before the palace drawbridge and reached into my medic kit to draw out the small metal box X-En had given to me to communicate with the Binoid at a distance; I ensured the device was turned on before I placed it back in the kit.

"Gin-Kouteki, please notify me at once if we are under attack or if you detect the presence of any unauthorized persons, and await my direction, understood?"

"Affirmative, Yukari."

I flew Masaru and I up to the balcony of the room assigned to the Chosen of Sapphiros, rather than entering through the front door. My intention was to avoid – as much as I could – anyone interested in the sudden return of the Chosen of Sapphiros and her Knight, who was apparently supposed to be under Deathsquad guard.

Masaru looked concerned when I placed him back on his feet in the somewhat lavish palace room, with its rich, red curtains drawn shut to conceal the various sleeping areas. "That was certainly odd about Sabien," he noted. "Do ye think we'll encounter more Deathsquad soldiers in the palace?"

"I'm almost certain of it," I answered with a grimace, "but for now, until they learn otherwise, you're not a Knight, just a Roughlander I'm travelling with, okay?"

Striding with purpose, I opened the door and stepped boldly out into the hallway, trying not to be intimidated by the presence of two Deathsquad soldiers guarding the room across the hall. Neither of them made any move to stop Masaru and I as we strode past them and through the door to the Knights' chambers. I was relieved to note there were no soldiers stationed within the room itself. In fact, the only people I found within the room were Jeth and Aysel.

"Hey, Yukari," Jeth greeted me with a smile from his seat by Aysel's bedside.

I walked right by Jeth in my haste to check on Aysel; the last time I had seen her, she had still been unconscious after the grueling amputation of her right arm. Now, however, Aysel was awake and propped up in bed, looking decently alert. "Yukari, it's good to see you again."

"I'm glad you're both all right," I told them, as I gave Aysel a once-over.

"I've felt better, but I'm healing," Aysel informed me. "Have you heard anything from my sister?"

I shook my head to indicate I hadn't spoken to Adel before I did a double-take and truly noticed Jeth for the first time.

"Sabien mentioned I was the first one back," I told Jeth. "Did you just get here?"

"No," Jeth answered simply, "I've been here since yesterday."

"Then where's Yue?" I asked.

"She was headed to Espearia last I checked," Jeth answered. "Why?"

"Because she was supposed to be with you, Jeth," I told him, exasperated. "You just left her alone out there?"

"She wasn't alone," Jeth protested. "She had the Chosen of Jedeite with her and she was going to meet up with Hotaru and Adel."

I glowered at Jeth for abandoning Yue and his duty to her as a Knight, but I didn't really have any further argument I could make given the circumstance. Honestly, I had just been worried about her and the others.

"Aysel?" Masaru paused, hands poised and dripping over an open barrel full of water in the centre of the room. I quirked a brow, inspecting it and noticing for the first time how out of place the object was in the otherwise elegant palace chambers. Masaru allowed the water in his hands to splash back into the barrel as the water within it spoke again, "Aysel, it's me, Hotaru."

"Yes, I'm here, go ahead Hotaru," Aysel responded, raising her voice a little so the barrel could hear her. I looked from Aysel to the barrel in surprise.

"Would ye look at that," Masaru marvelled, staring into the barrel.

Curious, I crossed the room to him and looked into the barrel myself. Sure enough, there was an image of Hotaru's face on the water, just like little Lilyth had appeared to us in the darkness the night before.

"Yukari, Masaru?" Hotaru questioned, proving she could also see us with this new power she had developed. "You're back already?"

"Yes," I answered her. "How are things in Espearia?"

"Better now. There's a lot to fill you in on, but I'm going to try to bring us back now, so I need you to give me some room."

Masaru and I did as requested. After a moment we heard a splash from within the barrel, followed quickly by sloshing as the water inside threatened to overflow. I watched in amazement as the water suddenly shot upwards and splashed over the side of the barrel, diving towards the floor and cascading into a puddle that coated the floor thoroughly. Moments later, the puddle reformed before my very eyes into several different people holding hands in a circle, when I had been expecting only Hotaru and maybe Adel.

"Aysel!" Adel broke away from the circle to rush to her sister's side, heedless of the rest of us – not that I blamed her.

Hotaru, who hadn't moved, looked a little worse for wear, with bruises, cuts, and a haggard expression, but she smiled with triumph, looking from me to the person on her left, whose hand she still held. The girl was busty and of medium build, though clearly still a teenager like us. Her brown hair had a reddish tint, to match the deep brown, doe-shaped eyes set into her round face.

"Mizu?" My jaw dropped in recognition. Suspicions rising, I looked to the other person. "Reiki?"

Reiki's head snapped up. Her expression was fearful. I took a few steps toward the girl I had known so briefly before I had left Earth, remembering her shy smile as she greeted me in the girl's change room before our big swim competition.

"It's me, Yukari," I told her with a tentative smile. "I know I must look so different."

I saw the moment recognition dawned on her face, followed by a sense of relief as the tension drained out of her, only to be replaced with the beginnings of tears. I enfolded her into the hug she likely needed.

"The Talons?" I mouthed over Reiki's shoulder to Hotaru, who nodded.

So Reiki and Mizu had also been trapped in the forms of the Talons, like Goji had been trapped as Fuzen. By the boyish cut of Reiki's hair, I had to assume she had been Arocoth, making Mizu's former identity, Zai-Aku. This left only the last Talon to be unmasked and freed – my least favorite person on this world or any other, except maybe the Vile Emperor himself – Kai-Een.

Unfortunately, this also meant we still had no leads to finding Kaji's missing girlfriend, Shuzhue. We had all assumed if anyone else we knew would be on this world, it would be her. I just sincerely hoped someone would get the chance to break this discovery to Kaji gently, and I worried the task was going to fall to me.

"What is this awful place?" Reiki asked, clutching me as she spoke through her tears.

"Shh…you're all right now," I told her, helping her to a nearby chair Masaru helpfully held out for her. I took another chair myself and brought it close to hers. "You're in the palace in Taiyou. It's a safe place, I promise." Though I said the words, I knew in my heart I couldn't actually guarantee that; the presence of the Deathsquad soldiers outside the door was a painful reminder.

"Why can't I go home?" Reiki asked the obvious question, imploring me with her eyes. "And who are all these strange people?"

I gave a sideways glance past Masaru to Jeth, with his one red-scaled demon arm and Adel beyond him in her full armour, as she spoke quietly with her heavily-bandaged sister in the corner.

"We're a long way from home right now, Reiki," I told her honestly, "but as for the people – this is Masaru."

"Hello there," Masaru greeted her and her eyes widened slightly at his unusual accent.

I smiled ruefully, remembering when we had first appeared on this world and realized Masaru and Dahlia's odd lilting way of speaking was our first clue to just how far from home we had come. "Masaru's one of the first people Hotaru and I ever met on this world," I told Reiki, "and he's really kind and not strange at all." I gave Masaru a look that told him to keep any strangeness he might have to a minimum.

Masaru pulled up a chair to Reiki's other side. "Aye, Yukari's telling ye the truth. We're not all bad here."

"Masaru, I really should go check on Goji after what Sabien told me. I would really appreciate it if you could stay with Reiki for a bit. I'll come back as soon as I can."

"Goji-sempai is here too?" Reiki asked.

"Aye, he is…and ye should hear what he's already managed to accomplish," Masaru began answering for me and telling Reiki all about the wonder that was Goji, so I could make my escape and see him. I hoped this mysterious illness that had befallen the one former Talon wouldn't begin to affect the rest of them.

Before I left, I took a moment to covertly use my power and give both Reiki and Mizu a visual once-over. Both of them had numerous bruises and shallow cuts, but also some more serious injuries, though they were healing well enough. Evidently they had already been somewhat taken care of – their bandages gave evidence of that – but from looking inside them I could also see they had been Flaqqered more than once. As odd as that was, what I was really looking for was the state of their hearts and I was right in my assumption they were just like Goji – neither of them had one beating in their chests, though, against all odds, they seemed just as alive as he did.

It was a simple enough matter to find Goji in the same room where he had first been placed the last time he had been unwell. This room was also guarded by Deathsquad soldiers. My mouth thinned to a line upon seeing them there, but it told me I had come to the right spot and they didn't try to prevent me from entering the darkened room.

Within, the curtains were drawn tight and it was only the outline of her wings that allowed me to identify Ris. I was able to bring her face into clearer focus by adjusting my eyesight with my power, to make use of whatever light I could in the room. I looked past her to the bed where Goji lay sleeping, blankets brought up to his chin to fight off a chill. Sweat beaded on his brow, but his obvious pain and fever were not what had me most concerned. Goji's eye-socket – the one now usually covered by the Fuzen's eye patch – was heavily bandaged, but still it oozed blood.

150

"How long has he been like this?" I whispered.

Since the rising of the sun, Ris mimed with her hands, *or a little before.*

Ris frowned – it was bad. Sabien had said Ris' magic didn't work on Goji and I wondered briefly why that was. From what I knew of the Talons – which was precious little – I knew he was here on this world in a different way from the rest of us. Was it possible his in-between state was what was interfering with Ris' healing magic?

I settled myself on the chair next to Goji and reached for Goji's hand – he didn't wake. I closed my eyes, concentrating, breathing slowly in and out. There was an answer here – I could feel it – and I remembered well the last time I was in this same spot and the glimpse of the hospital room in Tokyo I had seen. I wanted to see it again and this time I was determined my power was going to allow me to do so.

I could sense Goji's life force, though it was faint and seemed very far away. I let my consciousness follow after it, willing myself to find out where it led. When I opened my eyes the room that greeted me was blindingly bright, but the light held no warmth. Blinking to adjust my eyesight, I looked around slowly and with a surreal sense of wonder. I was back in the hospital. The fluorescent lights shone needlessly, adding to the already bright light filtering in through the open curtains. Goji lay in the hospital bed before me, his one eye covered in blood-soaked gauze – much like it was in Taiyou – and his position nearly identical to the way I had just left him.

Or had I left? I looked down at my own hand and realized I could see right through it; peering closely, it seemed I was no more solid than mist. Feeling faint by the very thought of the distance my soul had presumably crossed to be here, I stopped dwelling on the matter and returned to my examination of the room, determined to put my time here to good use.

A thin, light-blue hospital curtain had been mostly drawn around Goji's bed, but was open a little on one side. I floated over in that direction to see the rest of the room. The second bed in the room was empty and made up. Beyond it, I could see the main door to the room was about halfway open and the hallway beyond seemed quiet. My eyes lit on a clipboard fastened to the outside of the door – a hospital chart.

With mounting eagerness, I floated over until I was in the open doorway and able to lean in to read the tiny print. *Nakamura Goji,* it read in the Japanese style, followed by basic information such as height, weight and blood type. I skipped down to the bottom half and immediately discovered I wasn't looking at a hospital chart, but a police report:

Shinjuku High School students Nakamura Goji, Amori Mizu, Fuukara Reiki, and Harford Tim were admitted at two-thirty a.m. Friday, with reports of multiple injuries sustained as a result of gang-related activity in Hyuski Heights Park, allegedly involving members of the Yakuza. Police received a distress call at eleven fifty-five from one of the female victims, who gave detailed descriptions of her attackers, but when police arrived to investigate, only the victims remained at the scene. All four were found unconscious and required immediate medical attention.

My head spun as I read the rest of the document. There was no mention of the two policemen Kai-Een had murdered, but no doubt they would have their own files somewhere else. Otherwise, the description of events was entirely accurate as far as the police would be concerned. Somewhat frantically, I checked the date of the document against the date notated by hand in the top corner of the chart. The date of the attack was accurate, I remembered that well enough, which meant I was currently visiting Tokyo somewhere around forty-eight days later. Was that accurate? With the bounces, it was hard to tell exactly how long it had been since our arrival, but it was entirely possible time was running concurrently between the two worlds, which didn't exactly explain how we had arrived eight-hundred years later than we had been expected to.

As I tried to work it out, I felt myself begin to fade. I heard someone coming down the hall and I tried to hold on to see who it was. A nurse came around the corner and paused, her mouth falling open in surprise, as the misty image of a tall blue-haired girl in strange clothing faded out of existence like it had never been present at all.

A wave of sudden exhaustion and dizziness passed over me, as I became aware of the weight of my body in Goji's darkened bedchamber. I unintentionally squeezed Goji's hand in order to steady myself.

"Yukari," he said weakly, "you're back. Did you manage to bring back reinforcements?"

"Shh, don't worry about that now," I whispered. "I did and Taiyou is in good hands. You should rest now and concentrate on getting better."

Goji closed his remaining eye in obvious pain; I stood abruptly, motioning for Ris to come over and help me see to his bandages. I tugged at the corner of his eye patch to begin to remove the layers when he waved me off.

"Leave it," he instructed. "It's no use."

"You let me be the judge of that," I told him. "Just rest."

"That's all I've done is rest," he protested weakly. "I can't just lie here while Taiyou needs me."

"Taiyou's been here a lot longer than you have," I told him. "It'll get along just fine while you take the time to recover."

Goji grimaced but kept his mouth shut. I made quick work of his bandages, and then I left Ris to clean up, letting her know I had to go and speak with Narlhep before I, too, would rest. Stumbling to the door in the face of Ris' disapproving frown, I realized belatedly it had been nearly two days since I had last had any sleep. The walk across the desert had been so tense and filled with potential disaster that I had kept myself going. Now that I was back in the palace, those long two days were catching up with me and my trip to Tokyo hadn't exactly helped matters.

Righting myself, I tried to look alert, so I would not show any weakness before the Deathsquad soldiers. Out in the hallway, I discovered Hotaru, Masaru, and Kaji waiting for me. I greeted Kaji with a nod, glad to see he was back safely despite his many bruises, but too subdued and lost in thought after what I had experienced in Goji's room to make much of it.

"Goji's not doing very well, I'm afraid," I told them. "He's awake right now if you want to visit, but I'll warn you his headaches are pretty bad and he can't handle much light or noise."

"Reiki and Mizu are both fine," Masaru informed me before I could ask about them. "They're both fast asleep, so we came down here to see how Goji was doing. Yue is also back as well now, by the way."

"Mizu and Reiki?" Kaji asked, his mouth dropping open in shock.

"Yeah." Hotaru beamed proudly, though I could see she too was tired. "They were the Talons and taken captive in Espearia, but we saved them."

"The Talons?" I could see the wheels turning in Kaji's head and I knew before I even started to open my mouth to explain, it was too late; Hotaru had already bungled it.

I watched, unable to prevent the look of pain that crossed my friend's face, before he abruptly turned on his heels and stormed away.

"Let him go," I told Hotaru softly. "He doesn't want company right now. Go see Goji, or come with me to see the King. There's a lot to catch up on, apparently."

We waited for Hotaru to check in on Goji, which didn't take very long, before the three of us made our way through the palace to the throne room. The throne room doors were open when we reached them revealing that Yue, upon her return, had gone straight to the King. On either side of the doors there stood a pair of Legionnaires and a pair of Deathsquad soldiers, doubling the usual guard. Within the room there was an extra chair placed to the right of the triple thrones, upon which sat the familiar figure of Lady Mikura, kicking her heels playfully. The implications of this spoke volumes, but were also somewhat a mystery. I remembered Narlhep telling me Mikura was supposed to stay in her 'province', the Jade mountain – also known as the Temple of Jade – and only come to the city if it was to warn him of an impending attack.

There was also a newcomer in the room. A Roughlander by his dress, he could be none other than the Chosen of Jedeite Yue had gone to find. My mind whirling as I tried to piece together all I had seen since I had re-entered Taiyou, I ignored the guards as I made my way across the black and white marble tiles of the throne room floor, only half-aware of Masaru and Hotaru following behind me.

"Ao Kouen, Chosen of Jedeite, draw the sword and claim your rightful place," Narlhep announced, his voice muffled familiarly by his helmet, as he gestured to the sword sticking out of the throne beside him.

The Chosen of Jedeite stepped forward, his spine stiffening. "I will not," he stated. "I have no desire to end your life, or your reign, King Narlhep."

"You won't?" I could hear the shock and the sudden vulnerability of hope in Narlhep's voice; the sound of it broke my heart.

"No," Ao Kouen responded, sounding tired. "I'm not here to kill anyone, and if I'm supposed to be King of this place some day, then

I'm going to need you to show me how to do it. Please, stay as you are, King Narlhep, this country needs you."

Narlhep's helmet nodded imperceptibly and his shoulders slumped, the tension draining from his form.

"Well, now that that's all taken care of," Yue announced, sounding inexplicably chipper, "I've got a present for you, Narlhep, from the Vile Emperor!"

The room fell silent immediately following this pronouncement, interrupted only by the sudden clapping of Mikura's hands as she leaned forward excitedly in her chair, "Oooh, what is it?"

Yue pulled a single, coin-sized ruby from within her shirt and held it up for everyone to see. "I don't know what it is," she admitted.

"Why would you bring that here, Yue?" I asked, aghast. "You don't know what that thing might do!"

"The Vile Emperor asked me to," Yue answered, not taking her eyes away from the small ruby she held. "He said it was a test of my loyalty or something like that, and if I brought it to the King of Taiyou he would free the Talons."

Loyalty – whose? Yue's to the Vile Emperor? My mind screamed at me this wasn't right – it couldn't be happening.

Ao Kouen stepped forward and held his hand out to Yue, his face, which I saw for the first time as he turned in Yue's direction, set in a determined expression. "He said the King, he didn't say Narlhep. Let me be the one to receive it."

"No," Narlhep spoke, getting to his feet and stepping down from the dais. "It was meant for me and if the Vile Emperor intends for it to kill me, I was meant to die regardless. At least Taiyou will still have you."

"You can't seriously be meaning to accept this 'gift'," I protested. "No one has to die. We have three of the four Talons already. There is no need for this kind of bargain."

Narlhep's helmet turned. "It is true that I do not know what this stone will do to me, or anyone else. Anyone who fears it, or who does not agree with its presence here, is free to leave the room. Ao Kouen, I would suggest you depart as well. We will seal this room in Jade and hope any effects from the ruby stop at the doors."

With the exception of Ao Kouen, who nodded and walked past me on his way toward the open doors, no one moved. I would have left, not wanting to be a part of this, but without even realizing I had fallen, I sunk to the throne room floor, unable to support myself any longer.

It was simply too much. The past few days had been long and hard, with only the thought of safety waiting for me in Taiyou being enough to keep me moving forward. I had simply taken too many shocks without enough time to come to terms with them all and understand why these things were happening. I was sobbing and gasping for breath, all the horrors of the last few days weighing down on me, before I realized that Masaru had helped me to my feet and was half-carrying me from the throne room. I leaned into his arms and fought desperately to control myself – it wasn't like me to just fall apart.

The throne room doors shut themselves behind us with a shuddering finality. As Masaru led me down the hall I noticed distantly that one of the Deathsquad soldiers detached himself from the line of guards to follow after us; my emotions being all out of whack, I latched onto him as the most offensive thing within sight.

"What do you think you're doing?" I demanded, turning on the Deathsquad soldier.

"We have orders to follow the Knights of Sapphiros at all times," the Deathsquad soldier responded tonelessly.

There was no use denying that Masaru was a Knight of Sapphiros; no matter what Sabien had said, his rank by his continued association with me was fairly evident and I had to assume Mikura, at least, was aware of it.

"You may follow at a distance of ten paces," I instructed him coldly, but the Deathsquad soldier was not to be intimidated, not even by the Chosen of Sapphiros, and he stood his ground a mere few feet from myself and Masaru.

"I said ten paces," I repeated myself, my voice taking on a dangerous quality as between my hands a cyan glow began to form into an arrow. At this distance, I would not even need to aim to destroy this Deathsquad soldier and I sincerely doubted any of the others would attempt to follow us after that.

"Yukari..." Masaru interjected gently and my head snapped to attention at the sound of his voice. I saw myself briefly reflected in his eyes, my eyes alight with an unearthly cyan glow born of rage and I felt my will evaporate; the cyan glow disappeared.

A sob caught in my throat as I blinked and met his eyes again, my gaze this time filled with anguish instead of anger, as I realized what I had almost done. As a Chosen I had powers that made me able to defend myself, but I was not a killer. My unstable emotions shifted to shame and my powers activated with my need to run and hide – I hated the thought that Masaru had seen me this way – and I shifted suddenly to a cloud of mist to float away from him.

Thankfully, in this form I could not cry or speak, but still I was able to see as Masaru raised his hands to the Deathsquad soldier to indicate he wasn't going to give the man any trouble, before resuming his trek down the hallway at an unhurried pace. As mist I travelled a little faster than walking, and before long I was out of sight and drifting wherever my emotions chose to take me.

CH. 9 – BY THE LIGHT OF THE MOON

As mist, I phased through the door of the one room where I thought I might have the best chance to be alone. Thankfully, the room assigned to the Chosen of Sapphiros was as empty as I had left it – and still unguarded. Relief at finally being where no one could see me was enough to allow me to reform.

I was still somewhat unsteady. Putting a hand out, I leaned on the edge of the central table while I tried to gather myself and wipe the tears from my eyes with my other hand. I froze at the inexplicable feeling I was not alone. Without warning, all five red floor-to-ceiling curtains in the room drew back simultaneously to reveal five armoured strangers. Instinctively, I straightened my back.

"The Knights of the Blue Moon at your service, Yukari Namikoya," one said, stepping forward to bow.

My sense of unease was not lessened by their formality and I made no move to greet them. I was unsure of the strength of my voice and I dared not show any more weakness than I already had.

"We come bearing a message for you and a gift." The one who had spoken crossed the distance to the table in the centre of the room presented an ornate looking scroll case decorated with blue and silver engraving, similar to the colour and designs on the armour of these Knights. "Solve it and you shall have the answers you seek. Be careful, however, the Blue Moon Scroll must only be read in the proper light or it can prove fatal."

The Knight left the scroll on the table and proceeded to back up as a sudden gust of wind opened the balcony curtain wide. As light bathed the room, the Knights of the Blue Moon forms collapsed and they fell to the floor as no more than five piles of sand.

I froze, scanning the room in horror. Only the ornate-looking scroll on the far side of the table and the five inert mounds of sand scattered about the room gave any indication the strange Knights had been here at all. I was deeply unnerved by the strange visitation and it was all I could do to look about the room for a supply closet. Broom and dustpan located, I busied myself with the familiar and comforting act of cleaning the floor thoroughly.

I shuddered with revulsion as I finally reached for the scroll, unable to let it simply sit in the centre of the room any longer. Not looking upon the ornate and squiggly text, I opened the flap of my medic kit with one hand and shoved the scroll in with everything else I owned, pushing it in enough that I could still close the pouch.

I was startled by a loud, crashing noise coming from out in the hall. With my nerves on edge already, I didn't hesitate to rush to the door and fling it open. The first thing I noticed was the lack of Deathsquad soldiers. That, combined with the door having been broken off its hinges, was enough to raise my concern. Within the room, I could see Aysel holding tight to her sister's sword one-handed. Unbidden, my legs carried me forward and across the hall.

I spun slowly, taking in the tableau of chaos in the room and looking to see what Aysel had Adel's sword pointed at. To my left, Mizu and Reiki lay sprawled and unmoving, as if they had simply crumpled to the floor. Behind me, the two Deathsquad soldiers lay on the ground. One was dead from a bash to the head and the other's corpse still smoked slightly, a gaping wound visible through a hole that had been blasted through his chest plate.

My breath caught as my eyes lit upon Adel. The crash I had heard from across the hall had been the sound her armour made as it impacted with the wall. There was a definite indent where Adel's form had struck before she slid to lay in her current position.

I was on high alert, my senses sharp. I was waiting for the next attack to come, or for the attacker to show themselves, but whatever had happened here was somehow already over and I hadn't been in time to see it, let alone stop it.

"Adel?" Aysel's voice asked weakly, her sister's sword clattering to the floor.

I rushed to Adel's side and checked for a pulse. "She's okay," I told Aysel. "Sit down, don't strain yourself further. I've got her."

I inspected Adel briefly and was alarmed when my hand came away from the back of her head wet with blood. Making a quick decision, I used my power to turn her to mist. I walked slowly, guiding the mist over to Aysel's bed. I reformed Adel on the bed and laid her on her side, then I took a moment to dip some of the extra bandages Ris had on hand for Aysel into the barrel of water Hotaru had used to return here from Espearia. By the time I returned to Adel's side she was already stirring; a bad blow to the head was not enough to slow the tough Knight down.

"I'm fine, really," she said with a wince.

"Here, then." I handed her a handful of wet bandages. "Adel, what happened in here?"

"It was like nothing I have ever seen before, Yukari," she answered. "Your friends collapsed suddenly – the red-haired one was mid-sentence when it happened – and then the Talons seemed to rise up like spirits from their bodies. Zai-Aku came towards me. I tried to fend her off and draw her away from Aysel. The Deathsquad soldiers broke down the door because of the commotion. They tried to help me until Arocoth leapt into one of them and brought the Deathsquad under her control. I struck him down, but by then Zai-Aku had control of the other and she used her power to throw me across the room -"

"Um…Yukari?" Aysel interjected.

Reiki's legs and arms were twitching violently and unnaturally. Alarmed, I left Adel to her own devices and hurried to Reiki's side. Kneeling, I placed my hands on her to try and calm her sporadic movements, and was surprised to feel the heavy thumping of her heart within her chest – a heart that when I had initially inspected her earlier she – like Goji and Mizu – hadn't had. Unexpectedly, Reiki's eyes snapped open and her unnatural convulsions ceased with a sudden sharp intake of breath.

"Yukari?" she questioned, her eyes open but sightless. "Is that you?"

"Yes, Reiki, I'm here."

Her body felt strange under my hands, almost like she wasn't fully as solid as she should be. I abruptly recalled my surreal journey to the hospital in Tokyo. I suddenly thought I might have the answer to how all this was possible, as far-fetched as that answer was.

"Yukari, why do I feel so strange?" Reiki asked. "What's happening?"

"It's all right Reiki," I told her, hoping it was the truth. "Everything is going to be alright. You're going home now."

"You sound so far away. I'm scared, Yukari. Come back with me."

"I can't Reiki," I told her. "Don't be scared. All you have to do is open your eyes."

"The lights are so bright here…I think I'm in the hospital." Reiki was almost gone now; I could see right through her to the busy design of the carpet beneath.

"You belong in Japan," I told her, whether she could even hear me anymore or not. "Goodbye Reiki," I said at the last to the bare carpet before me, no trace there had once been a scared and battered girl lying there, wishing she could go home.

Sudden motion out of the corner of my eye drew my attention to Mizu – the spasms had begun for her. It would not be long now before she, too, would fade away, her soul reuniting with her body across the vastness of space. The Vile Emperor's promise to Yue fulfilled.

Goji – no doubt he would also be leaving soon if he hadn't already. Kaji would be devastated when he learned of it. It was hard enough on him to have lost Shuzhue; he didn't need to have Goji snapped away from him too. I let two message arrows fly; one to Kaji and one to Hotaru, letting them know what was happening in the barest and simplest of terms so it would not cause them any further distress. If they could make it in time to say their goodbyes it would be for the best, but my work here was done.

Nevertheless, I tried my best to calm Mizu down and ease her journey back to Japan by explaining the situation to her, whether she understood what was happening or not.

"Where did they go – the Talons, I mean?" I asked Adel when it was over, but it was Aysel who answered me.

"They left – out the window."

I nodded, absorbind this. "Aysel, for the next while don't let Adel sleep for more than a few hours at a time. She may possibly have a concussion. And, if possible, have Ris see to her. I need to get some sleep or soon I'll be of no use to anyone."

Aysel nodded, and I wearily left the Knights' room to cross the hall to the Chosen's room once more, and straight into Masaru's arms.

"Are ye all right?" He asked, concerned.

"Better now," I whispered, letting him hold me for a moment and not wanting for anything else. "Reiki and Mizu are gone, and likely Goji is too."

I quickly filled Masaru in before he led me over to the bed. I had more to tell him and it was important, too, though I couldn't quite remember what it was. I was fast asleep before my head even touched the pillow.

"Yukari," I was awoken by the sound of Masaru's voice, "it's nearly dark again and we're needed on the bridge to help fend off the Lillem."

"Did you get any rest?" I asked, sitting up and noting there was a blanket tossed over the chair in the corner of the sleeping area I hardly remembered choosing.

"Some," he answered, "but if ye're up we should probably be going – it's bad, Yukari. I've been talking to some of the Legionnaires, and the reason Lady Mikura's Deathsquad is here instead of up in the countryside is because they were needed to help defend the borders from the Lillem. Apparently the creatures are everywhere. Hotaru even had to face them in Espearia, only there they've now got a Chosen of their own to deal with the problem."

I swung my legs over the side of the bed, leaving its comfort only reluctantly. "What? Another Chosen?"

"Aye, of Damos – a little girl named Chikara."

"Oh," I answered, somewhat at a loss.

"Ye ready, then?" Masaru asked and I nodded, taking his outstretched hand and letting him help me to my feet.

He started toward the door, but I stopped him. "Are those Deathsquad guards still out there for you?"

"Aye, they likely are," he responded with a slight grimace.

"Let's take the window," I suggested.

By the last light of the setting sun, Masaru and I flew to the border of Taiyou, Gin-Kouteki following dutifully behind at my request, to join the rest of the forces assembled to keep the Lillem from overrunning the city. Those forces now included the Roughlanders, who had positioned themselves with their carbine rifles on the top of the city's outer wall. On route to the bridge we were joined by Kaji, who flew up piloting a Rubian Skyraider, accompanied by a Roughlander woman I didn't recognize.

"It was Fuzen's," Kaji informed Masaru and I, shouting over the wind and noise of his passage. "It doesn't make sense not to make use of what we have."

I nodded as he flew past and I dropped down to land next to Sabien and the other Knights just on the gate side of the bridge, where the Legionnaires had already gathered to form the front lines. The Deathsquad, I noted, with their General, Lady Mikura, among them, were separated from the rest of the pack and stayed back near the open gate.

"Save your strength, Sir Sabien," Lady Rhine, her staff of office in her hand as usual, was saying as my feet touched ground and my wings disappeared. "You and the Chosen, if they're willing, are going to form our reserves this time – we don't know how long this darkness is going to last."

"Four hours and four minutes," I supplied. "Each night should be one hour and one minute longer than the last."

"Lady Rhine is taking command of the Taiyoun forces during this night," Sabien informed me. "King Narlhep was not feeling up to joining us this evening, but we have been left in capable hands."

"Is Narlhep all right?" I asked, concerned, realizing the last I had seen him was before the 'gift' of the Vile Emperor had been accepted.

"Weakened, but as well as can be expected," he replied.

"Are the Lillem about in the city like they were in Espearia?" Masaru asked. "And is there anything stopping them from coming at Taiyou from the other sides?"

"Hotaru, along with the civilian reserve forces, have been supplied with weapons and armour. They will be patrolling the city as well as guarding the palace," Sabien explained. "There are some Lillem within Taiyou, but their numbers are thankfully few, and all civilians have been warned to lock their doors and stay inside during the darkness."

"Lord Rama's lands contain the only other bridge and his forces are more than capable. Also, the main brunt of the attack by these 'Lillem', as you call them, seems to be focused here, at the bridge. We're going to do this in shifts," Lady Rhine continued, "Legionnaires first, then, Sir Sabien, if your Knights would be good enough to relieve us at my signal. When you need a break we'll call in Lady Mikura's squad, understood?"

"I've noticed you don't have any lights or torches out here," I interjected. "Are you aware they fear light? Also, anyone who is killed by the Lillem will come back as one – we encountered creatures similar to these before."

"It doesn't need to be a killing blow," Rhine noted with a disapproving frown. "Any wound taken from these things will infect a person and make them turn on the people around them twice as fiercely as they fought before. It's the main reason for our losses."

Lady Rhine left us and strode forward to join the Legionnaires. Rama, I noted when the light from the tip of Lady Rhine's staff reached him, stood at the front of the pack with the few men of his Lion Brigade who had returned with us to the city. I let my wings appear, intending to fly up and at least light the way for them with my arrows as I had done for the Roughlanders before, but Sabien held me back. "Save your strength, Yukari. Our turn will come soon enough, and if last night's pattern is repeated the second wave will be worse than the first."

I couldn't just stand there listening to the screams and the clashing of swords in the darkness. If I couldn't help, then I had to at least be able to see. With a nod to Sabien, I flew over to Gin-Kouteki, who was stationed over by the wall nearer to the Roughlanders.

"Gin-Kouteki," I landed on his shoulder, "vid-screen on the bridge, please."

"Affirmative, Yukari."

The vid-screen swung out so I could see the green-tinged image of the front lines. The first of the Lillem had already reached the defenders and the siege had officially begun. I watched a Legionnaire impaled through on a Lillem's spiked talon. The change from human to Lillem was near instantaneous, but Lady Rhine was almost as fast. As soon as she glimpsed the wound being taken from the corner of her eye, her staff was in both of her hands and whirling to point at the fallen Legionnaire. The Legionnaire-turned-Lillem turned on her, intent on her death, but she shot forth a gout of flame from the end of her staff to engulf him.

"Target acquired," Gin-Kouteki spoke unexpectedly. "Should I engage?"

The scene on the vid-screen shifted beyond the bridge to somewhere further out in the sand. Beyond the Lillem stood a cloaked figure unconcerned for her safety - Ku-Roi.

"Hold your fire, Gin-Kouteki," I instructed him. "We don't want to provoke her."

As soon as the words escaped me, I noticed another figure the Lillem were also ignoring. The long coat, effortless grace, and lengthy katana were enough to identify Fuun as he strode between the Lillem, cutting them down like they were no more than weeds in his path to reach where Ku-Roi stood.

The screen offered me no audio, and it was unlikely I would have made anything out over the screams of the Lillem, but it was evident the two of them were talking. By their postures, the conversation, such as it was, was strained. All of a sudden, the hood of Ku-Roi's cloak fell back to reveal a wicked smile I could even make out from here on the somewhat grainy vid-screen image. Fuun's stance instinctively became defensive, as Ku-Roi lifted her hand. Fuun fell to his knees.

I didn't know what was going on, but I couldn't just let Ku-Roi destroy Fuun. Alarmed, I raised my head and looked around, but beyond the small bit of light on the bridge it was all just blackness out there. I squinted, narrowing my eyes as I peered into the distance, willing my eyes to focus and the world began to lighten. Thanks to my power, I was now able to see not as if it was daylight, but as if the darkness wasn't there. Locating Fuun with my own eyes, I turned him to mist.

"Target lost," Gin-Kouteki supplied before I had a chance to tell him to fire now that Fuun was safe. I checked the screen to confirm it, but there was no doubt in my mind that Ku-Roi had disappeared once again.

"Fall back!" I heard Kaji's voice above the noise as, all of a sudden, explosions went off further out over the bridge.

Kaji and the Roughlander woman were flying along the length of the bridge, dropping some sort of explosives over the sides of the

Skyraider to cover the retreat of the Taiyouns. The Lillem force were swarming the bridge now, falling and climbing over each other in their haste to get to where the humans awaited them.

I took off from Gin-Kouteki's shoulder and noted that, from the gate where they had waited behind Sabien, Masaru and the other Knights were surging forward to take their turn on the front lines, while the Taiyouns did their best to retreat without allowing the Lillem to overrun them. I felt I had to do something, though I didn't know what that something was. I knew that my light arrows would not be enough to even cause them pause, especially with the frenzy they were displaying this close to their prey.

Normal arrows wouldn't work, but maybe nets would be able to hold them back. At the very least, it would give the fleeing Legionnaires a second's respite. I centered myself, flapping steadily in the night air as I reformed Fuun on the ground somewhere below me. I formed an arrow with the intent that it would explode into as many nets as I could make. My arrow struck, forming a wall of netting extending across the bridge, only the nets weren't made of rope like I had been expecting, but of glowing, blue power instead – they stuck like a spider's web.

The Lillem struck the net and as they touched it they seemed to wilt. Sluggishly, the horde of advancing Lillem slowed, like water encountering a dam, the ones behind still frenzied and pushing on the ones in front of them while trying to surge forward.

Sabien and Masaru reached them first. "Hold," Sabien commanded. "There is no use in tiring ourselves needlessly."

Sabien was right, but unfortunately from up above I could see easily that my nets would not be enough to halt the Lillem's advance, although I had managed to slow it briefly. The Lillem were mindless, yes, but that mindlessness gave them a sort of perseverance and heedless of the damage they were doing to each other, they began to pile up and climb. Soon they would flow over the dam I had created.

It wasn't long before Sabien and the others saw what I had already determined and they backed up. What no one was expecting was for my energy nets to suddenly fail and wink out of existence. The pitched battle that ensued when the penned Lillem were released was worse than any of us expected. I lost track of time as I fired arrow after arrow to freeze pockets of Lillem in place and keep them from getting at the Knights. We were holding, maybe sufficiently, maybe barely – it was hard to tell – until one decidedly human scream broke through the inhuman sounds we had all grown so accustomed to hearing.

Sabien, his sword fallen from his hand, grabbed hold of the Lillem talon that had pierced through the shoulder guard of his armour. His face contorting with the effort – or the first sign he was turning – he ripped the talon off of the creature in a tremendous show of strength, before impaling the Lillem with its own extraneous limb.

Sabien staggered back, clutching his shoulder, before he doubled over, hunching in on himself. His left shoulder plate gave way with a crunch, revealing a Lillem talon sprouting from beneath to stretch into the open air.

I dove for him, hoping there was something I could do, but as my feet touched ground Sabien splashed to a puddle and before anyone could think to try and stop him he was off the edge of the bridge and into the lake of Taiyou.

"Fall back!" I heard the call in a familiar voice, as Rama joined the fray with the remaining members of his Lion Brigade to cover the Knight's retreat.

I wondered briefly about the whereabouts of the Deathsquad – weren't they the ones who were supposed to relieve us? – when I heard the steady marching of their boots. I lifted off into the air before a Lillem could get close enough to take me down. As soon as I was in the air, I saw the problem.

Rama and his men were tired, having fought long and hard on the first shift, and now the wave of Lillem had gotten much worse than before. The Lion Brigade was being butchered and it didn't look like they would last until the Deathsquad could reach their side – if they fell now while we were in retreat, the whole line of defense could fall.

Summoning my power, I fired off another row of those nets, hoping the delay would be worth the inevitable consequences, but I was unfortunately a split second too late. Rama took a wound to his side from a Lillem, there being just too many around him for him to face alone. Horrified and unwilling to lose another person I knew to these awful creatures, I acted on instinct and turned Rama to mist, hoping the transformation would be enough of a delay to keep him from turning for the time being.

Flying past Kaji's Skyraider as I shot back towards the gate, I called out to him. "Rama's been wounded by a Lillem!"

Flying hard, I landed on a clear spot on the foot of the bridge just before the gate and watched Rama, as mist, float to me on the wind. I didn't see Yue coming – I never could – but she appeared before me as Rama's cloud came to hover in my vicinity.

"Rama's been infected by the Lillem," I informed Yue. "Is there anything you can do to stop the transformation?"

"I don't know," she answered with a shake of her head, "I can try…"

That was enough for me; we had to try something. I reformed Rama at our feet and prepared myself for just about anything.

I let out a breath in relief as I noticed he didn't have any extra bone protrusions yet and the wound to his side wouldn't – under ordinary circumstances – have been a fatal one. Before I could exhale completely, Rama's head whipped around to face me, his expression contorted in a feral snarl.

This time I heard the snapping of his armoured shoulder plate as a Lillem talon shot out from beneath it, unfurling to reveal its deadly point and poised to strike. Yue, oblivious to the sudden danger, had her eyes shut as she hovered over his form, concentrating on manifesting some form of her power.

I dove for Rama and grabbed hold of the base of the talon to wrestle it to the ground. I held on for dear life, trying my damndest to avoid the wickedly sharp point of the talon as I was jostled from side to side. I heard the crunching from Rama's other shoulder and I knew it was only a matter of time before the second talon broke free – and I could not hold them both.

"Yue – it's not working," I told her.

"Move out of the way, Yue," I heard Kaji say.

The shoulder piece of Rama's armour at last gave way, but Kaji heard the sound and knew what it meant. He leapt onto Rama and pinned him to the ground before the talon could unfold enough to attack. "You're going to hold on, Leon," Kaji told Rama, "even if I have to beat the Lillem out of you. Leon Rama of Taiyou and the Raman province, you will not die tonight,"

Kaji directed his gaze skyward, toward the bright orb of the moon in the sky. "Sapphiros, hear me. This man is worthy of your power – grant it to him so he may fight off this disease."

Remarkably, the solid bone shaft in my hands turned abruptly to sand and Rama sat immediately upright, looking alert and human again, his wound at his side perfectly healed as if it had never occurred – save for the damage to his armour. I blinked a few times, staring at the evidence of the miracle I had just witnessed – Rama was a Knight of Sapphiros now and it had saved his life.

"Are you all right?" Kaji asked.

"I feel wonderful, Kaji, never better," Rama answered with obvious amazement, climbing to his feet.

I looked out over the bridge, taking stock of the situation. The Deathsquad, at Mikura's direction, fought in a very orderly fashion. They were in perfect rows, one line falling back to be replaced with the next with an almost dance-like precision. They were brutally efficient and organized; as a result, they took much fewer losses than the Taiyouns had.

I was grateful, of course, that they held the line and protected Taiyou where we hadn't been able to, but it was hard to watch the well-disciplined soldiers of my enemy and realize just how competent they were. If the Vile Emperor came to march upon us now, especially with Mikura's Deathsquad already here as an advance force, we would not stand a chance against him in our current plight. All we could do was hope that he, too, was plagued with similar problems while the Ruby City was covered by darkness, so he would stay home to deal with his troubles instead of creating more for us.

Ris was bathed by the light of the moon as she hovered over the edge of the bridge, gazing over the darkened waters of the lake of Taiyou. I could see the pain in her heart and the worry already eating away at her. My heart crying out for her, I crossed the distance between the two of us and put my arm around her.

"For you, I will," I told Ris softly, before I lifted my arms into the air and drew back a single arrow. *"Sabien."*

The arrow arced into the sky and I fought the desire to close my eyes tightly to shut out what it was going to tell me, but thankfully it did not explode. Instead, it split into a multitude of arrows which rained down upon the waters of Taiyou in a shimmering display of cyan light.

"He's alive," I told Ris, easing the burden on her heart as I looked out upon the moonlit waters myself, remembering my own dark time and wondering at Ris' strength. "He's out there somewhere."

CH. 10 – IT TAKES TIME TO BOUNCE

From the centre of the land of Taiyou rose the mountain of Jade, temple to the gem god Jedeite. Ao Kouen, his scarf billowing in the slight wind, stood atop the mountain on the platform which housed the foremost weapon of Taiyou. He contemplated the weapon for a moment, but it was not the answer to saving Taiyou from its attackers. Turning his back, the future King of Taiyou instead faced the land.

The wind picked up around the Jade mountain, whipping at the trees and the village below, spiralling as it expanded outwards. High on the mountain's peak a green glow became a pillar of light, shooting upwards into the sky, visible for miles. From that green glow a fire began; a cleansing fire born of the power of Jedeite. The green tendrils of flame whipped out from the Chosen of Jedeite to spiral down the side of the mountain and follow after the wind.

In the city of Taiyou, the green flame came before dawn and wiped through every city street and every home and business.

Citizens of Taiyou cowered before the sudden display of magic in their midst, but they were left unscathed when the blazing wall of green flame had passed, and they looked upon themselves and each other with wonder.

On the borders and at the bridge, the flames swept out as far as they could reach, eradicating each and every Lillem they touched. In the palace, the green flames swept through the halls, lighting none of the furnishings or the tapestries on fire and harming none of the people that lived or worked there, but consuming any intruders instantly.

Two Deathsquad soldiers and two Legionnaires stood guard before the throne room where King Narlhep sat on his throne. The fire passed right by the guards, leaving them alarmed but unharmed, and swept through the throne room doors to fill the Jade-lined room with green flames.

Ao Kouen found himself suddenly and inexplicably before the helmeted King of Taiyou, but slightly to Narlhep's left, his hands firmly grasped upon the hilt of the sword of Jedeite that had been placed in the centre throne to herald his coming. His eyes widened as he realized where he was; his gazed darted from Narlhep to the sword before him in a kind of panic. "No, I won't...I won't do it."

Take the sword. It is my will.

To his left, Ao Kouen saw Narlhep nod imperceptibly, and Ao Kouen knew he had no choice but to accept his own fate as well. The gem god's power – his power as a Chosen – would be needed now if Taiyou was to have a chance of surviving. He tugged once and the sword came free, and as soon as it was released, Narlhep was consumed by the fires of Jedeite, leaving only ashes in the place of the young King who had ruled so briefly.

"I know we've all received some shocks recently," I began after all of us, except Yue and Sabien, had gathered in the Knights' room, "but unfortunately there is worse to come and it's best I tell you now. Hotaru, can you slice the bottom off this melon for me, please?"

I placed the lid on the barrel of water in the centre of the room and the melon with the lopped-off side facing down on top of it so it wouldn't roll anywhere. "I know you've probably all been wondering about the darkness. Some of you remember when this planet had night and day, but to the rest of you, I know how unnatural it seems." I looked in particular at Rama, Masaru, and Pine. "Natural or unnatural, this darkness is still a very sudden shift in the planet's established cycle and there has to be a reason for it."

I fished my slightly dented apple out of the pocket of my Roughlander pants and held it up. "I'm going to use this apple to represent the planet and the melon will represent the sun." I repeated the earlier explanation I had practiced on Razor and Masaru. "Now, it's my theory something had to have happened eight hundred years ago – or thereabouts – to cause the planet's orbit to shift in the first place."

Hotaru put up her hand. "Well, Espearia crash-landed here from another planet. That's a whole country hitting this planet, could that have done it?"

I raised my brow and looked to Jeth, the only Espearian I knew, for confirmation. "Could be," Jeth answered with a shrug, "but there was still night and day when we all went to sleep."

"Well, it may have taken some time for the planet to adjust to its new orbit, so the change could have been gradual when it happened, or there could have been a delay before night disappeared." I noticed quickly I was getting a bit ahead of some people and decided to actually use the props I had set up. I held the apple next to the melon but a little ways out and began to spin it slowly with my hands while moving it around the melon. "This is what the planet's orbit probably would have looked like before anything happened to it – so let's just say eight hundred years ago or so," I explained. "If Hotaru's theory is correct, the planet could have been struck by something," I used my other hand to 'strike' the apple from beneath and push it upwards, "moving the planet either above or below the sun into a new cycle."

"If this was the case, then the same side of the planet would always see the sun, while the other side would always see darkness. Our side of the planet, the sunny side, would eventually dry out, which explains the Sand Lakes, while the other side would largely consist of frozen water.

"Now, eight hundred years pass, bringing us to a few days ago, and the thing I don't have any theories on is what changed to cause the darkness to suddenly fall now. What I can tell you is that since it first fell, the darkness has been growing longer by one hour and one minute consistently in every twenty-four hour period. If this pattern continues, then in twenty days from now we could have total darkness like this world has had total sun."

"You mean you don't think it will go back to having both night and day?" Aysel asked, looking horrified.

"It's possible," I agreed, "but unless we can figure out what's actually happening, and I don't really have the tools to do so, then we won't know for sure until the thirteenth night."

"Mifa has a telescope at her house," Kaji stated. "I don't know if it's working, but if it is I'm sure she wouldn't mind if you used it."

"That would help," I told him.

"So what you're saying is if we don't find a way to deal with these Lillem permanently, then soon we will be fighting them without the respite the sun gives us?" Rama asked.

"That's only one aspect of the problem, Sir Rama," I responded grimly, "one of the most immediate, but if I'm right about the situation on the other side of the world, then eventually this side will become a frozen wasteland, not just a barren one. That's of course presuming we live to see it, through the floods and natural disasters caused by the shift in the planet's orbit, and the melting of the ice on the other side of the world."

What I was describing was the end of the world, or at least of sustainable life, even without the undeniable threat of the hordes of undead creatures that came with the darkness. By the look on the faces around the room, I had made my point clear, but no one was willing to put it into words, least of all me, who had been burdened with this knowledge the longest.

I had finally found something in this world worth caring about and I felt like I was starting to belong here, to be accepted by the people here like I never was back on Earth. Now, due to some unexplained phenomena, I was going to lose it all.

The meeting broke up on the same subdued note it had begun, everyone needing time to absorb what they had just learned and come to grips with it, if they could. I, at least, having shared the burden of my dreadful conclusions with everyone else, felt a little better at having gotten them off my chest, even though it didn't change anything.

"I know you know your science, Yukari, but this time I sincerely hope you're wrong," Adel told me before I left.

"So do I, Adel," I responded quietly. "I would like nothing more than to be wrong."

Masaru was there waiting for me when I returned to the room assigned to the Chosen. I found myself drawn into his arms where he held me in a wordless embrace I hadn't known how much I needed.

"You've known since the third darkness, haven't ye? It's what's been tearing you apart inside."

I pulled away from him reluctantly – I didn't want to break down again. "I didn't want to worry anyone else until I was sure…"

"But there's still more tests ye can do, right? Ye're not quite certain yet, are ye?"

"Right, there are still things I can check," I told him, feeling a little frazzled and wondering where to start. If it was possible to save the world, I suppose that task would fall to us as Chosen. "Plotting the movement of the stars would help me determine how the planet is moving and how quickly, and of course we'll know either way by the thirteenth darkness."

"Well, there's nothing ye can do about it right this instant. I know for a fact ye can't see the stars unless it's dark out, ye told me as much when I asked about the little lights in the sky." I nodded in agreement. "Well then, ye have some time to get caught up on yer rest. Ye'll be able to think more clearly if you get some sleep."

I nodded again. I would need my wits about me to face the next darkness and to do what I could to work through this. Masaru led me over to the bed. "What about you? I can't just let you sleep on the chair again, there's no way that's comfortable."

"It was all right…" he answered evasively.

"Well, you should take the bed," I told him, deliberately not mentioning the four other beds in the other sleeping areas. "It's only fair you get a turn."

"Ye can't sleep in a chair, ye need proper rest," he protested.

"You said it was all right," I pointed out. "The other alternative is we share. The bed is big enough."

Masaru was oddly reluctant, but in the end I convinced him to take up his part of the bed. I felt better knowing Masaru was close and in no danger. I didn't remember dreaming, least of all working through any of the problems I had to consider, but when I woke, sometime still during daylight hours, suddenly everything seemed clearer than it had before.

I leapt up out of bed and scurried over to the table in the centre of the room, rummaging in my medic kit as I went. I pulled the Blue Moon Scroll out first, just to get it out of my way, and then I reached for the sheaf of blank paper I had picked up from the Temple of Sapphire and the pencil I had obtained at the same time. Laying the paper out on the table before me, I couldn't get to writing fast enough, almost knocking over the chair in my haste to get in it.

"What're ye doing over there?" Masaru asked groggily.

Without looking, I held a finger up to him to indicate I couldn't talk just yet. I drew quick diagrams and notations, working through vague theories and possibilities on the limited amount of paper I had at my disposal. At the edge of my perception I heard Masaru rustle about behind the curtain, before coming over to peer over my shoulder at what I was doing.

"I knew ye could do it," he spoke softly, placing his hand on my shoulder.

There was a knock at the door. I looked to Masaru to answer it, but he was already to his feet. Having mostly gotten everything down by this point, I rubbed my aching hand – I wasn't as used to writing as I had been on Earth.

"Adel!" I exclaimed, pushing back my chair and surging to my feet. "I was wrong!"

"That's good to hear," Adel smiled. "I'll be looking forward to hearing more about what's actually happening later, but I've come to let you know the other Chosen are down at the bridge trying to retrieve Sabien – I thought you might like to join them."

"Yes, if I can be of help. Thank you, Adel, and could you do me a favour and arrange for another meeting tonight before dark? I'd like to apologize to everyone for my error and let them know what I figured out."

"I will," she agreed and left, taking Masaru with her out into the hall.

I returned to my papers and looked over them for a minute. Writing small, I had filled nearly five pages on both sides. Knowing I was needed down at the bridge, but not wanting to leave all my hard work behind, I sat in my chair once more and tried reaching the bridge another way. I closed my eyes and concentrated on Ris..

When I could feel her presence – very similar to the way my message arrows always found their targets – I willed myself to follow it to her physical body the way I had followed Goji's spirit to Earth.

This time the sense of dislocation wasn't nearly as strong – I was only going from the palace to the bridge and not to another planet – but it was still present. I found myself standing behind Ris on the bridge, as she leaned out over the rail. Like in the hospital, my hands were transparent and now, having the chance to look a little closer, I realized this astral form of mine was made up of water particles like when I turned myself to mist.

"Whoa!" Hotaru exclaimed. "Are you really here?"

"Not exactly," I responded, "I'm still back at the palace."

"Yue's gone for a swim to see if she can find Sabien," Kaji said.

"I was going to try and talk to him through the water to see if he'll answer that way," Hotaru added.

Hotaru settled down cross-legged on the bridge, while I tried somewhat unsuccessfully to console Ris.

"Sabien?" Hotaru addressed the water in her canteen before her. "Sabien, can you hear us – we're worried about you."

"Take their blood..." It was the barest of whispers.

"What was that?" I asked as Ris' head snapped around at the sound as if drawn to it.

"Take their lives..." the sibilant whisper spoke again.

"Shh," Kaji instructed, holding up a finger, "I can just barely make it out."

"Take their land..." the whispery voice continued, insistent, almost compelling. *"Take their power..."*

Ris was nodding her head and gesturing frantically to Kaji. I translated verbally for Kaji's sake. "That's what Sabien's been saying over and over again in her mind. She wants to know what it means."

"Take their blood. Take their lives. Take their land. Take their power," Kaji recited. "I don't know, Ris. I wish I did."

Out in the water there was a sudden splash and we all whirled about, "Make him say it again!" Yue called out. "I almost had him."

"Sabien," Hotaru dutifully repeated the process of activating her power. "Sabien, we're here to help you. Kaji, Yukari, Yue, and I, we're all here and Ris is too. She's worried about you. Please talk to us and let her know you're okay."

By now Ris was crouched down next to Hotaru with her mouth open like she wanted to say something, but as expected no sound came out. The silence wore on, but then the lake of Taiyou responded, lapping against the side of the bridge nearest Hotaru and Ris.

"It's Sabien!" Yue called out, causing some more splashing herself as she swam the distance back to the bridge.

Sure enough, she was right – it could be no one else – as the lake itself rose up over the side of the bridge in only one spot and a man-sized puddle formed on the bridge. It took Sabien a few tries to pull himself together, and even when he did he still looked unsteady, as if he was going to splash back into a formless puddle at any moment. The most horrific part of his appearance was not his instability, however, but the singular Lillem talon that formed with him, the bone limb protruding from his left shoulder.

Ris scrambled to her feet and tried to rush to him, but Kaji held her back as Yue hauled herself onto the bridge behind them. She was covered in cloth wrappings over skin-tight leggings and was, of course, sopping wet, her dry Roughlander clothes still in a pile a little ways away.

"Don't come any closer," Sabien spoke in an unsettling double voice. His own voice could be heard, but beneath them was the dark, sibilant whisper, and I felt as if I could still hear it chanting, demanding to be obeyed. "I don't know how well I can keep control. It is easier now in the light than before, but I can still feel its presence."

"What presence, Sabien?" I asked. "Do you know what it is?"

"It is hard to describe," he answered, pausing as he took a moment to ensure he was still in full control, the Lillem talon twitching sporadically as he did so. "It is like a spirit. An entity has invaded my body and is trying to wrest my power and control of my faculties from me, only at the same time, it does not seem sentient enough."

"Can you fight it off?" Yue asked.

"I've been trying," Sabien admitted. "That's why I left, to keep you all safe. The best I've been able to manage is to not let it gain further control of me. I don't know if I'll be able to manage as much again when the night comes."

"I can store you in my Noh-space," Yue offered – I assumed in reference to the place where she put things until she wanted them again. "That way you'll be safe until we can figure out how to fix you. I've already got Dahlia, so it shouldn't hurt to have another person chilling out in there."

"You have Dahlia?!" I whirled to face her.

"Yeah," Yue answered. "I meant to give her to you already, I just hadn't gotten around to it yet."

Our discussion was interrupted by Sabien hunching over and stifling a hiss as the Lillem in him wrestled for control once more. I was distracted by the indescribable feeling of someone shaking my body back at the palace. I felt myself fading away from the scene on the bridge as Yue flashed in close enough to touch Sabien and make him disappear, putting him into her 'Noh-space' as she had called it.

My expression was mutinous when I finally opened my eyes. The anger I felt inside was not dampened by Masaru's concerned expression as he looked me over.

"Are ye all right? I couldn't get a response out of ye."

"I was at the bridge. Sabien's been found, but Masaru," I met his eyes and held them, "Yue has Dahlia."

I watched as Masaru's face went through a variety of emotions until he also seemed to settle upon a seething anger. "How long has she kept that to herself?"

"I don't know, but I promise you the next time I see Yue I'll be sure to get Dahlia back."

"You mean *I'll* get Dahlia back," Masaru protested, and in the mood we were both in I completely understood his feelings on the matter; it seemed, after a moment, he understood mine as well. "We'll get her back," he amended.

"And Yue's going to have some explaining to do," I added.

Masaru and I likely would have trekked down to the bridge that very minute to demand Dahlia be released, except as usual, there was something that got in the way.

"Unauthorized persons within range, should I engage?"

My wings appeared before I even thought of them and I was in the air, heading out the balcony and rising upwards toward to join the veritable flock of winged women that had somehow arrived in Taiyou. They didn't seem to be attacking anything or anyone, but I sure as hell didn't know who they were or how they had gotten here. Considering Gin-Kouteki's instantaneous warning, it fell to me to determine whether these strange newcomers were friends or foes.

"Excuse me," I said, selecting a winged girl at random. She appeared young and friendly, with medium-length blonde hair. "I don't mean to sound rude, but who are you all?"

"Us?" she asked, "Or them?" She gestured down towards the ground and following her direction I noted quite a few more women, these without wings, but wearing matching light blue cloaks instead.

"Uh, both I suppose," I answered.

"Why, we're the priestesses of Air, and down there are the priestesses of Water and Fire," she explained, her voice reminiscent of the accent the Knights of the Blue Moon had shared, like a southern drawl. "We've come from Espearia because y'all asked for our help."

"Ah," I answered, somewhat relieved. "Gin-Kouteki," I addressed the box in my medic kit, "please authorize these women as having access to Taiyou. They are our allies, the Priestesses of Espearia. Are you in charge here?" I asked the priestess I was speaking to.

"No, I'm not. You'd be wantin' the Head Priestess Arashi, but I believe she's inside talking with your fellow – I think he said his name was Kaji – one of the Chosen of Sapphiros. I take it that's what you are as well?"

I smiled, nodding and feeling better now I knew Kaji had this one in hand. I introduced myself formally to the priestess I had been speaking with, and took my leave of her to head back inside to let Masaru know everything was fine.

That evening the Knights' room was a bit more populated than I was anticipating. It seemed quite a few people had gotten wind of my breakthrough and were interested to have the darkness explained to them. As I entered the room, dinged apple in hand, and with Jeth on my heels carrying the bucket I had requested he fetch for my demonstration, I felt suddenly self-conscious; nearly everyone of import in the castle was waiting for me to arrive.

The curtains to the sleeping areas had been drawn back and every seat and bedside in the room was taken up, with still more people coming in with extra chairs. Mifa was there, seated with Kaji and a few of the members of Goji's 'advisory council'. Ao Kouen was present and flanked on either side by Lady Rhine, and Lady Mikura.

Masaru and Razor were there, and also Hitachi and Yuge. Likewise, several new arrivals representing our allies from Espearia. Arashi, like an angel with her white-gold hair and her white-feathered wings, was truly a beautiful sight to behold, but the other Espearians were almost as interesting to look at.

All of the Knights were also present, except Sabien of course, and even Ris looked attentive. Hotaru sat with Aysel, the wounded squire's one hand held in hers, and Yue was also present this time around, though to my annoyance her expression betrayed her obvious boredom.

Technically, even Hex and Gin-Kouteki were accounted for as I took the communication box out of my medic kit and placed it on the table left empty for me to use. "Gin-Kouteki, can you hear me?"

"Affirmative, Yukari."

"I would like to begin by apologizing to everyone for my error in this morning's presentation," I began, once I had everyone's attention. "I'm happy to announce I have reason to believe I was wrong about the nature of the sudden darkness. Though I still have work to do to prove the accuracy of what I'm about to explain to you, I am now of the opinion the change we have been witnessing is actually a sign the planet may be righting itself and returning to a more natural cycle of night and day.

"Those of you who attended this morning's meeting, I ask you to try your best to forget what I told you. For the benefit of everyone who is joining us for the first time this evening, I'm going to start at the beginning and make it as clear as I can."

I pulled my apple out once more. Using the same basic principles I had used earlier, I got my audience up to speed on the basics of planetary rotation.

"So, this morning I explained a theory involving the planet rotating at a level above or below where it had been before in relation to the sun," I explained. "Well, what led me to my current theory is what I presented this morning simply isn't possible. A force called gravity is what keeps the planet rotating a certain distance away from the sun and if the planet was to be knocked off that course and no longer held into place by that force, it might be sent off into space, but it would never settle into the pattern I described.

"The theory I propose now has to do with the Splitters. I was once told that while the Splitters are active, time moves the same on both planets. If this fact is true, then it implies that while the Splitters are active there is a connection between the two planets.

"To understand what is happening now, we must first understand what happened eight hundred years ago. Being that I, like the other Chosen of Sapphiros, am only fifteen and not eight hundred like some of us in the room," I paused for a bit of a chuckle from my audience, as with the Knights present there were more than a few people who were alive during the time period I was describing, "I haven't been around long enough to have all the facts, but I have done my best to piece together a timeline of what occurred and how it relates to the effects we are experiencing now.

"On the night we first encountered the Talons and the Vile Emperor, we also spoke to Yuko Seig, and it was she who took control of the Splitters to allow us to escape from the Vile Emperor. We should have arrived on this planet immediately, but while we were in transit from our world to this one something happened which delayed our arrival. I have reason to believe that while eight hundred years passed on this world, the same did not happen on Earth – in fact next to no time passed there at all.

"So what happened?mConsider two planets rotating around their respective suns and held in check by some unseen connection created by the Splitters. If that connection remains, both planets move at the same speed, but what would happen if that connection were to be suddenly, forcefully severed? Thanks to a recorded message left for us by Yuko Seig, we know she and the Vile Emperor were struggling over the control of the Splitters while we were in transit. At some point later, the Vile Emperor attacked the Temple of Sapphire and the Splitter program was abruptly terminated when the Binoid operating the system was cut down.

"I have asked Jeth to help me demonstrate what I think happened when the connection between the two planets was severed without being properly disconnected. Jeth?"

Jeth filled the bucket with water from the barrel in the room, and moved to the space before me.

"All right, now instead of the melon, picture Jeth as the sun," I instructed everyone.

"I am the sun," Jeth pronounced in an exaggerated fashion.

"The bucket in Jeth's hands represents the planet." I had Jeth spin slowly and rotate the bucket in his hands to indicate the planet turning naturally around the sun, just like I had with the apple and melon earlier. "Now I want you to imagine that the surface of the water in the bucket represents the side of the planet we are currently on and the bottom of the bucket is the other side of the planet. When the Splitter's connection was severed, I believe the resulting force was enough to cause a slingshot effect where one of the two planets – this one – was flung around its orbit at a greatly increased speed. Jeth?"

Jeth began twirling fasterand his arm rose and straightened as the bucket spun around and around until the surface of the water was perpendicular to Jeth in the center; due to the speed at which he was spinning, not a drop of the water spilled onto the floor.

"If you'll notice," I explained while Jeth was still spinning quickly, "at this increased speed, our side of the planet – the water – is always facing the sun and the other side is always facing away from it. That's because with the speed of the yearly rotation increased so dramatically, the daily spin is suspended and each bounce of the sun we see in the sky is actually the planet making its way halfway around its entire orbit.

"Now because of gravity and friction, which is created by motion, this level of speed cannot be maintained indefinitely. The planet would eventually slow down once the force that initially propelled it wore off."

"I am tired," Jeth supplied helpfully, much to everyone's amusement, as he began to slow down, carefully lowering the bucket once more.

"It is my belief that the moment the speeds of the two planets came to match once more, the Splitters may have reconnected – having never been properly shut down before – allowing us to finally arrive as we did. And having been returned to a more natural speed, the planet's daily spin would attempt to resume its course, only it takes some time for something as large as a planet to get moving again." Jeth brought the bucket back to its original speed and expended a comedic amount of effort to get the bucket spinning again.

"This would give us a lag period," I explained why the darkness hadn't fallen immediately upon our arrival. "Exactly forty-eight days after the four of us arrived on this planet marked the fall of the first hour of darkness. Seeing as each dark period is being increased at a consistent rate, if I am correct we should be able to prove we are back on a normal cycle of twelve hours of dark and twelve hours of light by the thirteenth night."

When I finished, reactions around the room were mixed. The Knights, as well as Kaji and Hotaru, having had some understanding of the basics of night and day, seemed to have followed along the best and most of them appeared thoughtful, like they were trying to absorb everything I had just told them. Yue, on the other hand was asleep, whether pretending or otherwise, just like this had been a boring lecture back in school she hadn't wanted to sit though.

The Taiyouns, including the serious-faced Ao Kouen, by and large were grim or reserved. They alone of the people gathered here this evening knew exactly what was at stake and how hard we would have to fight just to get through tonight's darkness, let alone the next handful of them. The only notable Taiyoun smiling was Mifa, and I'm sure in her case it was nice to hear a presentation on a controversial theory that didn't get immediately shot down. I had no doubt she had understood and followed every word with intense interest; my intelligent friend loved learning about the how and why of the world's workings.

The varied Espearians looked nonplussed, while the Roughlanders in general were beaming – presumably with the relief the rumours about the world coming to an end were false – but in Masaru and Razor's case it could have been pride. Hitachi was a different matter altogether, and his expression could only be described as suspicious.

"So the world isn't ending then, is it?" Hitachi asked. "That's what you're sayin'?"

"Right," I agreed, "if what I've told you is correct, then we'll end up with both days and nights in roughly equal balance."

"So alls we gots to do is find a way of survivin' the monsters every night and then we'll be all right, eh?"

"In essence, yes," I agreed, seeing where this might be going, "and of course keeping in mind there will still be quite an adjustment period for the whole world – natural disasters and dangerous weather patterns – but if the world has gotten through it once, it should be able to do it again."

"Oh." Hitachi paused. "So we got the Lillem bangin' on our doors every time it gets dark and you say the weather's gonna try and kill us too? Well seein' as yer so smart and all, how 'bout you tell us how we're gonna live through that, eh? What are we s'posed to do about it?"

"I know it's not going to be easy and I don't have all the answers," I responded, not just to Hitachi, but to everyone "but we have to do what we can to defend Taiyou while we work on a solution to the Lillem problem."

"That's where we come in," Arashi interjected, stepping forward. "We are your allies and we will ensure the borders are defended for this night. Y'all deserve a rest."

"Are you sure?" I asked her, somewhat alarmed. "Taiyou is rather large and the Lillem seem to be concentrating their attack here more so than they were in the desert."

"The Espearian priestesses will defend the city's borders." Arashi stated definitively.

"That's all well and good," Yue spoke up suddenly, awake and perfectly alert, "but that's only Taiyou – what about the rest of the world? We don't know how anybody else is faring. Are the Lillem attacking everywhere, or is it just here and Espearia? I don't know about anyone else, but I intend to go back to the Ruby City tomorrow and see how they are doing. I mean, the city is like a fishbowl with its magical barrier. If they've got Lillem in there with them, they could use our help."

"Our help?!" I exclaimed, shocked at the sudden turn in the conversation. "No one deserves the Lillem, Yue, but you're talking about the Vile Emperor here – the one who has been trying to kill us this entire time."

"But that's just it," she protested. "I don't actually think he's been trying to kill us. If he really wanted us dead, we'd be dead by now. But even still, the Vile Emperor has been around a long time, so he might have more information than we do about the Lillem. Am I the only one who thinks it's worth going to find out? Lady Mikura?"

"I don't know…" Mikura hesitated. "You're right about the Ruby City being in danger. As far as I know all of the other Generals have been called back home, but I don't know if my master would want to talk to you. I don't think he likes you guys very much."

"Well I, for one, would be willing to give it a try," Rama proclaimed. "If they are in the same situation we are then we have something in common, and maybe now, of all times, peace can finally be reached."

"So who's with me, then?" Yue asked.

"I think we have enough concerns of our own to worry about," I stated somewhat forcefully. I was getting a little sick of Yue's budding association with the Vile Emperor.

After that point, the meeting degenerated somewhat. Our allies and all those who intended to be on or around the bridge when darkness fell needed to be on their way, as through the opening of the balcony it was clear the sun was beginning to set. Others stayed behind to converse with each other about current events and what could be done about them. I was angry enough that I would have stormed out after having finished my part of the meeting, but the knowledge that Yue alone knew how to retrieve Dahlia stopped me.

As I made my excuses to the people who wanted to share their views about my presentation, I noticed out on the balcony that Kaji and Adel seemed to be trying to have a private conversation. I was surprised to note a look of absolute horror on Adel's usually stoic face as the Knight fell to her knees. Kaji looked distressed, but after a moment Adel recovered, and with another quick word to Kaji she fled and rushed right through the crowd. Concerned, but unable to do anything about it, I continued to make my way through the still fairly crowded room to where Masaru had already cornered Yue, but I was surprised to note it wasn't Dahlia's whereabouts they were speaking of.

"Do ye really think with all those Deathsquads the Ruby City would be in as much trouble as we are?" Masaru was asking as I joined them.

"I don't know, but I'd like to find out," Yue answered.

"Yue," I interrupted them. "Where is Dahlia?"

"I told you, I have her."

"I think you should give her back, now," I told her. "I would like to know for sure she's okay."

"I thought you might," she responded, "so I arranged a room downstairs for you to use as an operating room."

"Operating room?" I questioned. "Yue, is she that hurt?"

She grimaced. "I didn't get a really good look at her, but she didn't look good, so I put her in my Noh-space right away so she wouldn't be in any danger –"

"Ye mean ye don't know if she's okay?" Masaru sounded shocked, and then his tone changed to one of disappointment. "Yue…ye should have told us right away."

"Yeah, well, come on," she stood. "Everything's all set up."

CH. 11 – A WEDDING, A FUNERAL AND A CORONATION

I had to admit Yue had done well to set up a room on the ground level where I could see to Dahlia, or any other patients that might require my attention in the future. It was evident the room had previously been used for storage – there were still some crates containing who knew what lining the walls – but the spacious room had been cleaned thoroughly by palace staff and furnished with a couple of high beds, a few small tables, and a handful of chairs, all placed along the walls where they would be out of the way. Upon entering the room with Ris, Yue, and Masaru on my heels, I was introduced to yet another of the palace medics, who had apparently volunteered to be my assistant. He gave me a quick tour of the room and an inventory of what supplies we had at our disposal.

To be honest, I was a little overwhelmed by it all. I had gotten so used to just doing what I could to help people who were hurting with my hands and the meagre supplies Rama had gifted me with when we first met. But despite my sudden elation at the discovery of my new operating room, I was still worried about Dahlia.

"All right," I told Yue, "if you can make her appear on the bed that would be best."

"Actually, I was speaking to Mikura a little earlier and she suggested I have either her or Adel look over Dahlia before you start to work on her," Yue informed me. "I kind of got her back from the Ruby City, and according to Mikura they sometimes leave curses as traps on political prisoners."

I narrowed my eyes dangerously in Yue's direction, which she chose to ignore. "Fine," I stated, "But I'll go see if I can convince Adel to come. I don't believe that as a Deathsquad General, Lady Mikura would be the best person for Dahlia to see when she wakes."

Remembering Adel's strange behavior in fleeing the Knights' room not so long ago, I decided to contact her myself in person – more or less – rather than sending her a message arrow or sending someone out to find her. Taking up the last chair in the row along the wall, I lowered my head and closed my eyes. When I became aware of where I was, I realized I was curiously being tugged along down a palace hallway as Adel, before me, stalked forward at a determined pace.

"Adel?" I called and she froze, whirling about to face me, her stance indicating she was ready for an attack. "It's just me Adel, I'm sorry if I startled you."

"You didn't," she stated, her tone unfriendly. "What do you want?"

I narrowed my eyes in suspicion, wondering what I might have stumbled into. I looked around myself and realized we were very near to the palace doors, but off in a side corridor. "Were you going somewhere, Adel?"

"I was going out, which is my own business," she replied defensively. "Need I report my every movement to the Chosen, or is my will still my own?"

"Of course it is, Adel," I responded carefully. "I was just wondering if you'd be able to help me with a patient. Dahlia's been recovered from the Ruby City and I could really use your expertise to make sure there isn't some sort of magic on her that might get in the way of Ris' healing, or make it unsafe for us to touch her."

"Yes, you're right, I better have a look at her." Adel hesitated a moment, but then she seemed to give in. "I'll be along shortly, but if

I help you with this I want your word that you won't come looking for Aysel or I for a day or two. I require privacy and I don't want any interruptions."

"I can't guarantee something won't come up," I told her honestly, thinking about just how many things could go wrong in a period of two days, "and I can't speak for the others, but I can let them know. Adel, if something is the matter, please tell me. I'd like to help."

"Just make sure I am not disturbed," she stated coldly, "and I'll be along shortly."

I left her with directions to the operating room, my heart heavy. Adel seemed markedly more pleasant by the time she reached the operating room, which is to say she seemed willing to work with me at least. Before I let Yue materialize Dahlia, I shooed Masaru out into the hallway with instructions to keep anyone from disturbing us.

Dahlia appeared a ghost of her former self. Where before the competent Roughlander had been at the peak of physical health, now she was gaunt and skeletal, her skin pale and stretched tight along her bones. Her hair, once a vibrant orange, now lifeless and scraggly. There were not cuts, but holes over places where her more prominent veins were, as if she had been drained of blood.

Despite Yue's warning and the reason for which Adel was brought here, I couldn't help but use my power to continue my examination. My eyes adjusted automatically, allowing me to see into Dahlia and as if I was much closer to her. It was as I had feared, she had lost a lot of blood – far more than even Masaru had been missing when he had returned to me with the falling of the first darkness.

I noted too, that however they had tortured her, they hadn't used natural means. Dahlia's shoulder was badly dislocated and she had a few broken bones, but what I found most disturbing were incomprehensible tears in her muscle tissue and veins. Worst of all was the horrific level of damage done to her lungs; I watched as they struggled to continue to function. It was remarkable she was even still alive.

"She's fine," Adel said at last. "Go ahead."

I rushed forward and placed my hands over Dahlia's heart, activating my power to will her heart to keep beating then I peered into Dahlia's veins to check her blood, knowing I had seen that particular pattern of cells before; Neva.

"Yue, you're the fastest – bring me Neva," I said, "Razor should know where to find her."

I heard the double doors open and close, and Yue was gone at her usual speed before Adel spoke, "So that's it, then, you don't require me any further?"

"I always require your help, Adel," I replied somewhat distractedly, "but if you have something else that needs your attention, then go."

Adel left and Ris hovered behind me anxiously, waiting for her turn to be of use. Meanwhile, the palace medic saw to cutting away the torn and ragged strips that remained of Dahlia's Roughlander clothing so he could clean her wounds. Thankfully, Yue was as fast as I needed her to be, and before I knew it she had returned carrying Neva draped over her shoulders like a rag doll. She dumped her into a chair along the row against the wall, where she proceeded to topple over, barely conscious.

"What's wrong with her?" I asked.

Yue grimaced. "She's dead drunk. The Roughlanders are having some sort of party out there in front of the palace gates. I found her dancing up on top of that giant metal robot."

"Gin-Kouteki?" I asked, somewhat alarmed, but then decided it was perhaps better if I didn't dwell on what was going on out there. I had a job to do here, whether Neva was a conscious, consenting participant or not. "Thank you, Yue, she'll have to do as she is."

Turning my back on Yue, I instructed Ris and the palace medic in what I needed them to do. Before long, we had Neva propped up in the chair nearest to the bed with a thin line of tubing running from her vein to Dahlia's. Then Ris used her magic to encase Dahlia – and my hands – in a protective blue bubble of healing energy.

It was a grueling process and I could not tell you how much time passed before Dahlia first opened her eyes again. At almost that exact moment, the double-doors to the operating room burst open to admit the love of Dahlia's life and her mate, Krox, Head-taker of the First Spawn.

"Be careful with her, Krox," I cautioned.

"Are you the healer?" he demanded gruffly.

"Yes," I answered stiffly, refusing to be intimidated.

"See that she lives, then," he ordered, and turned his attention to Dahlia.

To my surprise, somewhere Dahlia found the strength to lift her hand up to Krox's snout. I backed up a few paces to give them some privacy.

Ris directed my gaze to the open door where Masaru and Razor stood waiting to be given permission to enter. Razor looked bleary-eyed and I could see an open canteen clenched tightly in his fist. Masaru, on the other hand, simply looked apologetic. "I tried to stop him, but I think ye know what little good that did."

"Come on in, both of you," I told them, feeling tired. "We've done everything we can for now anyway."

Razor got about halfway into the room before he stopped.

"Go on, Razor," Masaru nudged, "you've come this far."

Krox looked up with a growl in Razor's direction, which was immediately silenced by the faint sound of Dahlia's voice, "Razor, is that you there?"

Razor went to Dahlia's bedside where he was greeted warmly, by Dahlia at least, and Masaru turned to me. "The Espearians have the bridge well defended and there're no more Lillem within the borders of Taiyou itself, thanks to whatever it was Ao Kouen did with that green fire. But out in the Sand Lake they just keep coming with no end in sight. The Croatins have brought an army with them, over forty thousand strong, and they're cutting their way through the Lillem as we speak, clearing their way to Taiyou."

Having given his report, Masaru joined the rest of his family at Dahlia's bedside. I, on the other hand, took a seat beside the slumped-over Neva. I would have to remember to get someone to take her to a comfortable bed. She would probably wake a tad confused, but there was little I could do except ensure she was provided with enough food and water.

I was tired and needed rest, but Adel's odd behavior was nagging at me. I closed my eyes and concentrated on sending myself to Aysel. I knew I would be breaking my word to Adel by doing so, but if Adel wouldn't tell me what was going on, then maybe her sister would.

My power took me out of the palace. The small room with one small, draped window was not anywhere I recognized. The furniture was scarce and worn, but thankfully Aysel was alone on the faded rug. She sat amongst a handful of unlit candles and a few strange objects. She looked worried as she picked at a few loose strands in the rug.

"What's going on here?" I asked her and her head snapped up at the sound of my voice.

"You shouldn't be here," she hissed urgently. "You have to go."

"I won't stay, but can you tell me what's going on? I'm worried you're in danger."

"We're all in danger, Yukari, grave danger. But I'll be fine, you needn't worry about me. Adel will always take care of me. Now go, before you make her angry."

"All right, I'll go…" I would have said more, but at that moment the door slammed open and I instinctively snapped back to my body.

"Who were you talking to?" I heard Adel demand as I lost awareness of the strange room where Adel had hidden Aysel from the rest of us with no explanation.

Out of nowhere, Yue appeared before me. "I've got a Lillem."

"You what?" I exclaimed.

"I have a Lillem in my Noh-space," Yue clarified. "I thought you might want to have a look at it, so we can work out a way to fix Sabien."

"Uh, yes, you're right," I replied, a little caught off-guard. "But how do you propose we examine it without it trying to kill us?"

"Well, it can try," Yue stated boldly. "All we have to do is make sure it doesn't succeed. I've already talked to Mikura about it and she can use her magic to hold it in place for us."

I grimaced at the familiar way Yue spoke of the Deathsquad General. I agreed reluctantly; I had no desire to work between a Lillem and a Deathsquad General, but the chance to study one of the creatures that plagued us was well worth the risk. "But I want to make sure there is one of the Knights there with us just in case, and it has to be in a secure location."

"Would the palace dungeons do?" Yue asked with a sly grin. "Because I've already arranged for us to use one of the cells. Only Ao Kouen or the Visionaries can operate the doors, so we can seal it in there if we need to."

I nodded – against my better judgment – and stood to accompany Yue, all the while thinking of the small, enclosed cells in the palace dungeons lined with Jade and sealed magically so not even someone with powers like I had could get out of them. I reluctantly gestured to Masaru to come with us. I didn't want to take him away from his happy reunion, but Dahlia needed her rest, and I had insisted a Knight be present, so it might as well be him.

"The door has to stay open if I'm in there, Yue," I stipulated, as we reached the dungeon level in the basement of the palace and met up with Mikura, who waited impatiently between a Deathsquad soldier and a Legionnaire.

"Whatever you say," Yue agreed. "Thanks for coming, Mikura."

"No problem, dissecting a Lillem sounds a lot more fun than more boring meetings," Mikura answered brightly and then unexpectedly leaned past Yue to speak to me. "No offense intended, your meeting was interesting. I was talking about the council. I'm sure Ao Kouen doesn't want to have to listen to them either."

"Careful Mikura, the wrong person might hear you and actually be offended," Ao Kouen himself entered the conversation, as he approached us from the other end of the hall, dressed in his usual Roughlander clothes, even though with his new position I'm sure he could have opted for something more elaborate.

"Nah, they're just stuffy old men anyways," Mikura replied amiably. "So, what do you need me to do?"

Ao Kouen opened a cell by placing his hand on the door where a handle should be, while Yue explained the plan to the rest of us. Against my better judgment, I stepped just inside the cell as directed. Masaru was at my side with his blue energy knives drawn and Mikura positioned herself in the open doorway. Yue, furthest in the cell, gave a count of three before she released the monster into our midst and then flashed backwards out of the room. The Lillem didn't have a chance to even twitch its talons before it was caught in Mikura's magic and lifted up, suspended immobile.

Close up, the Lillem were a different matter altogether. By its near full suit of armour and helmet, all white and decorated with the dove emblem, this Lillem had, less than five nights ago, been a Legionnaire. Now it was a disfigured monster with powerful bone limbs protruding from its shoulder blades and two more jutting out from its hip bones that appeared strong enough to stand on.

First peering past the armour with my power, I found the face of a man, though it was a distorted one. The lower jaw jutted out unnaturally, and was elongated to the point the helmet was near to bursting. Twisting my vision, I looked inside the body of the former Legionnaire and I didn't find organs and blood as I was expecting.

"Sand," I said aloud. "They're made up of nothing but sand and the remains of bones – but *something* has to be animating them."

"Celine…"

Yue's head snapped upwards at the sound and she flashed forward. In a heartbeat, Yue had torn the Legionnaire's helmet off, tossed it aside, and placed her hands to either side of the thing's disfigured face. Her eyes glowed faintly through her closed eyelids and the mark of Sapphiros upon her breast bathed the room in a sudden glimmer of cyan light. In the sudden added illumination, I lighted upon a seemingly insignificant detail I hadn't taken notice of before. The left hand of the Legionnaire wore no gauntlet, and upon his finger there sat a silver wedding band.

Yue came out of her trance as quickly as she had gone into it, but when she walked away from the Lillem and turned to face us there were tears on her cheeks. "Put him out of his misery. I'll get another Lillem."

Nodding my acquiescence, I raised my arms and formed a cyan arrow charged with power and let it loose, reducing the former Legionnaire to the particles of sand that made up a Lillem.

With the experiment finished for now, we left the cell and had Ao Kouen seal it up.

Sleep was a welcome respite and I didn't wake until the sun was once again high in the sky. Taking our breakfasts with us, Masaru and I took a walk about the palace grounds. We found ourselves looking over the city and the fields of Taiyou beyond from the battlements, when Masaru broke the amiable silence that had fallen over us. "So have ye got anything ye have to do today?"

"Not really, no," I said, somewhat surprised that nothing came to mind. "Why?"

"Oh, well I was wondering if ye've got anything to wear to the coronation today or if ye'd like to go to the market with me."

"They're crowning Ao Kouen today?"

"Aye," Masaru replied, "I thought everybody knew about it."

"I've been a little busy, Masaru."

"Aye, I've noticed," he replied wryly, "but what d'ye think, would ye like to go?"

"I think I'm expected to go to the coronation," I replied, thinking of the political implications of one of the Chosen of Sapphiros and ally of Taiyou not making an appearance at such an important event.

"I know that," Masaru replied with a hint of a smile. "I meant the market, and then to the ball afterwards, with me."

I looked down for the first time in days at what I was actually wearing and I was disgusted to discover the state of my Roughlander clothes. Even before the first horrid hour of darkness in the desert, I had been practically swimming in blood and sand who knew what else. Now all of that had crusted and dried into my clothing, which, in the fight for survival the last few days had been, I hadn't even thought to clean.

I was embarrassed and disgusted with myself all at once, and as I shamefully met Masaru's blue eyes once more, I felt tears begin to well up as I realized all I had recently lived through to get to this day.

"This is all I have," I told Masaru dejectedly. "I'm not fit for a coronation or a ball or anything."

He chuckled a little. "Don't worry about it. We'll find ye something pretty to wear and get ye cleaned up. It's been a rough couple of days."

"But I don't have any krevels," I protested.

"I offered to take ye to the market," Masaru informed me in a tone that told me he wouldn't take no for an answer, "and I'd like to buy you something nice."

The marketplace was booming. White dove symbols were everywhere, from being sewn onto people's clothing to waving about on green or white flags. Considering current events, it was remarkable to see the joyous expressions on so many of the faces.

"What about Narlhep?" I asked Masaru. "Have they all forgotten his sacrifice so soon?"

"No, it's quite the opposite, actually. From what I understand, most of the celebration is about Narlhep. Don't get me wrong, they're happy to have a new king to take his place and help them through these troubled times, but from what I've heard they're celebrating Narlhep's life.

"Today is not just Ao Kouen's coronation," Masaru continued, "but also the wedding day Narlhep and Kosetsu never got to have, and their joint funeral. The parade is the funeral procession and it's set to start just after the noon bounce. It's all according to Taiyoun custom."

"Oh," I replied, placated. "How is it you know all of this?"

He grinned. "Well, I haven't been nearly as busy as you have, so I've been passing the time by talking to people." As if to prove his point, a merchant raised his hand to wave to Masaru from across the crowd. "Would ye excuse me a minute?"

Left to my own devices, I wandered over to look at racks of dresses set up at a nearby stall, thinking I might as well get started on what I had come here for.

"Hello there, beautiful lady," the portly merchant greeted me pleasantly. "Come to look for something to help you look your best for the celebration?"

He needn't have bothered – I had already found what I wanted.

The dress was cut in what I associated with the Chinese style, with a high collar and a form-fitting silhouette. The fabric was a creamy white, richly embroidered with even whiter doves, trailing in flight from the base to the neckline. The entire dress was finished with gold thread along the edges, including a lengthy slit on either side.

There weren't too many colours I could pull off well with my uncommon shade of hair, but white certainly qualified. There was only one problem; the dress looked very well made and richly detailed, and there was no way Masaru would be able to afford it. As far as I understood it, most Roughlanders made do with what was on their backs. Even though Masaru had been in Taiyou for some time now, he was still a Roughlander, and it wasn't like he had a job outside of being my Knight – and I sure didn't pay him for his service.

"Oh, you like that one, do you?" the merchant inquired, just as I was working up the willpower to walk away.

"Yes, it's lovely," I responded truthfully, "but way out of my budget, thank you."

He waved his hand at me. "Nonsense, you can at least try it on. It won't cost you any krevels to do that. And it's a festival day, I just might be willing to cut you a deal."

I hesitated, but he was right; it wouldn't hurt to try it on and then when it didn't fit me, I could walk away without a single regret. Asking the merchant to give me a minute, I backed up a few paces until I could make Masaru out beyond the rack of dresses. I waved to him and he grinned at me through the passing people. I pointed at myself and then in towards the merchant stall I was standing in front of. Masaru nodded his understanding and gestured for me to go ahead, so I returned to the merchant and let him direct me to his curtained-off changing area and took the gorgeous white dress in my hands, careful not to let it brush up against my filthy Roughlander clothes.

Unfortunately it was perfect and regrettably, no other dress was going to compare. With a sigh, I peeled the silky material from my skin and forced myself to climb back into my Roughlander ensemble, stiff with dried blood and none of it mine.

Masaru was waiting for me when I emerged from the changing area, talking with the portly merchant. As I approached them, I saw a pouch full of krevels change hands and the merchant reached for a box from behind the counter.

"You wouldn't want to get it all wrinkled before the coronation," he suggested, holding out the open box to me.

"What?" I asked, startled.

"Fit you like a glove, didn't it?" the portly man commented. "As I was telling your man here, I have an eye for such things."

"Do ye like it, then?" Masaru asked, smiling.

"Yes, of course, it's beautiful, but–"

"It's yours," he pronounced. "Come on, we best be getting back so ye'll have enough time to do whatever it is girls do to make themselves even prettier."

After I had a proper bath and made myself presentable, I felt like a wholly different person in my new and flattering dress, with my blue curls washed and behaving for once, held in place by two dove-shaped clips. With such finery, I hardly recognized myself either as the rough and ready medic and honorary Roughlander, or the anti-social high school student I had been back on Earth. It struck me that perhaps the person I was today was closer to Yukari Namikoya, Chosen of Sapphiros, than anything else I had been before now.

Masaru was resplendent as well in a new and well-made white shirt, with billowed sleeves and doves embroidered over his right breast and onto his shoulder. There was a pocket sewn into his shirt over his left breast, in which he had stuffed a blue kerchief – the same colour as my hair.

We formed up on either side of the silver-coated Jade throne room doors, Masaru and I to the left with Ris, Jeth, Hotaru, Sir Rama, Kaji, and Mifa with the rest of the advisory council. To the right stood Lady Rhine with her staff of office, ready to await the arrival of the new king and a host of Taiyou's other allies. We had gathered just in time for the procession to reach us, and we all straightened as fanfare erupted in the palace hallways.

Ao Kouen headed toward the throne room at a stately pace and with a solemn expression. I was a little surprised to see that his clothing was still Roughlander in style, though evidently newer and of much improved quality over his last outfit. He kept his same embroidered scarf, however, and as usual it came up just a little past his chin. When he reached us, I was taken aback by the intense green of his eyes. It hadn't fully struck me until this moment that the new King of Taiyou was a Chosen like I was with the power to match. It was a daunting thought that Kaji, Hotaru, Yue, and I were theoretically equal in status – or thereabouts – with kings and emperors.

Ao Kouen entered the throne room and the rest of us followed. The large throne room with its triple thrones was decorated as I had never seen it before. The trees at the far end of the room were in full bloom, covered in white flowers. Hanging from the ceiling at intervals were complex, coloured pennants denoting each of the provinces. Lord Rama's province was denoted by a silver lion head emblem on a blue backing and I watched as Hotaru accompanied Rama over to stand beneath his banner. Behind them hung a moss green-coloured banner with a symbol I didn't recognize, but beneath it stood a handful of Croatins, including Pine.

Across from the Croatins, there was a banner showing a green field and blue sky with a perfectly symmetrical green mountain overlaid in the center of the two. Beneath that telling symbol of the Jade Mountain stood Mikura, decked out in a frilly red dress with black ribbons. She was flanked to either side by a few of her Deathsquad soldiers, including her captain and a Kumori I recognized as one of the healers from the temple.

On the right hand side hung another banner whose meaning abruptly became clear when Masaru tugged me over to it. The depicted outpost building with a fenced-in yard could represent none other than the Roughlander Sanctioned Outpost, and beneath it I found Hitachi, Yuge, and Razor, who greeted Masaru and I warmly.

The chatter in the room was abruptly silenced and everyone's attention was drawn to a newcomer. She was of medium height and build, wearing white silk robes in the Japanese style with an elaborate belt of green silk tied around her waist. Her hair was dyed a striking white and her skin was painted white to match, making her appear ghostlike. What stuck out as the strangest part of her appearance, however, were the green, flame-like markings painted all over her skin.

The doors shut with a shuddering finality as the mysterious figure walked down the middle of those assembled. Just before she passed out of my view entirely, my mind supplied me with the one detail about her appearance that allowed me to identify who this was. Upon her breast, just visible between the folds of her silk robe, there was a spot where the paint stopped and reality showed the cyan blue diamond-shaped mark of Sapphiros.

Yue walked with purpose to the dais to join Ao Kouen. "We are all about to witness a return to the days when the Chosen of Jedeite ruled over Taiyou by the grace of the gem god of these lands. I have been commanded by Jedeite to preside as Mediator over the coronation of Ao Kouen, Chosen of Jedeite and the next King of Taiyou. As such, I will uphold the laws as decreed by Jedeite and the traditions of Taiyou for the duration of this night. Any person who is found breaking of those laws will be mine to deal with."

Ao Kouen stepped forward and drew the royal sword of Jedeite. The Jade sword glinted with a green inner light as it was revealed, before Ao Kouen plunged the blade back into the central throne. "Yue can confirm for everyone that I am this moment without any powers." The low authority in his voice carried over the silent room. "I have asked Jedeite to seal them away for now. I never asked to be Chosen and I never asked to be king, but if I am going to be either, I ask you to accept me for myself.

"I know not all of you are contented with the prospect of a king chosen for you by Jedeite," Ao Kouen continued, just as softly, "so I offer to any of you who believe they would make a better king than I to try and prove themselves worthy. King Narlhep in his wisdom declared that only the true King of Taiyou could draw the sword of Jedeite from the throne. Let that person step forward."

The silence in the room held for a moment, then all of a sudden three men of different provinces rushed forward, only to pause halfway to the dais when they realized they were not alone in their presumption. Ao Kouen waited them out. Eventually one, a burly-looking lord of a province I wasn't familiar with, strode forward, "I accept your challenge."

"It is not I who challenges you, but Jedeite," Ao Kouen responded.

Snorting, the nobleman advanced on the throne, rubbing his hands together in preparation for the feat of strength before him. The room watched with bated breath for the moment the man's skin came in contact with the hilt, and when it did he burst into a pillar of green flame and the screams of his agony filled the throne room.

Everyone flinched when another sudden spurt of green flame erupted in the center of the room, incinerating the former provincial lord's banner.

"More lands for the Croatins to return home to," Ao Kouen commented tonelessly.

Alone out of those forced to watch what had just happened, the Croatins cheered. The provincial lord's compatriots, I noted, were mostly down on their knees begging for forgiveness. One of the two nobles that had stepped forward to challenge Ao Kouen stepped back in fear, and when no one stopped him he scuttled back under his province's banner. The other was a robust man and his round, full face filled with rage that left the man shaking.

"I don't have to want to be king myself to disagree with you and your methods, Roughlander!" the man said, spittle flying. "I don't need the Sword of Kings to face you. In the name of Lord Viron, you will pay for what you have done!"

With that, the man drew his sword and it was as I feared. The man got within striking distance from Ao Kouen, then froze, as if he was held immobile by some unseen hand.

"I'm sorry," Ao Kouen spoke softly. "I didn't choose this, but I will be king."

I finally managed to look away and hide my face in Masaru's shoulder as the nobleman began to scream. It went on for quite some time, and it was nearly worse for the prolonged nature of it.

Ao Kouen crossed the dais to the central throne and stood before the legendary sword of Jedeite, before addressing the room at large, "Are there any further objections?"

Silence was the only acceptable response and the only one he got. With a solemn nod, he turned to face the throne and placed both hands upon hilt of the sword that had incinerated a man only moments ago. Ao Kouen gave a single tug to the sword. Remarkably, it did not just come away into his hands; instead that same sickening sizzle was heard and Ao Kouen's body hunched over, wracked with pain.

"No!" Lady Rhine called out, breaking the silence. "Will you accept no one, then? Not even the one you chose for us?!"

Inexplicably, it was Yue that answered in a voice barely her own. "It is not I who must accept," she said, stepping forward. "You must accept he who would be your ruler."

Lady Rhine's mouth thinned to a line. "I accept Ao Kouen as King of Taiyou and request you spare him."

"I accept!" Mikura added.

"I accept," and "Long live King Ao Kouen," echoed about the room. I didn't join in, but being as I was not Taiyoun, perhaps my vote didn't matter, as abruptly Ao Kouen was able to stand, a little singed around the edges, but sword in hand.

There was no fanfare to end the unorthodox coronation ceremony and no cheers in celebration of the new king. The people of Taiyou had gotten a king of immense power who would live forever unless his life was ended in battle – whether they wanted him in that position or not.

"It is done," Yue pronounced and the throne room doors opened, letting us all escape – grateful we had been spared.

Jedeite's law was 'civilized savagery', indeed.

CH. 12 – A REASON TO CELEBRATE

Masaru and I filed into the palace ballroom with everyone else; after the enclosed Jade of the throne room, the bright, open, and airy space filled with people in high spirits was a very welcome change.

The room was immensely large and only the far half of it was filled with rows of tables, the rest having been left open for milling about and presumably dancing later. I could see there was a band set up to play on a dais behind where a throne-like chair had been placed for Ao Kouen. The bar and serving area was to the right of the main entrance, just before that entire wall gave way to the pillars designating the beginning of the large open balcony, which had been decorated with gauzy white curtains.

As we discovered when we got closer, the tables were reserved and a place had been designated for Masaru and I on the far left table in the first row. I was not entirely pleased to note that Mikura and her captain, Grinkin – I learned his name by reading his place card – were already seated at our table, but my displeasure evaporated when I saw who was seated at the next table over.

"Dahlia?!" I hurried to her side, surprised to see her up and about so soon.

"Yukari, there ye are." Dahlia looked tired and wan and Krox was beside her, protective, but she was smiling and appeared comfortable in her uncharacteristic silk Taiyoun robes. "Krox mentioned what ye did for me and I wanted to thank ye."

"There's no need to thank me." I gave the Roughlander Corporal a hug. "I'm just glad to see you're doing okay."

Our table was mostly full by the time we reached it. Seated next to Mikura was Kaji, dressed as if he, too, were a representative of the Ruby City. I wondered where he had gotten his gold-threaded black and red noble's outfit and the fancy looking rapier he wore at his belt, but I didn't have to wonder long. "I'm so glad you accepted my gift, Kaji!" Mikura was saying as Masaru drew back a chair for me. "It looks wonderful on you!"

Between Kaji and myself, Mifa greeted me with a shy smile as I took my seat and I returned it with interest. As Masaru took the seat to my left, I looked past him to see Ris, who was picking somewhat desolately at a thread on the napkin before her. It was all too obvious who the empty seat next to her was supposed to belong to. Unfortunately, we still were no closer to solving the Lillem problem or finding a way to fix Sabien so he would be safe to let out of Yue's Noh-space.

I tried to focus on the people before me instead of problems I could do nothing about. "Mifa, Kaji mentioned to me the other day you have a telescope at your house."

"Uh huh," Mifa said with a nod, "it was a little run down, but Goji repaired it for me and now it works great."

"I was wondering if I'd be able to come by and make use of it. I still need to plot the stars to check on a few things for my theory."

"Yes, of course." Mifa beamed. "That sounds great. You can come by tomorrow, that is…if you're not busy with something else."

"Tentatively tomorrow then," I answered with a smile, "if I'm not needed on the bridge."

The food in Taiyou was generally simple, but it had the benefit of being very fresh and plentiful when compared with the dried and pickled foods more commonly found out in the desert. Melons and other fruits were still staples on this world, more so than they were in Japan, and due to the near constant heat most Taiyoun dishes were eaten raw or cold. Either way, the food presented to us was some of the best I had yet tasted on this world, with the exception of the popular Taiyoun desserts called crumblecakes. We were well into the meal when there was a sudden commotion on the far side of the ballroom near the balcony where the pillars began.

I watched Ris suddenly launched herself into the air, the ballroom being just large enough to make flight possible. Yue stood on the balcony, still in her outlandish costume, and under the arm of Sabien, who looked somewhat worse for wear, but who also no longer had a Lillem talon protruding from his shoulder.

Before I realized it, I was in the air and flying over the tables to follow after Ris and land at Yue's side, as she and Sabien reached the edge of the dance floor. Sabien looked wilted, like he was having trouble holding himself together. It was a little unnerving to see the way he drooped and sagged, looking solid one minute and like he was going to melt into a puddle the next. I fit myself under Sabien's other arm and together, Yue and I helped him across the room and into the chair designated for him where he flopped gratefully.

"Thank you," Sabien managed, holding the arms of the chair for support.

Ris fussed over him as I did a cursory examination. Other than the effort it was taking Sabien to hold himself together and keep from turning to water, there was absolutely nothing wrong with him. I looked about for Yue to ask her how she had done it, but as usual I was a few steps behind my lightning-fast friend and she had already flashed away to somewhere else. Sabien's return was much celebrated, even if no one knew how it was possible he had managed to be rid of the Lillem affliction. When asked, Sabien himself claimed to know no more than Yue had done it.

Through the rest of the meal I found my thoughts kept drifting and it was difficult to pay attention to any one conversation. As the meal came to a close I stood and excused myself from the table. I crossed the room, passed the pillars, and wandered out onto the open balcony, wanting to get some air.

Leaning on the balcony's rail, I looked out over Taiyou, which was as beautiful as ever. Rama had informed us that the defense of the bridge was being taken care of for the evening, so we could enjoy the celebration. Even still, despite its beauty the setting sun gave me a deep sense of unease as I watched light fade ever so slowly from the sky.

But the sun always rose again, didn't it? For every sunset there was a matching sunrise, and even though the nights of this world were getting progressively longer and longer – tonight would bring us to six hours and six minutes – the sun always came back up again. And if I was right in what I had discovered, it would continue to do so.

I found myself thinking of Narlhep. Though I had only known him briefly, he had been my friend, one of the first I had made on this world, and I knew all he would have wanted was to know Taiyou would be in capable hands. Today, Ao Kouen had proven he could be strong enough to uphold the ideals of civilized savagery as Jedeite required of him and I just hoped for Narlhep's sake, and that of the people of Taiyou, his strength would be enough to see this country through the trials it faced. Ao Kouen's methods and the display that had occurred today in the throne room were not something I could agree with, but I thought maybe Narlhep, with the coldness he had learned during the three days he had spent locked up in the Temple of Jade, would have understood their necessity.

Goodbye, my friend, I thought out to the setting sun. *You will be missed, but we'll do our best to protect the people you had to leave behind.*

I felt the sadness that had been tugging at me lift somewhat. Narlhep had suffered for Taiyou, holding on to await the coming of Ao Kouen, even though all his hopes for the future had already been taken from him. My friend was probably better off wherever he was now, with his beloved Kosetsu, instead of being here and having to fight every day to try to ensure Taiyou's continued survival.

The sun always rises again... I think I was coming to understand what the Roughlanders meant when they talked about 'bouncing like the sun'. Roughlanders had so many sayings, but not being from this world, that one had been the hardest for me to grasp. I supposed it meant even though dark times come, the living have to live in the light. Part of that living is not dwelling on the sadness that is a natural part of life, but moving on like the sun does after it touches the horizon. I mentally reminded myself I would have to thank Masaru for that piece of advice.

I felt a tap on the shoulder and whirled about, thinking perhaps Masaru had come to find me.

"Hey, how's it goin?" Jeth asked, putting an arm around me.

"What are you doing, Jeth?" I asked him, smiling.

"Nuthin'," Jeth answered slyly, turning me about slowly until I could see Masaru headed our way from between the pillars. "Just tryin' to see if I can make the boy jealous."

I elbowed Jeth in the ribs, even though with his thick skin he probably couldn't even feel it, but he let me go and walked away with a slight chuckle.

"What was that about?" Masaru asked when he reached me.

"Nothing." I shook my head. "Just Jeth being Jeth."

"Uh..." Masaru looked uncomfortable for a moment as I heard the beginning notes of the musicians striking up in the background. "I was coming out here to ask ye…if ye'd like to dance with me?"

I smiled, remembering a time when I would have been too shy to accept. "I would love to," I answered took hold of the hand he held out to me.

With an answering smile of his own, Masaru led me back into the ballroom and onto the dance floor, which was rapidly filling up with other couples as the musicians began to play in earnest. Much to our amusement, Masaru and I discovered rather quickly neither of us really knew what we were doing. Masaru quickly solved the issue, however, by taking me into his arms and holding me close, swaying in time with the music.

The ballroom around us seemed to fall away and it was as if there were only the two of us in the whole world. Masaru held me tenderly as if I was precious to him, and for the duration I lost myself in the wonder of being in his arms. The song had come to an end and another one already begun before I realized we had long since stopped the pretense of actually dancing and had been just holding onto one another.

"Can I cut in?" Razor interjected.

Flushing slightly, I stepped back to put some space between Masaru and I when I realized Masaru hadn't answered Razor's request because he was waiting for me to do so.

"Would you mind?" I asked Masaru, not knowing how Roughlanders felt about such things.

"Not at all," Masaru responded, stepping back.

As Masaru walked away and I was left facing Razor, I abruptly realized I may have made a mistake. "I'll warn you Razor," I told him, "I don't exactly know how to dance."

"You seemed to be doing quite fine with Masaru," Razor said with a sly wink."Don't worry," he continued, "I'll lead. All you have to do is try to keep up with me."

I wondered briefly what he meant by that as Razor took hold of my hand in his and placed his other arm about my waist, but I didn't have enough time to back out of the arrangement before the music picked up suddenly and we were off, practically racing across the dance floor.

Razor flitted the two of us about in a quick-footed manner to the increased tempo of the music and it was all I could do to keep myself from tripping over my own two feet. Being whirled about as I was, I felt as if I was on a carnival ride back in Japan, but the only thing holding me in place was Razor and I wasn't sure exactly how far I trusted his grip. But then I caught sight of his roguish grin, and I realized the terror he must be seeing on my own expression and I began to laugh, unable to help myself. It had all been on purpose, I was sure of it – I wouldn't have put it past Razor to have requested this song with this exact scenario in mind.

My sudden fit of laughter made keeping up with Razor that much easier because I had stopped worrying about where my feet were going to fall and just given in to his nonsense. I was struggling to catch my breath from exertion and laughter when the song came to an end and he finally let me go.

"Razor, wait." I took a moment to compose myself. "I wanted to tell you how grateful I am. I just wanted you to know how important you are to me."

"I understand," Razor said with a smile, but I noted the hint of sadness and it was that more than anything that told me Razor understood what I wasn't saying. I knew he had feelings for me, but regardless, I had chosen Masaru and that wasn't going to change.

With impeccable timing, Masaru returned then, punching Razor amicably on the shoulder. "Are ye done tiring her out yet?"

Razor grinned. "Nah, she's a Chosen, I'm sure she could run circles around you and me both."

In actuality, I was feeling a little winded, but I was having fun and so I stayed to dance for a while longer with Masaru. The subsequent dances were a little less intense than the first, so I was able to look around. I watched Rama dance with Hotaru and then a very red-faced Mifa. Jeth and Yue whirled about the dance floor much like Razor and I had done, except in their case the decision and energy to do so was more or less mutual. Halfway through, Yue switched off to pull a reluctant Pine onto the dance floor, while Jeth accosted a startled Lady Rhine, literally sweeping the stately woman off of her feet.

As the next song came to an end, Masaru went to get us something to drink, and I made my way back over to our table. I caught sight of Kaji off to one side of the dance floor swaying from side to side with Lady Mikura balanced on his feet to allow her enough height to actually dance with him. I wondered at Kaji's sudden change of heart. He had, if anything, been even more opposed to Mikura's presence in Taiyou than I was – had something happened for him to change his opinion of her? Nevertheless, there she was gripping tightly to Kaji's hands to keep herself upright and giggling playfully. It was endearing – if one could forget about exactly who Mikura was.

Kaji noticed the newcomer before I did. She was not tall, but she carried herself with a presence about her that indicated a certain nobility. Her dress was a deep, blood-red colour and form-fitting with a high neck. Stunningly, her hair was a matching red colour, framing the perfect oval of her face and drawing attention to the unlikely red of her irises.

"I hope ye like melon juice," Masaru interrupted, blocking my view as he leaned past me to place my drink on the table. "They had too many things for me to choose from."

"Mhmm…" I mumbled.

"What're ye looking at?" Masaru asked, trying to follow my gaze.

"She's quite stunning, isn't she?" Masaru commented. "Who is she? I don't think I've ever seen her before."

The mysterious woman had reached where Kaji and Mikura had been, and now she was leading Kaji out onto the dance floor. I pursed my lips together, wondering why this woman seemed familiar. "I don't know who she is, but she seems to know Kaji."

"Aye," Masaru replied, seemingly as engrossed as I was watching the way Kaji and this woman moved in response to one another. It was uncanny, the near perfect grace and elegance.

They whirled about the dance floor, putting the other dancers to shame, but not even noticing due to their preoccupation with one another. I felt my face flush in response, remembering how I had acted with Masaru, but it only deepened the mystery of who this woman was. The only person I knew whom Kaji would act this way about was his girlfriend from Earth, Shuzhue. But she couldn't possibly be…

I did a double-take as the song they were dancing to came to a close. Long, flowing red hair over round features and a diminutive build – could it be her? She looked much older, very much a woman, and different than I remembered her, but I suppose I had seen enough that this, too, was possible.

Kaji stood shocked to stillness as the woman who was possibly the person he had been hoping to find since we had arrived here turned away from him to make her exit, as swift and without warning as her entrance had been. I was on my feet before I knew it and had even taken a few steps forward before I realized I had lost sight of her through the lively crowd of dancers. The music picked up in tempo once more and the path she had taken quickly closed up behind her.

"Come on," Masaru said, striding past me.

I hurried to fall in step with him and the two of us rounded on Kaji as quickly as possible, but it was evident as soon as we reached him that for the moment, at least, he was unresponsive.

"Let's get him out of here," I suggested and we half-carried his unresisting form out of the ballroom.

We led Kaji to the room where we'd been staying and settled him in a chair. Taking hold of Kaji's hand on the table, I tried to force him to see me by locking my gaze onto his.

"Kaji, it was her, wasn't it?" I pressed him. "Did she say anything to you? Give any indication of what happened to her, or what's going on now?"

"Who?" Masaru asked. "What's going on?"

"Shuzhue," I responded.

"Ye mean someone from back on yer world?" Masaru questioned.

"I'll kill him for this," Kaji spoke in a low, dangerous voice, gripping my hand tightly in his.

"Kill who?" Masaru asked, still struggling to keep up.

I recalled the few days before we had left Earth, around the time of Shuzhue's mysterious disappearance. Inexplicably, I had seen the Talons of the Vile Emperor skulking around the Shinjuku district of Tokyo before I even knew who or what they were, or how dangerous they could be.

"The Vile Emperor," I clarified for Masaru, my tone unintentionally almost as dark as Kaji's.

The tension in the room was thick enough to be tangible, but it shattered completely when a green fire erupted brighter than anything I'd ever seen outside the window. Kaji screamed as he fell from his chair and tried uselessly to cover his eyes with his hands; his magic vision burned with the intensity of the green fire. Unable to do anything to help him, Masaru and I ran to the balcony to see what was happening.

The sky was filled with Jedeite's green fire, like a thick wall of flames encompassing the whole city, or maybe even the whole country. We had gotten maybe halfway to the threshold of the balcony when I saw what the green fire was trying to defend us from. There were massive mushroom-shaped clouds, tinged green from the light of Jedeite's fire, but unmistakable for what they were. There was radiation and radioactive materials on this world – I had encountered them before – so I knew that what I was seeing before me was possible. The explosions were at a great distance judging from their size, but it wouldn't take long for the radiation to reach us.

We had fought so hard, but Taiyou was finished by some unforeseen cause and our lives were forfeit. I caught sight of Masaru, his form illuminated by the green light and my heart leapt to my throat as I realized this was all we were ever going to have.

I was in his arms before I even realized I had moved.

IloveyouIloveyouIloveyouIloveyouIloveyou...

I held Masaru tightly, my eyes shut to the awful green light that spelled our doom and my ears closed to the awful sounds of Kaji's screaming.

I love you too, Yukari.

I thought perhaps I had heard something before all went silent. I took a single breath and then another, and when nothing seemed to happen, I opened my eyes slowly.

Masaru's hand was under my chin, lifting my face gently so I was looking into his eyes. The green glow was still present in the room, but it was less intense and I could no longer hear any sounds other than the softness of Masaru's breathing. I blinked a few times in confusion – surely we should have felt some of the effects of the radiation by now – from all I had heard, death was nearly instantaneous to everyone within sight of a nuclear explosion.

"I said I love ye, Yukari."

Masaru didn't wait for my startled response, he simply leaned in and kissed me with the passion to prove his statement and I, for a wonder, let go of my worries and kissed him back. Against all odds, we were still alive and for now that was enough.

"What made ye so scared?" Masaru asked when we both needed to catch our breath.

I turned my head to look out past him to the green fire and I could see no hint of smoke or destruction anywhere. I could even hear the faint sounds of the celebration still going on in the ballroom – it was as if the mushroom clouds I had seen had never even happened.

"It was nothing," I answered, still a little shaken. "I guess it's a good thing I'm wrong sometimes."

Masaru smiled and cupped my face in his hand. "I love you, Yukari," he repeated, looking into my eyes to ensure I heard him this time.

"I love you too, Masaru," I replied with a genuine smile.

It felt strange, but it was such a relief to say the words I had been holding in for a long time and knowing Masaru wanted to hear them. Somehow, remarkably, he loved me, and all it had taken was a little courage to discover it.

On the floor by the table, Kaji stirred and moaned. Masaru and I broke apart, startled.

"I can't see anything," Kaji said, holding the side of the table for support.

Kaji's eyes were glowing an intense cyan in the most unnatural way. Then he created a clone standing before himself and the Kaji before me unexpectedly splashed to water.

"Ah, much better," he said.

"If you're feeling better, perhaps you should head back downstairs to make sure everyone else is okay," I suggested. "Maybe see if you can find out what happened to make Ao Kouen light the sky on fire."

Kaji nodded, squinting past me at the glowing green sky, which must have appeared all the brighter to him due to his power. "You're right," he answered, "I'll go find out."

Once Kaji had left, I turned back somewhat shyly toward Masaru.

"Shouldn't we?" Masaru gestured after Kaji.

He was right, of course, but I was a little tired of always doing what was expected of me. I walked to the door, intent on closing it – the world could take care of itself for an evening – when a dark shadow stepped in the doorframe.

"What do you want, Fuun?" I questioned, not taking my eyes off of him.

"My gift to you," Fuun stated emotionlessly, raising his clawed, metal hand with a deliberate motion.

Shadow blacker than the night itself gathered around Fuun's outstretched hand and Masaru let out a sudden cry from behind me. I whirled about to see Masaru's feet raised a few inches from the ground and his back arched painfully. The same blackness that enveloped Fuun's clawed hand seemed to spew from his open mouth, like Fuun was drawing it out of him. It was done within moments, and the blackness dissipated in the night air. Masaru's feet lowered to the ground and his head slumped against his shoulders as he fell.

I was across the room in time to catch him before he could crumple to the floor. I instinctively felt for a pulse, which beat just as strongly as before, but Masaru's skin felt clammy. Holding him tightly, I snapped my head up to face Fuun. "It was you, wasn't it?"

"It was I who took him from you," Fuun admitted, not flinching, "but it was not I who poisoned him."

"Who, then?"

"Ku-Roi is the Chosen of Machalite," Fuun stated. "Only a Chosen is capable of making a Knight. There was a darkness in him. Ku-Roi saw it and wanted it for her own. I have made him free of the curse of becoming a Knight of Machalite. That is my gift to you."

My anger drained out of me; as was becoming the way of things, I had completely misunderstood what was happening and what it meant. "Why?" I asked, wondering why he cared at all.

"Ku-Roi is gone," Fuun responded, not answering the question I had actually asked him. "It is that fact alone which makes what I did possible. Cursed is the life of the twice-Knighted."

"You're a Knight," I ventured, piecing it all together, "of Machalite…and who else, then?"

"…Sapphiros," Fuun responded after a moment's hesitation.

"Where is she, Fuun?" I demanded. "Where did Ku-Roi go?"

Fuun's eyes were that curious blend of black and blue I had noticed before. "Earth," he replied simply, and I felt the wind knocked out of me as he flashed off down the hall – as fast, if not faster than even Yue could have managed – causing a wind to slam the door shut behind him.

Left alone with Masaru's unconscious form, I finally fell prey to the whirlwind of emotions I had just experienced, now that no one was around to see me crumble under the weight of it all. I don't know how long it took me to cry myself out, but in that time Masaru did not wake. When I had composed myself, I stood and brought my wings out to give me strength enough to carry him across the room and to the bed. He woke as soon as I had gotten him settled and laid myself down beside him.

"How did I get over here?" Masaru asked, sitting up abruptly.

I sat up more slowly, feeling tired. "Are you feeling all right?"

"I feel fine, Yukari," he insisted, holding my eyes with his own, "but what happened?"

"It was Fuun – he saved your life." I repeated what I could remember of Fuun's cryptic words and the awful revelation the woman who could wreak such destruction on a whim if she chose had now apparently gone to Earth, where they could in no way be prepared for her coming any more than we had been at the Temple of Jade. It made me angry just to think of it; that murderous woman had tried to make Masaru her Knight, when I had already claimed him as my own.

Masaru must have caught the rage in my expression. "Yukari, I am no one's Knight but yer own…and maybe a little bit Hotaru's."

I smiled a bit at Masaru's attempt at humour. I had been upset at the time, but with Hotaru it was different – she had been my best friend my entire life and so sharing with her wasn't nearly so difficult. Also, thankfully, Hotaru had been the first to understand my feelings toward Masaru and had done me the kindness of acknowledging that.

"There ye go, that's a little better, isn't it?"

I nodded and then realized where we were and remembered Masaru's reluctance to share the bed with me under normal circumstances. The pile of blankets and the pillow he had relocated to the bedside gave evidence to the fact each 'night' he slept on the floor, usually after I had already collapsed into insensibility.

"I suppose I'll let you rest," I said quickly, feeling suddenly self-conscious, and I turned to roll away from him to get off the bed when he reached out a hand to stop me.

"I think I may be feeling a little weak after all," Masaru pronounced with an exaggerated vulnerability. "I don't think I'm really up to going anywhere, if ye know what I mean."

"Well as your medic I wouldn't want you to experience another fainting spell," I replied, giving in easily.

"Fainting spell?!" Masaru protested. "I didn't faint, it was a manly collapse!"

I laughed suddenly, the tension of the evening evaporating with Masaru's lively good humour. Masaru was laughing along with me when his expression abruptly turned serious and he caught my arms in his hands, pinning me to the bed. "I love you," he told me with the utmost seriousness. "I've never felt so strongly about anything in my life, Yukari, and I want ye to know no matter what happens that's not going to change."

It had been a day filled with ups and downs, but Masaru abruptly brought my mind back to all of the better moments this evening had offered: the feast, the dancing, the relief of knowing we had both survived another horrific night, and the incredible fact he loved me.

"I love you, Masaru," I tried out the words deliberately, now that I was completely conscious of saying them, and found although I had waited so long to first say them aloud, it was easy now because all along they had been true. "I've been trying to tell you for some time."

His serious expression never changed as he leaned down to kiss me again and this time was still filled with the same passion, but it was intentional, not born out of the sudden fear we would never get another chance. This time we were alone and with nothing to interrupt us, it was some time before either of us came up for air.

CH. 13 – LET US IN

On Earth, the Sapphire Splitter began to glow with cyan light. Raved removed his dark glasses to reveal his cyan eyes as they reflected the light from the twirling diamond-shaped piece of Sapphire in the center of the Splitter pad.

"The Splitter is active. We have made contact," Raved reported.

"Understood, Raved," Corporal Zukatoro replied, noting the corresponding colour in the Splitter was red. "Form up – this is your last chance to back out. From this point onwards, there is no turning back."

Stony silence greeted this pronouncement as Corporal Zukatoro had largely expected, but because of the personal nature of the mission and its extremely hazardous nature, he felt for the first time in his career he needed to ask. Also, the Corporal recognized the fact not all the members of his assembled squad were military personnel. The squad formed up on the Splitter pad with all of their equipment and prepared for the journey to the other world, not one of them completely at ease with the thought of what might await them on the other side.

Raved initiated the sequence that would send the team back to his home world when something about the display before him changed. The panel before him and the corresponding crystal set into the topmost point of the Splitter inexplicably changed from a pulsing red to a deep and foreboding black.

Raved didn't know where the Machalite Splitter was hidden, but one thing was certain – every person and piece of equipment that had been standing atop the Splitter platform a moment ago had been sent to the Machalite Splitter and there was no way to get them back until the Splitter could recharge. Raved slumped, his shoulders sagging, when he heard something that made him lift his head. There, on the platform, stood a mysterious woman with lengthy blue hair, mostly hidden like her face by the cowl of her hooded cloak.

The deadly Ku-Roi, Chosen of Machalite, looked up, Raved's cyan blue eyes meeting her hollow black ones, and from that point it is anyone's guess how long Raved could have possibly survived after that. Of the thirteen members of the top secret Japanese military expedition that made the crossing through the activated Splitters to the other world, only eleven would survive the horrors of the Temple of Machalite where they landed, and one more would die needlessly when Fuun dropped them off without warning or explanation into what they believed was hostile territory...

Under the eerie glow of Ao Kouen's protective dome of green fire, the coronation ball was finally winding down. Hotaru stood alone on the balcony, looking out at the flames dancing in the sky. Something clattered to the ground at her feet, startling her out of her thoughts. Confused, she bent down to scoop up two identical metal chains and straightened once more, taking a few steps closer to one of the torches affixed to a pillar on the balcony in order to examine what she had found. They were identification tags, much like the ones issued by the Japanese military. In fact, the two she held in her hands were identical in style to the ones she knew both her parents had. Though the names on the two tags were written in Japanese, she didn't recognize either of them, and as she stood there puzzling over the how and why of what she held, the atmosphere around her filled with sudden tension.

"Hold your fire!" a familiar voice barked as simultaneously there was the impossible but undeniable sound of a gunshot being fired from the other end of the balcony.

Gripping tightly to the mysterious identification tags, Hotaru surged forward. The first thing she noticed was Krox, as the massive Croatin was hard to miss under normal circumstances and even more so when he was enraged as he was now. Beside him the source of his distress was evident as Corporal Dahlia, looking more delicate than usual in her silk Taiyoun robes, was gripping tightly to her right shoulder to try to slow the seepage of blood, which had already stained the white sleeve of her robe a deep crimson.

Hotaru's breath left her in a whoosh as she took in the cluster of people gathered defensively on the far end of the balcony with their weapons drawn. Their uniforms were the navy blue standard issue of the Japanese military. Even more surprising. Hotaru knew most of them.

Kaji's father, Corporal Zukatoro, had been the familiar voice to bark the order not to fire, but arrayed before him were both her mother and her father, and also the parents of the other Chosen of Sapphiros. Corporal Zukatoro's wife was also present, but kept to the back with two other soldiers Hotaru did not recognize. There was a deafening thud as Krox impacted with the ground in the centre of the dance floor and carried forward his momentum for another leap which, judging by the distance he had crossed in his first lengthy bound, would bring him to the gathered crowd of humans. Hotaru didn't know who would emerge the victor between the angry Croatin and the well-trained and disciplined soldiers, but she did know the situation had to be diffused before anyone else could get seriously hurt.

She didn't fully realize she was running forward until she heard her own mother cry out, "Hotaru!"

In a race against the Croatin's powerful legs, Hotaru slid in between Krox and her parents and used her power to throw up a shield wall of blue energy from one end of the balcony to the other. "Everyone stop! There's no need to fight, we're all on the same side here!"

Krox growled in response, but for just a moment he hesitated and Hotaru was certain she had gotten through to him, when all of a sudden she was grabbed from behind and forced to the ground.

Someone – she couldn't see who – pulled her arms painfully behind her back and tied them together with a plastic zip-tie.

In that moment, Hotaru had lost what brief grasp of control she'd had and Krox leapt impossibly high over the wall she had constructed to land amongst the surprised humans. Krox placed one hand on a soldier's shoulder and grasped the top of the man's head with the other. From her uncompromising position on the floor, Hotaru was spared the gruesome sight of the Head-taker doing what he was named for, but the sickening sounds painted a clear enough picture.

The soldier to the other side of Kaji's mother fired a shot and Hotaru had little doubt the entire scene was about to become a bloodbath, when armoured Sir Sabien, nobly-dressed Sir Rama, the mysterious cloaked Pine, and a bored looking-Jeth arrived and took up positions on the other side of the shimmering cyan shield.

"That's enough, Krox," Sabien said.

Krox, however, was not a Knight of Sapphiros. With seemingly little effort, Krox picked up the man who had shot at him and tossed him bodily over the balcony rail. The man's screams could be heard growing fainter as he fell two stories, before they were abruptly cut off with a deafening finality.

"Drop the shield, Hotaru," Sabien commanded tonelessly.

Hotaru obeyed and the cyan shield winked out of existence. Simultaneously, the Knights surged forward and they had everyone, including a glowering Krox, subdued in short order, which allowed Hotaru to notice the small audience of onlookers.

At the forefront of the crowd stood Yue in her theatrical make-up. At her feet lay the slightly quivering form of the soldier, who had the exceptional luck of surviving due to Yue's timely arrival. To Yue's left stood Ao Kouen, his lips pursed with displeasure.

"You have broken the peace of Taiyou this night," Yue declared.

"Yue?" her father interjected. "Is that you?"

"Any violent acts committed in Taiyou until the rise of the sun are considered to be committed against the King himself, and therefore are punishable by the Mediator," she continued in the same fashion.

"Yue, can you let me out of this?" Hotaru complained. "I didn't do anything wrong. I was trying to stop everyone from fighting."

"Release her," Yue commanded. "Knights of Sapphiros, you are pardoned for your assistance in this matter. As for the rest of you, your weapons and equipment are confiscated." At her words, Yue flashed between them, removing every gun or piece of military equipment she could spot and depositing them into a pile just beyond them all. Once she had everything all together, she caused the pile to disappear into her Noh-space where only she would have access to it. "And you will spend a full cycle in the palace dungeons to be released at dawn after tomorrow's darkness."

I spent the rest of the night and well into the next morning sleeping in Masaru's arms. My beautiful new dress lay draped across the bedside chair along with Masaru's discarded clothing and beneath the light covers I wore nothing but Masaru's usual white shirt, and he wore even less than that.

But we hadn't done anything I would regret later, unless of course one counted my regret we hadn't done more than we had. Masaru hadn't seemed to mind my asking him to wait; in fact he had been extremely supportive, but that fact almost made matters worse. I didn't want him to feel I was letting him down. Of course, Masaru being as important to me as he was, I wanted our first time together to be as special an occasion as possible. The only problem was I didn't know if we were ever going to have a night more special than the one that had just passed.

Unfortunately, I wasn't able to fully reign in my unruly emotions before Masaru woke and took notice of the tears streaming down my face. I tried to hide the evidence of my momentary weakness, but it was already too late and he took me into his arms.

"Oh Yukari, I'm sorry if I was too forward with ye last night," Masaru apologized, genuinely concerned.

"No, it's not that," I assured him, pushing away from him a moment to try and collect myself. "It's just…"

"Ye've never been with anyone before, is that it?"

"Well, no, I haven't," I answered honestly. "You're the first person I've ever felt this way about."

"How old are ye, anyways, Yukari?" Masaru interjected suddenly.

I was startled by the unexpected question, and looking back at him with an appraising eye, I began to realize perhaps Masaru wasn't as close to my own age as I had originally thought.

"Well, do you even count years here in the same way we do?" I narrowed my eyes. "How old are you?"

"Well, it's generally a difficult question for Roughlanders," Masaru answered in an off-hand manner, adjusting his position so he could lean back against the headboard. "Most of us don't know when we were born, especially if we're found out in the Sand Lakes like I was. But I worked it out once, so I've got a fairly good idea." He took a moment to count on his fingers, considering the question, while my mood improved watching him try to puzzle out his own age. "Well if Razor was seven then, I would've been about five and Tira three. That would make Razor…twenty-two now, which puts me around twenty."

"How long are your yearly cycles?" I asked, fearing I already knew the answer.

"About seven hundred and thirty one bounces, give or take a couple," Masaru answered promptly.

I quickly did the mental math. "So it's the same as ours then," I informed him, "three hundred and sixty-five days with an extra one every four years to equal it out."

"That's impressive," Masaru commented.

"No, not really, that was an easy question."

"So how old are ye, then?" He prompted.

I hesitated, avoiding his gaze. I pursed my lips, knowing I couldn't lie to him, but not seeing how I could get out of answering his legitimate question either.

"Is it that much of a difference?" He asked. I nodded, unwilling to say anything further. "Oh," he commented, the truth dawning on him. "I guess I always thought ye were older because of how smart and how mature ye are. Not to mention how well ye've handled yerself since coming here. I guess I never thought much about it, but ye've had to come really far to overcome everything that's been thrown at ye, haven't ye?"

I met Masaru's eyes, stricken, thinking for sure he wouldn't want anything more to do with me now, mature and intelligent or not. "We're fifteen," I told him, admitting it at last. "All four of us are only fifteen."

To my surprise, Masaru let out a sigh of relief, "Oh, well that's not so bad, then. As I said, I might have been off a little in my own calculations. For the sake of compromise, I'm probably more like nineteen, anyways."

"That's still four years difference," I pointed out, failing to see why it suddenly wasn't an issue any longer.

"Aye, well, Razor and Tira were about four years apart," Masaru explained. "It may be different on yer world, but among the Roughlanders that's not so uncommon."

He stood, wrapping the blanket around himself for cover, and offered me his hand. I took it, contemplating what he had said and I realized he was likely right; something as arbitrary as age would hardly make much difference to the Roughlanders, who lived such unpredictable lives and never knew when those lives would suddenly be cut short. I stood as well and relied upon the fact Masaru's shirt was nearly long enough to be a dress on me as we traipsed out into the common area, grateful to find the palace staff had, as usual, left a tray of fruit and baked goods on the centre table.

"I could get used to this," Masaru commented, looking at me, and I gathered it wasn't just the readily accessible food he was referring to.

I blushed and then my blush immediately deepened to embarrassment as all of a sudden we were no longer alone. The door never opened and neither did any of the curtains move, but suddenly and without explanation Rama was standing between us and the door. I had the urge to hide, but there was nothing I could do to make this scene look like anything other than what it was.

"Oh," Rama spoke, evidently just as startled himself, "well, that will teach me to knock before entering a room, won't it? Uh…"

"What is it?" I forced myself to speak.

"Yes, right…" Rama continued. "I…uh…was requested to inform you that some visitors have arrived for you. I believe everyone was quite shocked, but your parents arrived late last night and are currently being held in the palace dungeons. They're not allowed visitors for the time being, but they will be released at the next rise of the sun according to the Mediator. So I'll leave you to it then…" and his unusual power was revealed as he walked deliberately through the wall.

The wall itself seemed to be displaced for a moment by his passage through it before returning to its customary solidity. I stared after Rama with my mouth open, unable to form the words to express my disbelief, though truthfully his news was even more shocking. *My parents…here?*

"Yer parents?" Masaru spoke my thoughts aloud. "Here? But how is that even possible?"

I stared at him, my eyes wide. "I don't know…I suppose they must have used the Splitters…it's the only way I know of."

"That's amazing news, Yukari," Masaru stated, sounding kind of awed. "I'm sure once ye get over the shock of it, ye'll be real happy to see them."

I wasn't really, but I didn't dare tell Masaru that, since I knew he would have given almost anything to see his family again. I had somewhat recently begun to come to terms with the fact I was never returning to Earth and in my heart I had started to let go of the people and things I had loved there. Foremost of such, and the hardest to distance myself from, had been my father, whom I had always wanted to please more than anyone else. My parents being here – as impossible as it seemed – only meant now they were in as much danger as anyone else on this world, and perhaps more so as it was a place they did not understand.

We had been told our parents had lived here eight hundred years ago and, in fact, this was the planet we had been born on. However, I was certain Sabien could tell me the world as it was now was a far cry from how it had been then, and the dangers were vastly different – possibly even much more deadly. Unlike us, our parents weren't some mystical chosen ones who had been granted unusual powers just for coming here, and so they didn't have the same chance as we did of surviving and overcoming the obstacles placed before them. There was nothing else for it; I would have to find a way to send them home. In the meantime, I would have to have to prepare Masaru, for if they got wind of our budding relationship, which they would, I'm sure both my mother and father would have something to say about it – especially considering my recent discovery about our respective ages.

"I think I should warn you about my parents, Masaru. My father is a defense lawyer for the Japanese military." Masaru regarded me blankly at this pronouncement. "He's like a professional arguer."

"Oh. That doesn't sound very pleasant."

"No," I agreed, "and I'm sure he's going to have a lot of questions for you…seeing as we're…well, you know…"

"Seeing as we're a match," he said, using the Roughlander term.

"Right. Well, my father's always been rather strict," I explained, "but unfortunately, my mother's worse."

"Is she a professional arguer too, then?"

"No, but she can be rather…high-strung?" Looking at Masaru through slanted eyes and taking in the many healed scars from past injuries and knowing the only things he owned were behind him draped over a chair, I knew there was no way my mother would approve.

"I think I get it," Masaru informed me, "but hopefully when they get out they'll just be happy to see ye and it won't matter so much that I'm around ye."

I frowned. "That will depend, of course, on why they're here. I can't believe they would come all this way just to visit. Obviously the fact they're here means they somehow knew where we had gone when we disappeared from Earth. That worries me a little."

"They're yer parents," Masaru pointed out needlessly. "I'm sure everything will work itself out just fine."

Having lost his own parents so young, I got the impression Masaru had a much idealized concept of what having family around was like. I wasn't so sure I agreed with his optimism, but I let the subject drop, willing to let him form his own opinions of what my family life was like, since as impossible as it may have seemed beforehand, he was now going to get the chance to do so.

I spent the rest of the day with Masaru before following Mifa's directions to her house for our pre-arranged night of stargazing. Mifa's house was a quaint and homey two-storey white stone building decorated sporadically with free-growing vines. It was a fair distance from the palace, beyond the marketplace, but with my wings the distance was negligible. I was dressed once more in my sturdy Roughlander clothes, which had been thoroughly cleaned.

"Hi! I'm Felice. You must be Yukari – the one Mifa just won't shut up about."

Felice, whom I gathered was the older sister Mifa had mentioned a time or two, was average height with a round face and a dimpled smile, and I could have sworn I had seen her somewhere before. Her Taiyoun robes were blue and she wore an apron tied over them.

"Sorry if I got any flour on you," she apologized, taking in my outlandish appearance with an appraising eye. "I was just helping Mifa bake some crumblecakes…well, she doesn't really need my help – she's a much better baker than I'll ever be – but it doesn't hurt me to try and learn from the best!"

The sudden mention of the Taiyoun dessert reminded me of where I had met Felice before. When Yue and I had first arrived in Taiyou, we had joined a gaggle of girls at a café near the palace to try and get information about the city and current events. Felice had been among those girls. As Felice led me through the sitting room and into the kitchen, Mifa was happy to see me, but she was also apparently at a crucial point in the process of making crumblecakes, so she motioned distractedly for us to take a seat at the kitchen table.

As Felice and I sat across the table from each other, Mifa's sister studied me. "I feel like I've seen you before," she mentioned, evidently trying to remember where. "Are you part of the defense of Taiyou?"

I nodded, wondering what Mifa had told her sister concerning me.

"What division are you in? I'm with the reservists, myself."

"Uh… I guess the aerial one," I responded, thinking about how, now that the winged Espearian priestesses had arrived, there would be more people in the sky the next time I had to join the fight.

Felice's eyes widened a little. "You mean you're the pilot who flies the stolen Skyraider?"

"Uh, no. Didn't Mifa tell you? I'm one of the Chosen of Sapphiros. If you've been out there, you've likely seen my wings." I let my wings appear at my back for a brief moment to show her what I meant, but Felice immediately scraped back her chair to stand.

"I'm so sorry, Chosen," Felice said, bowing her head. "I didn't mean to presume."

"Felice, there's no need for that. I figured Mifa told you who I was. You do know she's been working in the palace with us, don't you?"

Felice nodded, but would say no more to me that wasn't 'Can I get you anything, Chosen', or 'Are the crumblecakes to your liking, Chosen?'. As Felice left Mifa and I to our own devices, Mifa watched her leave, frowning after her.

"I'll talk to her about it," Mifa volunteered. "I'm sorry if she made you uncomfortable. She's really quite taken aback by what I've told her of Ao Kouen and all the changes he's made. You see, other than me, most people didn't believe the gem gods even existed before. Now there's suddenly all these Chosen in the city with powers like you have and people don't know what to think, other than that they have to shape up and start believing or a Chosen is going to strike them down or something. It's silly, really, but the only Chosen anyone really knows much of is the Vile Emperor…and he's got a reputation."

I frowned, considering this, but what could I say? I couldn't blame Felice for her standoffishness, but I hadn't expected anything like it – I had gotten too used to everyone, at the palace at least, knowing who and what I was. Maybe being anonymous wasn't such a bad thing if it meant I didn't intimidate anyone.

At the top of the stairs leading to the second floor there was an open balcony with a table set out, covered in paper and writing utensils, and facing outwards. Mifa had evidently taken the time to take apart and clean her telescope until the ancient device gleamed. Walking over to it, I ran my hand along the length, wondering at the familiarity of its shape until I noted faded writing on the side of it: *NASA*.

"Do you know what this is?" I asked Mifa, as she placed a tray of freshly baked crumblecakes on the table.

"Goji called it a telescope. My family has always had it. It was just a fancy-looking antique to them, but Goji cleaned it up and found it still worked after a few repairs."

Of course Goji would have recognized it immediately. "It's from my world," I told Mifa. "It's in incredible shape if it's as old as I think it is."

Mifa was ecstatic at the discovery her family heirloom was even more interesting than she had initially believed. As I listened to my friend talk, I began to realize that during his somewhat brief stay in Taiyou, Goji had spent quite a bit of time with Mifa and the way she spoke of him said volumes about how much she missed him. "Goji made some other stuff too," she mentioned. "I've kept them all, though he only explained to me what a few of them were supposed to be for."

"I'd like to take a look at that later," I told Mifa, "but for right now the sun is setting, so we've got work to do."

Mifa nodded. "And there's this strange thing about the moon I wanted to show you. I could never see it before, but now that it gets dark it's really obvious."

"What is?"

"You'll see."

But when it got fully dark, I realized our error as Ao Kouen's wall of fire sprouted upwards from all directions to encompass the country in a dome of green flame for the second night in a row. I stared at the fire, feeling a little stupid for not realizing Ao Kouen was likely using the wall to keep the Lillem at bay – and likely would keep putting it up at night for as long as he had to. Remarkably, Mifa wasn't daunted by the green fire in the slightest. She lowered her eye to the telescope's eyepiece and she began adjusting the trajectory of the device.

"There," she indicated, stepping back to let me take her place. "Have a look."

Curious, I did so, and was surprised to discover that the green fire wasn't solid but a latticework of flames allowing us to see past it. What was more curious than that fact was what Mifa had set up for me to view.

I had already noted on previous nights that this world's moon appeared larger than the one I was used to from Earth. I didn't know if that was because this world's moon was larger, or because this planet was smaller – or perhaps it was simply that the two heavenly bodies were closer together. Either way, the moon was a lot clearer to see through the telescope than it would have been otherwise, and it wasn't completely round like I expected it to be, but rather looked like a bite had been taken out of it on one side.

"What happened to it?" I asked Mifa.

"I don't know," she answered, "but what's even stranger is that little light there – do you see it?"

I looked again to try and spot what Mifa was talking about, when all of a sudden there was a blinking white light on the bottom edge of the broken part of the moon. "What is that?"

"I watched it for a while," she said. "It blinks a series of patterns in six and a half second intervals and then it pauses only to repeat the whole cycle after another six and a half minutes."

"You've already calculated it?"

Mifa nodded and reached over to the table to hand me a piece of paper full of lines and dashes drawn in a precise hand. "I think it's some kind of code."

I was blown away by this new information and intrigued by it at the same time, but I knew I had more pressing concerns to deal with.

"All right," I told Mifa, "let's get this star charting started and then we can puzzle over that a bit as we wait."

We plotted the constellations and major stars on a grid Mifa had prepared. She pointed out to me what the various constellations were called, but I was already quite familiar with the shapes themselves from a puzzle I had figured out long ago to gain access to the Temple of Sapphire. It was curious to note the constellations of this world were not so different from Earth's, it was only that they appeared backwards from the way I was used to seeing them. There were also a few additional stars, namely those five said to represent the varying gem gods, which actually appeared to be tinted in colour to match the gems they were named after – Machalite's being denoted by a blank spot in space where there were no other stars.

As much as we tried, neither of us were really able to make heads or tails of the coded message on the moon. We had theories of course – distress call, ancient knowledge, lost treasure – but try as we might there didn't seem to be any reason behind the deliberate flashes of light so precisely timed.

The message on the moon abruptly reminded me of the Blue Moon Scroll I had been gifted with, despite my unwillingness to receive it. It still weighed heavily upon my conscience and physically took up much needed space in my medic kit. Glancing sideways at Mifa while she dutifully noted the progress of the motion of the stars through the sky, I convinced myself she of all people wouldn't judge or question where my puzzle of a scroll had come from, and she might even be willing to help me unravel its mystery despite the potential danger.

I cautiously pulled the scroll from my medic kit and pulled over a fresh piece of paper to begin making notes. I made sure the moonlight bathed the eerie blue and silver scroll in its light, taking the Blue Moon Knights' warning with the utmost seriousness. I then got to work copying out every inch of the scroll, so I could study it at my leisure without having to take the forsaken thing out again. To her credit, Mifa expressed interest in my task but didn't question my reluctance to explain it to her. It was very soothing to be able to spend time with a friend, even while working on such vital tasks, and I was almost reluctant to leave when the time came to return to the palace to face my parents.

I found Masaru sitting by Gin-Kouteki while the Roughlanders partied around him. It seemed the Roughlanders weren't needed at the bridge with Ao Kouen's barrier in place, and so had created a new tradition where they celebrated surviving each darkness by partying through it. Masaru wasn't participating, but instead he seemed to be conversing with Gin-Kouteki and reading something on a glowing screen set before him.

"Are ye going to see yer parents now, then?" he asked, shutting the screen down as Gin-Kouteki removed it. "The sun is nearly ready to come back."

I nodded, inwardly smiling at his attempt at coming to terms with the changes happening to his world. "We've got some time yet before they're released, so I was thinking I'd take another look at that Lillem down there, and see if there's anything else I can figure out."

"I'll come with ye then, if ye don't mind."

"Not at all," I replied, smiling – I had been hoping he would say as much.

Not wanting to bother Ao Kouen, we sent a guard to fetch a Visionary to open the cell for us so I could continue my research on the Lillem. Not having Mikura around this time to hold it still for me, I shot an exploding arrow at it first thing as soon as the door was opened and reduced the creature back to the sand it came from. I swept the scattered sand together into a pile with a broom I had requisitioned from a palace servant I had passed in the halls, and without touching the sand, I knelt down beside the pile.

"Are ye just planning to get rid of it, then?" Masaru asked.

I shook my head. "I wanted to examine what it's made up of to find out what animates it. Can I borrow one of your knives?"

I'm sure Masaru didn't know what I wanted it for, but he didn't hesitate in drawing one of the knives he kept on him at all times. I took the proffered knife from him and carefully lifted a small amount of sand onto the blade of it, before holding it up.

I directed my focus inward on the tiny particles of sand to see them better. Up close, the sand just looked like normal sand with nothing special about it, but maybe one in ten particles wasn't like the others, being glossy and black instead – volcanic rock?

The miniscule flecks of black rock were igneous, but beyond that, there was little I could determine from them. Maybe if I brought Kaji here he could tell me if they had any sort of magical energy to them, but there was no way for me to tell. Black could be an indication the power of Machalite was involved somehow, but the only volcano I had noticed labelled on the map was the one purported to be in the Ruby City itself where the power of Rubia reigned. It was possible the Lillem could have come from a different source entirely than the power of the gem gods, but if they did, then I had no basis for understanding them.

If it was these little black rocks that made the difference and somehow turned ordinary sand into deadly, animated Lillem, then the simplest way to try and overcome the problem was to devise a way of separating the black flecks from the rest of the sand and neutralizing them that way. I would have to investigate further. For now, however, I could hear in the hall that Yue and Ao Kouen had arrived and were addressing the guards stationed at the doors – it was time for our parents to be released and it was time I faced the fact they were here.

By the time I had emerged from the cell with the Lillem, one other cell had already been opened to release Krox from his confinement. He stalked off immediately upon his release, presumably to go check on Dahlia.

All four of us Chosen of Sapphiros had arrived individually for the momentous occasion. Hotaru looked worried, nibbling at her lower lip in distress, her eyes dark. Kaji appeared outwardly in control, but I could see the way his hands fidgeted with his clothing. Yue, stoic as usual, was difficult to read as she stood impassively with Ao Kouen. Ao Kouen placed his hand upon the doors, each of them opening at his wordless command. Slowly, the Japanese men and women emerged from the Jade-lined cells.

Hotaru's parents couldn't have been more excited. The two loving parents rushed their daughter and caught her up in a hug.

"Kaji," Corporal Zukatoro acknowledged his offspring in a formal tone.

"Corporal," Kaji responded just as formally before Kaji's mother broke the tense moment by taking hold of her son's hands and pulling him into her embrace.

I was distracted from that reunion scene by what I supposed was my own. My mother looked worried and tentative and she made no move to advance, though her eyes were trained on me. My father beside her looked stoic and patient, waiting to be acknowledged, and his expression gave away nothing.

Taking a deep breath, I walked towards them. I felt more than saw Masaru fall into step behind me. As I walked by the Noh family unit, I noticed Yue had also been swarmed by her parents, notably her father, who was always an exuberant man. In her case she didn't seem to want to give them the time of day and instead addressed the whole crowd of us in the hallway.

"The Knights' room has been prepared as a meeting room for all of us to use," Yue announced. "I ask that all present attend immediately for a debriefing."

I decided immediately that I wasn't attending this meeting of hers. Part of my reasoning was petty – I was still a little bent out of shape over her sleeping through my science lesson. However, the main reason was I wanted to be able to explain things to my parents myself and not in a group discussion format.

I nodded my head to my mother and father as I reached them. "Mother, Father, I can lead you to the meeting room if you wish to go, but I will not be attending. I will wait for you in the room across the hall."

Mother looked like she wanted to speak, but Father forestalled her. "That will be fine, Yukari."

I did as I said I would and led my parents through the palace and upstairs to the Knights' room. Masaru followed, no doubt wondering at our tense silence and why there was no happy reunion for the Namikoyas. I, on the other hand, tried to swallow my apprehension concerning what would await me after my parents had been briefed on the situation.

Turning to leave and cross the hall to wait for them in the Chosen's room, I noticed Ao Kouen approaching, and for once he was completely alone with no guards and no Yue. I watched with mounting confusion, which abruptly turned to sharp disagreement when I realized where he was headed.

"Where do you think you're going?" I demanded in a sudden flash of anger that hardly left any room for me to take into consideration who I was speaking to. "I thought you had released them. Why would you attend our private reunion with our families – haven't you interfered enough?"

I was immediately ashamed of myself; I suppose I was a little more distraught about the current circumstance than I had initially thought. My feelings of shame only escalated as Ao Kouen unexpectedly turned about without a word, his eyes downcast. I realized abruptly I had been thinking of him as solely his role and not as the person beneath. The person, I realized abruptly, I didn't even know one detail about.

"Ao Kouen, I'm sorry," I called to his back, but the new King of Taiyou kept on alone down the hallway and he didn't look back.

Masaru was wincing when I was finally able to meet his eyes. "Ye might want to take it easy on him," he suggested. I allowed Masaru to lead me into the room we had appropriated as our own, where we took a seat at the central table. "Ao Kouen's a Roughlander, ye know that, aye?"

I nodded, feeling numb and more than a little ashamed.

"Well, I was talking to him a bit while we waited for ye to fix Dahlia. Seems he's had a rougher life than the average Roughlander. Apparently he's a survivor from the massacre of Marble Ridge."

"What happened at Marble Ridge? Was it Deathsquads?"

"No, worse, if it's even possible for ye to believe it. It was sandcrawlers, a whole herd of them. More than anybody's heard tell of before in one place. It's gone down in history as the most thorough destruction of any outpost – there were no survivors."

"I thought you just said Ao Kouen survived."

"Aye, and until the other day, I hadn't heard of any. Apparently since then the poor kid had been wandering the Sand Lakes alone looking to join the rest of his people, but the world just wasn't co-operatin' with him.

"Now Jedeite's got a hold of him and he's suddenly King of this green land and a people he doesn't know. That's a lot of responsibility dumped on him all of sudden, especially when he'd all but given up hope before. Ye might find if ye talk to him the two of ye have a few things in common. He may not have been cut out to be a king, but he sure doesn't deserve yer scorn."

"I know," I replied softly, my eyes downcast. "I'll definitely have to apologize to him. I wasn't being fair."

Except now I had problems of my own to deal with and unfortunately I could only try and work out one thing at a time, even if new issues kept piling themselves at my feet. I hoped I could make it up to Ao Kouen and we would get the chance to start over on the right foot, since I had made such a bungle of his first real impression of me. I hoped he would be able to understand it was better I come to him a little late with my apology, than not at all.

CH. 14 – BETTER LATE THAN NEVER

I found myself thinking of a time not so long ago when I hadn't understood why my father would take me on a visit to the military base near Shinjuku. That seemingly insignificant visit and the events of that day had been a mystery to me then, but now, in light of everything, the tangled web that was the memories of my former life was finally unravelling.

"Yukari, over here."

To my surprise, my father was waiting to pick me up after school. I felt a mounting apprehension as I approached my father's nondescript black sedan issued to him by the military, but as I neared his window he greeted me with a warm smile.

"Is there something wrong?"

"No, of course nothing is wrong, Yukari," Father answered. "What would make you think a thing like that?"

"Nothing." I shook my head. "I was simply surprised to see you here."

I got into the passenger side of the car at Father's instruction and I tucked my school bag awkwardly between my knees as I buckled myself in.

I glanced sideways at my father as we rode along in silence. "Won't Mother be concerned if we aren't home in time for dinner?"

"I told her I was taking you somewhere today," Father told me. "I can't say she won't mind, but she knows where we're going."

"And where's that?"

"You'll see," he answered ambiguously.

We pulled in at one of the locations my father worked at. It was a small military base, located on the outskirts of the Shinjuku district. The guard at the gate waved us through and my father parked his car near a side door. Inside, the open concept warehouse housed the largest and most comprehensive obstacle course imaginable. As we walked along the length of it to get to the far side of the building, I couldn't help but notice the course didn't look humanly possible to complete. There were parts where one might need to be able to fly to get from one obstacle to the next and walls too high to actually climb without a rope or handholds, of which there were none.

My father led me into the observation room lined with computer terminals overlooking the obstacle course through a wall of floor-to-ceiling windows. I was introduced to a reserved man with an extremely professional air in dark sunglasses named Raved.

"What do you think?" Father asked me.

"Is it finished?"

My father smiled. "Not quite, but it will be soon. We were thinking we might get you and some of your friends to test it out for us."

I looked from my father back out to the half-finished course that would be challenging for even a top athlete. "I think you could easily find someone a lot more qualified than I. Gym isn't exactly my best subject."

I perhaps expected either a smile or a laugh in response to this, but my father instead just looked disappointed. "I suppose I could try," I volunteered unenthusiastically, trying to make up for ruining his enthusiasm about the project, "but if you were looking for someone inexperienced, wouldn't some newly recruited cadets be a better choice?"

"You'll do just fine," my father told me, obviously holding back some strong emotion and ruffling my hair like he hadn't done since

I was a little girl. "Come on, let's go home...we'll talk about this some other time..."

We left the base that day without any further words being spoken, Raved watching us go with an unreadable expression, and we never did speak of the obstacle course or the military base again until now, when so much had changed and it was already much too late.

"...And so Raved, as a Knight of Sapphiros, was supposed to be the one to train you," my father explained. "You were supposed to be trained on Earth after your sixteenth birthday when your powers were expected to manifest. We had thought we would have more time."

The four of us, my mother and father, Masaru, and I, were seated around the central table in the room where Masaru and I had been staying. So far my mother had done no more than stare curiously at Masaru, but my father had been too busy explaining his side of things to pay much attention to the oddness of his presence at a family meeting.

I nodded in agreement to my father's statement. It certainly had been a surprise, our coming here, one we might have been better prepared for had our parents told us the truth sooner. Unfortunately, there was no changing the way everything had happened and there was no use passing blame for something that was, in essence, inevitable.

"I'm not upset," I told my parents, as it seemed they thought I should be. "What's done is done. I'm here now and a lot of things aren't how they should be, but I have to concentrate on what is, not what was supposed to be. I know you said you used to live here and I was born on this planet, but surely you've noticed this isn't the same world you left."

My mother was the one to nod vehemently at this, and her voice when she spoke was hesitant, "Yue mentioned you've been here eight hundred years..."

"No." I shook my head and wondered what other nonsense Yue had tried to pass off as fact in her 'debriefing'. "It's been roughly eight hundred and fifteen years on this world since you left it. For us, we left Earth no more than two months ago and have been here ever since. My sixteenth birthday is still a month away, if I've got the timing right."

Before I knew it my mother was up out of her chair and giving me a hug, tears streaming down her face. I immediately understood she was relieved, but all I could do was pat her back awkwardly. Father paid Mother's sudden hysterics no mind, but replied to me as if she wasn't even there, "Well, that's a relief. I wish Yue would have made that more clear. We know the Chosen stop aging at a certain point in their lives, which is what allows them…I mean you…to live forever, so it was a simple misunderstanding."

I had known, theoretically at least, that Chosen lived forever. The Vile Emperor and, until I learned he was just a Knight, Fuun, were proof of that, but it was a different matter altogether to hear that immortality was a trait I actually possessed. More to the point, now that I thought of it, if Fuun was immortal as a Knight, then likely I had done the same for Masaru, and it was abruptly evident that provided we survived everything thrown at us, we had the potential of being together literally for eternity.

Mother seemed to recover her composure a bit and took a step back from me, but still held onto one of my hands as if she couldn't bear to break contact with me, now that she knew she had me back and hadn't missed the majority of my unbelievably long lifespan. I took a deep breath and figured since we were in the midst of getting all the shocks out at once, I might as well use this opportunity to introduce Masaru.

"Mother, Father," I began, taking in a deep breath and turning my head to include Masaru, who was to my right. His expression was wary and his chair was pulled back a little, so he wasn't exactly a part of the discussion, but that was about to change. "I would like you to meet someone very important to me. This is Masaru, he's a Knight of Sapphiros."

"Hello there," Masaru spoke, evidently feeling a little self-conscious. "It's nice to meet ye both."

My father was giving Masaru an appraising look, but it seemed Mother, at least, had already caught on. She was looking from Masaru to myself with a look of shocked disbelief.

"I don't remember you from the Temple of Sapphire," my father told Masaru. "Were you cryogenically frozen like Sabien and the others?"

"Masaru's from this time," I interjected. "He's a Roughlander, a part of the people Yuko Seig arranged to ally with us against the Vile Emperor."

Father looked confused. "Who Knighted him, then?"

"I did," I said.

Mother and Father exchanged identical looks of surprise. "Well, she always was a quick study," Father commented before turning once again to face me. "I suppose that means you have control of your powers now." I nodded, thinking about just how natural using my powers had become – it was remarkable I had really only discovered them a short time ago. "Good. I'm proud of you, though I knew you would be just fine."

I thought perhaps with this turn of conversation I had avoided any awkwardness concerning the revelation of my relationship with Masaru, but while my father had returned to the initial topic of discussion, Mother had been busy looking about the room.

"Are you two both staying in this room, then?" Mother asked, having noticed past the slightly open curtain the discarded clothes on the chair from the night before and the rumpled bed coverings.

"Uh…yes," I answered as Masaru spoke at the same time, "It's not what ye think."

My parents now eyed us both appraisingly. I felt my cheeks begin to heat as I realized what they must be thinking and how it wasn't too far off from the truth of the matter.

"I thought it was a little odd my daughter would have her personal bodyguard present for this," Father mentioned.

"You're not…" Mother began and I shook my head quickly to forestall the rest of her question.

"You said he was important to you," Father said. "How important are we talking, here?"

"Daddy…" I pleaded with him to understand and not embarrass me further by making me clarify things for him.

"What? As your father, I have a right to know."

I took a deep breath and I desperately tried to remember how it was I had planned to explain this to them. I had the whole day to prepare for this moment, after all.

"I love him," I declared, almost defiantly. "Masaru is one of the few things on this world that makes me happy. It's been a struggle every step of the way, but Masaru has always been there to help me through it, even when I thought it was too much to bear."

If my parents were taken aback by this bold declaration, they didn't show it. My father simply turned his attention to Masaru. "And do you feel the same way?"

"Aye," Masaru answered as confidently as possible under my father's stern gaze. "Ye have a wonderful daughter and I love her very much."

"Masaru, was it?" my father asked. "May I have a word with you for a moment on the balcony?"

"Aye..." Masaru replied cautiously, standing and giving me one last worried expression before following my father outside.

The navy blue sleeve of my father's military uniform could be seen as he tugged the heavy red velvet curtain shut, leaving me alone at the table with my mother, who was still staring at me as if I had grown a third eye on my forehead. When she finally broke the silence in the room, it was the last thing I would have expected to hear from my usually judgmental mother. "So...a boy, huh? He's kind of cute. A little rougher around the edges than I would have expected, but–"

"Mother!"

"Well, it's just I would have thought any boy you'd choose would be more like your father," Mother continued, incorrigible. "Oh, what am I saying? I'm happy for you, Yukari."

"You are?" I was surprised at her reaction. I knew my father was stern but I generally had his approval; it had been Mother I had believed would be more difficult to convince.

"I am," she replied. "You know we had always sort of hoped you would bring somebody home to meet us, but you never did...not even any friends, except Hotaru."

"I didn't like any of the boys in Shinjuku," I told my mother, a little awkwardly. "They only ever seemed to want to stare at me...and I never had any friends to speak of before coming here."

Mother smiled, though underneath her expression was a little sad. "It seems this world was really where you were meant to be the whole time. Can you forgive us for what our decision put you through?"

"There's nothing to forgive," I told her honestly. "I'm here now and I'm a different person than I was back in Tokyo. I don't think I would fit in there anymore, not like I ever really did. Mother, I have to ask, why did you come?"

"To find you, of course," she answered. "The military would like us to retrieve you and bring you back with us, but to tell you the truth your father and I just wanted to make sure you were okay. We weren't certain this was where you had disappeared to, but it was the only explanation that made any sense."

"Well, I'm not going back," I told her, not really caring if she or the military disagreed with that statement. I had too much to do here and the fate of this world was more important to me than the life I had left behind.

"Then we'll stay here," she stated. "We've come this far already."

"I don't know what it was like eight hundred years ago," I told her dubiously, "but this world is a very dangerous place now and every night we have to fight to survive. You wouldn't know it in the daytime, but at night this country is under constant siege by hordes of awful creatures that kill and infect indiscriminately."

"Then we'll help you," she insisted. "I may not be the best with a weapon, but the rest of the squad consists of well-trained professionals and we brought our equipment with us, if this Ao Kouen person will give it back to us."

I heard my father and Masaru coming back into the room. "I've become a bit of a medic since coming here," I explained, "and I don't think I could bear it if you or Father ended up being one of the people I have to put back together. I have to be able to focus to do what I have to do, and having you join the fight will only distract me. I'm glad to see you, both of you," I included my father now that he was fully in the room, "but can't you see it doesn't make sense for you to stay?"

"I understand what you're saying, Yukari," Father was the one to respond, "but regardless, we're not going anywhere for the time being. As I understand it, the Ruby Splitter is not an option and we came by way of the Machalite Splitter. We have no way or desire to return there, as that place nearly cost all of us our lives.

"Ao Kouen has allowed us to stay in his kingdom and he's promised us our safety, so for now we will take him up on his offer. Now," he changed the subject suddenly with a slight grimace, "is there somewhere we can go to get something to eat? We're nearly starved after spending all that time in the dungeons."

I abruptly realized that unlike usual, there was no platter of food laid out on the central table. Looking past the balcony curtain, I noted the sun had risen not too long ago and it was possible the staff had simply not gotten around to delivering it yet.

"Uh…yes, I guess so," I said, "There's a café not too far from here, but…"

"It'll be my treat," Masaru offered, seeing into the heart of the matter immediately – I still had not once had a krevel in my possession and he knew it better than anyone. "I know the place yer speaking of."

"That sounds lovely, Masaru, thank you," Mother responded politely, taking Masaru by the arm and leading him through the door and out into the hall.

I rolled my eyes slightly at Mother's blatant attempt to curry favour with Masaru and get to know the 'boy' her daughter was so interested in, but I realized very quickly her actions left Father and I alone together. He took my arm much in the way my Mother had Masaru's and began leading me toward the door as well.

"I approve," he murmured, leaning down to speak quietly for my ears alone, "but that doesn't mean I don't still want you to be careful, all right?"

I smiled, feeling suddenly much happier than I had until now, the knot in my stomach evaporating with his words of approval. "Thanks, Daddy," I whispered, giving him a slight squeeze of a hug, "I will."

The café where I had first met Felice and had been introduced to the wonder that was crumblecakes was within view of the palace gates and across the open courtyard where Gin-Kouteki was stationed. My father was intrigued by the giant robot as we passed it, but I promised him I would introduce him later.

Outside the palace we met up with Krox and Dahlia who, following their own reunion after Krox's time in jail, had apparently gone for a walk to build up Dahlia's strength as a part of her recovery from her awful ordeal. Masaru invited them along with us and the group of us took up a long table on the patio of the small café.

"Krox, are you all right?" I had noticed a trickle of deep purple blood from a small wound just above his metal chest plate.

"It's nothing," Krox stated. "Just a small wound causing me some discomfort."

I remembered hearing that Krox had been involved in the incident that had landed everyone in the dungeons the night of the ball and I realized what it was I must be looking at – a bullet wound. Instinctively using my power, I peered past Krox's metal plating and into his flesh, where sure enough, a metal bullet was deeply lodged.

"Krox, you can't just leave that untreated," I told him seriously. "That's a bullet wound." I looked to my father to back me up on this one.

"She's right," he stated. "It won't ever heal properly if you don't have the bullet removed, and if it stays in you too long it could eventually kill you."

"Remove it then," Krox barked. "You're a healer, aren't you?"

Krox was right; I was a healer of sorts and likely was the best person to deal with a problem of this nature. I grimaced with distaste, however, at his heavy-handedness. Excusing myself from everyone else, I stood and fished in my medic kit for what I would need. For modesty's sake I had Krox at least turn around to face me, so no one else would have to be put off from their breakfast. Regardless, those gathered around the table watched with fascination as I did what I had become adept at doing, treating the wounded 'on the field' so to speak.

With the help of my unique vision power and a pair of long needled tweezers I had the obstruction removed within mere moments. It was when I noticed my mother's aghast expression that I realized I had gotten so used to treating patients wherever and however I could, I hadn't even thought to pull on my gloves and my hands were now coated in purple Croatin blood.

"You should be all right now, Krox," I told him before turning to the rest of the table with a slightly sheepish expression. "I'll just go find somewhere to wash up, then."

To my surprise, Dahlia offered to accompany me to the ladies room and the two of us located the small, but pleasantly decorated, white room at the back of the restaurant.

"So how long is it you and Masaru have been a match for?" Dahlia asked with a sly smile as I towelled water off of my hands.

I froze, suddenly self-conscious. "Well, you've been gone quite a while, Dahlia," I told her, feeling my face heat a little. "I suppose it was a little after reaching Taiyou, though it hasn't been official for nearly that long."

"Have ye two joined, then?" Dahlia asked with immediate interest.

"J...joined?" I spluttered a little on the word. "I'm not a Roughlander, Dahlia, you're going to have to be a little more specific."

"If ye don't know what it is, then ye likely haven't," Dahlia stated, her sly smile returning. "It's a Roughlander custom, but they have similar ones in other cultures as well... like with the Croatins taking a mate." If anything my blush deepened at this pronouncement. I couldn't figure out why Dahlia would want to know if Masaru and I had 'mated' or not, but I was mortally embarrassed by the prospect of sharing that information with her.

"Ye know what I'm talking about, don't ye?" Dahlia continued as if she wasn't aware of how uncomfortable I was, or maybe it was just that she was enjoying it. "It's a ceremony of sorts where ye agree to be with each other and exchange tokens of yer commitment to one another."

I felt the breath I hadn't known I was holding whoosh out of me in relief. "Oh, you mean like marriage." I shook my head gratefully. "No...of course not."

Dahlia's grin immediately filled her face with sudden excitement as she took my hands in hers. "Oh good! I'm not too late then. Please tell me ye'll let me be the one to officiate for ye. I've been waiting a long time for the chance to preside over a Joining and I'm fairly certain Razor's a lost cause. Please, Yukari, say ye'll let me."

"Uh..." I made an uncertain noise, but Dahlia's enthusiasm was hard to deny. "Shouldn't that be Masaru's decision, Dahlia? I mean, we haven't even talked about...Joining or anything like that."

"Men," she snorted disdainfully. "They don't get to make decisions concerning this sort of thing. Masaru'll go along with what you and I tell him. I won't pressure ye, of course, but when ye decide to be Joined with him, let me know, all right?"

I nodded, feeling overwhelmed, and I let Dahlia tug me from the ladies room and back to the table where we found a plate full of crumblecakes had already been ordered and served. Also, to my mortification, I found my parents were already in the midst of telling embarrassing stories about my childhood escapades to Masaru.

"Ugh, what is that supposed to be?" Masaru questioned, regarding the remainder of his crumblecake in disgust. "It hurts my teeth just to bite into it."

His response elicited a laugh from everyone except Dahlia, who evidently agreed with him on the matter.

"It's sugar," I explained, smiling slightly at the Roughlanders' discomfort. "I guess that's another thing you don't have in the desert."

Though Krox was nominally a Roughlander himself, he didn't seem to have the same aversion to the sugary treats and was happy to polish off Dahlia's and Masaru's, as well as his own.

"So how is it you all know each other?" my father asked.

"Well, Krox is my mate," Dahlia responded openly, "and I've known Masaru here his entire life. I'm sort of like his older sister, though we're not related by blood at all."

"Dahlia's a Corporal for the Roughlanders," I added a reference my father could understand from his own military background, "so she's also Masaru's commanding officer."

"Aye, that's true," Dahlia continued, "and Masaru and I were the first to meet Yukari and the other Chosen when they arrived here. Can you believe they were–"

I shot Dahlia a warning glare before she could say anything further about the state of undress she and Masaru had found us in.

"Aye, well, ye've already told us an entertaining story about Yukari," Dahlia continued, changing the subject slightly, "let me see if I can think of a good one about Masaru to share, shall I?"

Masaru looked panicked, but in my estimation a tale about him was much better and of more interest than my parents discovering Masaru had already seen me naked, and within the first few moments of our acquaintance no less.

"It was before Masaru was old enough to know how to ride a mount properly," Dahlia began and I substituted the word 'horse' for my parents' sake before she continued her story. "Aye, well, he had watched me ride one a hundred times before and my brother Razor, who's a little older than Masaru, had been teasin' him about not being able to ride a mount on his own yet.

"Well, ye see, there was a trade caravan full of new recruits from the children's outpost expected to arrive and Razor convinced Masaru it would be a great opportunity for him to prove his prowess by going out to meet them on a mount. Now, normally, Masaru would've been wise enough to know not to touch my mount, but Razor had been pickin' at him for weeks now and he had had about enough of it.

"Generally speaking, we aren't supposed to mess around with the mounts. It can be a very tricky business and even Yukari well knows what can happen when a mount stops working, but Krox and I had been tinkering with my mount to make it go a bit faster, if ye get my meaning.

"Well, o'course when Masaru decided to take my mount out for a ride, he wasn't aware anything had been done to it. Also, around that age and just around the outpost, even Roughlanders are more apt to wearing something a bit more comfortable, more or less like what I'm wearing right now, actually." Dahlia tugged at her loose fitting Taiyoun robes to indicate what she meant. "So Masaru climbed on to my mount while it was still in the stables and he at least had the forethought to untie the thing before he kicked the throttle open.

"Now Yukari, do you remember what I told ye about the throttle?"

I smiled in anticipation of where this was going. "That the amount of pressure you give it is how fast you're going to go."

"Aye," Dahlia continued her story, "well Masaru kicked it full force. Let me tell ye, he was off like a bolt out of a carbine and it was all he could do to hold on while the mount raced off with him into the Sand Lake.

"It also just so happens it was a very windy day. As luck would have it the mount carried Masaru off in the direction he had wanted it to and he was well on his way to meetin' with the caravan of recruits. Only by the time he reached there the wind had had its way with him and he had not a stitch of clothing left on him!

"So there the poor boy was, butt-naked in front of a whole gaggle of younglings no more than twelve or thirteen years of age."

"Oh dear." My mother laughed, covering her mouth politely. "And how old was Masaru at the time?"

"Maybe about fifteen," Dahlia responded, laughing to herself at the memory. "Oh, but that was years ago!"

Unfortunately, my parents both caught on immediately to the fact Dahlia had let slip and I cringed as their gazes turned to me before centring on Masaru.

"And how old are you now, Masaru?" my father asked the question I had been dreading to hear, with a hint of the displeasure he expected to feel at the answer Masaru would give.

"Nineteen, sir," Masaru answered very carefully, his own face still a little red after the story Dahlia had told about him. "Yukari and I worked it out not too long ago. Ye see, Roughlanders don't pay much attention to age and a lot of us don't know when we were born."

"Oh, but Masaru's a wonder on a mount now," Dahlia interjected on Masaru's behalf, feeling the sudden rise in tension, if not knowing exactly what it was about. "He was a very quick learner after that, almost a natural. Ye should see him now – not many of us can ride while standing on our own mounts, but Masaru can and fire a weapon at the same time too."

"So you all are havin' a get-together, eh?" Hitachi's voice came unexpectedly from the courtyard side of the patio rail. "And you chose not to tell us about it beforehand? Well, that's not very nice, now is it?"

"That's all right, boss," Yuge responded. "That there's Yukari's family, that is. I 'eard they was all in the dungeons before. This must be a celebration for their release or somethin'."

I was saved for the moment by the necessity of having to introduce Yuge and Hitachi to my parents and explain to Dahlia how and when I had become acquainted with the two eccentric Roughlanders. Fortunately, Yuge and Hitachi were more than up to taking over being the life of the party, so to speak, so there were no more awkward questions or embarrassing stories about Masaru and myself.

Sometime before the noon bounce, Yuge and Hitachi wandered off to wherever it was they had been headed and we realized Dahlia and Krox had somehow remarkably managed to fall asleep during the conversation. It wasn't surprising for Dahlia, given she was still recovering, however exuberant she tried to appear. Krox, on the other hand, had spent an undoubtedly sleepless day and night in an eerily lit Jade cell with a bullet lodged uncomfortably in his chest to cause him pain, if worry over Dahlia hadn't been enough to keep him awake.

"Should we wake them, do you think?" Mother asked after Masaru had paid his krevels to our server.

I shook my head. "No, let them sleep. I can take them up to bed."

I stood and placed one hand lightly on Krox's shoulder and the other on Dahlia's before I willed them both to turn to mist. Where before there had been a woman and a Croatin, now there was only a cloud of moisture; my mother stared at me, mouth open in disbelief.

I tried not to pay any mind to her expression, though I felt decidedly odd using my powers so blatantly in front of my parents. It felt a little like I was showing off, though that wasn't exactly the case.

"Come on," I instructed. "Let's get going before they reform."

Before the palace gates, my father stopped once more to marvel over Gin-Kouteki, but my mother simply could not take her eyes off the cloud that was Dahlia and Krox floating along behind me.

"Masaru, would you mind introducing them to Gin-Kouteki?" I asked him. "I'm just going to take these two up to bed."

Masaru nodded and headed over to Gin-Kouteki with my father and with a shake of my head for what my mother would no doubt think of this, I let my wings appear at my back and I took off for the fourth floor balcony, Krox and Dahlia's sleeping forms still trailing after me.

The Knights' room was silent and empty when I reached it, though a few of the other curtained areas were closed, indicating there were possibly others who were asleep. Unlike Earth, the shifting cycle of this planet meant people slept when they could or when they needed to; there was no customary time. It was no trouble at all to reform Dahlia and Krox comfortably on one of the beds. Having done my good deed I turned about, intent on flying back out the way I had come in, when I noticed Rama on the balcony where I could have sworn he had not been a moment before.

"Good day to you, Sir Rama," I said as I came up beside him. "You know I just realized you and I have never really gotten a chance to speak to one another."

"And why would you bother now?" Rama responded rather coldly.

"I apologize," I replied stiffly, feeling stung by his immediate rejection of my attempt to befriend him. "It won't happen again."

"I'm sorry, Yukari, that wasn't fair of me," Rama allowed.

"No, I think your message was clear enough," I told him, my tone matching his perfectly as I flew up and turned about in the air to face him. "Just know I would've Knighted you myself to save you from the Lillem, if not for your own sake, then for Taiyou's, but at least the way it happened I can be thankful it isn't me who will be stuck with you for an eternity."

Having said my piece, I left Rama to his own misery, feeling a little ashamed, but also hurt. I hadn't thought I had ever given reason – before this, anyways – for him to believe ill of me, but apparently that was the way things were.

I landed just inside the palace walls but a little ways off from Gin-Kouteki to give myself a moment to compose my features, as I didn't want Masaru or my family to notice anything was wrong. Out of the shadows of where the trees came together Fuun revealed himself, stepping into my path with only his usual stony expression for a greeting.

"Fuun, is that you?" To my surprise, mother rounded the corner before me through the palace gates. I stood between them, but it was like I wasn't there at all – my mother was looking past me to where Fuun stood just out of the shadows.

"Hana," Fuun breathed my mother's given name. "Cousin, it is a pleasure to see you again."

Mother walked past me without so much as a glance and I turned to follow her with my eyes as she walked right up to Fuun. I was bowled over by the discovery that my mother was Fuun's cousin, which made Fuun…my second cousin?

Not wishing to interfere in their solemn reunion after eight hundred years – in Fuun's case, at least – and feeling uncomfortable where I stood, I forced myself to leave the two of them alone and continue on to where my father and Masaru sat by Gin-Kouteki. My mind was reeling with the implications of this sudden revelation and as it were to turn out, there were a great many things I didn't yet know about my mother and our shared heritage.

CH. 15 – HOPES OF SAPPHIROS

"It's a map," Mifa stated, thrusting a piece of paper at me.

It was much later in the day. I had gotten a nap in and my parents were soundly asleep. Upon waking, I discovered Mifa had been looking for me. By the simple expedient of a message arrow, I had her meet me in the courtyard where Gin-Kouteki was stationed and a couple of chairs had been set up, presumably by the Roughlanders, though none were present when we arrived there.

"The coded message on the moon," Mifa explained. "I've done nothing but try and crack it and I think I've finally gotten it figured out. It's a map."

"Oh," I replied, a little surprised she had managed to translate it so quickly, but I suppose considering it was Mifa, I should have expected as much. "What about the star charts?"

"Oh, yes, I finished those first, of course," she responded, handing me the rolled bundle of papers she carried as well, "and I'm also supposed to invite you back to my place when you've got time to spare. Felice wants to apologize for the way she acted and she's also put together a bundle of clothes for you, since I kind of told her what you're wearing is all you have. I hope you don't mind."

I looked down at my Roughlander clothes in surprise, realizing yet again I had forgotten they were all I wore day in and day out now. At least this time when I was forced to notice them, they weren't thickly coated in who knows what.

"No, I don't mind at all. I'll have to thank her. It's true I'm getting a little sick of this outfit." I smiled ruefully with a hint of a shrug for my sad lack of fashion.

"Unauthorized Skyraider detected," Gin-Kouteki behind us spoke unexpectedly, startling us both. "Should I engage?"

I didn't hesitate in leaving Mifa where she was and taking off into the air. "Hold your fire, Gin-Kouteki," I instructed on my way past his head.

I scanned the air to identify the threat for myself and sure enough, there was an incoming Skyraider flying sporadically and coming from the direction of the bridge. It was still at a fair distance, though thanks to my vision power I was able to see it clearly. It was evident the pilot was wounded and doing his or her best just to stay on as straight a course as possible.

"Gin-Kouteki, can you hear me?" I spoke into the communication box in the medic kit strapped to my chest.

"Affirmative, Yukari," Gin-Kouteki responded.

"Good, I'm going to investigate. You have my permission to engage should the pilot open fire or otherwise attack me, understood?"

"Affirmative."

I cut through the air in a sharp dive, picking up speed before levelling out and aiming straight for the incoming Skyraider. At the speed we were both going, it was not long before I got close enough to overshoot it and spin in the air to correct my trajectory so I was flying alongside it at shouting distance. I scanned the area, but from what I could tell – and my vision was excellent – there were no other Skyraiders or Deathsquad anywhere within view.

I glanced sideways at the pilot to try and see who I was dealing with when I noticed the dents and scratches in the thing's side and the way it sort of sputtered through the air. As I watched, the pilot – a woman by her slight form and wild orange hair – drooped limply and the Skyraider dipped forward suddenly in response.

I let myself be guided by instinct and I dove for the Skyraider. When I got within range of the pilot, I did everything I could to wake her, including shouting and shaking her shoulders to elicit a response. It was no use; the woman, though very much alive, was injured and not alert enough to right the Skyraider in order to save herself, and I had no idea how to fly the thing for her. Making a quick decision, I turned the pilot to mist and lifted off from the failing Skyraider.

"Gin-Kouteki, destroy that Skyraider."

A single precise shot from the Binoid was enough to explode the Skyraider and reduce to it to a shower of debris, instead of letting an object the size of a car plummet out of the sky onto the unsuspecting citizens of Taiyou. Breathing out a sigh of relief, I turned in the air and began racing away from the near disaster back toward the palace with the injured Skyraider pilot in tow.

Maneuvering deftly, I flew myself and my incorporeal passenger through an open window frame on the ground floor and didn't bother slowing my pace for anything as I glided through the palace halls, finally landing when I couldn't propel myself any further with my wings. Making a judgment call, I headed unerringly for the palace dungeons; at the very least I knew they were a safe and clean place to work. Upon my arrival, I fired off a quick message arrow to Ris to inform her I may need her healing abilities. The pilot, when I reformed her in one of the open cells under the watchful eye of a Legionnaire, was in rough shape, but her wounds didn't appear to be fatal.

At first glance, the woman had a strong resemblance to Dahlia, with her wild mane of fiery orange hair and her battle-hardened appearance, but her pointed features and Rubian-style armour quickly disabused me of that notion as I got to work. I pried the woman's armour off with deft hands – I was getting used to treating soldiers, and Rubian or not, most armour was constructed similarly.

Her leg was broken, but other than that most of her other injuries were fairly minor. As I was examining the woman, I felt the slight gust of wind that was enough to inform me Ris had arrived. *Why the dungeons?* Ris asked with her hands, having passed the Legionnaire at the door to stand beside me.

"She's Rubian and came in on a Skyraider," I quickly explained. "Her leg is broken," I continued, showing Ris where I meant. "I'm going to set it so you can heal it, all right?"

Ris nodded and I knelt over the woman's leg to get to work, when all of sudden her eyes snapped open, startling us both, as seemingly out of nowhere a Lillem talon shot like a striking scorpion tail protruding from the Skyraider pilot's back. Instinct, or perhaps simply my power, saved me; as the talon struck the space where I had been, it passed through my form, which had turned to mist just long enough for me to remain unharmed. Breathing hard, I faced the woman, reluctantly drawing an arrow to strike her down when I realized there was still a trace of humanity in her eyes and she hadn't struck again to press her advantage – she was trying to hold herself back.

"S…sorry…" She stumbled over her words and I heard the same eerie dual voice Sabien had displayed while he was fighting off his own Lillem infection. "Can't…fight it…anymore…so tired."

"Ris, back out of the cell, slowly," I instructed. "We'll have to get Yue. Hopefully there is something she can do for her, like she did for Sabien."

I sent for Yue and Ris and I waited impatiently in the hall for her to reach us, though with her speed it took mere moments. Yue refused us access into the cell while she did whatever it was she had figured out to stop someone from becoming a Lillem, saying it was too dangerous a process for spectators. Disgruntled, I continued to wait in the hallway with Ris.

Yue emerged looking drained, but even when I pressed she wouldn't explain her methods to me, not even in the name of science. "It's better you don't know, trust me," she insisted. "You better get in there and fix her up so Ris can do what she does best."

Ris did look a little impatient. Reluctantly leaving Yue to her own devices, I joined Ris in the cell and got to work. The pilot, a woman named Kichigai, seemed much more alert than before and she was nothing but grateful for our ministrations, despite the fact she knew she was in a cell of some sort.

"Why did you come?" I asked her.

"I'm looking for Kaji," Kichigai said. "Please, can you get a message to him for me? Tell him where I am and that I need to see him, please."

The mysterious Kichigai would say no more on the issue to me, simply insisting it was Kaji she had made her perilous journey through the Lillem-infested Sand Lakes to reach. There being nothing for it, I sent a message arrow to Kaji once Ris and I were through and we were back out in the hallway with the cell door shut behind us. For good measure I sent another arrow to Ao Kouen, leaving the matter of this Kichigai person in his hands.

Afterwards, I found myself curiously unoccupied, so I wandered back up to my room where I found my mother seated at the central table with a cup of melon juice, looking out over what she could see of Taiyou through the open balcony curtains.

"Where's Father?" I asked.

"With the Corporal and the rest of the squad," Mother responded. "They're having a meeting and I declined to attend. I'm not much for the military mindset."

I nodded; this, at least, followed with my knowledge of my mother's personality. No doubt the journey here had been quite a drastic change for her, but since her arrival she had seemed so different to me; at times, it was like she was an entirely different person.

"Oh, there was a rather rough-looking fellow that came by earlier," Mother informed me. "He left a present for you. He said his name was…Razor?"

I smiled, imagining my mother meeting Dahlia's charming, yet rough-around-the-edges brother. "Where is it?"

Mother stood, led me over to my own sleeping area, and drew back the curtain to reveal a long, rectangular wooden crate had been placed on my bed. I studied it curiously for a moment, trying to fathom what it could possibly contain.

"I found something we can pry it open with," Masaru announced, coming into the room with something that looked decidedly like a crowbar in his hands. "Oh, there ye are. I was beginning to wonder when I didn't see ye with Mifa out by Gin-Kouteki."

"Something came up," I replied absently, watching with mounting curiosity as Masaru pried my mysterious gift open.

I was surprised and touched by the contents of my present. Some time ago now, when Razor, Masaru, and the rest of us had all entered Taiyou, it had been under the guise of penniless refugees – not too far from the truth of matters then and now, all things considered. When we had entered by way of the main gate, the Legionnaires on duty had confiscated our weapons. At the time, the Roughlander bow I had obtained before we left the Central Sand Lake outpost had been my prized possession and I had been reluctant to part with it, even if I could make arrows with my mind.

Razor had somehow thoughtfully retrieved my bow, along with my quiver half-full of arrows, and returned it to me after all this time.

"Oh, it's yer bow," Masaru commented, "isn't that nice of him? I'm much more fond of the box personally. It's quite a nice box, and large enough I'm sure I could carry everything I've ever owned in it."

"You can have the box if you'd like Masaru," I noted.

Masaru happily appropriated the box and took off with it who knows where, and I was left alone with my mother who watched me care for my bow with a curious expression on her face. It wasn't until she spoke I realized she wasn't looking at me, but to the dress behind me, still laying draped over the chair where I had discarded it after the coronation ball.

"I noticed you don't seem to have any other clothes other than what you're wearing and that dress," my mother noted. "Where'd it come from, anyway?"

I flushed a little self-consciously under my mother's scrutiny. "Masaru bought it for me, for the king's coronation ball."

"That's a pretty expensive gift for someone who could fit his entire life's possessions in that box. He must really care for you."

"He does," I agreed. "What about Fuun?" I attempted an abrupt shift in the conversation to try and steer it away from more awkward questions about Masaru and I, especially where the night of the ball and that dress were concerned.

My mother sighed and her gaze became distant as she looked past me out the window once more. "Fuun and Sabien are my cousins–"

"Sabien?!" I exclaimed, immediately flabbergasted. "You mean the Knight Commander, Sir Sabien?"

"The very same." My mother smiled indulgently at me. "You mean you didn't know Fuun and Sabien are brothers?"

"Sabien never mentioned it," I whispered, working through the implications of this in my mind. Come to think of it, their deep voices were somewhat similar in quality and their colouring was the same.

"I'm not all that surprised, I suppose," my mother admitted with a sigh. "Ever since Fuun became what he is now by trying to kill Sabien, he's never referred to him as his brother that I know of, but it's true."

"Fuun tried to kill Sabien?"

"Perhaps I should start at the beginning," my mother said. "I suppose it's time you knew our family's history. We are all of us descended from the Blue Moon tribe, which was once located far to the south of this world on the easternmost mountain of the Mountains of Sapphire–"

"The Blue Moon tribe?" I interrupted her.

"Yes, have you heard of them since coming here? Did Sabien say if any of the tribe still lived?"

"No, I'm sorry," I told her. "I met a few of them, but they're all dead now. They gave me this." For the first time in front of anyone, save Mifa, I pulled the Blue Moon Scroll from my medic kit. "They said it was a gift, but I would have to puzzle out its meaning in the right light or it could prove fatal."

Taking my warning seriously, my mother did not try to read the intricately-tooled writing on the outside of the scroll case, but she did give the Blue Moon Scroll a once-over. "I've never seen or heard of it before," she admitted finally.

"What strikes me as odd about it was they delivered the Scroll specifically to me and not to the rest of the Chosen," I told her what I hadn't yet revealed to anyone. "They knew my name and they sought me out."

"It could be because of your heritage, dear," Mother hypothesized. "None of the others have a connection with the Blue Moon tribe like you do."

"I'm sorry, I didn't mean to interrupt."

"As I was saying, Fuun and Sabien are brothers, Sabien being the eldest of the two," she continued. "Myself, I'm a little younger than both of them. Now, both of them were training to become Knights of Sapphiros and they each took that training with the utmost seriousness. That seriousness bred a sense of competition that began to drive a wedge between them and would eventually tear them apart.

"Sabien, being the eldest, was bound to be elevated in status first out of the two of them, but what started the issue was when Fuun was told by his mentor and the current Knight Commander that he was not suited to be a Knight because of some inner darkness. When approached later, Sabien apparently agreed with this assessment, though grudgingly. He did, as far as I know, want his brother to succeed and one day be Knighted, but he accepted what the tribe's elders had decreed."

"That's awful," I commented, thinking of Masaru's turmoil when Sabien had pronounced seeing the same sort of darkness in him.

Mother nodded. "It gets worse. Fuun left the tribe, though I pleaded with him to stay and continue his training so he could prove them all wrong. Fuun apparently had a different method in mind for doing the same thing. When Fuun finally did return from his journeys, he was different.

"We began to hear tales of murder in nearby tribes, they were vicious and cruel deaths. Rumours spread that the Chosen of Machalite had surfaced once again. Only now can I assume those rumours were concerning Fuun, but back then I didn't know what he'd become.

"It came as a report from Yuko Seig as a representative of the Temple of Sapphire to the elders of our tribe. Sabien had been on his way to the temple for his Knighting ceremony and had been attacked on the road and left for dead. Yuko Seig found Sabien just in time and Knighted him on the spot to try and save him. Sabien turned to water as soon as the ceremony was complete and didn't reform for a full month. By that time it was discovered who had attacked him: Fuun.

"I had a hard time believing it and it wasn't until I travelled to the temple myself that I learned the rest of it. Once Sabien was announced the next Knight Commander, Fuun appeared and challenged his brother for acceptance as a Knight of Sapphiros. They fought and Fuun won, though barely. Sabien wouldn't agree he should be Knighted for the victory, but Yuko Seig did it anyway," Mother concluded her story. "The rest of it you should already be fairly acquainted with. The Japanese came from Earth, I met your father while I was at the Temple of Sapphire, and I stayed. Sabien was there and there was little for me to return to with Fuun gone. I had you, and Sapphiros himself blessed you as his Chosen when you were born."

"So you knew Sapphiros?" I asked.

My mother made a sound of agreement. "I knew *of* him, yes, and I even met him a couple of times, but by the time I came to the Temple of Sapphire, Sapphiros was already a very old man and close to death. It is said Sapphiros alone of the five gem gods wished to experience a mortal existence and so he lived among us for a normal lifespan. It was the end of his life once the last of you was Chosen and it is believed he gave the last of his power to do it, though I don't know how true that is, since a gem god's power is supposed to be infinite."

I remained quiet and thoughtful after she finished speaking, her words tumbling through my mind as I slotted the new information she had given me into place. I found myself gazing out the window as I tried to absorb it all when I caught on a familiar sight as Gin-Kouteki's voice rang out from the communication box in my medic kit.

"Four unidentified objects incoming," Gin-Kouteki announced. "Awaiting direction."

Through the window I could see four comets of identical size were converging on the palace of Taiyou. I instantly recognized the phenomena before me as the unusual travel method used by Mikura's Deathsquad and knew the comets were unlikely to do any actual damage when they landed. Their arrival, however, begged the questions of where they had gone and why they were returning.

"I have to go," I announced. Without further explanation, I left my mother as I launched myself into the sky through the open balcony. I hadn't flown far when I caught sight of Mikura and she was somehow managing with her peculiar powers to carry someone larger than herself dangling in her arms. I realized belatedly it was Kaji.

Mikura was coming in for a quick landing on the palace battlements and I angled my flight to intercept her. I had nearly reached Mikura when I stopped. A lone woman stood next to Goji's old Skyraider upon the battlements, her eyes taking in nothing save Kaji's limp form. Her hair was a deep red and waving loosely in the wind, and her dress, though still a dark red, was cut in a different style from the one she had worn to the ball – this was Shuzhue.

"Lady Akuma, he's hurt real bad!" Lady Mikura announced as her feet touched ground.

I dove and landed. "I can take care of him, Lady Mikura."

Akuma nodded, meeting my eyes with her intense gaze. "Leave him with his friend, Lady Mikura," she instructed, her voice richer, but otherwise much like I remembered it – this was Shuzhue, it had to be. She turned her attention to gaze longingly after Kaji. "I had hoped for a last goodbye, but I must go now that Ao Kouen has lowered the barrier for the day. Please, take care of him, Yukari."

I nodded slowly, and without waiting for further permission I turned Kaji to mist and dove off the battlements with him following me. Wheeling about in the air, I aimed for the balcony of the Knights' room and shot for it, hoping I would find Ris there – there was little I could do for burns, but the Kumori could fix them easily.

Surprisingly, the first Knight I came across was Adel. I sent a message arrow after Ris as I landed and headed over to the nearest bed to reform Kaji so I could take a better look at him. To my surprise Adel followed, seemingly interested.

"Are you back now, then?" I asked Adel, somewhat distractedly.

Adel's only response was a sharp intake of breath that caused me to take my attention away from Kaji for a moment to look at her. She had her hand over her mouth and her expression could be described as nothing short of horrified.

"Are you all right, Adel?" I asked her, surprised at her reaction. "He's badly burned, yes, but provided Ris gets here quickly he should be fine."

"That's not ordinary fire he was burned with, it's Hound-fire."

"What?"

"Hound-fire," Adel repeated. "See that sticky-looking yellow substance there," she pointed, "it's a bio-chemical substance in the fire that burned him that is produced by Lady Lilyth's Hounds, which can only mean one thing: the Lady Lilyth really is coming back, if she hasn't returned already."

"What are you talking about, Adel?"

But Adel would say no more on the subject. By the time Ris arrived by way of the balcony window as I had, Adel was already deeply involved in some sort of arcane ritual and I was loathe to interrupt her, knowing her temper. Using her sword, the Knight had sliced open one of her palms and held it in a fist over Kaji's right shoulder so the blood would drip onto him. That accomplished, she dropped some more on his right hand and then proceeded to do the same on his left side. Finally, she placed her open palm on his forehead and muttered some sort of incantation under her breath I didn't quite catch. Acting as if she was drawing something away or out of Kaji, Adel then brought her fist back to her own chest and I watched, confused, as she grimaced in discomfort and clamped her other hand down on her wrist to hold it steady.

"What's going on, Adel?" I asked.

Adel responded through clenched teeth. "The Hounds are Lady Lilyth's eyes and ears. The fire they breathe is especially dangerous because it can cause a person to hallucinate, and sometimes, if that person is very unlucky, it can even allow the Lady access to their minds." She winced at the pain in her clenched fist. "This technique is the only way I know of to remove the possibility of possession. Unfortunately, it is not a simple method and I am long out of practice."

"Is that why you went away? Because of Lady Lilyth?"

"She's coming, Yukari," Adel answered. "She's coming and she is stronger than us all."

Adel sank to her knees, gasping for breath and her fist unclenched suddenly. Ris rushed forward to see to Adel's hand, but Adel waved her on and pointed her in Kaji's direction. "You can see to him now. I am strong enough for that much at least."

"What is it that you did?" I asked Adel as I sank to my knees next to her. "Why does it cause you so much pain?"

"I've spent the last few days re-learning everything I'd ever forgotten with Aysel's help. This technique was among those things I thought I had put behind me forever. I used to serve Lady Lilyth when she ruled from the Ruby City, but I left. She wanted to make Aysel..." Adel struggled with the painful memory, unable to form it into words. "I wouldn't let her take Aysel, so I left. Eventually Jeth found us and helped us escape to the Temple of Sapphire.

"There was a civil war going on at the time, Yukari," Adel explained. "Everyone thought the Vile Emperor had been successful in his aims and had killed Lady Lilyth. Even I believed it. I was her Knight then, but it was as if the flow of power had been cut off. I can feel it again, now. She's not dead. I don't know how it's possible she survived, and how or why she's remained hidden all these years, but she's not dead like we all thought."

"You're right, Adel," Kaji spoke from where he lay on the bed. He looked weak, but Ris' blue field of magic was gone and so were the burn marks that had marred his flesh. "She's not dead, but she's not quite back either. I think it's possible her body was somehow frozen on the other side of the planet when the orbit changed and as that side of the planet melts, she gains more freedom."

"Kaji, whatever you saw," Adel cautioned, "no matter how real it seemed, it could have been a hallucination."

"I know that," Kaji said. "Regardless, there was a Hound at that outpost. Lady Mikura identified it for me."

"Outpost?" I questioned, trying to keep up.

"Lady Kichigai's outpost," Kaji explained. "She's the Deathsquad General that took over the outpost formerly run by that despicable fat man. The defenses there are solar powered and last night they finally gave out. The darkness just got too long for them to continue operating. Kichigai fled to the only place she could think of reaching to get help, but by the time Lady Mikura and I went to investigate the entire place has been destroyed. There was only one survivor we could find and he was just lucky the medical bay still had power enough to seal itself. The Hound got me when I tried to get into the outpost to let the surviving Croatin out. I got too close. It won't happen again."

"See that it doesn't, Kaji," Adel instructed. "The Hounds are more dangerous than you know. We'll have to hold another meeting so I can fill everyone in on what I know. If Lady Lilyth has indeed been alive all these years, who knows what forces she now has at her disposal."

We got everyone together at Adel's request. For my part, I used the simple expedient of firing off a multitude of message arrows with the same message, each sent to seek out a specific target. It wasn't too long before we had all gathered, but I was surprised at the additional number of people that arrived to hear what Adel had to say.

The entirety of the audience from my science lecture had somehow had gotten wind of the gathering and had made an appearance for this information session. In addition, there were also a few newcomers, namely Mikura's Deathquad captain, Grinkin, and the Deathsquad General Lady Kichigai herself, not to mention Corporal Zukatoro and the majority of the Japanese military unit. More chairs were yet again brought in and once everyone was more or less situated the meeting began.

Kaji, feeling much recovered, began the meeting by retelling the story about encountering one of Lady Lilyth's fearsome Hounds. "It was taller than me by maybe a foot or more," he described. "It had short, reddish-brown fur like a dog and a powerfully-muscled body with an oversized head. Its teeth looked large enough to be tusks and it had bone spikes protruding from its head and down its spine. These things are tough, my sword hardly even dented its thick hide."

Adel was nodding. "The Hounds are Lady Lilyth's most prized creations," she added. "She created them in much the same way a Chosen creates a Knight, by sharing some of her power. This fact makes them infinitely more dangerous because they are not just beasts or mindless creatures like the Lillem, but are capable of thinking on their own. The Lady was also capable of looking through her Hounds' eyes and for these reasons she considered them to be the generals of her army.

"The power she gifted them with is not varied the way Knights usually develop their powers. The Hounds' power is inherent in their breed, in the way they were formed, and so most have the same traits. Each Hound has a certain thickness of hide that makes them difficult to wound and a gem god's power has no effect on them. They also are capable of breathing fire. This fire contains a bio-chemical compound that can cause powerful hallucinations. If a person is struck by this fire, or the saliva of a Hound, they may also be in danger of possession by Lady Lilyth.

"I do know they can be killed, though it is not a simple matter to do so. Fire does not harm them as it is their natural element and I have already said magic is of no use against them, which I suppose leaves brute force. During the civil war and afterwards, the Vile Emperor instituted a common practice of hunting the Hounds and eliminating them, offering rewards for bringing their heads as proof of the kill. The last estimated count of Hounds had them at about a few hundred, but who knows where they have hidden for the past eight hundred years and what their numbers are like now."

"Wouldn't the Vile Emperor be the best person to ask about how to defeat them then?" Yue interjected. "If he's the one who was so well known for killing them, surely he knows how to do it properly."

"Are you suggesting we just walk up to him and ask him, then?" I countered. "You forget our two countries are at war, Yue. What reason would he have to share that information with us?"

"Yue has a point, as much as many of us don't wish to hear it," Rama agreed. "As it stands now, we have a common enemy and this might be our only real chance for peace between our two nations. If we can't band together for this, then there is no real hope of the fighting ever ceasing."

"What are you suggesting?" I questioned.

"I'm not saying it would be easy," Rama admitted, "but I am willing to attempt to talk peace, or at least open up negotiations for a sharing of information concerning this new threat."

"I'll go," Yue offered. "I've already said I wanted to make the trip down there to see how they were handling the Lillem and offer them help."

"What information could we possibly offer in exchange that they would consider worthwhile? Also, I think we've already ascertained the Vile Emperor has no liking for us. I doubt he would appreciate any offer coming from us, isn't that true?" I directed my gaze over to Mikura and Kichigai, who were conveniently seated side by side. Kichigai was out of her battered armour now and was dressed much as Dahlia was in a borrowed set of Taiyoun robes.

"You have to understand," Kichigai answered hesitantly, "to us, you are believed to be the Destroyers. It was long foretold that your coming would upset the balance of the world and send it into chaos. Even you must admit that what has been foretold is coming true. Look at the state the world is in and it only continues to get worse."

Destroyers? Foretold? I had never heard such superstitious nonsense in my life.

"What exactly was it you were taught concerning the Chosen of Sapphiros, Lady Kichigai?" I asked.

"It was taught by the ancient ones and passed down by the Teachers, there was once a great power in the world, and when it suddenly disappeared it upset the balance, causing a time of great suffering," Kichigai explained. "It was taught one day that power would return and bring with it chaos and destruction. Of course we were taught to fear you and dread your coming. How could it be any other way?"

"Do you hold us responsible, then?" I demanded, my temper fraying rapidly.

It was obvious to me the Vile Emperor had sown the seeds of this information eight hundred years ago when he knew the Chosen of Sapphiros had left this world, but would likely one day return. At the time, it no doubt seemed the best way to explain the planet's shifting orbit to the terrified populace of his city. However unfair it was to us now, that would be to his advantage – why not discredit your enemy with false propaganda if given the perfect opportunity?

"I would have you know, Lady Kichigai," I continued, hardly knowing what I was saying in my anger, "that the four of us were no more than toddlers when we left this world. Our parents or any of the Knights here can attest to that. Not to mention the fact our return here wasn't exactly our decision. Your Emperor attacked us on our home planet and if he had not done so, I dare say we would not have returned here in the manner we did and the planet's orbit would not have suffered for it."

"So you do admit the world's troubles are your fault?" Kichigai retorted, "That your coming here has set these events into motion?"

"Unintentionally, yes," I admitted with a bitter taste in my mouth. "Something to do with our return caused the Splitters to malfunction, which changed the orbit of the planet, but now we are here and that change is beginning to correct itself."

Kichigai's words suddenly came back to me and I had a sudden flash of insight. "Did your teachings ever mention the Chosen of Sapphiros directly? Is it not possible perhaps the great power suddenly leaving this world you mentioned was not the four of us, but maybe the Lady Lilyth? As I understand it, our powers were not to manifest until we were sixteen years-old. Surely four powerless and insignificant toddlers would have less chance of unbalancing the world by leaving it than the Lady Lilyth."

"It's true you didn't have much power as babies," my father spoke up. "It took everything the four of you had to power the Splitters to take us back to Earth, which is why you were not supposed to have any power until you turned sixteen."

"And Lady Lilyth is coming back," Adel added. "The presence of the Lillem and the Hounds are proof of that."

"I suppose you may be right," Kichigai admitted finally. "You say these Hounds are the Lady Lilyth's generals, and the Lillem, I assume, her army. It will take some time for me to adjust my thinking, but I can't disagree that the chaos and destruction I have witnessed have been at the hands of those monsters. I…apologize."

"I'm sorry I reacted so strongly, Lady Kichigai. If peace can be obtained between Taiyou and the Ruby City," I said, "then I support that whole-heartedly, but I personally will have nothing to do with the Vile Emperor, and I will not give him the satisfaction of begging for his help."

With that, I left the room – let them work out what they would say to the Vile Emperor to convince him to share his multiple lifetimes worth of knowledge. I, for one, believed he was the one person who knew exactly what was going on and seeing as he had eight hundred years to prepare for this moment, if he wanted to share information with the rest of the world he would have already done so.

Once within the welcome quiet and solitude of my own room, I settled down on the chair by my bed to look out the window and watch the sun set, trying to soothe my unruly emotions. Judging by the amount of sunlight remaining, the meeting would be over soon in any case. Tonight would mark eight hours, so few until night and day would even out once more and the Lillem would become a near constant threat. How long could we survive like this? And how long until the weather patterns became dangerous because of the changes taking place? Between the Lillem, the Hounds, the Vile Emperor, and the world itself, how was anyone expected to get through this unscathed?

We needed answers. Obviously, Yue thought those answers lay with the Vile Emperor. I didn't know if Kaji or Hotaru agreed with her, but I certainly didn't. There had to be another way.

I found myself drawn to the mystery of the Blue Moon Scroll where my mother and I had left it earlier on the night table. The light of the moon would soon shine on it, but I knew from experience that wasn't enough to make the swirly print on it legible. It still appeared to be some combination of Japanese, Taiyoun, and something older. My mouth setting in a grim line of determination, I picked up the scroll and carried it with me to the balcony where I decided I would work on it under the light of the moon until I unraveled its secrets.

There was a light, cool breeze on the balcony and I carried a chair out to make myself as comfortable as possible. Working mostly from the paper copy I had made, I set the actual scroll by my feet and settled in for the long haul. Sometime later, my mother and father returned from the meeting, and shortly after they were joined by Masaru, Dahlia, Razor, and Krox. I greeted them all from where I was, but my task was too important to interrupt just to socialize. The group of them fitted themselves around the central table, passing around the melon juice, and my mother brought a glass and a chair out onto the balcony to join me.

We chatted companionably while I worked and I was repeatedly amazed by how pleasant it was to be able to talk freely with her now. It was as if by coming back to her home world my mother felt as if she was finally free to be herself.

Dahlia and Masaru came out on the balcony to look out at the wonder that was Ao Kouen's green wall of fire. Mother was also distracted by the oddity of it, but somewhere along the way I suppose I had begun to take such magic and power for granted, though the vast lattice-work of protective flame was impressive in its scope. So it was that I was startled beyond belief when a drop of water landed on my nose, followed shortly after by one landing on my page of notes.

"What the—?" Masaru looked about himself in alarm.

Dahlia, looking just as confused, caught a few drops in her hand and carefully touched her tongue to her palm. "Masaru, it's water, and falling from the sky, no less."

I knew well what this was and what it meant. I had been waiting for a sign the weather patterns had begun to change and now that it had begun it was only a matter of time before it got much, much worse. Not to mention the rain would ruin the notes I had been working on so diligently. Gathering the pieces of paper carefully in my arms, I fled the balcony on my mother's heels as the rain began to come down in earnest.

Dahlia and Masaru stayed out on the balcony where I had unwittingly left the Blue Moon Scroll next to my chair. The two of them were laughing and splashing water at each other like this was the grandest occasion of their lives, and I supposed that to them, boundless water that fell from the skies was more than a reason to celebrate.

Out of the corner of my eye, I noticed Razor cross the room as he stepped out onto the balcony and raised his face to the sky. Krox was also drawn over to the threshold to the outside world by the phenomena and I came to wholly appreciate that to most of this world this moment was nothing short of a miracle.

Mother, Father, and I watched the Roughlander and it struck me that had Tira been here this night, then Masaru's entire family would have been together for this momentous occasion. As if he had heard my thoughts, Masaru turned and gestured for me to come and join them. Returning his smile, I turned to place my pile of papers carefully on the table when I was interrupted by Krox placing a hand on my shoulder.

"I think you forgot this out there." He spoke as quietly as he could manage in reverence for the occasion. "I hope it was not broken by the water from the sky."

I held out my hands for the pieces that made up the Blue Moon Scroll, my mouth open in shock. It wasn't broken, it was open — somehow the water must have…

Regardless of how it had occurred the Blue Moon Scroll lay open in my hands and its even more puzzling contents were at last revealed. Rolled up inside the scroll case was a letter on thick paper, written in faintly-glowing cyan and with it a slim, rectangular box.

> *My Dearest Children,*
> *Your friendship is your strength, as is your determination. I wish I was there to witness you all grow. I now tell you a great lesson; this scroll case is the key to understanding the Splitters, should you ever need to make use of them. I have made you each a gift and I hope you cherish them the way I cherish you all.*
> *Sapphiros.*

Feeling overwhelmed, I opened the slim box to peek at its contents, wondering what Sapphiros had left for us to be passed down through the ages. Inside were four identical-looking rings, seemingly made of glowing cyan light, but feeling infinitely more solid.

The rings, I also noted, were labelled where they sat inside the box: *Dedication, Passion, Honour, and Temperance.* I gathered they were meant for the four of us, but I had no clue as to which was meant for whom or what, if any, purpose they may have.

I closed the box and did the only thing I could think of; I headed straight for Sabien with the scroll case and the letter held close to my chest. I found him almost immediately in the Knights' room directly across the hall; wordlessly I handed him the letter and let him read it for himself.

"The Hopes of Sapphiros," Sabien spoke with a reverent tone.

"What are they, Sabien?" I asked.

"None of us knew exactly, except perhaps Yuko Seig," Sabien responded. "Sapphiros fashioned these four rings from Sapphire and wore them for the better part of his life, imbuing them with his power. He called them his Hopes and gave them to the tribal elders upon his passing with very specific instructions I wasn't privy to. How is it they have come now into your possession, Yukari?"

At long last I explained the strange visitation I had received from the Knights of the Blue Moon and how I had subsequently learned of their deaths shortly afterwards. Sabien listened carefully but afterwards there was little he could say that would make their strange actions any clearer.

"Have you shown these to anyone else yet?" Sabien asked and I shook my head. "Then we should do so now. Can you call everyone together? Summon the Knights as well. It is time we all regrouped, we have spent much time apart lately."

I nodded and sent out a multitude of message arrows to fulfill Sabien's request. As Sapphiros had written in his timeless letter that had been kept sealed away until now, 'our friendship is our strength', and for the past while we had been drifting further and further apart.

When we all gathered it was in my room this time – for myself at least, I had had enough of the tensions that usually resulted from meetings held in the Knights' room. My parents, Razor, Dahlia, and Krox hadn't minded vacating for a little while once I impressed upon them the serious nature of our meeting.

Soon all four of us Chosen had gathered, and with them the Knights also began to arrive. I was glad to see Aysel when she followed in after Adel. Kaji entered with Rama and Yue with Jeth, and perhaps not so surprisingly, Pine followed in behind them. I hadn't known Pine had been Knighted, but upon seeing him enter the room and registering the changes in the way he carried himself under his dark cloak, suddenly it seemed as if he belonged here.

"Sir Pine, I presume?" I said and he nodded. "Welcome. Who was it that Knighted you, Yue?"

"Kaji."

Beyond Pine's shoulder I realized suddenly Rama was watching the two of us. "If you'll excuse me," I told Pine and took a deep breath before addressing him. "Sir Rama, I want to apologize if I was harsh to you before. Welcome to the team."

Rama moved more quickly than I expected him to and, before I could so much as blink, he had pulled me in for a grateful embrace. "I apologize also," he said into my ear. "My remark was exceptionally callous and I want you to know your acceptance means a great deal to me."

He pulled back momentarily, leaving me feeling stunned. "So we're able to start fresh then?"

"I would love to."

"If I could have everyone's attention," Sabien announced.

We took our seats and Sabien retold the story of the Hopes of Sapphiros and the death of the gem god who was our benefactor before revealing the rings and the message I had discovered. "For

Hotaru, the Hope of Dedication. May your determination always see you through. For Kaji," he continued in the same vein, "the Hope of Passion, may you have the fervour to accomplish all you desire. For Yukari, the Hope of Honour, may your convictions lead you down the path to what is right and true. And Yue, may the Hope of Temperance always guide your thoughts and actions."

One by one we placed the Hopes of Sapphiros upon our fingers and for the first time since coming here, all four of us were able to look about the room and feel like a part of a team filled with purpose and hope. We had amassed good people with heart, determination, and skill, and although this world would try its best to knock us down, I sincerely doubted we would ever give up.

The double doors to the room burst open without warning to admit a very worried-looking Ao Kouen. "The Hounds are here," he announced with dreadful finality. "I can feel them disrupting my shield. If we don't do something to stop them they'll take it down and it won't be long before all of Taiyou is crawling with Lillem."

Ch. 16 – Trial by Fire

As it turned out, we were woefully unprepared to deal with the ambush awaiting us on the western border of Taiyou. Upon our emergence through Ao Kouen's barrier, we were at first surprised to discover only one Hound and no Lillem besieging this side of Taiyou. However, once Kaji and Yue bounded off together to engage the lone creature, another one began to haul itself out of a crag in the rocky ground. Ris and I took to the skies, and the remaining Knights and Hotaru were able to attack the second creature en masse. One would think that with such odds the forces of Sapphiros would have little trouble, but unfortunately that wasn't the case.

Easily seven feet tall, if not a little larger, the Hound's oversized paws were even more deadly looking than those of a lion and the claws soon proved themselves strong enough to crack rock and dig in, allowing the Hound to haul its massive body up out of the ground with ease. Wicked bone-like protrusions jutted from the crown of its head and a line of such spikes followed down its spine, affording it yet another layer of protection against the Knights' swords.

Rama prudently stayed well back out of the creature's reach, making use of his uncanny ability to manipulate his sword from a distance. Not having such gifts, Jeth, Adel, and Hotaru were forced to get in close to the beast, while Masaru hung back with Rama and awaited an opening to throw one of his knives.

Still, the Hound ignored the Knight's various efforts to wound it as if they were no more than a mild annoyance and the oversized creature opened its jaws wide to reveal grossly yellowed teeth. The curved and wickedly sharp points gleamed dully in the darkness before swiping forward to take a bite out of Adel, who had gotten in the closest. The Knight's instincts warned her in time and she rolled out of the Hound's way as without further warning it roared with an angry and vehement sound, belching out a spray of flames and tossing its head to and fro in order to cover as many targets as possible with its searing fire. The fire, as intense as it was unexpected, lit up the surrounding area and revealed yet another of the fearsome creatures sneaking up behind Masaru and Rama.

I could see from the air that the situation was getting dire quickly and, uncertain of what else to do, I peppered the hide of the newly revealed Hound with a handful of cyan arrows. Unfortunately, my arrows did nothing more useful than alert Rama and Masaru to the danger behind them as they simply bounced off of whatever aspect of the Hounds' making nullified a gem god's power. Rama and Masaru whirled about to face the new threat; however, the Hound before them had taken notice of a new target – me.

Lamenting my lack of forethought in not bringing my newly re-acquired bow with me on this particular mission, I desperately tried to think of what I could do against this creature as I faced its malevolent stare. To my shock and surprise, the thing suddenly geared up and leapt, and there was nothing anyone could do to stop it as it launched itself directly at me.

I dove to the side, once again underestimating it. The Hound roared once and shot jet of flame as it passed by in the air. The pain was so sudden and intense I dropped like a rock out of the sky with the shock of it. When I next realized where I was, Masaru held me cradled in his arms and Rama now wielded not one, but three swords. The swords, presumably somehow created using his power as a Knight, whirled in a deadly pattern around us and now there were Lillem surrounding us with their screams, where before the air had been silent. The Lillem were too close for comfort and they

270

tried desperately to reach us past Rama's whirling blades, their faces contorted beyond natural human expressions of savagery.

I shook my head to clear it, trying to fathom how so many Lillem had simply appeared. Remembering what Adel had said about hallucinations, I thought briefly the Lillem I was seeing now were a product of my imagination, but a wickedly sharp bone talon piercing briefly through Rama's defenses and coming dangerously close to striking Masaru was enough to disabuse me of that notion.

Noticing by my pained hiss that I was awake, Masaru helped me gently to my feet, though every motion hurt. I was covered in stinging burns from head to toe, much as Kaji had been when Mikura had flown him in, though not as badly.

"Are ye all right?" Masaru asked.

I would have assured him I was fine, but at that very moment the unthinkable happened and I watched in frozen horror as yet another Lillem talon pierced through Rama's attempt to shield us only to sink right through the center of Masaru's chest. I hardly had a chance to react or even to draw breath to scream for help before one of Rama's blades sliced through the offending talon, removing it from the Lillem, and therefore reducing it back to sand which fell, suddenly harmless, back to the ground where it had risen up.

Masaru's breath came in sharp, ragged gasps, as from the likely fatal wound in his chest came not blood, but a flowing cascade of sand instead. I had trouble comprehending what I was witnessing, but I watched the hole the Lillem had pierced through him fill up with sand before smoothing over nearly with flesh once more. I stared at Masaru in confused horror, waiting and dreading, my breath held unconsciously for the moment when he would begin showing the effects of transformation into one of the horrid creatures, but as impossible as it seemed, that didn't happen.

"Yukari, I'm fine," Masaru insisted. "Really, I'll be alright."

"A little help here would be welcome!" Rama spoke loudly in a tone that belied the current circumstance.

Turning his back to me, Masaru had little choice but to direct his attention to defense. I could tell our situation had gotten a great deal worse, though I could not see or hear anything beyond the screaming Lillem surrounding us. I couldn't fly – I hurt all over, and just the thought of trying to lift myself off the ground caused me pain – and therefore I couldn't see.

Lifting my arms hurt, but I did it anyway, choking back sobs as I drew back an arrow. I chose a Lillem right in front of me and let my arrow go; I didn't have the strength or the energy necessary to do more than that. The Lillem I had chosen fell, exploding into a cascade of sand, and then beyond it my arrow struck the next Lillem behind it, exploding that one as well before moving on. All in all, I reduced five Lillem back to sand and it was only for the briefest of instants, but I had cleared a line back toward the direction of Ao Kouen's flame barrier and revealed one of the things I had feared most to find. Hotaru lay face down in the sand, still wet from the rain, and she wasn't moving.

"Rama!" I pointed in the direction I had cleared moments before the surging Lillem filled that space and Hotaru's inert form was blocked from view. With a determined nod, he began moving our small but well-defended circle forward using his whirling swords to fend off the Lillem.

By the time I thought we had gone far enough I should be able to make her out again, we were well into the thick of the Lillem and had to fight hard for every step. My worst nightmares were coming true, but I refused to give up and leave Hotaru behind, whether she still lived or not. I raised my arms once more and fired off another arrow. Hotaru, once revealed, was in a sad state. She looked as badly burned as I no doubt did, but far worse, her body had been repeatedly punctured by the Lillem's talons as they propelled themselves over her.

I turned Hotaru to mist and let her drift to me on the wind. I couldn't afford to look her over now and see if there was anything I could do as my arrows were needed now more than ever to keep the Lillem from reaching us. Preparing myself for the pain, I lifted my arms and created five arrows in rapid succession, letting them loose on the Lillem around us. I watched with grim satisfaction as one Lillem after another exploded into sand and my arrows fanned out to find yet more targets to destroy.

In the suddenly cleared space around us, I was finally able to see beyond our immediate circle. Where before the sand and rocky ground had been desolate, now the area was filled with Lillem, and here and there I could see pockets of disturbance where one or more of our forces fought. Far more worrisome, there also seemed to be Lillem standing head and shoulders above the rest of their fellows. These Lillem were easily the size of houses and had no human features to speak of, their skeletal forms more like giant spiders made of bone. My gaze stuck upon three of these larger Lillem and the threat they represented – how were we supposed to fight something that monstrous?

I continued scanning the area now that I had the chance, looking for Hounds. I didn't see any in my initial inspection, but recalling how they had hidden from us at first I knew it didn't necessarily mean there weren't any around. What I did see, however, was that inexplicably Gin-Kouteki stood between us and the flame barrier. I noticed immediately by focusing my vision on him there were also a number of Roughlanders positioned on his shoulders, firing shots from their Carbine rifles at the Lillem trying to climb the massive binoid's legs to reach them.

I silently thanked Ao Kouen for sending allies to help us as I reached into my medic kit for my communication box. "Gin-Kouteki, aim your cannons at the larger targets. Also, communicate to the Roughlanders that they are to focus their efforts on any Hounds that show themselves and inform them I will do what I can about the Lillem."

I didn't hear the familiar response from the binoid, but the answering cannon fire was enough. Fulfilling my end of the bargain, I loosed as many arrows as I could stand to fire, forming nets of cyan energy all over the lower half of Gin-Kouteki to pin the Lillem there. As before, my nets slowed the Lillem until they seemed to almost freeze in place. There was an answer to be found there, but I didn't have time to dwell on it now.

In fact, there was no time to dwell on anything except struggling to keep myself moving despite the pain every motion caused me. I had never felt so awful in my life, but I pushed myself to keep firing arrows and to keep taking step after painful step toward the barrier with Masaru and Rama. My power was also distantly focused on keeping poor Hotaru safely floating along behind us.

Ao Kouen waited for us at the barrier he held open, guarded by a contingent of Legionnaires. Ris and Adel had made it back already; I could see them on the docks waiting for us with the ferry boat behind them. Still feeling disoriented, I remember trying to resist hiding behind the safety of Ao Kouen's barrier while there were still others out there, when someone pointed out to me the sun had begun to rise over Taiyou and this night's eight hours of darkness was now finally at an end.

Somehow, my impossible hope was revealed to be true and everyone made it back alive. I counted them as they passed me, waiting by the opening in the barrier with the faint light of the rising sun at my back. I waited still longer for Yue; in the distance I watched her kneel next to the corpse of a Hound and place her hand on the sand before her.

Yue manifested a power I had never seen before and she was suddenly surrounded by a thin aura of white fire, which then encompassed her hand before sinking into the sand itself and spiralling outward. The white flames swept the sand in ever-widening arcs, until they had nearly crossed the distance between us; then they died down as if they had never been. Feeling curiously numb, I hardly realized I had walked forward until I was nearing Yue's side. She looked up at me, her eyes mirroring what I suppose was my own rather blank expression.

Perhaps it was my distraction, or only my power had finally run out, but at that moment Hotaru reformed from the cloud of mist that had been following me, and when she did, she bore little resemblance to the friend I had tried to rescue. Her eyes glowed an intense cyan, the pupils and the white of her eyes hardly visible past the glow, and to my horror, blue Sapphire Lillem talons had emerged from her shoulder blades and now hovered menacingly before us.

I wasn't given a chance to react before Hotaru's new limbs struck out impossibly fast. I cringed, but the talon never pierced my skin; somehow Jeth got there first and put himself in the way of the blow. The Sapphire talon bounced harmlessly off the thick skin of his scaled arm and within moments Jeth had Hotaru wrestled into a hold, her dangerous new Lillem parts held immobile in his unyielding grasp.

Yue was on her feet in a flash and she wrapped Hotaru in her embrace, encompassing the two of them in the same white fire I had watched her use on the sand. Within moments, the Sapphire talons broke off in Jeth's hands and the light dimmed in Hotaru's eyes, bringing them back to the blue they had become since Sapphiros' power had filled our lives. Taking a limp, but Lillem-free Hotaru in his arms, Jeth headed back in the direction I had come from, leaving Yue and I alone once more.

"I got you something," Yue stated, holding out her hand to me.

Still feeling oddly detached from the world around me, I held out my hand to receive whatever Yue was trying to hand me. There was nothing there, but an instant later she caused something warm, sticky, and decidedly heavy to appear. I immediately felt bile rise in my throat and I dropped the mangled handful of purple and grey-coloured Hound remains. It was brain matter as near as I could tell, but I couldn't bring myself to examine it further. The disgust was enough to shock me out of my detached state and bring me forcefully back to reality, as I shook my hands to try and dislodge the revolting mess.

I caught Yue's affronted expression at my reaction to her strange gift before she flashed away, leaving me alone in the unprotected wastelands. Shuddering with revulsion, I began the walk back to the docks, wanting nothing more than to be away from the battlefield.

There were people all around, some injured, some not, and almost all of them faces I knew, but once I was safely within Ao Kouen's barrier and my feet hit the solid wood of the docks all I had ears for was the gentle lapping of the lake of Taiyou. My only practical forethought was to remove my medic kit before I less than gracefully walked off the side of the dock and into the lake. I drifted there, the water holding me up and soothing my pained body and I hardly noticed the passage of time until I vaguely registered a distressed voice calling my name in a familiar Roughlander accent.

"Yukari!" "Leave her alone, Masaru," Sabien's voice directed calmly. "Yukari knows how to swim and I'm sure she'll come out when she's ready."

I sighed, it was time to face reality once more. "Actually, Masaru, I could use a hand up."

All too soon I was back on land and the throbbing of every inch of me was getting more intense. I gritted my teeth against the pain and settled in for the long haul of dealing with the discomfort – I would be tender for quite some time, but I was sure there were others who would need Ris' attention more than I.

"Yukari," Adel's tone brooked no opposition, "come here. You're first."

"First for what?" I asked her, slowly climbing the ramp onto the ferry to join her at the rail.

When I reached her side, Adel touched her palm to each of my shoulders and as she reached for my forehead I saw her hand was bloody. "The same thing I did for Kaji," she answered. "Ris won't be able to heal you if I don't and it's possible through the Hounds' fire you are vulnerable to possession by the Lady. I won't take no for an answer."

I was too tired to argue with her, so I watched as she completed the ritual and her arm and fist seized up again, as if with her very body she was fighting off some hold the Hound had gotten over me.

"You'll have to do this for everyone that got hit by that fire, won't you?" I asked, watching her struggle.

"The fire, yes, but also anyone they might have bitten."

I hardly knew where I found the strength, but I drew back yet another cyan arrow and this time fired a net to encompass the arm causing her pain. The seizing in her hand beneath the energy net immediately seemed to ease somewhat.

"Oh, that's better," Adel commented, easing up on her hand a little. "How did you know that would work?"

"The nets I can fire drain energy," I told her. "I can't quite follow all you are doing, but I gathered it had something to do with drawing the power into yourself to fight it. I figured if I could drain the energy from whatever you were fighting it would make it easier on you."

"It does, yes," Adel agreed.

I stayed with Adel and every so often coated her arm with another net as the ferry began its journey back across the lake of Taiyou. I looked each of the Knights over to see if any needed to see Ris immediately, but honestly other than Hotaru, and I suppose myself, Ris was the worst of the bunch and it would be a while before the Kumori felt up to task.

"Ris and Sabien both should be taking it easy. They're not as young as they used to be," Adel commented, eyeing the Knight Commander.

"You should talk," Aysel, who had come with the ferry and had stayed on it while the rest of us were outside the barrier, retorted to her sister. "Look what that does to you!"

The energy-draining cyan nets had long since ceased working to ease the cramping in Adel's right arm, but thankfully we had seen everyone who had come into even minimal contact with a Hound.

"I thought the Knights were immortal, like Chosen," I commented. "Shouldn't their ages just plateau at a certain point?"

Adel grimaced and I gathered her expression wasn't in reference to the pain in the arm she held cradled against her chest. "Normally, yes, but it's different for Knights. We're immortal as long as the one responsible for Knighting us still lives. After that, we return to our normal life spans."

"And Sir Sabien was Knighted by Yuko Seig and Ris…" I trailed off realizing the implications.

"Ris was Knighted by Sapphiros himself while he still lived," Adel filled in.

"So you were put into cryogenics because in each case the person who Knighted you is dead," I stated, understanding at last.

"Well, perhaps not in my case as I was Knighted previously by Lady Lilyth," Adel admitted. "If she's not dead, then a part of my power still comes from her."

An awful thought occurred to me while Adel spoke. "Adel, how long do Kumori generally live for?"

Again Adel grimaced. "The oldest Kumori I ever heard tell of was a little over twenty."

"And how old is Ris?" I asked the inevitable question.

"She was sixteen when she was Knighted, but that was quite some time ago."

The dilemma became painfully clear. Sweet, silent Ris, the companion I had come to count on and the love of Sabien's life, was nearing the end of her lifespan and only the other Knights, except perhaps Masaru, knew it.

"Isn't there anything that can be done?"

"Perhaps," Adel responded. "It's never been done that I know of to be Knighted twice by the power of the same gem god, but it would be worth a try."

Cursed is the life of the twice Knighted, Fuun had once said concerning a person being Knighted by two different powers, but perhaps blessed would be the life of someone Knighted twice by the same power. Either way, Adel was right in saying we had to try – none of us would deny Ris immortality if it was in our power to give it to her.

I tried to speak to Ris once we had all laboriously trekked back up to the Knights' room in the palace, but she silenced me with a gesture, assuring me she was fine and well enough to see to the people who needed her before encompassing me in the blue field of her healing magic.

At some point during the healing process, I fell asleep and I was quite unaware of anything else for some time…

"Goji?"

Goji Nakamura, former student council president of Shinjuku High, sat with his back to a tall maple tree out in the school yard. He eyed his can of pop with distrust, questioning his own sanity, before he darted his eyes from side to side to make sure he was alone. The other students crossing the school yard paid him no mind so he gave into his curiosity and spoke into the can before him.

"Hotaru? Is that really you?"

"Yes, it's me," Hotaru's voice came undeniably from the pop can.

"Mizu told me you had discovered a way to talk to her, but until now I hadn't really believed it. Hold on." He stood, seeing that another student was coming dangerously close to his tree. There were already enough rumours flying around concerning his long period of hospitalization and his new permanent injuries; he didn't want to add insanity to the list of reasons people now avoided him. Taking his cell phone out of his pocket, he stuck the device to his ear to give himself an excuse to be talking. "All right, go ahead."

"How are you, Goji?" she asked. "How has everything been going there?"

As she spoke, he picked up his lunch bag, slung the strap over his shoulder, and put some distance between himself and the other students, his feet taking him out the front gates and away from the crowded school yard. "Not good, I'm afraid," he answered, for the first time feeling as if he could share his troubles, because unlike anyone else on this world, Hotaru understood.

"What's going on? Has Ku-Roi attacked Earth?!" Her alarm was evident even through the tinny reverberation caused by using a pop can as a communication device.

"Who's Ku-Roi? No, no one's attacking Earth that I can tell," he responded, glad he had taken the precautions of heading away from other people before having such an unorthodox conversation. "It's just things aren't the way they used to be here, and after I was gone so long…it's hard to settle back in, you know?"

She took a little while to respond and he instantly regretted having brought up his own petty concerns. Surely whatever Hotaru and the others were going through was much worse than any ostracism he was experiencing. "Forget I said anything–"

"Are you unhappy there?" she interrupted unexpectedly. "What I mean is…would you come back if you could?"

"In a heartbeat," he answered.

He had been thinking of little else since his somewhat uncelebrated return. Before the 'incident', he had been well-respected, head of the student council, and known in the community for his charity work and his connections. Had he never left, none of that would have changed and he might have really made something of himself, but now…

He was shunned. The newspapers had released information concerning the mysterious attack on four teenagers who attended Shinjuku High. They said the attack was related to gang activity, possibly involving members of the Yakuza. Even if their names weren't expressly released, those four students had been hospitalized with serious injuries and there wasn't a soul in Shinjuku who didn't know who the papers were referring to.

He had lost his left eye in the 'incident'. Now it looked as if his connections weren't in the community, but with gangs. Some said Goji Nakamura had traded too many favours and was paying the price for it; others said he was a Yakuza member himself and deserved what he got.

"Hurry up and get to a place that has more water, then," Hotaru instructed, "and you might want to make sure it's private because I'm coming to get you."

"What?! Are you serious?" He spluttered, looking about to make sure no one on the street was paying attention to the crazy man yelling into his pop can with a cell phone for a prop.

"I can do it," she insisted. "I know I can. I just need to try harder and I can make it to Earth. Are you in a secure location yet?"

"Hold on, hold on. I'm going," he placated her as he ducked into the convenience store he found himself in front of.

"Can I use your washroom?" he inquired politely of the man behind the counter and was given the key. Going around to the back of the building, he worked the door open with his free hand, having tucked the cell phone under his ear. Once inside the small room, he placed his cell phone and his lunch bag on the counter.

"All right, I found a bathroom, is that good enough?"

"Perfect. Turn the water on and stand back."

Feeling the tiniest spark of hope, but also feeling a little silly, he did as he was instructed and turned the faucet on full blast, plugging up the sink so the water would pool there, presuming Hotaru needed it for whatever she was going to attempt.

"All right, it's on."

"Okay, I'm coming."

Some instinct caused him to turn toward the door as he remembered he had neglected to lock it behind him before it smashed inward, propelled by a kick delivered by heavy combat boots. The man revealed was perhaps only a little older than Goji, but he held the butterfly knife in his hands with a confident manner.

Goji put his hands up to show the punk kid he was unarmed and didn't intend to cause any trouble, and backed up a few steps to prove it. The sink to Goji's right and a little ways behind him had completely filled with water and was now beginning to overflow onto the floor, filling the room with the sounds of running water.

"You're going to regret claiming to be a member of the Yakuza," the punk with the knife threatened. "You think losing your eye was something? How about a hand?"

Goji backed up another step, his mind working frantically. He never claimed any connection with the Yakuza, but he knew beyond any doubt it would be pointless to try debating with this madman when everyone believed it to be true. There was only one way in or out of this room and the door lay beyond his attacker. He desperately scanned the room for anything he could use to get out of this mess, but the little room was surprisingly clear of debris. There was only a toilet, a sink, his discarded cell phone, now floating in a few inches of water at his feet, and of course, the mirror on the wall.

Really looking at the mirror for the first time, he mentally did a double-take, for it showed not an image of himself, but a face somehow even more familiar to him than his own – Lord Fuzen, Talon of the Vile Emperor.

Inexplicably, though the image of Fuzen with his long black hair, eye patch, and rugged features stood in the exact spot where Goji should have been, Fuzen's expression was not the one of panic or terror Goji knew was visible on his own face. Instead, Fuzen looked calm and serious, and when he was certain Goji could see him, the Talon directed his gaze pointedly to a bug zapper on the far wall – the wall that in reality would be to Goji's left, which he hadn't taken notice of because of his missing eye.

"Goji! Goji, are you still there?" Hotaru's voice echoed from all directions, the water she was using to speak through now filling the room. "It's not working, Goji!"

As if in slow motion, the Yakuza member surged forward and Goji dove, his left hand outstretched for the cord to the bug zapper he knew would be there, even if he couldn't see it. His hand closed around the thick cord and he gave it a yank, satisfied when it came loose in his hands and he caught the sparking of the live wire out of the corner of his remaining eye.

The gangster before him froze. "You're not crazy enough to do it, are you?"

"Try me," Goji countered, lowering the wire slowly toward the water to test the gang member's resolve. He had no intention of electrocuting them both – after his long stay in the hospital, Goji was certain he wanted to live, even if it was on Earth and not in Taiyou – but his attacker didn't need to know that.

Then he abruptly began to feel a little strange about the knees. He felt as if he was sinking, but his mind could supply no rational explanation for it. Concerned, he spared a glance downward and was alarmed to discover his legs were rapidly turning from solid to liquid and he was melting into the water around him.

"What the hell?!" Goji heard the gangster exclaim as the splashing of the man's boots caused Goji to look up. The live wire slipped from Goji's hands as they, too, became water and painful light filled his awareness as electricity surged through him and the water on the bathroom floor, and likely the Yakuza as well.

"Hold on, Goji…" Hotaru's voice pleaded with him and then another voice, louder and stronger took its place in his mind. "Take my hand, Goji," Lord Fuzen's European tones demanded, and Goji mentally reached out without hesitation, accepting his former identity's help for the second time.

"Goji's back!" I came awake to the sound of Hotaru's jubilation.

I found myself in my own bed with the curtain drawn shut. Feeling somewhat disoriented, I sat up slowly and checked myself over. I remembered the intense pain after my encounter with Lady Lilyth's Hound, but my burns were gone and though I felt a little sore, I was otherwise perfectly fine. I silently thanked Ris before standing and drawing back the curtain to see what was going on out there.

"I'll go get Ris," I heard Masaru announce moments before he noticed me. "Yukari, how are ye feeling?"

"Much better, thank you. What's going on?"

"Yer friend Goji's back," Masaru explained with a shrug that said he didn't know how it was possible either, "but he's in a bad way and Hotaru's not much better. She was supposed to be resting."

"You go get Ris, then. I'll take a look at him in the meantime."

Goji had an entrance and an exit wound, with burn marks that indicated an electrical current had passed through his body, though there was nothing I could think of that would account for that here. Regardless, a little bit of time under Ris' healing field and Goji would be as good as new, though he would likely be some time resting.

Hotaru was simply exhausted. I sent her off to bed after looking her over, though she tried incessantly to explain to me how Goji had arrived. "You can tell me later. Get some sleep, Hotaru. You won't be fit for much if you don't."

Once that crisis had been dealt with, I headed back to my bed to pick up the bow and quiver of arrows that rested beside it. I had been unprepared for the battle with the Hounds last night and had paid the price for it – I wouldn't be so caught off-guard again.

"Penny for your thoughts?" my mother interjected, looking me over from where she stood in the curtained opening to my sleeping area.

"I was just thinking how I need to pick up some more arrows," I told her.

"That's how it is for you now, isn't it?" Mother asked with a sad smile. "All work and no time to consider anything else."

I realized she was not just speaking in general terms, but referring to something in particular as she looked me up and down. I flushed with embarrassment and didn't bother to follow her gaze – I knew the sad and likely disgusting state my Roughlander clothes were in once again. In fact, after the blast of fire I had taken from the Hound, it was a wonder my clothes were still intact; I suppose I had the many belts to thank for that.

"They're the only clothes I have," I mumbled shamefully. "I can't very well be out fighting in my dress."

"I know that, dear," Mother said with a sigh, "but you can't go around like that. I have an extra uniform that might fit you. We all brought a change of clothes."

I had dressed in my Mother's navy blue army-issued uniform before I remembered what Mifa had said about her sister preparing me a bundle of clothes. "Mother, are you doing anything in particular at the moment?"

"No, dear, I was worried about you," she responded with a grimace.

"I'm sorry if I caused you to worry, Mother. I can't say it won't happen again, but I was wondering if you wanted to come with me. There's someone I'd like you to meet."

"Sure, I'd like that," she answered, "but I have a request of my own. If we're going somewhere together can we walk there? Flying makes me nervous."

I laughed, though I knew she was absolutely serious; she had always hated the thought of flying and had always blatantly refused to board an airplane.

Mifa's house was a welcome refuge of happy domesticity. Felice was more than enthusiastic to show me to her wardrobe and the clothes she had set aside to give to me, while Mifa entertained my mother by showing her how to make crumblecakes. Felice kept me busy chatting, though I wanted a chance to give Mifa the happy news that Goji had returned.

When the doorbell eventually rang, I had the instant intuition of who it must be, and excusing myself from Felice, I scurried down the stairs to get to the door before Mifa could.

"Kaji? What are you doing here?" I demanded.

Kaji's awkward silence, in contrast with his usual confident demeanor, was enough to tip me off. "You? With Mifa?" I questioned. "But…Shuzhue…and Goji…"

"Is this the part where I only have ten seconds to explain myself?" Kaji mumbled.

I was a little hurt by his reference to a callous comment I had made the time he had discovered Shuzhue was missing, and had wanted to stay in the park to continue searching for clues to her whereabouts. *You have ten minutes, Kaji, then we're leaving,* I heard my own voice echo in my mind and wondered at a time when a very different Yukari had been so cold and unforgiving when it came to matters of the heart.

"No," I whispered, feeling the shame I should have felt then – the night when all this started. "I'm sorry, Kaji…I just didn't know. I assume you're going to tell her Goji's here? Go on then, just do me a favour please and don't hurt her, okay?"

"You've changed," Kaji stated. "The old Yukari wouldn't have said that, but to tell you the truth I like this version of you better."

"So do I," I agreed with a slight shake of my head; so much had changed in the past few months, not only me. "Go on, Kaji. I see Goji coming…I'll stall him for you."

Goji was indeed walking down the street toward us, dressed somewhat comically in one of the velvet curtains from the bedroom where I had left him, wrapped around him like a toga. Goji, ever one to bounce back from any trial, seemed jovial as we met on the street before Mifa's house. I had no choice but to tell him the truth, so he would be prepared, but curiously he wasn't upset. "I'm glad at least he was there for her when I couldn't be," Goji confided. "Kaji's a good friend, Yukari."

When Goji and I entered the little house, the group of us left Goji and Mifa alone in the kitchen while we retired to the main room to give them some privacy.

"Ah, young love." My mother sighed.

Felice giggled and their chatter continued. I tuned them out, having no wish to gossip, and found myself looking out the window instead, realizing I had slept the day away and now the sun was setting once more. This night would mark nine hours. As I watched the setting sun, I hardly noticed Goji and Mifa return from the kitchen together – I was lost in a sudden epiphany of how the Lillem could be combated.

"Yukari, are you coming?" Mother asked and I looked up to see everyone else had moved into the kitchen, following the warm sweet scent of freshly-baked crumblecakes.

"I'll be along in a minute. Save me one, okay?"

She left me alone and I let my head slump and closed my eyes, sending my awareness to Ao Kouen. I faded in behind him as he stood alone, halfway down the length of the bridge of Taiyou. I was awed once more at the sheer amount of power it must take for him to erect his barrier and maintain it, and I wondered if even the four of us Chosen of Sapphiros together would be able to accomplish something of the same magnitude.

"Ao Kouen." I said.

He whirled about to face me, surprised. "What is it?"

I realized abruptly I had yet to apologize to him for my behaviour at our last meeting. "I'm sorry," I told him.

Ao Kouen shrugged. "It's all right, I'm getting used to it."

"No, that's just the point," I countered, irritated by his tired acceptance. "It's not all right. I was out of line and I shouldn't have spoken to you that way. No one deserves the way I treated you. I suppose what I'm saying is I'd like the chance to be able to start over, if that's possible."

"Sure, why not?" he responded with a slightly lop-sided smile. "Is that all you came to tell me?"

"Well, no, not exactly. I came to tell you I think I've figured a way we can make headway against the Lillem–" I cut off abruptly, noticing motion in the distance. "What is she doing?"

"Yue?" Ao Kouen asked, turning about to face the barrier and trying to see who I was referring to. "I let her out with Jeth and Arashi before I put the barrier up because she said she wanted to try something…that's not Yue."

"No, it's Hotaru," I clarified.

For no reason I could fathom, my friend placed her hands on Ao Kouen's shield. How or why she had gotten that close to the flame barrier, I didn't understand, but either way there she was and the moment her hands came into contact with the fire, Ao Kouen dropped to his knees and gripped his head. "Stop her," Ao Kouen pleaded. "I can't hold it!"

I made to take off into the air before I remembered I wasn't fully there; right then as I was, my awareness was tied to Ao Kouen and I couldn't do much more than drift away from him slowly. I watched, unable to prevent it, as Hotaru somehow walked through the fire barrier. She must have been using some sort of power to accomplish it, but whatever it was she did caused a sort of ripple to occur in the shield.

Unaware of the chain of events she had set into motion, Hotaru walked away from the barrier. The shield behind her rippled and buckled, growing more and more erratic as Ao Kouen thrashed in pain at my feet, holding his head like his hands were the only thing keeping it attached to his body.

The ripple in the barrier surged outwards and the green flames began to solidify into one ribbon of power, gyrating wildly in the air, a weapon looking for a target. With the green haze of the shield missing, it was now possible to see into the dark desert beyond and the horde of Lillem shying back from the dangerous green energy. The colossal ribbon of power whirling in the air wasn't meant for them, though, I understood that immediately. The power, taken so forcefully out of Ao Kouen's control, was now searching for the intruder and it found it in the form of Hotaru, obliviously striding forward to engage the Lillem before her.

The weapon – for that is what the power had suddenly become – shot downwards in a deliberate arc. I watched, horrified and unable to intervene, as the power of Jedeite sought to destroy my friend. Somewhat surprisingly, it was Yue who came to Hotaru's rescue. In a sudden flash she was in the air between the ribbon and Hotaru, having leapt at her usual speed to intercept the blow. Extending her arm, Yue did the impossible and absorbed the power the way she had done with Fuzen's ruby eye, directing it through her body to emerge out her other arm and fire the weapon off into the air away from anyone who might get hurt.

I felt myself begin to fade and I whirled about to see what this was doing to Ao Kouen, only to watch him lose consciousness before I faded out completely.

Before I had even fully adjusted to the disorientation of returning to my body, I was up out of my chair and running for the door. I was flying well above the city before I happened to look down and realized somehow Kaji had used his power to attach himself to me as I left. He dangled impossibly in the air below me, though I didn't feel any weight from his presence. I was flying due east as fast as my wings could carry me. The western edge of Taiyou should be relatively free of Lillem, thanks to our efforts there the night prior and Yue's cleansing of the sand. The southern entry point into the country was well guarded by the Legionnaires and our allied forces. There was nothing I could do about the northern border, being so far away, but the eastern bridge, I was concerned about.

Halfway there, I stopped and hovered in place high up in the air; with my enhanced vision I could see the Raman Bridge clearly from here. On the far side of the bridge stood a sizeable force of Lillem, all pushing for their chance to cross into the lands kept from them until this very moment. On the near side stood the Lion Brigade, Rama's countrymen, formed up to face the threat head on.

Forming a single cyan arrow, I took aim on the distant skies and unleashed my power. My first arrow struck exactly where I intended it, directly above the Raman Bridge into the shadow of low-forming clouds that had gathered there, almost as if to give my arrow a target to connect with. From that cloud, hundreds of cyan arrows fell like rain, exploding on contact with the unfortunate Lillem below and destroying them before they could cross into Taiyou.

"That's my cue," I heard Kaji announce from below me, and I looked down to see that far below us, one of Lady Lilyth's Hounds was running full tilt across the plains.

Kaji didn't move, but a clone of himself appeared between the Kaji attached to me and the distant ground. The clone – or I suppose that was Kaji, now – drew a thin-bladed sword from the sheath at his waist as he fell and held it pointed downwards as he angled himself to strike the Hound.

I silently wished Kaji luck and let loose a second arrow to follow after my first. That accomplished, I whirled about in the air to head back the way I had come. I thought I had left Kaji behind me with the Hound until I heard him calling my name over the wind of our passage.

"Yukari! We have a problem!"

I turned about to see what was the matter; a streak of green lit up the sky as the energy Yue had fired off to save Hotaru came whipping back through the air. Be that source Yue, Ao Kouen, Hotaru, or Taiyou itself, regardless, the country and the people would pay the price when the weapon struck. Putting on as much speed as I could muster, I raced Kaji and I back to the city. I didn't know what I could do, but I was determined to reach where I could be of use.

Thankfully the palace was near the northern edge of the city and so it was the first place we reached. I skidded to a landing in the courtyard before Gin-Kouteki, where I found a crowd of nervous-looking Roughlanders eyeing the green beacon in the sky and wondering what it meant. Kaji disappeared nearly as soon as his feet touched the ground, his clone splashing to a puddle as he re-appeared somewhere else. Spotting Masaru with Yuge, Hitachi, and Razor at the front of the crowd, I broke into a run to reach them.

"It's Ao Kouen's power," I stated breathlessly. "It got out of his control when Hotaru walked through the shield. It tried to attack her, but Yue sent it away – now it's come back and–"

"And nothing will survive where it strikes," Masaru finished. "Yue told me about what happens when power forms a ribbon like that. The weapon Taiyou had before, that Lord Viron was going to use against us. It fired a ribbon of power like that which could destroy a whole outpost."

"Get everyone together and tell them to hold hands," I instructed. "I'll need contact if this is going to work."

It was a measure of the Roughlanders' growing respect for me that it took no time at all for every single person in that courtyard to grab hold of someone else. My face held high with determination in the face of the destruction coming for us, I took hold of Masaru's hand on my left and Razor's to my right and closed my eyes. I took a deep breath and tried to feel the people connected to me. In less than a moment, I could feel them like individual drops of dew on a spider's web made from my power that fanned out over the whole courtyard, and maybe even a little beyond. There were three hundred and fifty-two people; though some felt different – eight were Croatin.

I hardly knew how, but I grabbed hold of them all with my power and when I felt the concussive force of the weapon striking down the palace of Taiyou, I turned us all to mist to float as safe as anyone could be along the aftershock of the great green wave of Jedeite's power gone awry.

CH. 17 – THE CALM BEFORE THE STORM

66"Yukari! Yukari!" I heard Masaru frantically calling my name.

I struggled to sit up. I wasn't hurt exactly, but my body felt like lead and it wouldn't listen to me. I opened my eyes, though they felt gritty. I had an awful flashback to my first few moments on this world when I had arrived in the center of the Sand Lake with no protection whatsoever from the searing sun, but here and now it was dark and surprisingly chilly.

I was damp, I realized, and lying in sand with someone – a Roughlander I didn't know – draped over my legs, which is why I hadn't been able to feel them. I forced myself to sit up just a little, but abruptly felt weak and dizzy, and cautiously settled myself back down.

"Masaru," Razor's voice called out in the darkness, "she's over here!"

Razor reached my side first and pulled the Roughlander off me as Masaru arrived and pulled me into a grateful hug.

"Ye did it, Yukari!" Masaru exclaimed. "Ye saved us, all of us."

I shook my head, feeling tears I couldn't control welling up. "Not everyone, just those I could reach. Is Taiyou…?" I couldn't finish my sentence; I couldn't put the devastation into words.

"Taiyou looks fine from here," Razor interjected, "though I'd be surprised to see the palace still standing after that. How're you feeling?"

"Fine," I answered, feeling somewhat relieved at Razor's pronouncement, "just tired, that's all. Masaru?"

"Yes?" By his tone, I gathered I had him worried.

"Even if our room…" I swallowed hard. I couldn't bear to think of the palace being destroyed. "Can you just take me somewhere I can rest?"

"Of course," Masaru answered, taking me into his arms and standing in a fluid motion – it seemed I was the only one weakened by our desperate flight.

I looked about from my vantage point in Masaru's arms. We were out in the darkened desert and there was not a Lillem in sight, nor even in earshot. Somehow, the desert seemed even darker than it usually did and as I tried to focus on the way before us, I realized it was because none of my powers were working; I was simply too exhausted.

All around us were Roughlanders of varied descriptions and other citizens of Taiyou I hadn't even known were in that courtyard or the palace before disaster struck. Most people were getting to their feet now, some more disoriented than others, but none quite in the state I was, having used every drop of power I could command to get us here.

The green shockwave had carried us a long way, but conveniently southward and not too far past the bridge of Taiyou. Even with my weight potentially slowing him down, it wasn't long before Masaru reached the bridge of Taiyou and began to cross it. I felt a cumbersome bother, but I didn't quite have the energy to be anything else, so I settled myself comfortably into Masaru's chest and took advantage of the silent night to close my eyes for just a moment.

When next I opened them, I became aware of a heavy silence and the fact that more time had passed than I expected. The tense quiet was broken only by the clinking sounds of people in armour going to and fro with some urgency. Somehow in what had felt no more than a moment for me, Masaru had traversed the length of the bridge of Taiyou and we had reached the space before the gates, where the Legionnaires were stationed to guard Taiyou.

Now around us were not only Taiyoun Legionnaires in their white, dove-themed armour, but intermingled with them in almost equal numbers were members of Mikura's Deathsquad, supervised by their Captain, Grinkin. Mikura herself was draped over a fallen Deathsquad soldier and crying uncontrollably. Beside them, I watched as a Legionnaire and a Deathsquad worked together to lay another body beside the first; this time, a Legionnaire. Mikura looked up at the disturbance and began wailing with doubled distress.

As much as I may have once considered Mikura an enemy, the scene before me still tugged forcefully on my heartstrings. It was suddenly, painfully clear to me now, as it perhaps had never fully been before, that the Deathsquad soldiers were just as fully human as anyone else, as were their generals – Kichigai and Mikura came to mind, specifically.

Judging by the state of disarray the Roughlanders I rescued had landed in, I could well imagine what had happened here – when the green wave hit, no doubt the concussive force was enough to scatter the Deathsquad and Legionnaires. By the manner of death – drowning – it was likely these two, if not more like them, had been thrown into the lake.

There being nothing I could do to help, had I even the strength to be of use, I closed my ears to the sound of Mikura's crying and buried my face back into Masaru's chest to shut everything out until I had the energy to deal with it.

"Make her fix him," I heard Yue's voice demand sharply from out of nowhere and I felt Masaru's hold tighten around me.

"She's not really in a state to help anyone else right now," he replied defensively. "She's done more than enough for one night."

I fought my closing eyelids and turned my head to see what they were arguing about, only to find angry tears falling freely down Yue's face. In her arms she held a limp Ao Kouen.

Masaru was right in saying there was nothing I could do. Whatever had brought him to this state was no doubt tied to the malfunction of his shield, and therefore had been caused by his own magic. Yue would be best to bring him somewhere he could rest and then find Ris to see if the Kumori could discover more. I opened my mouth to tell her this, when I noticed her malevolent expression. She was staring beyond me now, her eyes dark with rage. As I watched her, it felt as if the air around her had gone still, yet despite this her impossibly long hair began to drift and move of its own accord and the shadows those strands caused seemed to grow longer – was she using some sort of power?

I craned my neck with some effort to follow Yue's gaze, only to realize I knew full well where Yue's rage would be directed – Hotaru.

"Yue!" I said.

Her attention snapped to me and in that singular instant I saw hurt and sadness behind the rage in her eyes. Masking over her brief moment of vulnerability almost as quickly as she had shown it, she flashed away faster than my eyes could follow. I didn't know where she was taking Ao Kouen, but as Masaru resumed motion my brain sluggishly brought me to the conclusion that otherwise would have been nearly instantaneous – Yue loved him.

I remembered my own reactions each and every time Masaru had been in some sort of danger and I immediately understood that Yue had shown a remarkable amount of restraint in regards to Hotaru. My oblivious friend was safe for the moment, but there was no telling if the storm of Yue's anger would pass before the two encountered each other again.

After a long and sleepless day, Hotaru was at the end of her rope emotionally and mentally. Sabien had been frustratingly patient in his efforts to explain to her the scope of the damage she'd inadvertently caused. She now knew every detail of the devastation that had resulted from her actions, but Sabien's refusal to scold her only amplified her feelings of guilt and left her unable to rest with her unbelievably heavy conscience.

Wandering the halls of the palace of Taiyou in the late afternoon, Hotaru found herself hesitating on the threshold of the Jade throne room. "I…" Hotaru began, unsure of how to put her feelings into words. In the end she settled on the simplest thing to come out the tangled mess of her thoughts. "I'm sorry, Ao Kouen, terribly sorry."

"There are a great many people you owe an apology to Hotaru," Ao Kouen told her, "but thanks to what you've done I don't have the luxury of forgiveness."

She had known explaining herself to Ao Kouen wasn't going to be easy, but never had she realized it was going to be this hard. "I don't understand," Hotaru admitted. "Are you saying you won't even let me try to make it up to you?"

"It is I who am responsible for what happened to my power," Ao Kouen stated tonelessly. "My weakness was not your fault, Hotaru, so in my mind there is nothing to forgive. I would suggest you let the subject drop and be cautious around Yue."

"So would it be possible for us to be friends again someday?" Hotaru asked, but Ao Kouen didn't wait to hear her out; he was already taking himself out of her presence.

Fighting back the tears that threatened to come again, Hotaru took refuge in the empty throne room before she had to go out and face the world once more. Yesterday she had been somewhat of a hero, bringing Goji back to this world, but today she was the worst sort of villain and she didn't know how she could possibly make people like her again.

"You dare show your face in here?" Hotaru stiffened as Yue's voice came from behind her and she felt the air in the room take on a dangerous stillness.

Hotaru turned about slowly, dreading the expression she was sure to find on Yue's face. "I came to apologize," she volunteered cautiously, Ao Kouen's warning fresh in her mind, "but I'll be going now."

"You came to apologize to Ao Kouen, *but not to me?*" Yue questioned, her voice darkening mid-sentence.

Yue's hair, always impossibly long, had been dyed white ever since Yue declared herself the Mediator of Taiyou on the day of Ao Kouen's coronation. Now that white hair seemed to have taken on a will of its own, wafting on a nonexistent wind, and its colour was contrasted sharply by deep shadows that had no rational explanation for their presence.

"What's going on?" Hotaru asked, surprised to hear the fear in her own voice. "Why are you doing this?"

"Why did you take down Ao Kouen's shield? You put all of Taiyou at risk!" Yue's voice continued to deepen until it was no longer recognizable. Her hair was wildly out of control now, whipping about her face as Yue herself seemed to grow and change.

Every inch of Yue darkened and seemed to pulse outwards until she was more than seven feet tall and looming darkly over Hotaru. Her long hair turned from white to the darkest shadow and fanned out behind her to appear as wings made up of dark, rippling tendrils. Her face elongated grotesquely, until it appeared more demonic than human and only the eyes were recognizable, due to the eerie cyan glow that marked them as belonging to a Chosen of Sapphiros. Yue's terrifying transformation completed with her fingers curving into wickedly pointed claws and her form taking on an almost animalistic appearance as it backed into a crouch, seeming ready to pounce if Hotaru even considered trying to flee from it.

"You will not do such a thing again," Demon-Yue stated as if her words were already fact.

"No…of course not, I…" Hotaru managed.

Without warning, the thing's clawed hand shot out and wrapped itself around Hotaru's head before she even had a chance to react. *"You will promise."* It demanded obedience. *"Never again."*

"Yue…you're hurting me…" Hotaru whimpered, having a hard time believing in the reality of the thing before her, even if the sharp claws around her skull felt real enough.

The demon snorted in disgust and with a sudden sharp downward motion released its hold on Hotaru, sending her plummeting to the unforgiving Jade floor below.

Thanks to the efforts of the other Chosen, only the topmost level of the palace had truly suffered from the impact of Ao Kouen's power returning in such a forceful and unorthodox manner. Gin-Kouteki, stationed where he was, had also felt the force of the blast, his legs finally giving way after the damage they had sustained in the fight against the Lillem the previous night.

Upon waking and having discovered the damage to the palace was not as extensive as I had believed, I hurried down to the dungeons, intent on confirming my theories concerning the Lillem when I came across Hotaru on my way back upstairs. She was walking, though barely under her own power, leaning heavily on the wall and sort of shuffling along down the hallway.

"Hotaru?" When she turned at the sound of her name, I saw the purpling bruises developing on her face. "What happened to you?!"

"It was Yue..." she managed to mumble through her tears. "She tried to kill me, Yukari. I know I deserve her being mad at me, but..."

"Shh..." I tried to calm her as best I could. "No one deserves what she did to you, Hotaru. You made a mistake, yes, but you didn't hurt anyone deliberately."

"The worst part is...she was my friend...and I don't think I'll ever be able to trust her again now. Even if she didn't mean to–"

"Don't," I interjected, a little more forcefully than I intended. "Don't trust her, Hotaru. Not anymore, not after this. I'm not even sure how far I trust her myself and I have less reason than you do."

"But–" Hotaru tried to protest.

"Just stay away from her if you can manage it, Hotaru. I know the four of us have to work together sometimes, but if you're around her make sure you keep your guard up so this doesn't happen again."

Hotaru nodded, subdued, and I offered to turn her to mist and carry her upstairs to Ris, thinking for the time being it was best to keep this incident to ourselves and see which way Yue was going to jump. Yue had always been hard to read and even more difficult to understand, but something kept telling me this was something else entirely and I was determined I would get to the bottom of it, if only for Hotaru's sake.

That evening the skies turned dark and foreboding even before night officially fell. For the first time in hundreds of years, dark clouds rolled in, threatening a storm infinitely more fierce than anyone in Taiyou had ever experienced, save perhaps those who had been on this planet eight hundred years ago. No one, not even those of us from Earth, could have predicted just how violent the weather would get and how quickly.

When the clouds rolled in with a dangerous suddenness, Masaru and I were at the Roughlander Sanctioned Outpost spending some time with Razor, who it seemed had been staying there with his gang, among others. Mostly due to my lectures on the subject, Razor and Masaru understood the warning in the skies better than most, and together the three of us were able to warn the Roughlanders present so they could take cover before the storm got too dangerous.

Immediately worried about the rest of the Roughlanders, who would have no frame of reference for storms, Masaru and I left Razor in charge of the outpost as we hurried back to the palace courtyard where we knew most of the others would be. By the time we reached the palace, the wind had already picked up to the point where it wasn't practical for me to fly anymore and lightning flashed occasionally through the sky, followed by loud peals of thunder.

The party on and around Gin-Kouteki was in full swing, with the Roughlanders unaware of the danger growing around them and seeing only the miracle of rain and enjoying the extraordinary effect of light flashing across the sky. From my vantage point down in the open courtyard, I could make out Neva among the other Roughlanders, dancing and carousing without a care in the world, high upon Gin-Kouteki's broad shoulders. The wind and water whipped about her, making her footing on the binoid's slick metal treacherous at best, but it wasn't until hail began to fall that a few of the Roughlanders began to realize what sort of trouble they were in.

"I'll get them down from there," Masaru said.

I nodded absently to him, trying to direct those who could hear or see me while still keeping my eyes on the people up above. I distantly noted Masaru hoisting himself up onto the Binoid, but my attention was drawn to Neva who, having taken a solid hit from a particularly large hailstone, lost her footing and was pitched from the giant robot.

Instinctively, I turned Neva to mist before I had taken into consideration how ineffective using almost any of my powers would be in these hazardous conditions. It was a mental struggle just to hold her together against the wind and eventually I had to realize there was little hope of bringing her safely to me. Reforming her in the air, I took off like a shot, fighting the wind and hail for all I was worth with my wings until I managed to grab hold of her and pull her in close. Wrapping my arms around her, I tried desperately to keep us from ramming into anything larger than a hailstone as I mentally formed an arrow and shot it downwards. The arrow whizzed about erratically, trailing a length of white rope behind it, and I kept a tight hold to the other end. I didn't care where the arrow landed, so long as it stuck in and I could use the rope to haul us both safely to the ground.

Thankfully, my desperate ploy worked, and once our feet touched the cobblestones of the courtyard, I ushered Neva over the drawbridge and into the main doors of the palace. That accomplished, I turned myself back around and headed back out into the storm.

The pieces of hail had gotten visibly larger, but were now less frequent and interspersed with a heavy rain. I peered through it all upwards at Gin-Kouteki, searching for how Masaru was faring, but no sooner had I located him, standing with Yuge upon the gun barrel, did the unthinkable happen. The Binoid's large metal form fulfilled its role as the best conductor Taiyou had to offer and when the first bolt of lightning struck low enough to reach ground, it was to Gin-Kouteki it was inevitably drawn. I stood frozen, unable to react, as lightning arced through the metal robot and before my very eyes Gin-Kouteki's two shoulder cannons exploded with concussive force.

The shock was enough to nullify my powers and make me in effect as useless as I felt. When usually my vision power allowed me to compensate for almost any conditions, now at the worst possible time I had to rely upon the infrequent flashes of the storm to make anything out. Masaru was visible in the afterimage of the explosion, but he was gone when the lightning flashed again.

I felt all the breath in my body leave me in a whoosh as I absently felt my knees make contact with the wet ground beneath me. It was like I was choking; I just couldn't seem to get enough air. I scanned the area around the explosion for any sign of what had happened to him – he couldn't just be gone.

The lightning and thunder were coming closer together now and the next couple flashes revealed horrific scenes of mangled corpses and people still alive, calling and reaching out for help amidst the wreckage. Scraps and wires that had formerly made up Gin-Kouteki's shoulder cannons and other more substantial pieces that had been his arms lay scattered about, but I saw none of it.

"What are you doing?!" I heard a familiar voice ask from just behind me – Hotaru. "How can you just sit there when there are people there who need your help?"

Her words barely registered with me – something was happening out there. I knew whatever was causing the water to swirl against the current in the center of the cobblestone courtyard couldn't be explained by rational means – and that meant power.

When I saw sand moving in the water, my first thought was to wonder if somehow the Lillem had found a way into Taiyou, but as the sand coalesced and reformed from the ground up, I realized I was very much mistaken. The sand drew together and painstakingly formed every minute detail of him. His sturdy rough hide pants, his loose shirt, and every last notch of his numerous belts. It formed a perfect sculpture of him, though lacking any colour save the soggy brown of wet sand, as if it was mocking what I had lost.

I stared at the apparition before me, unable to breathe for fear it would just fall apart and leave me with nothing, not even the semblance of him, when unexpectedly the sand solidified and Masaru was there – really there.

Unbeknownst to me at the time, as I had been staring at the scene before me, Hotaru had left my side to do what I hadn't been functional enough to accomplish. Turning herself to water, she had flitted about the wreckage as a puddle and turned each and every person she came across to water with her, making her puddle grow in size to save as many people as she could and bring them to where the healers could have a look at them. At the very same moment when Masaru appeared, Hotaru had arrived by my side once more, determined to rescue me as well, or perhaps just snap me out of my shocked state. At first, as I melted against my own volition, I had trouble comprehending what was happening. All I knew was Masaru was before me and I wanted desperately to reach him to make sure he was real, but I was being tugged away from him as if in a horrible dream where my legs wouldn't obey my commands.

In fact, the whole mess felt like a nightmare, from the sudden storm to the explosion of Gin-Kouteki to Masaru's strange re-appearance. It wasn't until Hotaru reformed us all in the operating room and I saw the sad state the Roughlanders were in that I started to once again believe any of this was really happening.

Not sparing a glance for Hotaru, and forcing myself to ignore the suffering around me, I spun on my heels and fled the room as soon as I was able, but he wasn't in the courtyard any longer and neither was anyone else, thanks to the still growing storm. I kept running into the wild wind, heedless of the rain pounding down all around me and only distantly thankful there wasn't hail any longer to slow me down further. I ran until I was forced to take shelter under an overhanging arch of a building, unable to even see through the rain in front of me, and realizing at last that running around out here blindly was not doing me or Masaru any good.

I forced myself to calm down. My powers were the only answer now. I considered briefly firing off a message arrow, but I knew watching that arrow explode because it couldn't locate him was the last thing I would be able to handle, and trying to follow even a glowing cyan arrow in this weather would be nearly impossible, regardless. No, I needed something a little more direct, and for that I needed concentration. Settling myself down on the wet ground, I forced myself to remember the meditation techniques Sabien had taught me when I was first learning to master my powers.

Remember fear, Sabien's voice echoed in my mind. *Remember fear and then use that fear to defend yourself.*

Then, the fear I had drawn upon to be my strength had been the horrific visage of the guardians of little Lilyth's valley, but for quite some time now my fear had not been mastered like I had thought; it had evolved into something much more complex. I feared losing Masaru and that was what had reduced me to such a useless state to begin with, so that was what I would have to overcome in order to find him again.

Water cannot be injured. Something else Sabien had taught me. *Water cannot be stopped, it flows where it will.* Sabien was right; essentially, I was water and my will would allow me to flow to where I needed to be. My power activated and all of a sudden I knew exactly where Masaru was; not his physical location as if on a map, but I could feel his presence nonetheless. I held onto that presence and sent myself to him.

He was on the ground floor of the Roughlander Sanctioned Outpost, looking just the same as he always did, if sodden from the rain. "Yukari?" he was calling up the stairs; he had been looking for me.

"I'm here," I spoke softly from behind him and he whirled about to face me.

"Oh, there ye are," he sounded relieved until he noticed my incorporeal form highlighted by the fact that when I was mist like this my wings were always visible, "but ye're not actually here, are ye? Where's the rest of ye?"

I wanted so badly to physically be where my astral form was right now that my power manifested on my behalf and granted my wish. I felt myself grow solid and knew somehow my body halfway across the city from here had drifted into nothing but mist, as if it hadn't been there at all.

"I'm here," I stated again, this time with more conviction.

I hardly noticed crossing half the distance to him when I realized he was doing the same and I put out a hand to stop him before he could wrap me in his arms.

"What is it?" Masaru asked.

I tried unsuccessfully to meet his eyes. "Your power…"

All I could see in my mind when I looked at him was the way Lillem crashed into sand when they were defeated, the way they rose from the sand that created them each night, and the horror I had felt when the Blue Moon Knights had dissipated into nothing but piles of sand.

Masaru seemed to grasp my meaning immediately. "I'm still the person ye know," he insisted.

I struggled with a realization. Lady Lilyth had created her Hounds and likely the Lillem as well by sharing some of her power with them – hadn't I done the same to Masaru? Had I made him something less or more than human – something altogether different?

Though a part of me feared what I would discover, I forced myself to look Masaru up and down using my power to see beneath his skin. All I saw was flesh and bone and not a hint of sand, but Masaru cut my examination short, reaching out a hand to put it under my chin and force my eyes up to meet his.

"Yukari, look at me," he pleaded. "I know what it is ye saw, but I promise ye nothing has changed. I love you–"

"Whatever you are now," I raised my hand and took a deep breath before continuing, "I made you this way and that makes me responsible for it." I knew as I said it that it also meant I couldn't turn my back on him – not now or ever. I couldn't hate or fear him for what I had done to him, inadvertently or otherwise – I simply wouldn't let myself.

Masaru took my outstretched hand and placed it on his chest above his beating heart, drawing me closer to him in the process. "And you've saved me in so many ways."

"I love you, Masaru," I told him and I meant it.

We stayed in each other's arms for some time, until our moment together was interrupted by the shaking of the outpost building around us. I was surprised, but Masaru's expression was beyond shock and he immediately crouched to the ground, putting his hand flat to the floor.

"What is it?" I asked him.

"It feels like a whole herd of sandcrawlers approaching, but from way underground," Masaru informed me. "I've never felt anything quite like it."

"I don't think it's a sandcrawler, Masaru," I responded with a frown, instinctively examining the outpost tower for structural integrity and to see if that first tremor had damaged it. "That felt very much like an earthquake. I hope we don't get any more of those or that they don't get any worse." I crossed the ground floor of the outpost to look out the doorway. "It looks like the rain has stopped for the moment and the wind has calmed down. This could be just the eye of the storm, but let's try to get back to the palace while we can. I don't think this building is the safest place to be and there are injured Roughlanders who could use my help back there."

It was a long, hard night and many people had been injured in the storm, having not been aware of the dangers the weather could pose. The Knights had dispersed themselves as best they could within the city to guide people to safety or rescue people. The city guard stations became safe havens for the displaced and Sabien and Hotaru spent most of their night flitting from location to location as water to relay information, people, and supplies as needed. I spent the night with Ris and the other medics in the palace helping the poor victims of the unfortunate incident involving Gin-Kouteki.

Rama had been struck by lightning not once, but twice. When Rama found me in my rooms – that is to say when I found him running through the curtains in my room in his attempt to be patient and wait for my return – he insisted nothing was really wrong with him.

"It's just I feel rather funny and I can't seem to sit down for even a minute," he announced, speaking very quickly, the speed and his accent making him almost impossible to understand. "Kaji said I should come to you, so here I am. Can you do anything?"

"First of all, when and how did this happen?" I asked.

"First, I was down at the bridge," he began. "I was wearing my armour, you see, with the other soldiers and Legionnaires, and it wasn't until I got hit that Adel realized what was happening and made us all take our armour off. Thankfully, Ao Kouen has gotten the defenses of Taiyou sorted out and we're not so much needed to defend the bridge any longer even without the flame barrier. Did you know that the Lillem didn't so much as do anything when the storm hit, they simply stood there and let those white balls from the sky take them out one at a time—"

"Rama!" I interrupted his flow of speech and directed his attention to me once more.

"Yes?"

"The second time? You said you were struck twice. When was the second time?"

"It was afterwards. I thought the worst of it was over and I was making my way back to the palace when I stopped at that café across the courtyard to take cover from the rain for a moment. It sought me out, Yukari, I swear to you. It came at me sideways while I was under at least partial cover and I was wearing what you see me in now."

I took in Rama's appearance fully for the first time since I found him here. He was not wearing his usual armour or his finery, but plain clothes and he wasn't even fully dry yet. "What have you been doing this entire time, then, if you haven't slept?"

"Walking. Around," he answered evasively. "Doing laps. Going through walls. I can't stop. I've honestly tried everything."

"All right, I get it." I put my hand on his shoulder to try to get him to settle down and I got a shock for my troubles. "All I can think is that you're still charged somehow. We need to ground you and since the ground itself isn't working for that," I said as I eyed his feet, which were bare as he had left his armoured boots behind somewhere, "we'll have to bring you to water."

"All right, let's go!" Rama tugged me enthusiastically out the door and through the palace halls. It was an exercise in futility to try and calm him down, but I did my best, talking calmly and slowly as we walked and I forced him to keep to my normal pace. On our way down to the Lake of Taiyou, I lectured him about storms, lightning, and electricity, and the science behind them. When we had almost reached the bridge I began to explain to him in detail how to swim.

"So you'll just have to float for a little bit and don't worry, if something happens I'll be there to help you out," I concluded, reaching the rail of the bridge near enough to the place where Yue had gone swimming while trying to find Sabien.

"What? You want me to go in there? Swimming?" Rama questioned in his rapid-fire way, which hadn't slowed in the slightest even during our lengthy walk across the city. "I haven't been in water since I was a little boy. I don't know how to swim."

"Unfortunately, it's a part of your treatment," I informed him mercilessly, "so you're just going to have to do it. Hopefully it won't take more than a minute."

I figured Rama would hesitate, but before I had even so much as blinked the man was in the water splashing about. I watched him flounder for a moment, thinking maybe he would get the hang of it, but he didn't. Within moments, the Knight was under the water and sinking fast, his flailing limbs slowing dramatically as he drifted away from me.

I dove in the water after him and two strokes later I had him in my grasp and was hauling us both upwards. I wasn't a strong person, but I was a strong swimmer, so it didn't take me too long to break the surface and pull him up with me. Holding onto him with one hand, I hauled myself back onto the bridge with the other and then dragged him up after me. At last, I had the sodden Knight laid out beside me and I was panting with the effort, but Rama hadn't drowned badly enough that he needed any encouragement to cough up the water in his lungs. I left him to it, taking my own moment to enjoy simply breathing.

"You okay?" I asked him once the coughing had eased.

"Much better, thank you," he responded after a moment, sounding subdued, "but tell me the truth, was that strictly necessary?"

I laughed, surprising myself. "No, I suppose it wasn't. A bathtub would have done just as well."

Rama met my laughter with his own and for once the two of us were able to simply enjoy the other's company. For a good long while we stayed there on the bridge of Taiyou in the sun, drying off at nature's pace in silent companionship.

Just before noon, when the sun was high in the sky, we were interrupted by Ao Kouen, of all people. The King of Taiyou was striding down the bridge with Kaji, Yue, and Hotaru behind him and, upon reaching Rama and I, he asked the Knight if he could speak to me in private.

"What's going on?" I asked.

"I have a request to make of you," Ao Kouen said. "I've arranged a meeting with a representative of the Ruby City and I would like all the Chosen to attend."

I raised an eyebrow at this. "Don't you think there would be diplomats better suited to this kind of meeting than the four of us?"

"Perhaps," he admitted, "but none of them have as much at stake in this as we have and we also have something of value that can be offered in exchange for the Ruby City's co-operation. I know how you feel about this, Yukari, you've made that clear, but I need someone with your viewpoint to be able to pick up on what others may not see."

"All right," I agreed cautiously. "So when and where is this meeting taking place?"

"Now," he answered, gesturing for the others to join us, "just outside of Taiyou. If you've noticed, I've reinstated the original defenses with Jedeite's help, so we can leave now and return to the country at will, and only those with negative intent to Taiyou will be prevented."

I could never have anticipated who the Vile Emperor would send to meet us, but in retrospect, the decision made a great deal of sense. Lady Akuma Kijo, as we were introduced to her, was accompanied by a Deathsquad General for her protection. The General was a large man of few words and dour expressions, but the confidence with which he held his dual-bladed staff and a mask that looked like it might just double as a shield immediately indicated he was likely a fierce fighter.

"My name is Bastion," the broad-shouldered man announced in a thick European accent.

Shuzhue, by contrast, was not armed or armoured in any way, unless one counted the symbol she wore openly on her chest marking her for what she was – Chosen of Rubia. The telltale red diamond with the topmost tip as a stylized flame sat visible above her low neckline.

"I am very grateful you have come to speak with us, Lady Akuma," Ao Kouen began once the introductions had been completed. "I believe it is possible we could be of some help to each other in the current unfortunate circumstances."

Akuma offered Ao Kouen a slight nod of her head. "I would like to formally thank you for your hospitality in housing two of my Generals and what remains of their squads, but other than a formal cessation of any hostilities between us, I fail to see what we can offer each other."

"Information, mainly," Ao Kouen responded. "I'll put it as bluntly as I can manage – are you currently experiencing the same level of difficulties as we are each night? I'm sure your Generals have reported our circumstances to you."

"Indeed they have," she answered cautiously and then, taking a deep breath, seemed to relax her reserve a little. "Yes," she admitted, "my city is under great duress each night. Your request for a cease fire is commendable, but you have little to fear from us as we have recalled all of our Generals, save the ones you have here."

"Lillem?" Ao Kouen ventured. "Hounds? Or is it both?"

Akuma grimaced. "Hounds have been sighted, but they have yet to attempt to breach our defenses. It is the Lillem we must contend with, only we have more than just the sand Lillem you have encountered. There are ones far worse than that."

"And the weather?" Ao Kouen pressed. "Has it gotten out of control in your part of the world?"

"The weather last night was nothing in comparison to what is to come," she stated, "but the world has survived it once before and it will do so again because it must."

"Either way," Ao Kouen continued, "I still feel we can be of use to one another and it cannot be denied we have a common enemy."

"The Lillem?" she asked with an arched brow.

"The Lady Lilyth," Ao Kouen answered, meeting Akuma stare for stare, "but we can start with the Lillem if you'd prefer. Yukari?"

I stepped forward and offered a nod of my head in Ao Kouen's direction, still studying Shuzhue out of the corner of my eye.

"You told me you had discovered a way to make headway against the Lillem threat," Ao Kouen commented.

"Yes, I did," I said, "and I finally had the opportunity to test it. I'm glad to be able to say it works, though I don't know if just anyone can learn to do it."

"You have a method of successfully combating the Lillem?" Shuzhue asked me, her expression betraying doubt and hope in equal measure. "So they don't just return the next night?"

"And more importantly, both Yue and I can cure someone who's been infected by the Lillem," I added with only the slightest hint of smugness – I had worked long and hard at discovering a method of my own to do what before only Yue could.

"We've done our best to keep the casualties to a minimum, but we've still had to kill too many of our own to stop them from turning against us," Shuzhue admitted. "You must show me how it is done if it is possible to stop them."

I reached down to pull up a handful of sand. "It would be simpler with a microscope," I mentioned casually, watching her red-tinted eyes for a reaction and getting only a knowing look for my troubles, "but you'll just have to look as closely as possible."

I sprinkled some of the sand from my right hand to my left and examined it for the black specks and, using my finger, tried to move a few into a clump so she could make them out. "Do you see them?"

"The black bits?"

I nodded. "Yes, it's igneous rock from a volcano and it's that which animates the Lillem."

"It's Ruby," she corrected me.

I gave her a knowing look of my own. "Yes, well…if you can eliminate the Ruby that animates them, then the Lillem can't reform. And when a person is pierced by a Lillem talon, the Lillem injects bits of this rock into that person's body and the power within it is strong enough to mutate them, and then usually take over their minds with simple commands."

"Take their blood, take their lives, take their land, take their power," Kaji supplied helpfully.

"So how do you get rid of the Ruby?" Shuzhue asked. "Gem stones are near to indestructible."

"The only way I've been able to discover is to fight magic with magic," I stated. "Burning them out, or neutralizing the power they have with your own. That's why, for now at least, only Knights or Chosen might be able to learn how to defeat the Lillem as they have the power necessary."

"Show me, then," Lady Akuma of the Ruby City commanded, "and you shall have any help I can offer you in return."

Ch. 18 – The Ties that Bind

Yue's cleansing fire was a little easier for Shuzhue to wrap her head around than my mist, as it had to do with fire, which was an element she more readily identified with. One moment Yue and Shuzhue were seated cross-legged on the sand facing each other, surrounded in a spiral of white and red fire in an attempt to cleanse the land, and the next moment Fuun had Shuzhue hauled to her feet with a sword held to her throat just close enough to draw a trickle of blood.

"Hello, Akuma," Fuun greeted her in a deadly monotone. "I see you've finally decided to leave the protection of your city."

There was not a soul among us who didn't freeze at Fuun's sudden arrival, momentarily struck with the fear that he could ruin everything we had worked for with a single stroke.

"Fuun," Akuma acknowledged him coldly and as if her words had been some sort of signal, several things happened at once.

Yue flashed to her feet as Kaji and Bastion surged forward and Hotaru drew her swords, but it was Shuzhue's response that mattered most. She simply activated her power as a Chosen of Rubia, causing Fuun to fall immediately to his knees, wracked with instant pain in every inch of his body. Kaji reached her side first, but Bastion arrived shortly after.

"Are you all right, my Lady?" Bastion questioned

"Yes, Bastion, I'm fine." Akuma stepped back from her would-be killer and put a tentative hand to her throat, which came away wet with blood.

But Fuun wasn't – I could see it from here.

"Please, whatever you're doing to him, stop it," I pleaded.

Thankfully Ao Kouen backed me up. "Yes, Fuun is our ally and therefore our responsibility. Let him go and we will see he is suitably punished for interrupting these proceedings."

"See that he is," Akuma said coldly and then tore her eyes away; Fuun's spasms immediately eased, though they did not stop.

Dismissing Shuzhue from my mind as best I could, I knelt down before Fuun and spoke to him in a low voice as I looked him over, "Please, Fuun, co-operate at least until we get you back into the borders of Taiyou. This meeting is very important to Taiyou's defense and it would be disaster to us if you harmed her now..."

I trailed off as I noticed what exactly was wrong with Fuun – what Shuzhue had done to him. She had used her power to take control of every drop of blood in his veins and made them travel the opposite direction of how they should. Had she done so any faster or for even a second longer, she would have easily killed him. It struck me immediately where I had seen this phenomenon before, or at least its aftermath. When Dahlia had been returned to us from the Ruby City, her blood had been manipulated impossibly through her body, causing tears in her veins as it tried to escape the torture, and then finally, she had been bled dry.

My eyes narrowing, I studied Shuzhue covertly from where I knelt over Fuun. She was doing her best to act the victim, but thanks to Dahlia, I knew who she really was now. I would be better able to keep my guard up in her presence and not be fooled by who she used to be back on Earth.

"Yes, I will speak to Adel concerning the Hounds tomorrow, if she's willing to meet with me," Akuma was saying to the others as the meeting had evidently continued without me. "Ao Kouen, would you please do me the favour of telling Yukari I need to speak with her before I depart."

"No need," I spoke, standing and turning Fuun to mist – he was recovering, but was clearly in no state to resist my power. "I will take Fuun back to the palace dungeons myself. What is it you would like to speak to me about?"

"I have a parting gift for you all," Akuma announced, "but I hear Yukari would be the best person to receive it. Consider it an act of good faith."

Akuma nodded to Bastion who suddenly seemed to leap and disappear in a beam of red light, before reappearing moments later with a person held limply in his arms. My breath caught in my throat as I realized who I was looking at – Tim Harford. On Earth, Tim had been a British exchange student at our school and now he was the last of the Talons to be returned to us, though I was at a loss to understand how and why he hadn't been freed with the others.

Tim was unconscious in Bastion's arms and it was obvious he wasn't well by the pallor of his skin. His blond hair was spiked and his clothes were those I remembered from his alter ego. Seeing him like this, I couldn't help but see Kai-Een, the Talon he had been for eight hundred years, and not Tim Harford, the poor abducted high school student, and it shamed me.

"I'll take care of him and bring him back to health if it can be done," I promised, turning Tim to mist along with Fuun.

With that, the two Ambassadors from the Ruby City took their leave of us on Bastion's strange beam of red light and I nodded to the others before taking flight in order to get my passengers where they needed to be. I dropped Fuun off in a cell in the palace dungeons as I had promised, though I didn't bother to shut the door. Not waiting to see what Fuun would do with his freedom, I quickly made my way down to my operating room to reform Tim as well.

There was little I could do for Tim, as he was in much the same state Goji had been after Yue had freed him from Fuzen. For good or for ill, all I could do was make him comfortable and wait to see if he would come around on his own. Instructing my medical assistant with what he would need to know, I left the operating room to meet the others in the Knights' room as there was much to discuss.

"Let's do this, then," Yue stated. "We're all here now, there's no better time."

"Do what?" I questioned, having just entered the room and missed what the current topic of conversation was. I crossed the room, noting everyone was indeed present, including all of the Knights as well as Aysel and Ao Kouen.

"Re-Knighting the old Knights," Kaji supplied, "so they're Knighted by all four of us."

"And the new Knights too," Hotaru added. "And while we're at it, we can Knight Aysel as well and show Ao Kouen how it's done, so he can make his own Knights."

"No." I hadn't even realized I had spoken aloud until everyone in the room turned to face me. "Not about Aysel, or the re-Knighting of Sabien and the others that were cryogenically frozen," I clarified, immediately worried they might mistake my meaning. "I don't think the new Knights should be re-Knighted."

"Why not?" Masaru asked, regarding me with some concern. "I thought it sounded like a good idea. That way if, gods forbid, something were to happen to one of ye, the Knights ye left behind would still be connected to the rest of ye and looked after the same."

I nodded, my lips pursed as I considered how best to approach what I had to say. "Yes, I can't deny there are benefits, but I'm not sure if any of you have considered as closely as I have what it means to Knight someone. That person is changed, forever."

"What do you mean, Yukari?" Hotaru asked from her seat next to Aysel; I gathered by the way she held Aysel's hand that she had been trying to convince Aysel to agree to the honour of being Knighted.

"Well," I began, "We know we share some of the power given to us by Sapphiros, right? The best analogy I've been able to think up will be perhaps lost on Masaru, but I think it adequately represents the flow of power – water.

"If Sapphiros is the ocean, and the Chosen are inland lakes fed constantly by rivers, then when we Knight someone we are making a stream to create a pond and constantly flowing water into it through that connection. When we die our lakes dry up and that pond, though it still exists, is no longer being fed fresh water and has no means to grow.

"Now, if another Chosen comes along and re-connects their lake to that pond, then a new stream would send a surge of water into the pond, making the amount of power that Knight has greater. Take a Knight already connected to a Chosen and add more Chosen and more connections and the pond grows, fed from multiple different sources at once. I'm not saying it's a bad idea to make our Knights stronger and ensure their immortality," I clarified, "but please keep in mind how much we've changed since we've developed our powers and remember we were born to them. A gem god's power changes a person and makes them no longer really what they were, maybe more than what they were, but still not the same. None of us are really human – or Croatin," I allowed for Pine, "any longer, and in addition to that we are immortal and will remain this way forever.

"All I'm saying is a decision this life-altering should not be made lightly. The person you Knight will be with you forever and is your responsibility."

"I agree," Fuun stated, stepping fully into the room from where he had been lurking just beyond the balcony curtain. "The decision to Knight or to be Knighted should not be taken lightly."

"Fuun," Yue acknowledged him with a nod of her head, "would you join us, then?"

Fuun did not answer her immediately, but directed a look in his brother's direction before replying, "I have been a Knight of Sapphiros for a long time, but I would give almost anything to be a true Knight, though I do not deserve it."

Sabien considered Fuun for some time before Ris elbowed him in the ribs and he nodded, then reached out his hand. "I would be honoured to have you with us, brother.

"As for myself," he continued, "I dedicated my life to Sapphiros long ago and I am more than willing to accept all that entails. You four have made me very proud and it is my wish I continue to serve as your Knight Commander as long as I am able."

Ris took hold of Sabien's hand and nodded, indicating she felt the same and would not be parted from him in any case. Unexpectedly, Pine was the next to speak up. "I have been granted a second chance at life thanks to Kaji," he spoke in his usual whisper. "I may not know all of you as well, but you have made me feel welcome. I am thankful to belong among you and I consider you like my family."

"I, too, would have died without the interference of the Chosen," Rama added, placing a hand on Pine's metal shoulder. "I am eternally grateful and I willingly accept the responsibility being a Knight of Sapphiros brings. I am with you all until the end."

Masaru stood. "I've already accepted what it means to be a Knight of Sapphiros and I would do the same a thousand times as long as ye'll have me."

"I'm just here to watch, if no one minds," Ao Kouen interrupted, causing a laugh.

The others deliberated, but I remained largely silent as my mind and attention were drawn over to Aysel who sat near her own sleeping area, leaning slightly in her chair to automatically compensate for her missing arm. Her expression displayed a mixed set of emotions; on the one hand looking awkward and hesitant about whether she belonged here or not, and on the other looking hopeful and proud of her sister's accomplishments.

Across the room from Aysel, Adel was speaking with Jeth and I made my way over to them as I realized they were the only two to not have openly declared a desire to be re-Knighted.

"Adel, may I have a word with you?" I interrupted them.

"Yes, of course. What is it, Yukari?"

"I know you may not feel the same way," I began, "but I've been meaning to tell you for quite some time that I believe Aysel is as much of a Knight as any of you, and if it is her desire to be Knighted, then I think you should support that."

"Tell *her*," Adel replied and I could hear the emotion thick in her voice. "I know it already. Don't think I haven't tried to convince her, but she thinks she's not worthy and nothing I say seems to change that."

"I will, Adel," I responded, giving her a quick squeeze on the shoulder, "I'll tell her."

I began crossing the room once more, intent on Aysel, but I realized halfway there that if Adel's concern was any indication then Aysel's stubbornness would take more than simply my words to dispel, so I detoured back over to Kaji and the others. "We have to convince Aysel we feel she'd make a good Knight and I figure she won't be satisfied unless it comes from all of us."

Hotaru nodded. "I've been trying to convince Aysel to let me Knight her since the Temple of Jade."

"Of course she should be Knighted," Kaji replied instantly and Yue simply flashed over to Aysel's side, leaving the rest of us to scurry over after her.

"Aysel, we think you should let us Knight you," Yue was saying. "There's no doubt you deserve it."

"See what I've been telling you?" Hotaru added.

"You really think so?" Aysel asked. "All of you?"

"Of course we do," I answered. "You've been with us from the start and your dedication speaks for you if nothing else does."

"But my sister is so much more qualified than I," Aysel countered, giving only the barest glance toward her missing arm. "I'll never be as good a fighter as she is, or any of the other Knights."

"It's not always about fighting, Aysel," I told her. "We need people with other skills too. Look at Ris, for example."

"And you have the biggest heart of anyone I've ever known, Aysel," Hotaru added. "We need someone like you."

Aysel looked to Kaji as he was the one person who hadn't yet spoken. "Do you agree with them, Kaji?"

"I've never understood why you weren't already a Knight when we met you, Aysel," Kaji replied, "so in my mind it's past due."

Aysel nodded slowly, joyful tears running down her face. "Well, if you all really feel that way…I would be honoured."

"Sapphiros.
Our friend and father
Our patron and our benefactor
We lift up our Knights towards you
We seek to give our gift of your blessing
To these worthy individuals
To assist in keeping balance
Hear us, Sapphiros!"

I alone of the four of us kept my eyes open during the ceremony, so I was able to watch as one by one, the symbols on our chests and our eyes lit up with a cyan glow, and when the ritual words had been spoken, the blue eyes of each of the Knights flared in turn as the power took hold of them.

Aysel, perhaps struck the hardest by the sudden influx of power she had never experienced before, swayed, and Adel instinctively reached out to catch her. Adel helped Aysel back to her feet, but by the time she had her upright once more the change had already occurred. Aysel looked down with a bewildered expression, opening and closing her new fist as easily as if it had always been a part of her. The hand, made completely out of Sapphire, floated in the air where it should sit had there been an arm attached to it, but as it was, there was only a field of cyan energy between Aysel's shoulder and the hand her power had manifested on her behalf.

There was as much congratulating of Aysel as there was general good humour, which was a welcome change from the tension that had plagued us all of late. As I looked about the room, I realized that maybe it had been today, maybe earlier, but somewhere along the way we had become a family. Families didn't always all get along, as mine was a perfect example, but when it really came down to it they stuck together and were there for each other.

Everyone else seemed to be settling down and striking up conversations, or partaking of the remaining food set out by the palace staff this morning, when Masaru fit his arm in mine and led me toward the door. I went with him, but I was a little confused as to why he would want to leave the gathering. Once back in our room, however, we discovered we temporarily had the space to ourselves, Felice having invited my mother out with her to give Mifa some time alone with Goji – the note on the table left in Japanese telling me as much.

"A few of us were wondering where the four of ye disappeared to without saying a word," Masaru said at last.

"Oh, I'm sorry," I apologized, somewhat startled I hadn't thought to give him the news yet. "We went just outside of Taiyou to meet with the Ambassadors from the Ruby City."

"I thought ye said ye weren't going to go if there was going to be talks with the Rubians?" Masaru interjected. "And why all the secrecy? I was worried about ye when Rama told me ye'd gone off with Ao Kouen."

"No, it's not like that," I told him. "I was as kept in the dark as you were. I wouldn't have prevented the Knights from coming. In fact, I expect I would have felt better with you there, but as it was the Ruby City only sent two representatives and we outnumbered them already with five Chosen."

"So it's not a secret, then?" Masaru asked.

"Not at all," I said, "and I have to say it went better than I expected, until Fuun showed up."

"Fuun was there?"

"Well he wasn't exactly invited, but yes."

"Go on," Masaru encouraged, "tell me the rest of it."

I spent the next little while filling Masaru in on all that was said at the meeting and my thoughts on the various matters we had discussed. "As I was leaving, I overheard Lady Akuma tell Ao Kouen she would be coming to Taiyou to meet Adel and share information about the Hounds," I concluded. "So I presume that means Fuun's attack didn't ruin everything."

"Thank the gods nothing worse happened to ye while ye were outside of Taiyou's protections."

"Masaru, there were five of us Chosen out there – six, if you count Shuzhue," I told him, smiling slightly. "But I know what you mean and next time I'll try to make sure you come with me."

"I know ye can take care of yerself," he said as he smiled wryly in my direction, "but it's always possible something could catch ye off-guard."

As if to prove his point, Masaru tackled me, trying to wrestle me to the bed. I, of course, hadn't been expecting it, but regardless my power activated and just as his hands closed on my shoulders I felt myself shift abruptly to mist, only to reform a moment later still seated upright as I had been before, with Masaru toppled over next to me.

"That's uncanny," he noted, turning his head to consider me a moment. "I hope ye don't do that every time."

"I can't help it," I mumbled, blushing at the subtle implication in his tone, but his words reminded me of what I wanted to talk to him about, though I wasn't certain I was brave enough to bring the subject up.

"Masaru," I began hesitantly and he looked at me expectantly, "I've been thinking a lot about something recently…"

"About Knighting, ye mean?"

"Well, yes, sort of," I admitted. "It's actually something Dahlia said that got me thinking in the first place, though I didn't realize it at the time."

"Dahlia?"

I nodded. "At the café, the night my parents arrived, she mentioned a Roughlander custom called…Joining?" I couldn't meet his eyes as I spoke the word aloud and I felt my face heat.

"Oh…" Masaru coughed, sounding a little embarrassed himself, though I didn't look up to check. "Did she now?"

"Yes." I took a deep breath; now that I had brought it up, only the hard part remained. "And after what I said to everyone in the Knight's room I realized something…" I swallowed hard, unable to continue, and I backed up a little to try it from another direction.

"I'm not sure if it's the same thing or not, but on my world we have a similar concept called marriage, where two people commit to be with each other for the rest of their lives. I realized that…well, I may not have fully known at the time what it meant when I Knighted you, but Knighting is forever and compared to that commitment…I…"

"Yukari," Masaru interrupted my failed attempt to get my point across by putting a hand beneath my chin to lift my face enough that I had to meet his gaze. "Will ye join with me, then?"

My breath caught. I had been trying to tell him I was willing to stay by his side forever, but I hadn't been expecting to actually hear those words. My heart pounded in my chest and I couldn't form a single useful thought, but it was the easiest thing in the world just to say, "Yes."

Though as soon as the word had escaped my lips and I saw Masaru's answering smile, I realized the enormity of what had just happened between us.

"Oh my god," I gasped, placing both hands over my mouth. "What in the world am I going to say to my parents?! They'll never agree to it…"

I had to explain to Masaru that although among Roughlanders my being fifteen and him nearly twenty was not an issue, my relative age on Earth meant I was still considered a minor and far too young for that kind of commitment.

"I'm not going anywhere, Yukari," Masaru assured me. "If ye're parents don't agree to it, we'll wait. It's as simple as that."

"But that still means we have to tell them, doesn't it?" I asked, only partly joking. "I was hoping my father would let me live to see my sixteenth birthday." That brought a laugh from Masaru."You may think it's funny now, but you'll have to face him with me. I'm not doing it alone."

That sobered him up immediately – Masaru had already had the pleasure of being subjected to one of my father's interrogations. "Aye, I suppose ye're right at that."

We stayed up talking much later than I thought I would be capable of, considering the long day I just had. I had a number of questions about Roughlander customs and what I was to expect of a Joining ceremony, and Masaru tried his best to explain it to me. "Generally the matched pair involved chose two people to stand with them, ye know, in case something should happen to either of them. Is that something that's done on Earth?"

"Um, maybe?" I answered, a little unclear as to what he was referring to. "Do you mean 'stand with them' as in during the ceremony?"

"Well, it's a little bit more involved than that," Masaru admitted. "It's so that if one of the pair dies, the one standing for them would be there to look after the one left behind. It's unfortunately a common enough occurrence among Roughlanders that the role is a necessary one."

"You mean, romantically, not just as a friend?"

"Aye, it usually turns out that way, but not always," Masaru replied. "Also, sometimes the two standing for the pair end up a match themselves, which is always convenient."

I was fascinated and overwhelmed at the same time by the culture I suddenly found myself immersed in. I had always had a great respect for the Roughlanders ever since I had first been introduced to their way of life, and I had even hoped to fit in with them, but never had I anticipated doing so in quite this way.

"So I was thinking of who I might choose to ask to stand with me, and I was wondering if ye would object to Razor?" Masaru asked suddenly, watching closely for my reaction.

"Razor?" I found myself picturing Razor's roguish smile and how since I had met him he had always been there for me whenever I needed him, and also how he had saved Masaru's life on more than one occasion. Moreover, Razor and Masaru were like brothers and there wasn't a single person on this world or Earth I could think of who would make a better choice for what Masaru was proposing. "No, he's the perfect choice," I answered honestly, "though I suppose if you choose Razor it means I would have to choose someone as well, doesn't it?"

Masaru nodded, though I could see he was a little hesitant to hear who my choice would be. I considered the question briefly, but there was really only one option I could see that made any sense, though I'm sure she and Razor would never be 'a matched pair' as the Roughlanders put it.

"Would you object to my choosing Hotaru? She's my best friend and though we'd have to explain it to her, I think she'd understand. Besides, she'd still be around a thousand years from now when we might need to consider the possibility of the two of us not being together any longer."

"I'm glad ye said Hotaru, though I couldn't for the life of me guess who it was ye might pick," Masaru admitted. "There's no one else for me but you, but do ye think Hotaru would mind once she knows what it means to stand for ye?"

I smiled at how oblivious he was. "Hotaru liked you before I did," I told him. "She told me so herself right before she encouraged me to claim you for my own."

"Really? I never knew," Masaru admitted. "I thought she liked someone from back on Earth."

"She did, but apparently you reminded her of him," I explained. "I don't think it was all that serious, but she was very upset when you were ill and I think she would take good care of you if I wasn't around to do it myself."

"Well, then I suppose Hotaru would make the best choice," Masaru admitted, trying to hide his embarrassment by changing the subject, "but how do ye think she feels about Razor?"

We fell asleep in each other's arms, night having fallen outside our window, and we were oblivious to any sounds my mother and father might have made when they came back to the room. It was a surprising luxury to be able to sleep while it was dark for once, and relax in the sure knowledge that we were safe in Taiyou and Ao Kouen's defenses would be enough to warn us of any danger. The greater luxury, of course, being that I had Masaru with me and if we had our way that was a fact that would never change.

I started becoming aware of my surroundings again to the odd sensation of Masaru gently ruffling my blue curls, when I was fully startled awake by Dahlia sticking her head in through the curtains covering our sleeping area.

"Good morning, you two!" she announced joyfully, giving us a knowing smile and wink to follow it. "I thought I might find ye still abed."

"Shh," I cautioned her, worried she might say something to upset my parents who, if they were in the room, would have no trouble hearing when she spoke at such a volume. "Come in."

"Don't mind if I do," Dahlia commented, letting herself in without opening the curtains at all and settling on the end of the bed. "So…have the two of ye got something ye want to tell me?"

I directed a surprised look in Masaru's direction, but he looked just as baffled as I did. "How did ye know?"

Dahlia laughed. "I didn't, but you just told me! So…give me the details."

"Details?" I questioned worriedly.

"Ye know, the when and where, and are ye going to let me officiate?" Dahlia adjusted her position so she was able to include us both in her intense gaze. "Oh, and have ye decided who's going to be standing for ye?"

"Well we've only just made it official–" Masaru began at the same time as I said, "We haven't told anyone–".

We stopped, realizing we were babbling, while Dahlia waited expectantly for us to sort ourselves out and answer her questions. "Well?"

"Razor," Masaru answered, "but I haven't asked him yet."

"And Hotaru," I added, "though she doesn't know a thing about Roughlander customs."

"And?" Dahlia said expectantly.

I smiled at her insistent attitude; it didn't seem she was going to accept no for an answer. "And yes, you can officiate for us, Dahlia," I told her what she wanted to hear, "there wouldn't be anyone better."

"Well, ye're right about that!" She agreed with a sharp nod. "Oh, come here you two, I'm so happy for ye!"

Never mind that Masaru was shirtless and I was wearing no more than Masaru's discarded shirt once again, Dahlia pulled the both of us into a hug and her strength was such that there was no use resisting her embrace.

"So what do ye think?" She pulled back and examined us both. "Could we get this ready in time for tomorrow, or would the next day be better?"

I stared at Dahlia with my mouth open in shock for a moment and I was forced to recall that waiting wasn't something Roughlanders generally bothered with. "Uh…"

"Ye might want to hold on a little bit Dahlia," Masaru said, coming to my rescue. "We've only just decided this last night and we haven't yet had a chance to even tell anybody about it. There's also some concern about how her parents might take the news."

I realized abruptly that having told Dahlia, the cat was now out of the bag, so to speak. "Dahlia, please do me a favour and keep this to yourself for now, okay?" I pleaded with her. "I'd like the chance to talk to my father first before anything is decided."

"Oh, well in that case," Dahlia commented, getting to her feet, "ye'll never get a better chance. He's just outside. I'll leave ye both to make yourselves presentable," she added with another wink, "but don't take too long at it, or I'll tell them myself."

"Dahlia!" I hissed after her, but I was too late; she had already let herself out through the curtain and I was not dressed enough to follow her.

Taking the top article of clothing off of the pile Felice had gifted me with, I quickly dressed for the day in a light blue dress that laced up the front. I hadn't realized Felice and I were so close in size, but the dress fit well and though I didn't have a mirror at hand, I thought it looked rather nice. Smoothing the fabric and attempting to settle my unruly hair, I found myself hoping I wouldn't have to fight today and risk ruining my appearance – today was a good day and I intended to try and keep it that way.

I took a deep breath to settle the butterflies in my stomach and turned to look in Masaru's direction. He had also dressed up a little with his newer white shirt – the one with the doves to commemorate Taiyou – and he smiled at me as I caught his eye, and I felt my nerves settle completely. We could do this, together.

Masaru took my hand in his, then together we pulled the curtain back and stepped through. Seated around the table in the centre of the room were Dahlia and Krox with my mother and father talking amiably over breakfast. Heading over to the table to join them, Masaru let go of my hand after giving it a little squeeze, so he could pull out a chair for me. I took a seat as Masaru went back into the curtained area to fetch another chair for himself and in his brief absence I found Dahlia was giving me a pointed look.

"Daddy, I–" I began and the room went silent, my father turning to look at me with a surprised expression – I hardly ever called him Daddy, and almost never in front of anyone else.

Masaru came back in the room, chair in hand, and paused on the threshold of the curtained area as I realized everyone was waiting expectantly for me to continue. I felt my face begin to flush, but I opened my mouth to try again when I was interrupted by the strangest and most unexpected thing flying into the room through the open balcony. It was a rather large bird – about the size of a raven – except it was clearly not a real animal, but made entirely of cyan energy like my arrows were. As I watched it fly straight for me, followed by another just like it heading for Masaru, my brain belatedly supplied to me one of us must have developed some sort of new power.

I stood to try and get out of its path, but the first bird landed on my shoulder and the second on Masaru's no more than a beat later. Together the birds opened their beaks and both began talking at once; mine was a little sooner than Masaru's, giving the message a slightly doubled quality.

"I need your help!" Yue's voice emanated from the birds, answering the question of whose power had sent this particular message. "Little Lilyth is here, in Taiyou. The Hounds came to find her in her valley and she came here to escape them, but she used up all her power to get here and now she's unconscious. Without her, the guardians she brought with her won't listen to me. I'm in the courtyard before the palace gates – Hurry!"

My eyes met Masaru's across the room. "Excuse us," I said, "but we have to go."

Less than a split second after I had spoken, I had crossed the room with the help of my wings for speed and scooped Masaru into my arms before taking the two of us in a dive over the balcony rail, leaving my bewildered parents behind. I distantly noted Ris flying out from the balcony next to ours and Krox following behind me to make the four-storey leap to the ground with his powerful legs.

The scene before the palace gates was utter chaos. The courtyard was filled with people and it seemed the sudden arrival of little Lilyth and her strange-looking friends in the space before the ruins of Gin-Kouteki had been enough to draw curious onlookers closer than it was safe to get. There were Deathsquad soldiers and Legionnaires trying somewhat ineffectively to keep the citizens out of harm's way, but there obviously weren't enough of them, and something told me the soldiers didn't know exactly what they were trying to protect people from. Ris and I landed side by side and Masaru ran over to begin filling them in.

The guardians weren't yet going after the citizens of Taiyou like Yue had feared, but instead the five of them Little Lilyth had brought with her seemed to be keeping in a tight cluster, guarding something between them. Oddly, it wasn't little Lilyth herself; I could see her draped limply in Yue's grasp, unconscious, but seemingly unhurt.

In the end, the guardians were no more than animated matter, so I used my power to see right through them. Ticket was a Roughlander Croatin of the Seventh Spawn, one of the smaller varieties that looked like a walking tree frog. He lay motionless on the ground in the centre of the cluster of guardians, and in their attempt to keep him there the guardians had stepped on him, repeatedly. I couldn't tell from here if he was dead or dying, but I knew if he should cross that line, he would also become a guardian also and there would be no saving him. Simultaneously firing off five arrows, I created energy draining nets to hold the guardians in place then I turned poor Ticket to mist and drifted him over to me.

"Ris!" I called out to the Kumori as I knelt down on the cobblestones and reformed Ticket before me.

Ris was beside me in moments, but Ticket was in rough shape. From my cursory examination I discovered he was still alive, barely, but he was beyond my abilities; I just had to hope Ris' power would be enough to save him before he turned.

The Kumori wasted no time, but when she lowered her hands to place the blue bubble around Ticket the magic simply dissipated. I looked at her in concern, but by her expression Ris was just as confused as I was.

"Don't waste your effort," Adel informed Ris, pushing past the Kumori to get a closer look at Ticket. "See the gash on his arm there? That was caused by teeth and those things over there don't look like they do much biting."

Adel was right; those teeth marks looked large enough to be caused by a Hound's bite. Before I had the chance to process what that might mean for Ticket, Adel had already begun the procedure that would allow her to fight off the Hound's control and enable Ris to heal him. When the last drop of Adel's blood came in contact with Ticket, the Croatin began thrashing wildly. I could see in Adel's expression and the way she clenched her fist that she was using everything in her to fight on Ticket's behalf. I let loose another energy net to surround Adel's arm, but it seemed to have less effect than usual.

Ticket's thrashing only grew in intensity, but as I watched him, a red haze coalesced around his form. The haze began to take shape and before I knew it, I was looking at the incorporeal form of a full-sized Hound. Scrabbling, I got to my feet and backed away from the terrifying beast, but it wasn't after me. The image of the Hound began to claw its way forward, intent Akuma, who had evidently arrived for her information session with Adel.

No one moved as we watched the Hound painstakingly struggle to cross the courtyard – and then Kaji appeared. He must have used his clones as simultaneously a Kaji appeared by Shuzhue's side and another appeared brazenly before the Hound itself. The one before the Hound threw all the force he could muster into a single punch directed at the Hound's incorporeal head. Somewhat surprisingly, it connected and the Hound reeled with the blow before disappearing.

"There," Adel panted, holding her arm gingerly. "Heal him."

Ris did as instructed, and before long we had Ticket more or less in one piece, with everything as under control as one could expect with a crowd of undead still waiting patiently in the centre of the courtyard. Remarkably, we discovered the guardians would listen to Ao Kouen, of all people, and with him commanding them I was able to turn both little Lilyth and Ticket to mist and lead them all to the Jade throne room, which was the safest place any of us could think to place the lot of them.

Hotaru, belatedly answering Yue's summons and coming out of the palace, met up with us and followed us to the throne room, where Ao Kouen released the guardians to wander and I settled the sleeping forms of both Ticket and little Lilyth beneath one of the trees that decorated the Jade room. "Are you going to stay here for when they wake?" I asked Hotaru.

"Sure," she answered, "I'm sure they'd both want to see a familiar face."

Satisfied, I stood and turned to leave, when I noticed Ao Kouen's back stiffen and his expression turned to one of horror. "The Hounds..." he whispered fearful. His eyes seemed sightless, focused on the distant borders of Taiyou as only he could, before he noticed my look of concern. "Yukari...it's too late. We're surrounded."

CH. 19 – THE FALL OF TAIYOU

I sent myself to Masaru as mist – it was the fastest way to get outside – and once I was fully standing beside him in the courtyard, I raised my arms and sent out a flurry of message arrows.

Ao Kouen could sense the Hounds on the border of Taiyou; according to him there were hundreds and not just here, but all around the country. We hadn't yet discovered if the Hounds, could simply walk through Taiyou's defenses, but if it was possible...we were in big trouble.

*Sabien, Sir Rama, Pine...*I listed off each name as I formed the arrows I would send to them, *Adel, Aysel, Yue–* I was startled out of my concentration as Yue's arrow exploded into a multitude of sparks and showered down to the ground.

Masaru rounded on me. "Whose arrow was that?"

I could hardly comprehend what I just witnessed. "Yue's," I answered him, feeling numb. "Has anyone seen her?"

I desperately wracked my brain for Yue's last known whereabouts and it occurred to me I hadn't seen any sign of her since I had taken little Lilyth from her. Masaru quickly asked around, but none of the Knights, or anyone else, had any idea where she had gone after that.

I was worried, but given the current circumstance I couldn't allow myself to think of what that failed arrow might mean. Forcing myself to concentrate again, I numbly fired off the rest of the message arrows to call the defenders of Taiyou to war – we were going to need everyone at our disposal.

Masaru and I accompanied Dahlia and Krox to the Roughlander Sanctioned Outpost to ready the people there and get the Roughlanders on the wall with every carbine rifle they had to spare. In record time, the combined forces of Taiyou and every ally who had gathered to defend the Lands of Jade stood ready to face the forces of Lady Lilyth, but as I flew up to survey what awaited us, I learned that if the barrier went down, it was unlikely any of us would survive the numbers she had brought to bear against us. There were several hundred Hounds in sight of the bridge alone – more than any of us had even known existed.

It was daytime, but even still the Hounds were outnumbered many times over by Lillem. They stretched as far as the eye could see in every direction, waiting hungrily for the chance to maim, kill, and destroy. Among them I could even make out the forms of the larger ones.

I drifted back down to the ground where the Knights and the other Chosen awaited my report and I recounted what I had seen in an emotionless tone. Without Gin-Kouteki, and with my allies, the Roughlanders, already prepared thanks to Razor and Dahlia, I felt out of place amongst the hustle and preparations for war. Turning and seeing Masaru looking to me for direction, I realized what I had to do. "Masaru, guard my body a moment, would you?:

I let my head slump and concentrated on locating Yue. I didn't know if I could reach her, but I couldn't go into this battle not knowing what had become of her. *There...* I could feel her, but she was distant somehow, shrouded. I reached for her, relieved there was something for me to find. Then I felt it – there was another presence blocking me from Yue – and before I knew it I didn't feel as if I was reaching beyond it to reach Yue, but that it was reaching for me to swallow me whole.

It was like I was being dragged under water and all the colours and sounds of the world became muted and far away. I was aware of what was happening, but I couldn't stop it and I didn't know the cause – nothing like this had ever occurred while using my powers before.

"Yukari?" Masaru sounded concerned. "Are ye all right? Did ye find her?"

"What's wrong with her, Masaru?" Hotaru asked as she approached. "Yukari? Yukari, what's wrong? Talk to me."

When reality snapped back in with a brutal clarity, there could be no rational explanation for where I found myself and I wondered briefly if this was also where Yue had disappeared to. I found myself in a familiar hallway, but my brain felt muddled and I couldn't explain why I felt so out of place here. It was late – the moon was out in full – perhaps that was the cause of this feeling?

"Yue?" I called her name out into the darkened hallway of the third floor of Shinjuku High. I couldn't for the life of me remember why we were here so late at night, but I knew I was looking for Yue and for some reason it was very important I find her.

"Yukari, you're scaring me," Hotaru whined. "This isn't like you, please stop it."

Hotaru cried out suddenly and stiffened as if in immense pain, her eyes displaying the shock and betrayal she felt and I relished her distress, revelling in it.

This wasn't right. I had wandered the halls looking for Yue, but every corner I took simply led me back to where I had begun and the layout of the school wasn't as it should be – there were no stairs down, for one. No way out of here. I stopped and considered this a moment, belatedly realizing the feeling that had been nagging at me for some time now – I wasn't alone here.

"Yue?" I called out tentatively and then, feeling foolish at my own cowardice, I raised my voice and tried again. "Yue, this isn't funny!"

"Yukari, this isn't funny!" Masaru stated, ripping Hotaru out of my grasp. "We have more important things that need our attention."

Hotaru gasped with the shock of having my talons removed from her. I had been so close; I almost had her, too, but no matter.

Masaru – yes, that was his name – was right; I had more important things that needed my attention. It was time to move on from here. I took off into the air and was pleasantly surprised when wings appeared at my back to carry me aloft. It wouldn't be long now until everything was mine.

I stood frozen in place with my back to floor-to-ceiling windows overlooking the courtyard below, watching the shadows before me stretch impossibly to cover the floor that should still be lit by the pale moonlight. I couldn't back up any further and there was nowhere to run as the shadows themselves seem to take shape and form an image of something both familiar and terrifying. It was Yue, though not the Yue I thought I had come here to find. This Yue was made from darkness and her long hair writhed like shadowy tendrils in a nonexistent wind. An eerie cyan light glowed in the place where her eyes should be as she took a menacing step forward.

Taiyou...beautiful Taiyou – the only place of beauty left on this rock of a world. I flew over it and saw how these humans had wasted the beauty they had stolen from me. Wasted and squandered it until it was nearly bled dry. That would all change today, when my children took it back for me and the humans became nothing more than my slaves until I decided to rid myself of them.

The palace – it was no throne of lava and fire, but it would do for now. Yes, it would do nicely. I dove through an open window and I could feel my destination growing ever closer, pulsing at me. I was almost there and nothing – nothing – would stop me from taking what was mine.

No, this was wrong! All of it was wrong: the glass windows at my back, the pleated cotton skirt I gripped in my hands, and the shadowy demon creature before me. None of what I was seeing and feeling could possibly be true. I was a Chosen of Sapphiros now. I had powers; I was different. I wasn't this scared high school student with square-rimmed glasses and my hair pulled back into a tight bun to control my curls. And Yue wasn't my enemy – her glowing cyan eyes and her powers weren't something to fear; she was just like me. Her powers made her different and changed, yes, but she was still the same person on the inside, like I was.

But if this wasn't her, then where was she? I had to believe my powers had led me here – wherever this place was – for a reason.

"And where do you think you're going?" Rama questioned, placing himself between me and my destination.

"Get out of my way," I hissed, not bothering with playing nice this close to my goal. "You move or I make you." I raised my hands to strike at him and a glowing cyan arrow formed itself between them. An arrow – that would serve my purpose very well. "Well? What's it going to be? I don't have all day."

"Make me," Rama said, deadly serious. "That's my choice, I'm afraid. You'll just have to make me."

I let the arrow loose, aimed directly at his head. Uppity Knight; I bet he expected his precious 'Chosen' would never turn her power on him. Well, he was wrong about that.

Rama did not move or attempt to avoid the strike at all, and when the arrow reached him it simply passed through him as if he wasn't even there. The unobstructed arrow continued into the throne room beyond where it landed solidly into Adel's shield.

"I'm afraid you'll have to make me as well, my Lady," Adel stated. "I won't stand for this."

In a flash someone new was on the scene and despite the speed at which they had arrived, this wasn't Yue either. It was a creature, not human, but not frightening like the shadowy demon before it. It was of human height, but covered in short, white fur, complete with strange patterned markings like little diamonds all in cyan to match its eyes. It winked at me in a friendly way and it abruptly reminded me of Ris, but where she was a bat-person, this creature was more of a fox-person, complete with a fox-like bushy tail flowing out behind it. The fox sniffed me once and then smiled, taking up position between me and the demon creature before us, and raising its paws as if it intended to fight it off, boxing style.

"Adel...my daughter," I called to her.

"I am not your daughter," she responded between clenched teeth and raised her sword at me, "and you will release my Chosen."

I laughed, finding the humour in Adel's betrayal as I was hardly surprised by her actions – she had always been delightfully willful.

"My dear, you should know better than to send Knights after Chosen."

I felt a sudden lancing pain in my right arm and whirled, placing a hand to the cut which came away bloody. "You..." I hissed, glaring over at Rama, who had used his power to throw a sword at me. "You will pay for that."

My power had brought me here, so it could presumably take me from this place and to Yue for real this time. As the demon and the fox wrestled, neither one seeming to gain the upper hand in their struggle, I closed my eyes and forced myself to shut it all out.

Silence, then...

"What are you doing here?" Yue's voice.

I opened my eyes and looked around myself, but my surroundings were like nothing I had ever seen before. Yue sat before me on the bottom step of a stone staircase leading up to a platform with nothing more atop it than a myriad of different-sized stone pillars. What caught my eye and disoriented me more than anything was that the grass was blue and the sky conversely was a deep purple, broken up here and there by the orange of treetops.

"What the...?" I questioned. "Where are we, Yue?"

"Does it matter? I'm stuck here anyway," Yue avoided the question with a bored sounding sigh. "And besides, it's not like you're real."

"I'm real," I responded, affronted.

"Yeah, that's what they all say," she retorted.

"Listen, Yue, something is wrong and we need to find a way out of here," I told her. "Taiyou's in a lot of trouble. We're surrounded by Hounds, Lillem, and likely worse, and everyone needs our help. They're counting on us."

Yue's eyes met mine, startled. "You really are here, aren't you?"

"Of course I am! Now, where are we and how do we get out of here?"

Her expression turned abruptly mulish. "Why would you want my help now? You've never wanted it before."

"That's not true," I protested, "I–" I cut off, realizing this was no time to argue. "Please, Yue. If you won't help for my sake that's fine, but at least realize there are others out there that need us and to help them we need to get out of this place."

"All right, I'll try," she agreed, "but I make no promises this will work, I've been trying to get out since I got stuck here."

I was bleeding from various points on my stolen body, but to my satisfaction the Knights were doing much worse and every cut, bruise, and broken bone they dealt to me only served to maim the one they sought to protect. The fight had ranged into the throne room itself, the place the Knights had been trying so valiantly to keep me from and my final destination. Within this room my enemies had so thoughtfully placed together both of the things I sought; soon I would have them and then I would have everything I wanted. All I needed to do was to eliminate these two nuisances.

Rama was panting with the effort of remaining standing after having to expend so much of his limited power just to keep me from killing him, and Adel was less tired but leaning heavily on one leg – the other was riddled with the last handful of arrows I had sent after her. I had them right where I wanted them. I lifted my arms and summoned two arrows – one for each of them – which was all I would need. I had gotten the hang of these stolen powers now and I knew how to best use them to my advantage. A slow smile spread across my face and I let the arrows loose on their targets, knowing the power would ensure the arrows sought them out until they struck, no matter how they dodged and weaved.

I came back to the reality of my bruised and broken body a lot faster than when I had left it. There was no transition; one moment I was concentrating with Yue, trying to break free of the dreamscape where we had been imprisoned, and the next moment I was watching two of my arrows whiz after Rama and Adel, intent on their destruction.

"NO!"

I screamed, but neither my voice nor my power could stop my arrows once they had been fired. Somehow I had turned on my own Knights and attacked them – with intent to kill.

Rama phased through the floor as he was wont to do, but his arrow, instead of sticking into the place where he had been, made an abrupt turn and whizzed out the throne room doors and down the hallway. Adel's arrow struck her shield, penetrated halfway through it, and then exploded with concussive force, sending her flying backwards into the Jade doors.

"Adel!" I rushed to her side, and skidded to my knees beside her crumpled form. I made as if to turn her over so I could have a look at her when I realized my left arm was broken.

"You're too late." My head snapped around at the new voice and I was surprised to see it was little Lilyth who had spoken as the voice hadn't sounded anything like her child-like one. The harmless-looking little girl stood before the triple throne of Taiyou with a scornful expression contorting her features.

"What?"

Little Lilyth didn't bother to answer; instead she simply smiled and backed up a few steps on the dais until she was close enough to raise herself into the centre throne of Taiyou and settle herself upon her new seat of power. "I've won."

The disaster that followed would come to be known by the survivors as the Great Red Wave. The wave of energy that washed over Taiyou and bathed it in a crimson light spelled defeat for the Taiyouns more completely than anything else leading up to the moment the Lady Lilyth had stolen her own daughter's body to seat herself upon Jedeite's throne.

Out on the battlefield, Yue walked with the Hounds as they converged on the bridge of Taiyou. Suddenly, she seemed to snap out of the mindset that had put her with the enemy troops and started bashing the heads of the Hounds around her. She got the upper hand by surprise, but there were too many of them to take on by herself.

Ao Kouen, standing at the forefront of everyone on the bridge, started forward when he felt a hand on his shoulder. "I've got it," Sabien informed him gently. "Command your people and I'll protect mine."

"Roughlanders!" Ao Kouen called out, knowing the message would be passed back by the relays that had been set up. "Target any Hounds that set foot on the bridge – no Hound will enter Taiyou! "Legionnaires, Deathsquad – we take the Lillem and hold the line!"

Hotaru rushed forward to engage the Lillem and moved through them confidently, destroying them with her swords made from ice and water. Up ahead she could make out Fuun doing much the same, and she fought all the harder to reach his side to prove she, too, was strong and skilled enough to make a difference. The Lillem were one thing – they fell before her blades and she had been fighting them enough now she knew the pattern of their movements – but Hotaru hadn't considered what she would do if she came across any Hounds. So when the ground shook and a Hound unexpectedly hauled itself out of a crag in the ground before her, Hotaru froze, realizing her error.

The Hound reared up and took in a deep breath, ready to spray its deadly fire in her direction, and Hotaru desperately thought of what she could do to defend herself against this creature, when at the last moment a winged angel dropped down to take the brunt of the blast meant for her. "Arashi?" Hotaru recognized the identity of her unlikely savior seconds before her beautiful wings lit up in flames.

Shocked and not thinking straight, Hotaru instinctively used her power to summon water, but in her haste to put out the fire that had taken hold of the Espearian priestess' wings, she summoned quite a bit more than she needed and was somewhat surprised to see the tidal wave that crested over her shoulders and crashed into Arashi. The force of the water at Arashi's back and the shock of it was enough to knock the Head Priestess off-balance and send her rushing forward.

Beautiful Arashi, scorched and battered, was helplessly whisked nearer to the Hound by the water, who did not waste the opportunity presented to it. The Hound picked up the fallen priestess in its teeth and, as quickly as it had appeared, carried her back down into the ground.

"Arashi, no!" Hotaru cried, stricken, and ran forward after her.

"No, kiddo," Jeth said, stopping her by placing a heavy hand on her shoulder, "that's what they'd want you to do. You'd never survive down there."

"I can't just leave her, Jeth!" Hotaru exclaimed.

"Go back, Hotaru, I've got this one," Jeth told her, absently destroying a Lillem that tried to get too close to them. "I'll get her back, don't you worry." And with that, Jeth left Hotaru, leaping into the hole in the ground after the Hound that had taken Arashi, and the ground closed up behind him, leaving Hotaru unable to follow.

The Great Red Wave began in the palace, where it swept through the halls before expanding outwards. It was visible for miles, so those further out were more likely to see it coming. Yue, for one, noticed it, being as she was so far out among the enemy forces, and thinking fast, she vaulted over the Hound she was facing to grab hold of Sabien, slinging him over her back in a feat of immense strength, borne of adrenaline or her power or both, and proceeded to run away with him at a speed only she could manage.

Hotaru, on the other hand, alone and fighting a veritable horde of Lillem to keep herself alive, didn't notice the red light coming for her, and as it washed over her she was already lost to thoughts of defeat because of what she had let happen to Jeth and Arashi.

Masaru's eyes were quick and he had been watching the direction of the palace for signs Yukari might be returning ever since Rama had informed him he would go after her and keep her safe. He hadn't seen any sign of her cyan wingtips, but he was the first one of the defenders to notice the wave of red energy approaching and the first, and maybe only one, to realize no one, save maybe Yue, would be fast enough to outrun it.

"Take my hand," Fuun said, appearing suddenly at his side. "I have a promise to keep."

There was no time to hesitate – Masaru did as instructed – but they weren't quite fast enough and the red wave reached them just as Fuun tried to sink them both beneath the ground.

The wave continued pulsing outwards, and Kaji only registered something was coming for him when he saw Ao Kouen whirl around to face toward the palace, sink to his knees, and place the sword of Jedeite before himself, seemingly as a form of protection. Then he felt more than saw the level of magic surge around him, and rather than be blinded again this time, Kaji pre-empted that effect by creating a clone of himself in the first place he thought of, which incidentally was back in the Knights' room,

Kaji's awareness shifted to his clone in time to realize something truly awful must have happened here to explain the scene he found waiting for him. Akuma lay crumpled on the ground, surrounded by a thick field of red energy, and standing over her with his hand outstretched – obviously maintaining that field – was the Vile

Emperor himself, complete with his menacing helmet and deep purple set of spiked armour.

"The Lady Lilyth has returned," the Vile Emperor stated, his deep voice reverberating from beneath his helmet. "This is her doing."

Kaji felt himself shaking with rage. Shuzhue – Akuma was alive. The Vile Emperor had protected her somehow from the effects of the red wave with his field. Protected her when Kaji hadn't been there to do so, and it galled him to admit it. When Adel had told them all of the past, she had mentioned everyone believed the Vile Emperor had been the one to kill Lady Lilyth in the civil war and end her reign for good, but it was common knowledge now that wasn't the case. Right now, Kaji didn't care about Lady Lilyth and he didn't care about the war or anything else. He cared about Shuzhue, and finding a way to strike back at the Vile Emperor for taking his girlfriend away from him and making her suffer here for the past eight hundred years.

"If you're going to kill somebody," Kaji spoke scathingly, having no better weapon at his disposal than the truth, "you should do it right."

In his preoccupation, Kaji had neglected to dismiss the clone he had left behind on the bridge, and by the time the red wave had cleared, he, too, felt its effects and the Kaji in the palace before the Vile Emperor splashed to nothing but a puddle.

By trusting in Jedeite, however, Ao Kouen had been able to resist the power of the wave, only to be taken down by the horde of Hounds and Lillem as they surged into Taiyou with little to obstruct their passage. A Hound tossed the limp body of Ao Kouen into the throne room to skid along the floor and stop at Lady Lilyth's feet, where she sat upon the Jade throne.

Resisting the wave had drained Ao Kouen's power, and the Hound's teeth and rough treatment had done a number on his body, reducing him to the sad state of barely being able to stand under his own strength. Despite all this he was still conscious and he fought to hold on to that last semblance of control over his situation, even when faced with the usurper of his throne.

Lady Lilyth was both beautiful and terrifying in equal measure; she stood easily nine feet tall, and made taller by the fact that she stood on two Lillem-like talons protruding from her waist. Her body was undeniably feminine and she wore no clothing to cover it, having instead a natural armour in the form of a thick exoskeleton. Her hair writhed like a head of snakes, and from her shoulders protruded thick limbs of bone, more in the shape of wings with no membranes than the simplistic talons of the Lillem. The most striking thing about her, however, and the place where Ao Kouen's gaze was undeniably drawn, was a massive red gem inset deeply into her chest, as if it was her heart on display for the world to see – hard and without a single flaw to mar its red crystalline perfection.

Not deigning to use her hands, Lady Lilyth instead drove one of her talons into Ao Kouen's shoulder, causing him to cry out, and she used that hold on him to drag him across the floor and lift him into the air to get a closer look at him. "Such a pathetic excuse for a Chosen, not even worth eating," Lilyth pronounced, bringing the rest of her multitude of talons around to surround him like a cage of claws with the razor sharp tips pointed inwards. "Perhaps I should just kill you now and be done with it."

"No!" Ao Kouen snapped his head around sharply at the sound of someone defending him, only to see it was Mikura. She held in her hand a ball of crackling red and black energy, ready to strike. "You won't hurt him!"

"Maybe I won't hurt him," Lilyth smiled wickedly, "but you will – kill him, Mikura, it is my will."

Mikura trembled before the will of Lady Lilyth, but she held her ground. "I won't," she stated. "The Emperor made Ao Kouen my Keeper and I'm magically bound never to harm my Keeper, so I won't do it."

A sneer crossed the perfect oval of Lilyth's face, contorting it wickedly. "Well then, Mikura, it's your lucky day because I free you of the magic of your Keeper – kill him!"

Ao Kouen was at a loss to what was going on here – he was Mikura's Keeper? It was the first he'd ever heard of it. But what Ao Kouen did know was his life was in the balance and every second that kept Lilyth from killing him was a precious one – he didn't want to die now that he had a country and a people to live for.

With a shaking hand, Mikura lifted her crackling ball of energy higher and drew her hand back to toss it like a ball. The wickedly charged spell launched through the air, but not at Ao Kouen, like Lilyth wanted, but at the usurper herself. Mikura shielded her eyes as her magic exploded, but when the smoke cleared she saw her gambit had been largely unsuccessful. Ao Kouen lay crumpled on the ground now, Lilyth having had to drop him to shield herself from the explosion, but it hadn't been enough to damage her in any way.

"You little impertinent—" Lilyth rose out of her protective crouch to her full and menacing height. "You will pay –" she cut off, looking suddenly beyond Mikura to someone else. "You!"

Mikura wasted no time now that Lilyth's malevolent gaze was no longer upon her, and she rushed forward to Ao Kouen's side, picked him up with her magic, and whirled around in the process to see what was happening in the rest of the room and if it would be possible to make any kind of escape.

The Vile Emperor himself stood in the doorway of the Jade throne room with his hands raised and prepared to launch everything he had at Lilyth, but in her rage, she reacted first, scuttling forward on her back talons to pierce him through the heart. Half an inch from striking through his metal chest plate, Lilyth froze unexpectedly, as Akuma entered through the doorway behind the Vile Emperor.

"I have you in my power now," Akuma stated, concentrating fiercely to control the blood flow to Lilyth's limbs. "Now!"

At his Chosen's command, Bastion ran up behind Akuma and the Vile Emperor, placing a hand on each of their shoulders and turning the three of them into a beam of red light, which would take them swiftly out of Taiyou and back home to the Ruby City. Mikura fervently wished they had thought to take her and Ao Kouen along with them, but there was clearly no time to waste; she had to find a way out of here before Lilyth remembered her presence. Speaking of Lilyth, the horrific beauty was lost in a wordless scream of rage, flailing her talons and stabbing them into the air wildly, like a child lost to a temper tantrum.

"Mikura," Ao Kouen spoke as loudly as he could to be heard over the screams, despite his weakened condition. "There, on the floor between the trees. There's a hole to the lower level."

Mikura spotted it and floated the two of them through the hole as silently as possible, escaping the wrath of Lady Lilyth so they could live to fight another day. With the King badly wounded and on the run, and the defenders by and large taken care of, Lady Lilyth had gained what she had been after all along – control of the place we had defended so fiercely, Taiyou.

As for me, I had been too close to the centre of everything to avoid the red wave of power emanating from the throne of Taiyou, though I tried my damndest to save Adel and myself by turning us both to mist in the final moments. This red wave, so like the green one Jedeite's power had created, was not nearly so easy to escape, however, and as it struck me I lost all ability to know what had become of Adel, myself, everyone else I cared about; even Taiyou itself.

Had I retained some semblance of awareness, I likely would have been tormented by the thoughts of what my failure would mean for everyone else. The hopes of every single person in Taiyou, including those allies who had come to help us defend the Lands of Jade, had been riding upon the Chosen to see them through whatever troubles beset the land, and despite how hard we had fought, we let them down. Especially me; there was hardly any way of knowing if I could have prevented Lilyth from taking over my body, even had I known what was happening at the time, but regardless Lilyth had so easily managed to make me the vessel for her success and ultimately the defeat of Taiyou.

That truth was bitter to swallow.

Taiyou suffered because of my weakness and Lilyth's exploitation of it, and with it, everything and everyone I loved. There was no way of knowing the fate of my parents, Masaru, Dahlia, Razor, Krox, Mifa, Felice, Goji, Kaji, Yue, Hotaru, our Knights, our friends, and our allies. We had each held on so tightly, weathering each and every storm, and all the things that threatened to destroy us, only to have it all taken away by something we couldn't possibly have foreseen. Our powers hadn't been enough – I hadn't been enough – to protect the land or the lives in my care.

I, and in fact everyone, had been blind-sided by one thing after another from the moment darkness had unexpectedly fallen on this world, and from there our troubles had only worsened. For every step we took, our enemies simply marched closer to defeating us, and in the end it hadn't mattered how high we had built the walls around Taiyou, or how many allies we had gathered to help us, we were still destined to fall as we hadn't known enough about our enemy to possibly be prepared to face her.

So much was still a mystery about the Lady Lilyth, the Vile Emperor, and every other dark secret this world possessed, but if there was one thing I had learned through overcoming all this adversity it was that as long as I still lived, I would not give up. I would fight for what I believed in and the freedom to live in a world safe from those who sought to destroy or rule it through tyranny.

I was a Chosen of Sapphiros now. I had power. I was not invincible by any means, but I had the ability to defend myself and those around me, and as long as I had the opportunity to try, I would continue to do so. Hopefully one day, it would be enough.

End of Volume 2

To Be Continued in

CITY OF RUBY

About the Author

Justine Alley Dowsett is the author of ten novels and counting, and one of the founders of Mirror World Publishing. Her books, which she often co-writes with her sister, Murandy Damodred, range from young adult science fiction to dark fantasy/romance. She earned a BA in Drama from the University of Windsor, honed her skills as an entrepreneur by tackling video game production, and now she dedicates her time to writing, publishing, and role-playing with friends.

WHO WE ARE...

Mirror World Publishing is a small independent publishing house based in Windsor, Ontario. We publish quality paperbacks and ebooks that feature other worlds, times and versions of reality. Our novels are for all ages and are creative, unique, imaginative and engaging.

We pride ourselves on our originality and 'outside the box' thinking, while taking a good look at the question, 'what if?' Our stories are never ordinary, the dialogue and action engaging, the characters believable, and there will always be some element of romance, adventure, science or magic. We are dedicated to bring our readers novels that will not only entertain them, but also teach them something about the world they live in by showing them one that mirrors it. We hope you'll consider picking up a novel from our collection today so you can see for yourself what we're all about.

You'll find a wide variety of our wonderful titles in our online bookstore and you can also purchase or review them through most major retailers worldwide.To learn more about our authors and our current projects visit: www.mirrorworldpublishing.com or follow @MirrorWorldPub or like us at www.facebook.com/mirrorworldpublishing